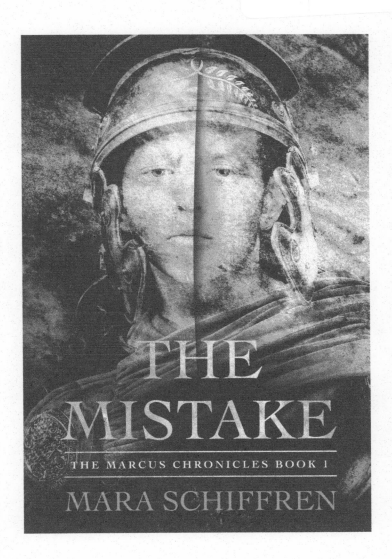

THE MISTAKE

THE MARCUS CHRONICLES BOOK 1

MARA SCHIFFREN

THE
MISTAKE

BOOK I IN THE CHRONICLES OF MARCUS

MARA SCHIFFREN

woodhall press

Woodhall Press | Norwalk, CT

woodhall press

Woodhall Press, Norwalk, CT 06855
WoodhallPress.com

Cover design: Asha Hossain
Layout artist: LJ Mucci

Library of Congress Cataloging-in-Publication Data available

ISBN 978-1-960456-11-3   (paper: alk paper)
ISBN 978-1-960456-12-0   (electronic)

First Edition
Distributed by Independent Publishers Group
(800) 888-4741

Printed in the United States of America

For my mother, Rita Lehman Schiffren, 1935-2018,
who cheered on this project from its early
days in every way she knew how.

Table of Contents

Cast of Characters

Marcus

Julius, his father, optio to Marcellus

Miriam, his mother

Silius Rufus, Julius' chief aide

Leos, weapons master

Ammon, expert tactician

Xenon, cohort doctor

Daniel, Miriam's father, Marcus' grandfather

Yehonatan, Daniel's son, Miriam's older brother, Marcus' uncle

Noemi, Miriam's maid

Ennius Andronicus, Julius' secretary

Vincius, a guard in Julius' century, later an aide

Octavio, a soldier

Drusilla, a camp follower, expert herbalist

Rufinus, the Syrian master arms man in Caesarea, Marcus' teacher

Tullian, Yehonatan's friend and business partner, bodyguard

Galenus, the Roman military governor of Ashqelon

Arianus, one of Julius' soldiers

Rabbi Chanon, a mystic and well-known rabbi in Sura and Yavneh, a connection of Yehonatan

Naphtali, a friend of Marcus from Yavneh

Binah, the sister of Naphtali

Itamar, Naftali and Binah's father

Tzipporah, Naftali and Binah's mother

Gad, the younger brother of Naphtali and Binah

Demetrius Ezekiel, a business connection and friend of Yehonatan

Rabbi Eli, Rabbi who is a friend of Itamar and his family

Rabbi Ariel, a Rabbi near Caesarea, a mentor to Marcus

Devorah, Rabbi Ariel's daughter

Critias, a Greco-Syrian friend of Marcus in Caesarea

Glaucon, Critias' father.

Dion, Marcus' friends, friends with Critias

Phoenix, Marcus' friends, friends with Critias

Antinous, a sophist and rhetor

Helen, the older sister of Phoenix

Rabbi Yo'el, a teacher of Marcus in Caesarea

Scipio, Vincius' aide

Argos, Marcus' horse

And the LORD said to Rebecca,
"Two nations are in your womb..."

– Genesis 25:23

Prologue

It had been forty years since the fall of the Great Temple in Jerusalem, destroyed ruthlessly during the Jewish revolt. Built by King Herod, the Temple had been one of the Seven Wonders of the World. But in the year 70, the Roman army, led by Titus, son of Emperor Vespasian, besieged Jerusalem and one by one by one destroyed the three layers of defensive city walls. Finally, he attacked and breached the Temple itself, the heart of Jerusalem. He set the Temple ablaze and as it burned, the remaining citizens in Jerusalem were hounded through to their deaths through the houses and cellars and sewers.

Nigh on a million Jews were killed. Nearly 100,000 were captured and enslaved. Some died as gladiators for the amusement of the Romans. Others were shipped throughout the slave markets of the Mediterranean, such a glut of slaves that the prices in slave markets all around the Mediterranean Sea collapsed.

They left the Temple a ruin, its beautiful structures plundered and burnt down and its great stone walls overturned.

In the years that had elapsed since its destruction, the Jews, hoping for miracles, prayed continually for the Temple's restoration. Forty years later, lightning struck and destroyed the Pantheum statue in Rome. From the point of view of the Jews, it was a small enough instance of divine requital on their behalf. Yet, in the end, seemingly, it provided encouragement enough. As a few years afterward, Jews living throughout the Mediterranean basin and beyond, in Libya, in Egypt and its neighbor Cyrene, in Cyprus and even in distant Mesopotamia, took up arms against the Romans and their other countrymen and rebelled.

Yet our story begins in Sardis where the Jews chose not to rebel. Sardis was an ancient city even then, a city whose true history lay buried under the impress of myth. Rich in gold, she had first risen to prominence as the capital of Lydia, under the Mermnad dynasty. Sardis' most famous King, Croesus, known to the ancient world as the inventor of money, had converted the ample supply of gold dust that washed up onto the banks of the Pactolus River into coin.

Bequeathed to Rome by the last Pergamene king, Sardis had for over 200 years been part of the Roman Empire. And there she continued, wealthy and quiescent under continuing Roman rule, a home to traders from all over the Empire.

PART I

CHAPTER 1
Genesis

Julius had had enough. The crude wooden table before him reeked of spilled wine and raw onions. Barley crumbs and the tiny skeletons of smoked fish lay scattered down its length, adhering to its sticky surface. He surveyed the length of the room, caught the eye of Silius, his deputy, and nodded. Julius peeled his sleeve from the table-top, then wiped his fingers through hair that felt salty damp and pushed himself to a standing position. Down the table, Silius followed suit.

On the benches all about him, his soldiers sprawled and talked loudly and hooted, some ogling the few servants in their midst. One young soldier slept, his head drowning in a puddle of wine, his mouth fallen open, his loose arm hanging down. Small favor, Julius considered idly, that no one had retched yet and added that acid stench to the accumulating aroma of drunkenness and unwashed male sweat in the humid room.

"Men," Julius said. He pitched his voice to lance through the noise like a scythe slicing through grass. And now the double rows

1

of faces, red with wine and blur-eyed, lost their slack as they turned to him. Even the sleeping soldier, yawning, shook himself awake and the wine spattered off his short, dark hair like a dog shedding rain.

"It's been a damn strenuous month of exercises. And you've handled it all with the steady excellence that Marcellus and I expect of you. Congratulations!" Julius wondered again where Marcellus, their centurion was. He had promised to stick his head in at some point and give this toast to the soldiers. But he had never appeared.

As optio, second in command to the centurion, Julius had spent the last month since his appointment running the cohort through tactical maneuvers wearing full battle armor, using javelins and short swords, on horse and on foot, day after day, old exercises and new routines, marching for tens of miles a day, testing for speed and strength and accuracy. Their cohort from the famous Xth Fretensis Legion was new to this area. Trajan had stationed it here in Sardis to discourage any restiveness among the population. Though from what Julius could gauge, the city enjoyed its status and stability and did not go in for rebellion. Still, the past month of maneuvers would have allayed any nascent rebellious tendencies, which had been a major point of the display. The men were now exhausted from the training, but happy to be done. No wonder, then, that they had quickly succumbed to the effects of the unwatered wine produced for them in the barracks.

So had he, Julius realized belatedly, after he had sent them off to the taverns and brothels of Sardis to enjoy their chosen entertainment.

Julius chose to walk off the effects of the wine by climbing one of the high hills of Sardis and watching the sun drop slowly over the long horizon. Just visible from the top of the rise he saw the ancient burial mounds at Bin Tepe, circular and mysterious. Julius leaned against a tall outcropping of rock, watching the drooping sun illuminate the mounds with long, golden streaks. Rumor murmured about the labyrinthine corridors within, the kings lying buried at their heart, with their tall horses and fair wives and the heaps of jewels that only

2

grave robbers had ever seen. But, then again, he rarely listened to murmurs. His line of work had left him disdainful of mysteries. He preferred the world of practical fact and solid existence.

After a while, Julius picked his way across the rocks until he sat out with his legs dangling off the western cliff edge and gulped more wine. The air smelled of evergreen and damp soil. When he turned to leave a few minutes later, his eye caught some dim scrapings behind a myrtle bush on an upright stone. They looked unnatural. Curious, Julius brushed the leaves back and wiped the stone with his sleeve until he could just make out crooked letters. And then he laughed out loud.

> *He grew up by his father's will,*
> *Hail to you Dionysius with your many grapes.*

It was an altar to Dionysius crudely carved into the stone of the hillside. On a whim, Julius picked up the flask someone had left as an offering to the god and poured a libation. He partook of a draught himself. To his surprise, this wine, unlike tavern wine, was heavily spiced and the herbs tasted earthy and unfamiliar. He took another swallow, then another. Suddenly moved by the beauty of his environs, Julius walked around the hillside, until he came to a stone ledge, pulled himself onto it and sat down with his legs spread out in front of him.

Time passed as he sat thinking, expanding and contracting into a fluid dimension, a visual field. When he looked next at the trees, they seemed particularly vibrant and alive. The lichen, in silver green and mauve, suddenly appeared to him like woodland faces looking his way, an animate dryad in every tree. Everything around him felt more alive, more profound. Slowly, he rose and took in the wealth of beauty, the living universe, as though the hand of the god was sealed on his heart and helped him breathe.

3

He stumbled back at last onto the homeward path and began to meander slowly down the hillside, his eyes gripping hard onto the rocks whenever his feet slipped.

A swish of leaves sent his gaze flying forward like a hunting dog pointing its prey. He located the rustle a bit above him and to his east. And then, from a lilac shelf of rock, a fair complected maiden arose suddenly into his sight, full-born atop the pink earth, with the glints of setting sun tinting her skin and hair roseate. Goddess or nymph, Julius thought wildly, enthused. An answer to his random prayer.

"Lady," he intoned, and ascended through bushes and rocks to her side.

He heard her catch a startled breath. But her face was still, and she did not utter a word.

When he touched her flesh a moment later, it was warm.

Of course, he thought. And with his hand clasped firmly on the real, the solid, an earth maiden, he shook the vision from his head.

They proceeded in silence, walking back home towards Sardis. Julius shared the remains of the libation wine, then silently poured out its last measure onto the earth in thanks to the Great Dionysius. Rounding the corner of the twisting path, they looked before them at the view, and stopped as one. Together, they sat at the rise of a deserted field to watch as twilight descended on the town, casting the white stone buildings below in a dusky grape tone. The vaulted sky above them melted into shades of lilac, and then luminescent green. And the wintering birds in the barren trees on the hillside behind them piped their farewell to the day. Then, turning before his luck changed, he kissed her softly, then roughly, then softly again. And she kissed back.

She tasted sweet, of ripe young flesh and wine. And, his *daemon* murmured in his head, perhaps a little of fear. Be kind, it told him. So he was. After, when he stood, he saw her maiden blood spilled onto the drab winter earth, fresh and red as poppies.

4

"A mistake." Julius hissed the word through his teeth late at night when he was alone, and the strange enchantments of the late afternoon had long since faded from his mind along with the effects of the spiced wine. Then, as something deep bored into his gut, he twitched. The fear that he had drawn Dionysius' attention for his impiety by stealing the libation beverage suddenly felt like a living force within him. Julius breathed out hard through his nose, then shook his head. "No," he said aloud. "I will fix this."

To propitiate the god, to ward off disaster from striking him, he would offer a month's salary to maintain the Temple of Dionysius in Teos, not far off. Further, he would make sure that flasks of exotic spiced wine were provided for the altar above Sardis. A heavy price, indeed, for such a mistake, wine-induced from start to finish. But he would pay that and more to mollify the god.

Dissected and accounted for, all wrapped up as far as he was concerned, he deliberately dismissed the incident from his mind. Instead, as a diversion from too much thought, Julius picked up a scroll of Seneca he kept by the side of his bed. He read by the light of an oil lamp, as the smoke from the lamp fogged the air and made his eyes red and itchy, before wafting into the rafters and staining them black.

"*I never come back home with the same moral character I went out with; something or other becomes unsettled where I had achieved internal peace; someone or other of the things I had put to flight reappears on the scene.*"

In the circumstances, the words comforted Julius. He closed his red-ringed blue eyes at last and fell into a deep sleep.

Alas, his sleep was not to last long that night. For a knock at his door sounded an hour later. He ignored it, but it continued.

"Go away," he grumbled at the door, in the grips of exhaustion.

"Emergency, sir," called Silius' voice loudly. "You are needed downstairs in riding gear. Immediately."

The "sir" was new. Julius wondered about it as he dutifully rose from his bed, dressed and paced wearily down the oil lit stone stairway behind Silius. At the bottom of the stairs, near a doorway, stood a clutch of veteran soldiers, Silius' contemporaries. These were the favored clique of Marcellus, their centurion, all highly trained and trusted. Despite that, it was he who had recently been promoted to optio, second in charge after Marcellus, not these older men who were closer to retirement. And that had created tension within the cohort and an ongoing labyrinth of resistance for him to navigate. He was young, but Marcellus, at the end of his third decade, still had many years left ahead of him. And he was the one being groomed to assume command.

"There's been a murder," said Leos, their weapons master, looking straight at him. The older man's face, always angular, was broken into stark plains of light and dark.

Whatever tiredness Julius felt fled immediately.

"I wager it was an execution," said Ammon, their expert tactician. "Not a simple murder."

"Poison," said Xenon, the company doctor who also served as a soldier.

"Who was killed?" said Julius.

"Marcellus."

Julius' jaw fell open. "What? Marcellus? How? Who?"

They told Julius the details on the way to the tavern where the body had been found. "Marcellus had a meeting earlier this evening at The Inn of the Three Sparrows close to the forum. He advised us that he was collecting information about Parthia from one of his sources. The man he was meeting was a long-time resource, and a man he knew socially as well. Knew slightly socially. He always met him alone."

"Do we have a name for the source?"

"Galenus."

"Galenus," Julius repeated slowly. The name meant nothing to him. "And where is he from?"

"He's Roman," said Leos, "a rotten branch of an aristocratic family. Years ago, they sent him east to Parthia to fend him off on the wars. To everyone's surprise, he's turned out to be an excellent soldier with a gift for command. He stayed afterwards to make trouble for the Parthians on the frontier. But every few years, he rides back west. Since he's heavily connected to the highest tier of Roman civilian families, he came to the attention of Emperor Trajan in Parthia. Trajan appointed him to his current position as Supply Master for the Eastern Army.

"Is he a suspect?" said Julius.

"Ask us again," said Xenon, "once you've seen the body."

Upstairs at the inn, one of their soldiers was standing guard over the room Marcellus' body was in. And then Julius was through the door.

His eyes swept the room and noted details. On the marble table were two sets of dishes, two glasses half full, a plate of stew untouched. The chairs lined up evenly. The room was well kept and homey, except that Marcellus' body was lying still and prone on the floor. There was no blood near him. "Turn him over, Cratus," said Ammon.

Marcellus' face was ash and dun, like a bog in some misbegotten landscape. His face, so recently full of life force and command, was already beginning to decompose and fall in on itself. "I think," said Xenon, "it must be some exotic poison. There is no entry wound that we noticed. No blood. Let's test that hypothesis." And he pulled a living mouse from his surgeon's pouch and, using a cloth, forced a dab of the liquid that had been in Marcellus' cup to the mouse's mouth. Then he placed it back in the pouch.

"How long do we leave it?" said Julius.

"Until it stops wriggling," said Xenon.

"We estimate he's been dead a few hours, the barkeep's daughter found him like this. When she screamed, her pater rushed upstairs and then sent a message to the barracks. Marcellus was a frequent guest here. They told us they touched nothing and were dead afraid their food or drink would be blamed," said Leos. He was leaning back against the wall of the room, his arms crossed over his leather cuirass, surveilling the room, his face once again fractured into planes of light and dark. But now the dark was winning.

As far as Julius could see there were no other clues in this room. The bed was yet pristine. Whatever nighttime activities Marcellus had planned for himself had not been executed. "Did he have a favorite whore or a mistress?" Julius asked.

Ammon lifted his eyebrows. "I'm still boggled he appointed you optio when you know so little." He took a deep breath and said, "No. The job rotated. No favorites. Not for five years or more. There was a time... But no."

Xenon pulled his pouch open and fished out the mouse, now dead. "It's poison then, just as we suspected, perhaps some exotic Persian or Egyptian kind I'm unfamiliar with. At a guess. Which to my mind relieves suspicion from the barkeep."

"Unless he was threatened or bribed," said Leos. "But I think we have seen enough here. Ammon, go down and interview the barkeep and his daughter. Threaten to lock him up with the lions if he doesn't tell the truth.

"There haven't been lions in Sardis for 20 years," said Julius.

Ammon raised his eyebrows. "We can always import more. Meanwhile get some sleep. Tomorrow, we go in search of Galenus."

But the next day, Galenus was nowhere to be found no matter how far and wide they sent sorties to search. And a week afterwards came the order confirming that Julius was to assume command of the cohort as centurion. He felt entirely unprepared. So he did the one thing that had never failed him. He blocked out all distractions, sat down and got to work.

PART II

CHAPTER 2

A Proposal of Sort

Five months later, in the fading light of a spring afternoon, Julius was sitting at his wooden desk in the barracks studying a recent report of army activities in the district. He heard soldiers squabbling outside like so many herring gulls scrapping over the remains of fish. Mildly amused, mildly irritated, he docketed the incident in his mind as minor trouble over women or dicing to be sorted out later and continued reading his report. Yet long moments later, Julius gritted his teeth as the disturbance continued and this time right outside his office. When his door suddenly burst open, he looked up, surprised and displeased. A man and a woman entered, followed by his aide, Silius, whose half-armor glinted amber in the golden afternoon light. Silius, whom he had known for nearly twenty years, and who had also worked for his father, approached his desk warily, looking apologetic in the extreme. Julius wryly marked the display of caution.

"The man insisted," Silius communicated briefly. "Personal matter." He shrugged and looked around, his face refusing to speculate.

9

"Personal to whom?" Julius asked his aide, frankly annoyed. Then he looked past Silius' left shoulder to where the man and the woman lingered in the shadows by the doorway. Failing to recognize either of them, he shrugged back at Silius.

He cleared his throat about to send them about their business, when the man caught his eye, and stepped forward, propelling the woman behind him into the light. Julius noted that the man, of middle height, was a little stocky and had short gray hair. His linen clothing was fine quality, yet plain. Turning his head, Julius looked at the woman just as the man removed her cloak. And then he got a clear glimpse of her face and figure and full recognition bored deep into his gut and began to squirm. The girl, beautiful still, was several months gone with child.

Was this, he wondered, the god's revenge for his impiety, here to doom his days? His heart began to reverberate. He felt every separate beat. His mistake, so carefully dismissed from his mind, had not escaped the accounting of Dionysius after all. It had come to fruition regardless, as does fertile seed furrowed in fresh earth. But what would grow from the seed, he wondered? Something good or bad? Julius, his face blank, looked at Silius, dismissed him with a nod, and then he looked back at the girl's figure, transfixed.

The man waited until Silius closed the door and then spoke, articulating each word distinctly. "We had a hard enough time finding you, as she didn't know your full name. But, I see, at least, you recognize that this is your work."

Julius removed his eyes from the girl, her face and her figure, and transferred them to the man. Their gazes locked onto each other and held. "I acknowledge it," he said, flushing slightly, "though it was just the one time. A mistake I deeply regretted."

"What you are prepared to do about it," the man said, his voice gravel-edged, "as regrettably, your child is now on its way." After a few seconds he added, "It is your child, so don't start doubting it,"

10

responding more to the flow of Julius' thought than to anything he had said aloud.

Julius broke the gaze, got up from the chair and walked around the desk towards the girl. She looked warily back at him and stepped closer to the gray-haired man whom Julius presumed was her father. She was, indeed, comely, with her wide-set green eyes, even complexion and her fair tresses in little braids wound about her head and falling to her shoulders. Though today she was looking piqued and anxious, away from the roseate light of the winter afternoon on which they had met and mated in a frenzy of alcohol and lust. He could not summon her name to mind.

"Miriam," the man said, reading his hesitation. "She learned your name from one of your men in town she saw in your company. That's how we finally found you. My own name is Daniel." A beat later, he added, "I'm a merchant here, in Sardis."

Julius nodded and took the girl's hand in his despite the fury in her father's eyes. "Miriam," he repeated. Calmly, with the slightest of smiles, she removed her hand from his. She glanced back and forth between the two men, attempting to display composure, but visibly ill at ease nonetheless, unsure of her stance in what threatened to be a battleground between them. Julius reminded himself he was a battle commander and positioned himself to make up lost ground. He leaned back against his desk casually. "I am prepared to make some sort of arrangement if the child is mine."

"If," Daniel repeated, his voice cold.

"She was a maid before me, but that is no guarantee she hasn't had others since. She came to me easily enough," said Julius.

"After you plied her with heavily spiced wine," Daniel replied, contempt in his voice. "Do you always woo young girls with herbed libations before you bed them?"

"Father," Miriam exclaimed, tugging at his arm, breaking her silence at last. She turned to Julius and said, "I don't wonder that you're

11

suspicious, but the child is yours." She swallowed. "I tried to convince my father you would likely not help. Not after what happened."

Her words rankled him. But she was right. His impulse had been first to negate what had happened on the very night it had happened and then, here, today, to shirk whatever responsibility he might bear in this confrontation with her father.

The girl continued to look him full in the face as she said, "He insisted we come, against my will."

Against her will. Julius watched horrified and enthralled as her skin changed from wan to patchily red. He felt his own blood surge into his cheeks in response. She had tasted of fear that night, his *daemon* whispered in his head, niggling him.

"We could marry. Then divorce following immediately on the child's birth," Julius said, as surprising to himself as anything he had ever uttered in his whole life.

Silence shattered the room. Yet, since those incredible words had been uttered somehow, had wafted out of his mouth unchecked by his brain, he felt too uncomfortable to grab them back. But he wanted to.

"It is possible I misjudged you," Daniel said at last, his face a stonewall. "Perhaps. But marriage is not an option at this point. Not without conversion."

"Conversion," repeated Julius. "To what?"

"We are Jews. We only marry other Jews."

For the first time, Julius relaxed momentarily. He wasn't going to convert to anything. But to stall he asked, "What does conversion entail?"

"It requires a belief that our God is the one true God. My own wife was a convert. It is a ritual easily performed. Also, for a man..." His voice trailed off.

"For a man?" asked Julius.

"Circumcision, to mark your entry into the covenant with God."

12

"Circumcision," Julius spat out. "Never." The idea of that for himself and any future son of his made him cringe. "No marriage," he added, turning his shoulder. "Better for all of us, I suspect." Only once he was facing away from them, did he allow himself to breathe out heavily. After a moment, he walked back around the desk and sat back down.

"Whether or not you convert, I will raise this child as a Jew. Whatever support you offer, or fail to offer," Daniel stated.

"As long as you are raising him, that is fine."

Julius turned back to look at Miriam and considered the price that was being set on the folly he had briefly, oh so briefly, participated in one warm winter afternoon. He'd never confuse her with a goddess today. She looked pinched and earth-bound. And he was neither raving drunk nor enthused. Still, he was an honest man who prided himself on taking responsibility for his actions.

Pious Aeneas, refugee from fallen Troy and the forefather of Rome, was the model of the Roman citizen. However hard Aeneas's sort of civic and domestic virtues were to emulate, Julius had always seen it as his duty to try. As a fighting man, he admired Achilles, with his breathtaking, moody courage. Yet, as a proud Roman citizen, Julius had disciplined himself hard to the performance of duty, even when it was of a homely nature. Here and now, the implication of this stance was that he must do something for the girl. This is what he had repeatedly counseled his men when they found themselves in similar predicaments. He sat still for a few more moments thinking, looking nowhere, then at the stone floor, then at the wall.

At last, looking at Miriam, Julius said, "I will assume part financial responsibility for the child if it is a boy, and will help house you with the child under the condition that while you live under a roof I pay for, you have relations with no other man. Except for me. If I hear or see or find out anything to the contrary, I throw you out and take the child. Do you agree?"

13

"Not with you either, unless we marry."

Not with him unless they marry. Then what in hell was he doing this for? Julius opened his mouth, then shut it. Ah yes, the unborn boy. But what did he care for some theoretical child? Julius opened his mouth again. "Then you must give me access to my son whenever I want it."

"If you, in turn, take an oath that the child will be raised as a Jew and allowed to study our traditions," she responded coolly.

Julius, irked at being bargained with by the girl, argued some more, but he finally agreed to take an oath. More than that, in his own mind, he resolved to fulfill it.

Late that night, as the oil lamp burned black smoke by his bed-stead, it occurred to Julius that the reason he had been willing to make that astounding settlement, even offered marriage, however lightly, is that he himself had been the result of such a casual union. He regretted that he had not known his own mother, that his father had not thought to bring her back with him from Germania. Or, per-haps, she had been unwilling to leave her people and go to Rome. He shook his head to stop his mind from speculating futilely. The need to adjust himself to the mischances of life uppermost in his mind, Julius picked up a copy of Epictetus's writings that he had found in a market booth owned by a seller of second-hand papyrus scrolls. *"All philosophy lies in two words, sustain and abstain."* Resisting sleep, he read on through the night, narrowing his concentration to what was before him on the page.

For the following three years that they dwelled in Sardis, Julius continued to live in the army barracks with his men. After the birth of the child, he helped to house Miriam and his son Marcus apart from himself in a small stone house towards the outskirts of town.

14

The house, typical of its neighborhood, had two stories. The ground level contained a reception room whose cold stone floor was covered by richly colored rugs and cushions. The room above served as a sleeping alcove for Miriam and the child. A small courtyard surrounded the front of the house with flowering trees planted in large stone pots. From there, the scents of roasting meat and spices drifted upwards, penetrating the walls of the house, along with the gurgle and chatter of Miriam's visiting friends and the servant girls who helped her with the cooking and did the wash.

Miriam's father Daniel visited the stone house frequently, though it was at a distance from his own large villa, situated on a hillside with a view of Sardis city. Daniel came from a line of merchants who specialized in dyes, spices and pepper. His family had originally been based in Judea. After the complete upheaval following the Jewish civil war in Roman controlled Judea, forty-five years earlier, with the attendant national, religious and economic disasters, the family business had been largely wrecked. Daniel's family had recovered by moving much of their business outside of Judea, sending brothers abroad to establish branches in Asia Minor, Babylon and southernmost Arabia, the central axis point of the worldwide trade in frankincense. Each of these locations possessed a long-established Jewish community.

Even now, Daniel had sent his only son, Yehonatan, to Babylon, where he had been trading for the last five years.

During his visits to the stone house, Daniel spoke to the toddler for hours at a time in Hebrew. He had perfected his knowledge of this language in his youth when he lived near Lake Tiberius, studying and debating in the courts of religion and law and learning the family trade amongst his cousins. Daniel also taught Marcus, while still a very young child, how to fashion Hebrew letters with a stylus on wax tablets, to write his own name and to read his first Hebrew words. As the child grew older, Daniel came to the house with more frequency, delighting in the opportunity to tell Marcus the tales of their people.

15

When his daughter was unoccupied, she would sit and listen to the stories with Marcus. Daniel remembered very well how, when both his children were young, he had loved teaching them the stories. For he was a born teacher and narrated them beautifully. Later, when they were older, he had taught both Yehonatan and Miriam texts from the Torah and parts of the law.

Daniel considered this to be his legacy. He dreamed that his stories would be passed on through his progeny. The family business produced wealth for them to live, but he always believed that his stories were the true gold.

———◆———

When Julius came to see the boy, he arrived in the early evenings, after his work for the day was finished. Often, he was tired and his temper not always even. He never stayed long, however, preferring the masculine atmosphere of his camp with its tight discipline. Sometimes during the day, Julius would send his aide Silius to pick up the boy. And when Marcus arrived in camp, Julius would take him around and show him, with great pride, his soldiers exercising their fighting skills. Occasionally Julius would don his gear and let Marcus see him fight in exhibitions as well.

The boy was blue-eyed and brown-haired like him. Marcus buzzed about from place to place, yet was sturdy on his feet, with a mind like quicksilver. He absorbed everything he was taught. Julius had his armorer fashion a small practice sword for his son and he began to teach him the same exercises that his father, Lucilus, had first taught him long ago before his father had gone back to the wars and left him, brokenhearted, with his aunt.

After three years of this comfortable and stable existence, tidings arrived that Julius' cohort was now posted south to join the Xth Legion Fretensis. They were moving to Syria to serve for a stint under

Hadrian, governor of the province and commander of the Roman forces stationed there. After a considerable amount of persuasion, Julius talked Miriam into allowing him to bring the boy, in whom he was beginning to feel a fierce pride, and to come herself to continue caring for Marcus.

⸻◦⸻

A day before what he privately referred to as the Great Exodus South, Daniel came to the small stone house for a farewell visit with his grandson, Marcus. But for tomorrow's sendoff, it would be the last time that Daniel would see him for a long while, perhaps the last time ever. He was furious Miriam had decided to allow Julius to take the child and herself with him. His sweet daughter, so beautiful, so intelligent, so accomplished, and she would always be an afterthought to that man.

God knew it was clear Julius was attached to his son, but since the boy had been conceived, it was also transparent to him that the man had never given a moment's thought to Miriam. And never, even then, had he thought about her welfare, only his own pleasure. Daniel had prayed hard for Miriam to marry a Jew after she had carried Marcus, but the looming shadow of Julius, Roman, martial and forbidding, had so far proven an immovable stumbling block despite Miriam's beauty and his wealth. So, instead, Daniel had made it his policy to do what he could to implant in this child of mixed blood pride in the heritage of his mother's people, whose laws, God willing, he would follow.

Now Miriam and the boy were moving south. What hope for them there, without him? Daniel sighed once and pushed open the door.

"Marcus," Daniel called as he entered the cool stone building, and the child came scrambling, love and eagerness shining upon his face.

"Saba," he cried. Daniel gathered the child into his arms, held him a minute, then sat on a rough-hewn stone bench below the

17

window. Marcus looked at him, waiting, his eyes glittering. Daniel handed the small boy a tightly curled papyrus scroll he had brought with him and showed Marcus how to unfurl it carefully. And when the small boy turned his face up at him, his expression curious, Daniel spoke to him softly, stroking his brown curls, silken and rough mixed together.

"Marcus, here is a history of our family for the last two hundred years, in the land of Israel, in Babylon and in Sardis where we live today." And taking the boy's hand, Daniel moved his finger over the names. "Here towards the end is my name, here is your uncle's name, Yehonatan, your mother's name, Miriam, and here, upon the last line of the scroll, your name, Marcus, is marked. See. You can read it there. When you have sons and daughters yourself, add them here, below your name." Then, moving Marcus' finger to the next column, he continued. "And here, to this side, your uncles and aunts are named and your cousins. You may meet them, one day."

And then breaking off, he transferred his gaze, solemn, sad, longing, back to the boy's face. Such a little boy. How could he ever remember all this? But even so, Daniel persisted, slowly and methodically. "Marcus, I am making you the keeper of this scroll. Remember, it tells the story of your family. It is the Book of Life for us all. Guard it all the years of your life and pass it to your oldest son in time."

Through the window, a voice rose in excitement then dropped. Then Daniel heard another voice lifted in response, a voice that was distinct, a voice he recognized. He grimaced, realizing his time with Marcus was about to be cut short. Daniel placed his hands over the boy's head and began hurriedly to intone a prayer for his wellbeing. After a few seconds he slowed down, and Marcus recited the end of the psalm with him, as was their practice.

"Behold, the Guardian of Israel neither slumbers nor sleeps..."

They finished the last words together, and Daniel removed his hands and bent to kiss his grandson's brow.

A second later the door was thrown open and Julius stood below the stone lintel, tall, vital and wind-tossed. His eyes moved first to his son, then to the old man and back to his son. He stepped neatly between them. As Marcus turned to him, his face rosy with excitement, his eyes gleaming, Julius swung him high and around, his wine dark cloak diffusing the scents of wood-fire, frankincense and blood into the dry air. The scroll in Marcus' hands, disregarded, went flying through the air, struck the wall and dropped to the ground.

Julius said, "The auspices for the trip could not be better. I have just returned from having them read on behalf of my cohort. The priest was astounded by the good fortune he saw for us." His eyes moved to the old man, challenging him.

The old man stared back, his expression stony. Stooping, he picked up the scroll and placed it onto the table. His eyes still hard, he looked back at Julius. Then, his eyes moved to his grandson, held firmly in Julius' arms and his expression slowly changed. He reached out and touched the textured curls once more and bade his grandson goodbye. "Remember, Marcus. Guard the scroll."

"Goodbye until tomorrow, Saba," Marcus' voice piped at him.

"Until tomorrow."

Daniel walked over to the door. "Julius," he nodded, and closed the door behind him.

Outside, Miriam sat in the cool air of the late winter day staring east at the hill. On top of it, the acropolis shone golden in the strong afternoon light. His daughter seemed pensive. The flowering trees around her in the courtyard were barren of leaves in their stone pots. Their branches, encased in ice, dripped silvered drops onto the mosaic floor that lay beneath them, like a very slow fountain. Miriam glanced at her father as he approached, her expression rueful. Taking her arm, Daniel drew her to the closed door of the courtyard, outside the hearing of anyone nearby.

19

He said, "I see now it was a mistake for me ever to insist that we look for Julius. But I was crazy with anger at you. And your brother's advice to me arrived months too late. He blames me. I blame myself. God blames me too, otherwise you and Marcus would stay with me now." He kissed her, his sight momentarily unclear, as the sunlight shining on his face refracted twenty different ways. Daniel rubbed his eyes and then touched her beautiful fair hair bound in braids.

"I blame myself for it," Daniel said to her one last time, as he pulled open the gate and left the courtyard of the small stone house forever.

PART III

CHAPTER 3
On the Road

Still groggy, Miriam pulled open the curtains of the wagon she had slept in overnight, breathed in deeply and looked out at the world around her. The weather had warmed considerably in the last few days and that change was reflected by the vista in front of her. Hills, softly angled, rolled past, from one horizon to another. The hills before her, brown, green and blood red, smelling of spring and damp earth, were profligate with poppies. The flowers had first appeared two days ago, the very morning after the snows melted away all in one day from the heat of an unseasonal sun. Runoff from the snow formed rivulets that raced down the slopes of the high hills and careened off boulders, drenching the horses and carriages and men below them. It turned the road on which they traveled into a quagmire of ruts, churned mud and newborn ponds. The central command called a day-long halt while the earth absorbed the runoff before the long column of soldiers, wagons, women, children and animals was able to proceed on its way.

21

"Miriam," she heard someone calling in the distance. Moments later, Julius was at her side, on horseback, dressed in half armor, with Marcus seated before him, his eyes wide, his cheeks flushed, his face betraying excitement and wonder. Miriam straightened her linen gown as best she could while sitting. Then she pushed her legs over the side and jumped down to the ground. Her fair hair, still unbraided this morning, fell loose about her shoulders and down her back. She shook it out, using her fingers to smooth it down roughly, as the sun shone behind her, bathing her in morning light. As she finished, she observed Julius staring at her out of the corner of her eye. As she caught his glance, he turned his head away. Julius lifted Marcus out of the saddle and placed his quick little body into her arms. Then he swung off his tall cavalry horse, holding it by the reins. The great black horse was restive this morning, fired with energy.

Julius stood close by Miriam's side as she admired his horse. His armor glinted in the golden light and she could feel warmth emanating from him. She looked Julius in the face and when he looked back at her, she felt goose bumps. After a few seconds, she stepped backward, looking away from him towards the field of virgin poppies in the distance, spilling red down the hillside. Her arms around Marcus tightened, but when he squawked, she let him slide down the length of her body to the ground. Miriam looked down at her son as he stood clinging to her, hugging her legs with his little arms. When she looked back at Julius, he was standing still as stone, with a frown on his face.

"Have you eaten yet today?" she said.

"Yes. Marcus has eaten as well." An awkward silence developed. "Well, then, I'll be off for the day." Julius mounted his horse and looked at her again. Then he turned his horse and made a circuit of the area, addressing some of the soldiers he met on the pathway before he galloped back towards the campsite where the command was stationed.

Miriam watched Julius depart, he and the horse in perfect balance one with the other, a marvel of fluidity. She shook her head and slowly released her breath. Taking hold of Marcus' hand, she walked down a slope to one of the central cooking pits. The smell of fresh bread and meat and wood fire wafted towards her. Miriam, careful even in isolation to obey the strictures of her people, never ate the meat at these campsites. But she retrieved her morning allotment of spiced bread dipped in olive oil and dried fruit and filled her earthenware mug with rainwater from a barrel. Then, with Marcus at her side, Miriam sat on a fallen tree trunk away from the chattering, raucous crowd of men.

After a while, as she ate, Marcus got up and humming to himself, began to investigate the clearing in which they were sitting. He settled nearby and began to pull apart the bark of the tree she was sitting on, hunting dreamily for bugs in its rotten innards.

Miriam looked around her. Here, by this cooking fire, the expansive vista she had glimpsed this morning was cut off by the slope of the hillside and a stand of tall evergreen trees. The area was still in deep shade, as yet unwarmed by the rays of the sun. She knew no one in this group except Marcus. Miriam shivered involuntarily, then grabbed for Marcus and hugged him close. When he protested, Miriam picked him up and marched back to the wagon towards the sunlight and the few faces already familiar to her. It was time to wash herself and Marcus as best she could in the snowy runoff and to pack everything up. The Legion would be moving shortly. She had learned early that no malingering was permitted in a Roman camp. The cohort she was travelling with was well disciplined, the men worked together with precision.

As the days passed, Miriam slept and woke and slept some more. She had been travelling for a few weeks now, from Sardis east towards Cappadocia. The view had been unchanging for some time. Up and down the rolling hills, sheep stationed themselves in groups, their

23

coats marked out in light and dark tones. Less frequently, she caught glimpses of goats and cows and an occasional shepherd seated near a flimsy hut.

As Miriam had brought her own horse from Sardis with her, a dappled gray mare, part of the time she rode on horseback. The remainder of the time, when she was too weary or too sore or when Marcus was too restless and difficult to control on top of a horse, she traveled in the wagon that she slept in. In the wagon were her luggage and her maid, Noemi, an orphan girl from Sardis, who had worked for her during the past year. Noemi, who was short and thin with dark eyes that often hid behind her curly dark hair, had been more than willing to accompany Miriam abroad despite the rigors of the long journey. For the first time in her sixteen years, her time with Miriam had given her a solid position each day. Her gratitude, though unmentioned, was palpable. Miriam too, was glad of Noemi's presence, however shy she was. There was only a small number of women traveling with them but very few that Miriam could address. Most of the women were located at the very back of the camp, a place that both her father and Julius had forbidden her to visit. On this particular issue, Miriam had no interest in contravening their commands. Her own position was tenuous enough.

In the wagon, she and Marcus and sometimes Noemi would sing songs, or Miriam would tell Marcus the stories and fables of their people that she had learned at the knees of her father. On those occasions, Noemi listened intently as well, her head cocked forward, her ears absorbing everything Miriam said. The girl was silent, Miriam had realized, but intelligent and hungry for knowledge. It made Miriam conscious anew how sweet was learning and how privileged her early life had been. Noemi had not been lucky in her lot, deprived of so many things that Miriam took for her due. But she did not seem unhappy. Did not the Sages say: *Who is he that is rich? He who rejoices in his lot, happy shalt thou be in this world, and it shall be well with thee in the world to come.* Noemi, who did not desire a life beyond her state, was in this way far richer than she.

On the road, Miriam made up a song with the letters of the Hebrew alphabet so that Marcus would not forget them. By now, Noemi knew it and sang along as well, her voice sweet and high. Once or twice, Miriam attempted to work at the stylus and wax tablet with Marcus, but the wagon jostled too much. So she abandoned her attempt, even though there was no other time in the day for Marcus to practice and boredom was a feeling that consumed them frequently. In the late afternoons, when the caravan stopped for the day, the boy needed the time to run around and lose the feeling of confinement he was now subject to daily as he sat in the wagon or rode on the horses.

She thought often of her father's words to her the day before she left. "I made a mistake," he had told her at last, years too late. Whenever she thought of her father's words, her lips pursed. In sadness? In regret? In exasperation? In anger? All of them, certainly. She worried about her father though, particularly now that she was away. With her and Marcus gone, Daniel was entirely alone for the first time, no family around him at all. Her mother had been dead long over a decade. And her brother Yehonatan was not due to leave Arabia to return home for several years. He was still in the East, learning the business of trade at one of its centers.

Miriam had envied Yehonatan in the past. As the only son, all the golden opportunities were naturally accorded to him. Sent abroad in his youth to study in the famed centers of learning in Babylonia, he had traveled the world, working hard on behalf of the family, even occasionally fighting. Nothing of the sort had been offered to her until Julius had told her that his Legion was being posted south and that he proposed to take his son. And this she had decided to grab at with both hands, to withstand the whirlwind of opposition she faced: anger, tears, prayers, every familial weapon had been used against her.

Daniel, her father, regarded her action in leaving as a personal betrayal, and refused to see it as the dawning of new opportunities for her.

Miriam had never been averse to change. She possessed a restless energy, a true inheritance from her mother. Her mother, her father had told her, had traveled often in her youth with her people, riding on horseback and in wagons across vast sweeps of land. She had heard of it so frequently; she had developed a dream of that for herself.

Yet, Miriam did not like hurting her father; with palpable hindsight, she realized now that whatever new existence she was wandering into would be far more fragile and less protected than the one she left behind. The one that her father had supported. It worried her. At night, she lay awake, staring at the black sky, the great dome awash with the milky white of innumerable stars, too troubled to sleep. Celebrating the magnificence, she would recite to herself, *"When I behold Your heavens, the work of Your fingers, the moon and the stars, which You have set in place. What is man, that You have been mindful of him? And mortal man, that You have taken note of him?"*

Miriam sighed again. She was not enjoying the axis around which her thoughts repeatedly ran these days.

One day, exactly like every other, Miriam, bored of endlessly sitting still, had chosen to ride horseback. She easily outpaced the wagon containing Noemi and Marcus and the young guard posted by Julius to oversee them, riding far ahead of their regular cohort. It was late in the day and the glaring afternoon sun slanted down upon her from over the tree line and flashed into her eyes. Miriam closed them for a moment and, holding the reins steadily, stretched out her back. She felt the onset of a headache.

A foot soldier brushed against her, jostling her out of her momentary reverie. She opened her eyes and looked down at him. She recognized him. He had marched in her vicinity for several days past; and when they exchanged glances and pleasantries on one or two occasions, he had been friendly and well-spoken. His name, she thought, was Octavius. Today, however, for all his pleasant looks, he looked grubby and disreputable. Like all of the men, he needed a bath. To be fair, though, he could not help that, she thought as the light glinted off of the soldier's golden hair and his shiny mail and into her eyes, dazzling her suddenly. So, Miriam shook her head to clear her thoughts and smiled down upon the man by her side.

High above the trees, a hawk circled once, then swooped below into the woods, hunting for prey. In a long whoosh of gray and brown feathers, the hawk passed far over her head, for a glorious instant, washed golden by the sun.

Octavius caught Miriam's smile and looked back at her intently. Suddenly, he turned fully to her and grabbed at her hard. Leaning his weight in, he trapped her leg against the horse. The horse, confused by conflicting signals, stopped suddenly. Miriam looked at Octavius bewildered, momentarily alarmed. She tugged on the reins, tried to move her horse away.

"What do you want?" she asked, but it came out as a whisper.

As though in invitation, Octavius placed his dirty hand inside the bottom of her robe and slid it, rough, callused, filthy, up all along the length of her white leg. His eyes devouring her, he squeezed her brutally near the top of her inner thigh, his soldier's fingers trained to an awful strength. He let go of her thigh and began wiggling his hard fingers slowly until it touched her private parts. His breath grew jagged. "You," he said.

Frozen, Miriam did not react at first. Belatedly, blood rushed to her face, staining her face, her throat, her chest. Only then, with impeded strength, did she push his head away, kick at his head when she got more leverage, urge her horse into a run, far away from him. "You wanted it, whore," she heard him call after her, "I saw how you looked at me." Stunned by his words, she turned her head over her shoulder. As she glanced back at him, he put his fingers in his mouth and licked them clean. And then he looked in her face and smiled slowly. Jerking face forward, her complexion drained, Miriam heard the bark of his mockery, malevolent and threatening, following her.

In the woods, the hawk alighting on its prey, rose into the air once more, screaming its victory song.

Miriam kept her horse moving at a brisk trot, at the side of the host of marching men and horses. When the road narrowed, carved between two abutting hillsides of limestone cliffs, Miriam was forced to pull her horse back into the column, far ahead of where she had stationed herself earlier. Focusing neither to the right nor left, Miriam locked her eyes straight ahead, at the road. The sun pierced through the tree line once again, brilliant, blazing, blinding. Reflecting off the white limestone, the sun's light, shining into her face, was magnified a hundred-fold. Miriam shut her eyes. She could still feel that man's eyes on her as she rode far ahead of him on the road; his eyes and others as well, hungry eyes, probing eyes, curious eyes, unfriendly eyes, male eyes. The constant din of marching men and horses, their weapons clashing, the wagons jerking up and down on their metal axles, was suddenly unbearable. Miriam exhaled once and began to shake. She breathed in and out deeply to calm herself, but the smell of unwashed men and animals surged up through her nostrils, penetrating, overwhelming, unrelenting. It sickened her.

Biting down hard on her lip, Miriam wished herself back home in Sardis where she could sink into a hot bath in her father's villa for hours and close out the rest of the world for a very long time. But she was here in the province of Cappadocia marching with the Roman army. With Marcus and Noemi to sustain. And it was futile to desire privacy in a travelling camp, even one in which she barely knew a friendly soul amongst all the host of thousands. Her thoughts, trapped, began circling once again, this time at a frantic pace.

In the sky above, the hawk, sated, sat on the topmost branch of the tallest tree and cleaned its feathers of blood.

At dawn the next day, Miriam sat on a boulder, sharing the morning meal with Marcus and Noemi, each of whom were seated close to her, one at either side. This morning, she had chosen to eat by the wagon and not near the raucous, chaotic cooking pits. She put the bread in her mouth and chewed and tasted nothing.

There was a faint crackle of wood snapping in the surrounding trees and Miriam jumped, her heart already racing. She looked up and saw Julius approaching. Her whole body tensed. She had scarcely seen Julius to exchange more than a polite greeting to him as they handed Marcus back and forth for days. Sometimes he did not even come himself but sent Silius, his aide, instead. Last night he had sent Xenon, the surgeon to see her but she had refused to talk to him. Xenon had done a funny thing then, countermanded Julius' orders and sent the leader of the camp followers to see her, a middle-aged woman named Drusilla. Miriam had sent her away too.

"Miriam," Julius said, standing opposite her in the clearing, "good morning." He nodded at Noemi and smiled at his son. Marcus got up, dropping his food, and ran, chortling, to his father, who picked him up and threw him in the air. Marcus' voice rang out, clear and jubilant. Julius laughed once and then handed Marcus to the arms of Noemi, who stood to receive him. Julius bent down and picked up the piece of bread that had fallen to the ground and handed it to the girl, dismissing her with a gesture. She walked off, silent as a shadow, with Marcus in her arms, squealing at the top of his lungs as he tried to escape back to his father.

Miriam looked up at Julius quickly and back down at her food. She felt a mixture of intense anger and shame and right now she did not want to see him at all.

"May I join you here?"

Miriam nodded and continued to eat.

"Miriam, I want you to ride with Marcus up near my men today. Or in the wagon if that suits you better."

Miriam wondered with ire which of the soldiers stationed around her had reported yesterday's incident to him. She also wondered what version of the event Julius had heard and what he had made of it. Even now she knew him so slightly.

"Miriam," he said at last, "look at me."

"No," she said, chewing her tasteless hunk of bread, "go away."

He reached out and gently brushed his hand against the tiny braids she had furiously plaited throughout her hair early that morning. Miriam sidled away from him to the furthest end of the limestone boulder on which she was seated. As she moved, her green, thin wool gown rode up on her thighs, exposing her white legs to the light. She looked down and saw a dark bruise where that man had gripped her yesterday. Then she looked up and saw Julius staring at her naked legs, transfixed. It made her fierce with fury, so she jumped to the ground and pulled her green gown into place. Slowly, he reached out and took hold of her wrist, his fingers firmly positioned around the narrow bone. She looked at him icily and pulled once at her arm. He let go of it suddenly.

"Miriam," he said, "listen to me for a few minutes, then, if you still want me to, I will go." She nodded and sat down on a boulder some distance from him in the clearing.

Julius hesitated, swallowing, modulating his voice. "As long as you ride alone, an unmarried woman, with a child in an army camp, plenty of men will think you are a camp follower. Or, more precisely, they will think you are my whore, and that you can be bought for money or even for lust. Many of them will be looking for a way to get a chance with you for themselves."

She looked at him and laughed, her voice impregnated with vitriol.

"Believe me," Julius said carefully, "I, of all people, know well you are not a whore. We both know what happened and why and how long ago it was. And that it has not happened since. But your presence here with Marcus gives the appearance of something else altogether.

30

We are far from Sardis now, far from your father and his objections to me. And I think even he would not object to our marrying if he knew your safety was concerned."

She heard him out to the end. Over their heads, a brace of swallows patrolled the sky together, challenging each other, scolding, declaiming their possession of the land. The early morning sun shone through the trees, creating a play of light and shadow on the ground, as the leaves tossed upon the wind.

Miriam said, "How little you know me even now, if you think I did not marry you only because of my father's objections. My father objected to my coming with you as well, and yet here I am. Though I must say, it is beginning to look like I should have listened to him after all. I have learned anew these last few weeks that his objections have more weight than I sometimes permit myself to acknowledge."

Julius flushed bright red and stood up. He paced around the clearing once, twice and then circling to where she was sitting, he stood before her. He took her hands gently in his and said, "Okay, they were your objections to me as well as your father's. Even so, the situation has changed."

Miriam let go of most of her anger, holding back just a little bit in reserve. "Yes," she agreed, "the situation has changed." She pulled her hands away, firmly. "Tell me Julius. I have hardly seen you for days. And yet here you are now asking me again to marry you after several years. Can you tell me why? Is it only because you are concerned about my safety?"

"I..." he began, and then broke off. "Have you wanted to see me? After the first couple of days, I did not think so."

Miriam shrugged. "I hardly know anyone else here among the thousands of soldiers, do I?"

"Why did you come with the army? I never thought you would."

She looked at him incredulously. "You threatened to take my son with you."

31

"I would not have, of course, if you did not come."

There was a shattering moment of silence during which the hard mask on her face fell off, like a farmer shearing a lamb's coat and holding up the soft underbelly to view. She did not speak.

"I see how you are with him. How much he loves you. Marcus would be miserable without you." The silence between them continued unabated. "I wouldn't do that to a son of mine. I never had a mother myself." And then Julius added, his voice hard, probing. "Was that the only reason you came?"

"No," she said and looked away. Then she looked back, directly into his eyes. "I wanted to see the world and…"

"And?"

"I don't know," she shrugged. "A fool has his reasons. So did I. In retrospect, they seem just as empty-headed."

Julius stepped closer to Miriam, pulling her up until she stood before him. He circled one arm around her back and laced the other one delicately through her plaited hair. Bending his head forward, he kissed her hard on the mouth.

After he broke it off, he said, "I have been wanting to do that for quite some time. I thought you knew that, Miriam. But I didn't dare while we were anywhere near your father," he said, and gave a lopsided smile, full of charm and lust. "In any case, we are fast approaching Caesarea, the capitol of Cappadocia and I think once we reach there, you should marry me. I hope that you will." He looked at her and saw that she still seemed uncertain. Taking her small face between his hands, he said, suddenly serious. "You will have a similar problem in any city we live in as you do here. The appearance will be against you, against Marcus, against me. I don't want that for you. It will be better for all of us if you marry me, if you are my wife," he said, and bent his head once again to kiss her.

"No," she said, and pulled away from him, "not here. Too many can see. I don't want anyone looking on and thinking I am your *whore*."

32

Then her voice softened. "Not until we are married." At the word, blood ran bright through her cheeks, but she steeled herself again. "I will marry you, and according to Roman rites, Julius, if I must. But know this. I won't relinquish my traditions afterward. And I'll continue to teach them to Marcus. If you can't stick to that bargain, say so now and we won't marry." At the stubborn look he gave her, she added, "You swore an oath Julius, if you remember. Marcus will be taught Hebrew and the customs of my people."

Cursing, Julius stood up, his cheek tendons pulling taut. After some moments he stretched out his jaw and reset his face. "Damn the gods, well do I remember I swore an oath to you. I've kept it too, even as I regretted it. Remember that Marcus will be Roman as well." His eyes were narrowing, as his face reddened. "Just make sure you keep the marriage oath you will swear to me in a few days as faithfully as I've kept yours." His voice went deadly low. "Because I'll find out if you don't. You understand me, I suspect," he said, his face and voice like glinting swords. He turned and stormed away, a small tempest whirling furiously on the hillside. When he reached the very edge of the clearing, he held himself still for a few moments before turning to look at her. When he spoke, his voice was even again. "I want you riding up near my men today. I'll send Silius back to fetch you and Marcus. And in a few days, we'll marry."

As he turned away from her, towards his camp, he added, his voice barely audible. "The man who did that to you will be punished." And then he left, disappearing through the trees, with only the rustle of his light tread upon a bed of dead pine needles to mark his departure.

Miriam let out her breath and sat back down on the boulder. For the moment, the tempest had subsided. A fury of wind fomented whole from some future storm, not yet in sight. She could not afford to harness the gust of that prospective anger at this strange juncture. There was ill-wind enough, already blowing on her horizon, that could end up scuttling her. Still, one way or another, with a marriage now in

33

view, she felt such relief after the events of yesterday that she let out a strange half cry, half laugh as she wrapped her arms around herself.

Marcus ran up to her just then, naked and wet after being bathed in a nearby pool. He was damp and warm and delicious; she picked him up, a small struggling boy in her arms, his dark hair a wet nimbus of curls. She kissed him and threw him up in the air, like his father did. He laughed for her then as he laughed when his father threw him in the air. "Again," he demanded, like every happy child from the beginning of time. She tossed him again and laughed right back at him, chasing him around the clearing until she was sweaty faced and out of breath. Turning suddenly solemn, she waited until she caught her breath and said to her handmaid, "It seems I am to marry Julius after all. In a few days."

Noemi did not look happy for her. Miriam could see the fear starting in the corners of her eyes though she tried to conceal it. With his martial air and his commanding voice, the girl, she suspected, was too intimidated to feel anything but trepidation and obedience in his presence.

"But mistress, how will we–" Noemi said, but could not bring herself to finish.

"Don't worry," Miriam said in as reassuring a voice as she could muster. "We'll keep to our traditions. I've already told him so and made him agree. But I'll be his wife, so we'll be safer. Don't worry," she repeated, this time with a small smile at Noemi, chiseled half from pain, half from courage. "It will be better for us. If I hadn't been such a fool, I would have foreseen it before I left." She shook her head to move them both past their nerves. The release of tension from the exercise had been evanescent after all. She said with focused practicality, "Well, we had best finish packing. Silius is coming soon to move the horses and our wagon up the line."

Julius emerged from the woods and walked straight towards his camp. It was not much past dawn. Truth to tell, he wanted a few minutes of privacy in his tent before it was disassembled and loaded on to the wagons for the day. Many of the soldiers he passed saluted him, glancing his way for a friendly look from their centurion. But he schooled his face and tarried neither to talk to his men nor to enquire after their wellbeing on the long march. Most mornings and evenings he spent some time riding a circuit around camp to keep up the morale of the men under his command, but he supposed today he would postpone the activity to the evening. Or better yet, he would send Silius to do it for him. Julius grimaced. Silius was becoming ever more invaluable to him. He had better check this tendency in future. Too much reliance on any one of his subordinates established a pattern of weakness and might diminish his authority in future.

Julius reached his tent. One of the Legion standards, a leaping white dolphin in a sea of blue, was at its post, ready to be carried at the front of the column by his men. "Vincius," Julius barked. Vincius, the recent recruit left on guard at his pavilion was facing away from him, slouching, relaxed, at his ease. At Julius' command, the soldier straightened up immediately, and turned sharply towards Julius.

"Yes, sir."

"Send Silius to me."

"Yes, sir. Immediately." Vincius loped off in the direction from which Julius had just come, before disappearing into the throng of soldiers milling around the morning cook fires.

Julius watched this half maliciously. He and Silius had a running bet as to how long it would take to knock Vincius into shape. He had predicted a long time. Right now, it looked like he was going to win. Then he bent his head and entered his tent. The air inside was cool, the night air still trapped inside, refreshing. Soon, too soon, with the heat rising, the air in the tent would stifle him. Better let the men disassemble it shortly. Then he could ride outside, in the morning breeze. Julius sat down on a folding chair and stared at his armor.

"It will be good to have *my son* and the girl nearby me all the time," Julius said aloud. "They will be safer that way. Especially her." He looked down at his feet, down at the ground and sat very still, breathing in and out softly. He thought, *"Nothing can come out of nothing, nothing can go back to nothing."*

Silius entered the tent at last.

"It took you long enough," said Julius, still looking at the ground. "Come help me with my armor."

"It went well, sir?" Silius approached him.

"Yes," Julius responded, looking at the ground. "They are moving up the line today. You are to go in a little while and escort their wagon up to the front of the column. Take however many men you want to aid you. In the evenings, for the next few days, set up their tent near mine. But not too close. I don't want any additional gossip arising among the men. And post a guard outside of it nightly as they sleep." Julius stood up and stretched.

"Yes, sir," said Silius, picking up the mail from the camp table on which it lay and positioning it over Julius' head, on his shoulders, over the light brown, linen tunic he was wearing. "Is there anything else I am to know?"

"She will marry me in a few days. But that's just between ourselves. I don't want the men privy to it beforehand."

"Congratulations, sir. And about time. It will be good to have the youngster nearby, proper-like. And your lady."

"Yes," said Julius. After a moment Julius glanced at him.

"Sir," asked Silius?

"We paid off that soldier generously who reported to you last night?"

36

Silius smiled cynically. "All too generously. I wish I had his wages this week."

"And he knows to keep his mouth shut so the talk doesn't spread any more than it has already."

"Sir, as I understand it, it happened out in the open, and there were plenty to see and to talk about it after, so without paying off a quarter of the army..." He shrugged.

"Yes, I see," said Julius. "Then, under the circumstances, we will manage as best we can. I want that soldier... What was his name?"

"Octavio. Under Serapio's command."

"Octavio," Julius repeated to himself. "If we cannot shut mouths any other way, I want him publicly whipped. A hundred lashes. That will make the men think, and, perhaps, stop their prattle and any other ideas..." He shrugged. "We won't have to worry about that after they see him punished."

Silius said, "You have considered with one hundred lashes, sir, the man is likely to die."

"Have I considered it?" Julius laughed, mirthlessly. His ice blue eyes flickered, then narrowed. "It's the reason I chose that number."

Pacing, Julius made a circuit around the inside of the pavilion. He positioned himself, face toward his pallet, his back towards Silius, and stood very still, his fists clenched at his sides. "Did you find out whether there was any truth to the man's accusation that she wanted him to act familiarly with her? Were there any rumors of misbehavior on her part?"

Silius waited silently.

Julius added at last, "Did she toy with him to treat her so?"

"Nothing, sir. The guards we posted near her say she is quiet, doesn't talk much to the men, but friendly when she does."

Julius spun around and glared at Silius.

"Not too friendly," Silius added. "Not that way."

"Good," said Julius. He frowned and swiped at his brow with the back of his hand. "It's like Hades in here, a dark and humid hellhole. Let's finish securing this armor. I want to get out of here. And you can be on your way to fetch my son to me." Julius paused. "And my bride."

CHAPTER 4
Wedding

It ended up longer than a few days before Miriam and Julius were finally married. All that next week, as the army column led by Julius and his fellow officers traversed the province of Cappadocia, sweeping towards the capitol city of Caesarea in Asia Minor, the sky shone a cloudless and benign blue and the air felt temperate for early spring. But, at night, when the sun disappeared from her world, the temperature still dipped precipitately, and Miriam found herself shivering and tense, and not only from the cold. Nightly, she withdrew into her dark tent illuminated inside by an oil lamp that burned until morning. She had Noemi and Marcus for company. She talked to them for hours, telling stories, and then watching through the night as first Marcus and then Noemi drifted into sweet sleep.

Occasionally, Silius joined them inside the tent in the early evening and told stories of his own, of his younger days when he campaigned in Britain and Germania. Marcus and Noemi would listen to his fabulous tales with wide-open eyes. Miriam, more worldly than the other two, sometimes wondered about the truth of Silius' stories; the great skirmishes waged against blue-skinned warriors, led into battle by fierce, blue-haired maidens riding chariots and wielding swords. He spoke, too, of a great wall that vaulted from one side of a gigantic island to another, built at the end of the civilized world to hold back these strange devils who summoned the very elements, dense fog and ceaseless rain, to aid them in their defense.

Miriam knew, of course, in some societies the women went out to fight; she had learned Herodotus' tales of the Amazons by heart: the women of Sauromatia who bestrode horses, taking to battle with javelin and bow, before they mated with Scythian men. Her brother, Yehonatan, had traveled to those parts once and written home to tell them of his finds. And so, as Silius told his tales, her thoughts wandered to her brother, an ache inside like a suppurating sore, tender and unhealed. He had been gone years already, and she missed him beyond measure; nor did she expect to see him any time soon. Once she settled somewhere, she hoped at most for a letter a year.

And then her eyes would alight on Silius again and bring her back to the present, a stolid and kindly presence, and one with whom she was already familiar, talking to ease their isolation. But after he left at night and the other two sank into their easy sleep, Miriam lay awake, perturbed by every stray rustle that came to her ears, her pulse jumping wildly until she deciphered what was happening outside of her in the dark around her tent.

One night after moonset, Drusilla presented herself again at the entrance to the tent. She was a petite woman with long brown locks mingled with a few gray strands who radiated a powerful presence. Tonight she wore a rough woolen cloak, undyed and well worn. This time, Miriam, at her wit's end, invited her into the tent and served her wine. They sat in a corner, while Noemi and Marcus slumbered, and their quiet talk quickly turned purposeful.

"Xenon sent me to teach you, if you wish to learn," Drusilla said.

"I do," said Miriam. And Drusilla proceeded to instruct her on how to prevent pregnancy through the use of herbal tonics and even how to get rid of a pregnancy in its first few weeks. After Miriam exchanged payment, Drusilla removed a vial from her cloak filled with a tonic for her to use and promised to come again to teach her. "I thought you would be interested when I heard what happened," she said. "A pregnancy on the road is no good."

"A pregnancy on the road would be disastrous," Miriam said, taking Drusilla's hand in her own. It was a strong and capable hand, much like the woman herself, who was a font of knowledge about herbal remedies. She sighed loudly once. "Thank you so much. If only I had known a woman like you when younger, it would have saved me from..." Miriam stopped herself. She was not particularly maternal. But she loved Marcus too much now to wish he had never existed in her life. Still, she made a silent vow to herself to aid women in like circumstances just as Drusilla had helped her. "I've been very lonely," Miriam admitted.

Drusilla looked into her eyes and nodded. "And very frightened too, I believe."

"Terrified," Miriam replied. She drew in a deep breath and looked down at the floor of the tent. "Please come see me again very soon. I'm to marry Julius when we stop in Caesarea, later this week." Her beautiful green eyes became large. "I have so many questions. I need to know..." And she looked down at the floor of the tent.

This time Drusilla took her hand. "Your mama never prepared you?" Her voice was rich and soothing, like a pan flute piped by a master. And on her wrist was a copper bangle with blue stones. Their color shone forth like the night sky near twilight's end when the planets first emerge, then stars.

"She died when I was very young, you see," said Miriam. Her brow furrowed as she looked inwards. "She was young too." Miriam looked up then. "If ever I can do anything for you in return, let me know."

41

"You can, lady," said Drusilla. By the light of the oil lamp, her face was half in shadow, but her deep brown eyes flashed. "Xenon says you read and write. Would you teach me? I can offer you this." And Drusilla pointed to the bracelet on her wrist. "It's the most precious thing I own."

"Of course, I will," said Miriam. "I'm already teaching my son and Noemi. But you keep the bracelet. It's beauty so befits you. When you come to teach me, I'll teach you as well."

Drusilla's eyes softened then and began to glow with inner light. "Thank you," she said. "It's what I've wanted more than anything. But until now, no one I asked ever said yes."

And so, a plan was formed between Miriam and Drusilla that lasted the rest of the trip and continued for many years afterwards, as Xenon and Drusilla later wed. But that's a story for another time.

As the days passed, the landscape around Miriam changed radically. Cliffs colored variously in white and beige, gray and black, surrounded her. The white cliffs rose out of the ground, spiraling up and out into jutting fingers, pitted and crooked, like the gnarled hands of a village elder. Elsewhere, the land had molded itself into odd, white cones of differing heights, which had formed, she was told by a soldier, after soft volcanic ash had spewed out of a mountain to the north. Miriam's eyes soon adjusted to the sea of white and gray enclosing her, eternally frozen into frothing crests and lofting peaks. And she realized belatedly as she looked at the cliffs each day, that some of the hills concealed high caves, inhabited by people whose faces she saw from time to time, peeking out at them from tiny crevices as the column passed. Whether the country people felt nervous or hostile to the Roman army riding by their homes, she could not tell.

The land, Miriam noticed, looked fertile and abundant for early spring. The bright green plants she saw around her appeared remarkably verdant against the white backdrop of the soil and cliffs. And as the farmland Miriam passed began to proliferate, as the inhabitants grew thicker on the ground, this signaled to her that the army was approaching the city of Caesarea.

Julius' superiors planned a stopover of several days to rest the horses and the men, to restock supplies and to overhaul the wagons bearing the heavy military equipment, the catapults large and small and the ballistae, machines that fired darts in rapid succession. Some of the wagons, drawn four hundred miles, carrying their heavy loads were now in poor repair, the wood splintering, their metal hinges needing maintenance. The heavy weaponry, in contrast, was in perfect shape as none of it had been utilized during the long trip.

The province of Cappadocia, like the area around Sardis, was securely held by the Roman Empire. Troops were only necessary en masse in the borderlands. And, except in the immediate aftermath of storms or floods, the provincial roads were well maintained.

Miriam had spent the week sitting in her wagon, discreetly guarded by Julius' men. Because of her lack of freedom, she looked forward to the relative autonomy she would be granted in Caesarea. She wanted to walk around the city for a few days, to sleep a little later without the daily need to wake in the small hours each morning only to be shut up in a wagon and traveling by dawn. She, Marcus, and Noemi were to be billeted to a house in town, she had been told, not to a tent. And a house, of all mundane things, suddenly seemed like a real luxury to her.

This final week, Miriam realized the toll the trip across Asia Minor had taken on her; she felt strained and exhausted. Her clothing was looking worn with the hard travel and the primitive washings it had endured, the dyes already faded. And in the past week, her garments had begun to hang on her loosely, as though they had been fitted to someone else's figure, not her own.

Miriam saw Julius during the days, but never inside her tent in the evenings. He had his reasons, no doubt, and she did not question his decision. The idea that she was to marry him in days, be his wife, cleave to his flesh, still felt unreal to her.

Late one afternoon, fifteen leagues outside of Caesarea, the column halted in its square formation preliminary to setting up camp for the Legion's final night outside of the city. As Miriam watched from her wagon, standing, stretching her arms and legs as her tent was pitched, she saw Julius beckon to her from the high ground where his tent was stationed. Surprised, she let herself down from the wagon and walked slowly over to him. He had never summoned her to his tent before.

"You wanted to see me?"

"Yes, Miriam, please come in." Julius smiled at her briefly and retreated into the tent, so that she could enter behind him. When she had passed inside, he leaned his upper body back outside. "Vincius," he said to the guard, "see that I am not disturbed for the next while."

"My pleasure, sir." Vincius grinned broadly.

Julius stared back at him, his eyes hard and unwavering, until the suggestive grin on Vincius' face slowly dissipated leaving behind an irresolute expression, like a pristine blanket of snow melting into a wintry mix.

"Yes, sir," Vincius said.

Julius stepped back inside and sealed off the entrance to the tent carefully. When he turned back to face her, Miriam's face was mottled red.

"I thought we would...," she said. "Didn't you say...?"

Julius bit off a laugh. "Don't worry, that is not what I had in mind," he said, and looked her over intently, noticing the lank fit of her robe. "Tomorrow night, once we are in town, and with time to spare, it will be a different matter. So, ready yourself." He sat down on his camp-folding chair. "No, I wanted to discuss the marriage arrangements with you. Of course, I realize it would have been more proper to discuss this with your father."

Miriam sat down opposite him on the camp bed and raised her chin, so that her head was held high. "I am perfectly competent to discuss the arrangement on my own," she said.

"I hope so," Julius said and nodded at her. He paused, a minute, two minutes, before he finally spoke again. "As I see it, Miriam, there is a problem. And it is best that you are informed of it now instead of two days hence, when it will be too late, in case you find the situation is not acceptable to you." Julius paused again. After some moments he resumed, this time looking at her straight in the face. "As you have previously informed me, our marriage cannot be legal by Jewish law. Unfortunately, it will not be altogether legal by Roman law either."

Miriam absorbed this without change of expression. "I don't understand."

"Marriage is only recognized by Roman law when one Roman citizen marries another. It is quite like Jewish law that way, as you've explained it to me. Only we don't have a system for conversion. The only way an exception comes about by law is if the Emperor grants citizenship to the party who is not Roman. Unfortunately, I'm too lowly in status to count on getting such a favor from the Emperor." Julius slight grimace was self-deprecatory. "But we can still be married. And it will be recognized as such in the army, but our future children will inherit your status and not mine."

"Oh," said Miriam. "So, then Marcus..." Her eyes widened.

"Yes, Marcus," said Julius, his eyes glittering like frost. "But, as my son, any future children we have will become Roman citizens as soon as he joins the army. Like I did. Like Marcus will." He broke off, then resumed after a moment. "I am less concerned about any girls we may have. Let them be content with your status and be Jews."

"Like you did?" said Miriam.

Julius glanced at her. "Have I never told you my parents weren't married when I was born?" he said, then closed his eyes, his anger nearly gone. "We'll have plenty of time for conversations like this

45

soon, so let's continue to discuss the marriage arrangement. It is a fact that our marriage won't be recognized in Rome. But it's unlikely in the extreme that the Legion will be posted to Italy for any reason. We've already been stationed in this part of the Empire for close to a hundred years. So, you see, it hardly matters. Such a marriage will be recognized well enough in the army, which is used to such mismatched marriages as ours will be, and in the provinces. Although, it is best that you know that it will never be considered wholly legitimate by Roman law."

"Not wholly legitimate," repeated Miriam, staring at the ground. She shrugged once. "But you tell me it will be recognized by the army," she said looking up at Julius.

He nodded once. "Yes, absolutely."

"Julius, why didn't tell me about this before?"

Julius asked, "What choice do we have, really? You mean to marry me, don't you, Miriam, and I mean to marry you. To tell you the truth..." Julius paused.

"Yes?"

"I wanted to calculate my chances of receiving official permission to marry you. But that would necessitate you being granted Roman status, which could take a long time, or it could never happen at all. We are better off simply marrying now, and not bringing it to official notice. Later, if the opportunity arises, we might be able to arrange the next step more easily, if we are still married by then." He shrugged.

Miriam sat still, thinking about what Julius had just said to her. Finally, she looked up. "But, if we are not to be married according to either Jewish or Roman law, there is still a question about what rite we shall use?" asked Miriam.

"Yes, that is a bit of a problem," said Julius. "But it seems to me that by both Roman law and Jewish law as you have explained it in the past, the two most important elements are the financial settlements and the bedding. We can work out the financial settlement

46

tonight, and the bedding tomorrow night and then we will be more or less married."

"More or less married," Miriam repeated, her eyes on the floor. She pursed her lip and held herself very still.

"Yes, it is unfortunate, but a legal impediment exists on both of our sides." Julius shrugged. "This is the best we can do at the moment." He broke off, frustrated. "So, we won't be precisely using either Roman or Jewish rites, but we will be writing out a financial settlement that I will vow before witnesses to honor even if we later decide to divorce. Normally," said Julius looking straight at her, "such an agreement could be contested, since our marriage will not be legal according to Roman law. So, I want our agreement written in a way that binds me. To put you at ease."

Miriam met Julius' eyes, squarely. "Thank you for that, Julius. But this is not what I wanted for myself."

"On that point, Miriam there is agreement between us. Nor is it what I wanted for myself either. But you're a realist. It is something I've admired about you at times in the past. And this is the situation we have to work with." Julius shrugged. "I admit this is my fault. For one, I should never have let you come along. It hasn't been good for you. I was selfish, I admit. Silius tried to warn me, but I didn't listen. I wanted Marcus with me and never thought ahead. So, now we must marry before anything else happens. I can't permit you to remain in a situation where you are neither fish nor fowl, hence unsafe. You are under my protection here. I am responsible for you."

Miriam stared at the floor, hugging herself, her face bright red. Outside the tent, she could hear some soldiers arguing loudly as they passed by. Another contingent of soldiers approached and there was the clash of metal on metal. Miriam heard a raucous laugh, and from somewhere else, the sound of orders barked at a junior guardsman. When she spoke again, there was a tremulous edge to her voice despite her attempts at control. "I heard you had that man beaten until he almost died."

Julius closed his palms into fists and held them tight at his sides. "Yes. I did. He may yet die. I hear he is still quite ill." He watched to see her reaction. "Does it matter to you?"

"No," she said, tears running silently down her face. "I still don't understand why...how," she broke off as the tears continued to run.

"Once you are married to me, you won't have to understand it. Such a thing is extraordinarily unlikely ever to happen to you again." Julius stood and walked over to a table placed against the tent wall, his back towards her momentarily. When he turned towards her again, he was carrying two earthenware cups. He handed her one and sat down again. "It's wine," he said. "Take it and drink."

Miriam drank her wine slowly, looking down at the ground, at the walls, at nothing at all. When she finished at last, she looked back up at Julius, her face still blotched with color.

"And now," he said, "I suggest we start negotiating whatever financial settlements we can arrange. I warrant," he said, and smiled gently, "it won't take long as neither of us have much. And when we are done, I'll call in my secretary to draft the agreement formally. Tomorrow, I'll have the cohort's legal advisor look it over. Then we can both sign it by the afternoon. If, Miriam, that meets with your approval."

Eyes down on the ground again, at last she said, "Yes."

All that afternoon, Julius and Miriam sat together in the tent arguing over every financial contingency that occurred to either of them. Initially, Julius was surprised by Miriam's sharpness in negotiating with him. She was the daughter of a merchant, though. Her father must have trained her to deal with business matters far more extensively than he had ever realized. He wondered, then, what other surprises Miriam had in store for him. And whether they would accrue to his advantage or not.

When late afternoon had stretched into evening and evening into night, Julius called to his guard. Vincius, still stationed outside the tent, stuck his head into the tent to receive Julius' command. He looked around the tent, seeing only two fully dressed people seated at a table amidst the casual disarray of parchment, ink and an unpacked tent. When Vincius looked straight at his commander, the disappointment on his face was palpable even to Miriam who hardly knew him. Julius' eyes met Miriam's and they shared a grin.

"Vincius," Julius said, "if you have had your fill of peeping around my tent would you be so good as to send for our dinner. And when you have finished that strenuous duty, kindly summon my secretary here with his writing gear."

Vincius glanced at Miriam before saluting Julius, right hand to chest, and left the tent.

The food, already prepared and waiting for them on a tray, arrived in the tent almost immediately, carried in by a servant. Miriam ate simply, flat bread with a spread of spiced beans and olive oil, fish sauce, some fruit. She envied Julius his roasted lamb, whose heavily spiced perfume lingered in the tent as he ate. Miriam swallowed her food and lifted her cup of wine to her lips. She drank the wine slowly, savoring its taste, as she warded off the scent of Julius' meat. The method of its slaughter prohibited her from eating it according to the law of her people.

Towards the end of their hurried meal, Julius' secretary, Ennius Andronicus, arrived. The secretary arranged his writing supplies on a folding table he had carried in with him, setting out his ink and some pieces of papyrus. Then he waited patiently while Julius finished his meal, stealing glances from time to time at Miriam from under his eyelids. The secretary possessed a wizened, dark face and small brown eyes, with almost no white surrounding them. As his eyes stole over her repeatedly, he looked, thought Miriam, exactly like a weasel peering nervously out of the ground on the lookout for prey as he watched his own back for predators. Julius insouciant, thought Miriam, was concentrating only on his food.

Julius finished eating, wiping his mouth slowly. He looked from Ennius Andronicus to Miriam and back to Ennius, his mouth taut, his eyebrows lifted. Ennius glanced once at Julius. Looking down suddenly, Ennius began reshuffling the bits of parchment he had brought with him. So, Julius had noticed, Miriam thought, but had bided his time before interceding.

Rising, Julius poured more wine for Miriam and himself from the beaker. He drank his wine straight off, then began to dictate to Ennius the financial settlements from Julius to Miriam and those from Miriam to Julius as they had agreed to them. Then they waited until Ennius transcribed the document into a form that satisfied each of them. Julius, pleased, looked up from the bit of parchment and dismissed the secretary. But he took firm hold of Miriam's arm when she rose to follow the man out.

"Stay here another moment, if you will," he said, his eyes only on her, as the heavy covering to the tent fell shut behind him once more. Turning, Julius secured it, then stood facing Miriam. Raising his hands, he caressed her face slowly, from her cheekbones to her chin. Then, tilting her face up lightly, with his index fingers, he kissed her, slowly, lingeringly. Miriam could taste the wine he had drunk and the meat he had eaten. She breathed in his scent. One of his hands slowly looped around her shoulders, before he pulled her against him, hard. She could feel the tension coiling through his body. He kissed her and kissed her. And at last, Miriam kissed Julius back.

When she lifted her arms a few moments later to place them around his shoulders, Julius broke off their embrace suddenly and pushed her away from him. She reeled backward as he stared at her, his brow tense.

"Julius?" said Miriam, moving a step closer to him.

He moved back a step half of a beat after her.

50

"I don't understand," she said.

"Nothing," he said. "We'll wait for tomorrow night. This is not how I planned things would go. Not now."

She continued to stare at him. Her face, she thought, must reveal everything she felt.

Julius looked away then moved to the door of the tent. He stuck his head out of the door. "Vincius," he bellowed.

As Vincius approached, Julius stepped out of the tent and held the door open for Miriam to follow him. "Escort the lady to her tent now," he ordered Vincius. He turned back to Miriam, who had not yet fully emerged from the doorframe of the tent. She was still staring at him. "Good night, Miriam," he said. "Until tomorrow."

Miriam stood without moving, looking up at him, her face exposed. Julius reiterated his command, this time to her. "Vincius will escort you to your tent." And turning back to Vincius he said, "Vincius, take her now." Julius walked off several paces into the dark.

"Yes, sir," said Vincius, stepping up to Miriam. "Come with me, ma'am," he said, just failing to look her in the face.

"Yes," said Miriam. She looked up at Vincius' face. He has a kind face, she thought to herself, and stepped out of the tent. She smiled at him and he smiled back. "We'll go together," she said and took his arm.

———◆———

From his vantage point some steps away, Julius watched Miriam as she departed with Vincius at her side. Then turning sharply on his heel, he walked back to his tent, and stuck his head inside for a moment. He stared blankly at the dishevelment in the interior of the tent and breathed deeply. He could still smell her scent. Shaking his head, he pulled out of the tent altogether, inhaling the cool night air. He looked up at the sky, but the stars were obscured by clouds. *The stars have lost their fires,* he thought, *the heavens have no brightness but only mists on darkened skies.* Julius looked a moment more, then changing his mind for no apparent reason, he went striding off to take a late-night tour all around the square perimeter of the camp.

"Silius," Julius said, when he came face to face with his chief aide. Leaning against a wagon, drinking wine from a silver cup in the shape of a gladiator that he had acquired during his service in Gaul, Silius was watching a game of dice in progress. "Keep company with me as I walk."

"Sir," agreed Silius amicably. And falling in next to him, Silius walked with Julius, in silence, pace by pace.

CHAPTER 5

Bedding

Julius stood staring down a precipice at the water-logged wreckage below him. Soldiers and horses and wagons had fallen down a muddy cliff, and the wounded horses, now dead, lay sprawled near the bottom of the ravine. They would lay there forever more, while vultures picked at their flesh and their bones slowly turned to dust.

His soldiers, his horses, his wagons.

His anger was beginning to boil into rage.

Julius had been riding three miles ahead of the troops, on his way to Caesarea and Miriam, when a messenger had reached him to turn back.

"Breugos," Julius yelled down the slope to the new weapons master who was hurrying back up towards him. Breugos had recently replaced Leos, but he had none of Leos' easy competence. "What happened here? What caused this disaster?"

"Sir," said Breugos, huffing slightly as he pulled himself up the last bit of slope. "The axle from the wagon split apart on this curve where some stones have been removed from the road and it needs maintenance."

"Why were the stones removed?"

"That needs investigation. Looks like malice, to cause an accident on the steep slope here. Then, as I was saying, the wagon tipped and fell down the cliff, pulling the men and horses."

"How many men killed?"

"Five men outright. And one woman. Eight wounded. Four serious." Breugos waited a beat. "The fall must have caused the ballista to begin showering bolts at the troops. A multiplication of misfortune."

"A woman?" said Julius. "Did she–?

"She was busy, I understand," Breugos interrupted. "She didn't cause this."

"Busy," repeated Julius with asperity, "in the wagon? With the men and the ballista?" He looked straight at Breugos, freeing his rage so it showed in his eyes and the set of his face, "Why was the ballista loaded during transport?"

Breugos hemmed and hawed and fear began to show in his eyes. But he had no proper answer, swearing he had overseen the disassembling of the weaponry after their last drill. Except it had not been disassembled today. Julius demoted him on the spot and ordered him back down the hill to help the others. More punishment, he avowed, would follow swiftly.

Julius' rage now felt incandescent. Why had Leos chosen this incompetent to replace him? Was it a parting gift of animus on a matter that Leos had never forgiven him for? His promotion? Or the fact that Marcellus' murder had never been solved?

He left Vincius in charge of recovery and followed Silius to the tent where Xenon, with an aide, was working so hard treating the wounded, he barely had time to consult.

Xenon looked up at Julius and they each nodded to the other. "I have two men here with broken bones, one broke an arm, the other

54

a leg, both set now. Two more are unconscious. Those are serious. One, I'll wait to see if he wakes up. The more severely injured had his skull bashed in."

"Any chance he'll recover?" Julius knew that Xenon had successfully performed trepanation before, skull surgery to remove bone fragments and to release inflammation, but he had done so in Sardis. The odds were against this soldier surviving with his cohort on the move.

"If he survives the trip to Caesarea, it's possible. I don't want to operate on him here," said Xenon letting out a deep breath. "The rest have wounds that are less serious. They'll all be fine."

The funeral was held later that day, with Julius choosing to bury the dead rather than burn them because of the absence of sufficient dead wood in the vicinity. Julius gave a short eulogy, "Men, the deaths today were not in battle. They were utterly preventable. That is the tragedy. Nevertheless, these men gave their lives for the service of Rome, to spread civilization, and that is worthy of great merit in this realm and in the next. And now we must say goodbye to these soldiers as they go individually to their gods and their fates in the afterworld." Then Julius read out all the names and closed by saying, "I know you have worked hard these last six weeks. But we must all do better. Here and now, I vow to you that I will too." He then called an early halt to the day, so that they could stay here for the night with an extra drink ration.

All this day, he had taken note of his men's weariness, the slowness of their responses. The trip, 400 miles thus far, had been trying. That reflected the poor conditioning and readiness of everyone involved, not least, he admitted to himself, his own. No longer were they the crack troops Julius Caesar had relied on, as when, nigh upon a century and a half back, Caesar had famously hauled the Xth Legion forty miles each day in Gaul only to fight and win repeatedly at day's end. Having read Caesar's memoirs, he felt dispirited by the lack of discipline in his cohort and saw his own flaws of leadership quite plainly.

"Silius," Julius said, "When was the last time I made an offering to Dionysius?"

Silius thought a moment, then counted back on his fingers. "The month before we left. That's two and a half months back, sir. You don't think...?"

Julius felt fear boring into his gut again, the particular kind that occurred when he placed himself at the mercy of an angry Dionysius, who rained down chaos at will. But he made his face show nothing. He needed to calm the situation lest it get out of hand and the exhausted men turned restive.

He turned then to speak to Silius. "I should stay."

"No," said Silius. "You go, all will be well this evening. You'll see."

Night had long since fallen by the time Julius, torch in hand approached the small house in Caesarea Cappadocia where Miriam was lodging.

Assembling his thoughts on the condition of the Legion, thinking of improvements small and large that he could implement during the next stage of travel, Julius rode through Caesarea, looking about him by the light of a waxing gibbous moon. He was searching for the small house he had been directed to which was a way station for Roman officials to use when passing through Caesarea, nicer and more private than the accommodations available in camp. Silius had accompanied Miriam into town earlier that day, then arranged for her baggage and Julius' to be transferred to the house.

The city of Caesarea Cappadocia was dominated by Mount Argaeus to its south, rising thousands of feet above them. Julius had been eyeing the mountain for days. From a small mound far off at the end of the horizon, the mountain had grown to dominate their skyline, looming larger daily. An ancient volcano, but one that no longer rumbled, for which thank the gods, who had seen fit instead to decorate the plateau with tufts and turrets, like small fingers creeping up towards the heavens. Out of these soft conical formations, dotted here and there with black basalt caps, the natives had whittled themselves living spaces. What a strange and primitive thing to inhabit a cave instead of a house! Though, he supposed, it would be warm enough in winter and cool in summer. And better than a tent.

Finally, Julius saw the small house and the posted guard who looked half asleep. When the man caught sight of him a few seconds later, he straightened quickly, Only, then, did Julius cross the street.

"Hello, Arianus."

"Sir." Arianus sketched a salute, his right hand barely touching his chest.

"All quiet here?"

"It is now."

"You've had your dinner, I hope?"

"Yes, sir. The ladies inside provided me with camp rations."

Julius nodded. "Any trouble at all to report on, then?"

"A couple of drunken men walking by is all. I sent them off in another direction. They didn't seem too happy I was interfering with them."

Julius stepped in close and looked over Arianus. The young Spaniard was coltish, his body tall and lanky rather than well developed, with dark hair, a lengthy nose and a prominent forehead. Julius had always found his work competent. "All right, then, get some sleep. But I want you and Atticus back on guard here tomorrow at midmorning."

"Sir," said Arianus, relieved. He stifled a yawn, took Julius' horse, and saluted one more time – a proper salute this time – before setting off.

Alone, Julius stood outside the house, watching the empty avenue idly, until Arianus disappeared from his sight. At last, Julius turned. Then firmly pulling the door open, he stepped inside.

57

Inside the house, Miriam sat downstairs on a wooden bench in the atrium of the small house, awaiting Julius. With its plain, white-washed walls, the house possessed little in the way of furniture or other amenities. There were a few benches downstairs, and a rickety wooden table large enough for a few people to sit together. Miriam had substituted the pallets and blankets upstairs with their own, since she suspected them of being cleaner than what she had found in the lodging. She had not touched Julius' belongings. Noemi and Marcus were already upstairs, sound asleep. Miriam leaned her head back against the wall, closed her eyes and nodded off.

Sometime later, she came suddenly awake. She heard two voices outside, breaking the silence. One of the voices, Miriam recognized, was Julius. There was the sound of someone marching away and then silence. A while later, the latch to the door lifted.

"Julius," she said, as he entered. She stood up to greet him. "There's wine for you waiting on the table."

Julius stood near the stone lintel, regarding her, then closed the door behind him. He fastened the bolt, walked over to the table, and poured a glass of wine. She looked down at herself, at the wreck of her own clothes, unchanged from earlier in the day and felt a stab of unease, until she remembered what she was about.

"Shall I pour you some wine as well, Miriam?" asked Julius.

Wine might help, she thought, but then remembered all this trouble had first started with some shared wine. Wine would not be her ally tonight. She shook her head. "No, not now, Julius," she replied and sat back down.

He walked over to her then, coming to sit next to her on the wooden bench. Miriam shifted away, closer to the edge, giving him distance, room for both of them to sit comfortably. He drank his wine down slowly, savoring the taste on his tongue. When he was done, he placed the earthenware cup on the soft stone floor, and leaning back against the wall, Julius circled her waist. Slowly, he began to rub her back. His hand strayed up, down, around, up down and around, slow, sensual movements. Miriam stayed upright on the bench.

"Some wine might help," said Julius at last.

Miriam did not reply.

Julius continued to move his hand along her back and waist, taking in new terrain, always with that gossamer touch. Finally, he turned his body to her, placing his two hands on her shoulders, and began to draw her to him softly. She did not move. She could feel his surprise at her resistance. He looked down at her, then put a hand on her breast, squeezing lightly, rubbing his thumb up and around, up and around. At last, he moved his head in to kiss her. Miriam turned her head away from him.

"What is this, Miriam?" Julius said.

She said nothing.

"I told you last night to prepare yourself for this."

"You did tell me that last night," she said, and her eyes flashed with anger, "along with a host of other things."

"If there was something in the agreement we made between ourselves yesterday that you objected to, you should have told me last night, or earlier today. There was plenty of time to change any facet of it before we signed it, earlier."

"No, Julius," she said, "it isn't the agreement I object to tonight." Miriam's eyes slid to the left, then down to the ground. "It is just that...," she said and hesitated. Then she exhaled roughly and continued, "I can't, not tonight. I have my menses."

Miriam felt Julius' gaze on her. He was studying her. Her face and neck flushed crimson red.

"A little blood, Miriam, that's all it is. I am a soldier. I deal with blood all the time. It's not something that concerns me tonight."

59

"No," said Miriam, "not now. Not tonight." Her eyes had not budged from the ground.

"Damn you, Miriam," said Julius. He rose straight off the bench, like a hawk unfurling upwards into the air and threw himself at the wall. Turning, placing his back against the wall to her left, Julius faced Miriam at an angle, scowling. "You had plenty of time to let me know this ahead of time. You had all day and last night also. Why wait until now?"

Miriam did not answer him. She had not moved.

Julius checked suddenly. "And last night also," he repeated to himself. "So, this wasn't a problem last night? Or was it, Miriam, and you were too caught up in the moment to remember or care?"

Miriam said nothing. Her skin color, if anything, had turned an even deeper red.

"You know, I would not have come here at all had I known this." Julius paused, looking appraisingly at every inch of her body. "And certainly not with the expectation of fucking every bit of you all night long and tomorrow morning too."

Miriam started, but kept her eyes adamantly on the ground.

Julius laughed nastily. "Well, that got a reaction, at least. Why suddenly so shy, Miriam? You know and I know you were ready to go at me hard last night. And you would have, if I hadn't stopped you, so be damned to your modesty." Julius paused, one hand on his hip, the other braced against the wall. He was still looking at her with hostility. She felt his eyes, like fingers, raking over her body. "You must know, I already sent away the guard for the night. So that now I am trapped here, with you, all night long. The way I am feeling right now, I would just as soon leave you here and go find myself a nice, clean, conformable whore somewhere in this town to do your work for you. So, tell me again, Miriam. I think I have the right to know. Why did you wait to let me know this?"

"It's a good question, Julius," Miriam said slowly, looking up from the ground, meeting his glance. "When someone has information that will affect someone else, why not share it immediately with the other person?"

Julius pushed himself off the wall and stepped in closer to her, bristling with physicality, like a hedgehog extending its quills. "Is this your revenge for what I told you last night, that our marriage won't be real under Roman law? And yet last night you wanted relations"

Miriam shrugged, then looked down, away, at the ground, her color still high. "No, she said, "or, at least, not entirely. There's still the problem I mentioned." Her eyes slid back to his, to gauge his reaction.

Julius stepped back from her and leaned against the wall once more. "And when, Miriam, do you suspect this problem will be resolved?" He spoke precisely, enunciating every syllable.

She shrugged again. "Soon," she said, "tomorrow or the next day."

"So, it was a problem last night as well. But it slipped your mind." Julius laughed. "All right, Miriam, I'll desist for now. I have no intention of raping you on our first official night together, although there is an ample tradition to do exactly that under Roman law, as you may know." Julius raised his eyebrows. "But keep in mind, the next time this occurs you will let me know beforehand. That's an order. Don't trifle like this with me again. If you do, I won't answer for the results, except for the fact that you won't like them."

The silence stretched on and on.

"So, how, then, do you propose to entertain me, tonight?"

Miriam looked up at Julius perplexed, "You want me to entertain you tonight, Julius?" said Miriam. "But how? I don't know what you mean."

Julius looked her up and down. He breathed out once, then licked his top lip. "Oh, go to bed upstairs. Get out of my sight. If you're not going to let me screw you, I don't want you here to look at. You'll just distract me." He stepped towards her again. "And then maybe I'll take you tonight anyway, your modesty be damned."

Miriam jumped up and scrambled towards the narrow staircase. She scurried halfway upstairs, but stopped when she realized Julius had not budged from where he was standing. He was, however, still watching her intently. Pausing for a moment, she said to him, "I hope for your sake there are blankets and a pallet in your gear. Otherwise, it will be a cold, hard night for you."

⁕

Miriam's voice wafted down, light and mocking. He had wondered yesterday what additional surprises Miriam had in store for him. Tonight, he had discovered another one. He was not sure he wanted to find out whether there were any more.

He had the whole night to get through, though, and he still felt worked up, with no outlet in sight. Walking over to the table, Julius poured himself another cup of wine, drank it off quickly, and poured a third. He sat down on the bench and drank the third cup slowly, cursing under his breath. When he was done, he got up and unpacked as much of his gear as he needed for the coming night. He lay down on the pallet, pulling the wool blanket over himself, and stared at the ceiling, rearranging his body to find a comfortable angle, then twitching into a new position when he did not succeed. His eyes on the ceiling, a self-mocking grin flit over Julius' lips, tarrying a moment or two. *"Torn between my humiliation and admiration for my manliness and self-control,"* he said aloud.

Sometime later, Julius was still awake. Chagrined, he sighed once, to be stuck again tonight with the very kind of problem marriage was meant to solve. *"Come hand. Serve as mistress of my pleasure."* This was a ridiculous quote he had by heart. But suitable for the occasion. Unfortunately.

He moved his hand slowly down his body, shutting his eyes gratefully. After a while Julius yawned, his body now at ease.

———◇———

Miriam lay still on her pallet with her eyes closed for a few moments, chasing her dreams as they evanesced into nothingness. Only then did she open her eyes to a new day with cheerful sunlight filtering in through a window. Downstairs, Noemi was speaking with Julius in a hushed tone with Marcus piping in occasionally, his high voice carrying further. Julius did not sound angry. That was good. Although, Miriam supposed, he would hardly target Noemi if he were. Julius' temper struck swift and hard, but he was not unjust whenever he slowed down enough to think. And last night, he would have had ample opportunity to think.

Miriam grinned, half mischief, half malice. Rising from her pallet, she dressed herself quickly. Today, she promised herself as she braided her hair, arranging the long individual plaits for the first time into a coronet around the crown of her head as befit a matron, she would find time to visit the city baths and luxuriate within the warm, scented water for hours.

———◇———

Julius, seated downstairs on a bench located between the wooden table and the wall, had Marcus perched on his lap, Noemi seated across from him. He looked up as Miriam descended carefully down the narrow white stairs, carved, like the rest of the house, out of the soft, white volcanic ash that covered all the land around Caesarea. At least, Julius thought as he watched her emerge fully into the sunny atrium, he no longer felt the burning rage he had experienced last night.

"Good morning, Marcus. Good morning, Julius, Noemi." Miriam nodded at each of them. She walked over to the table, seated herself, and ripped a hunk of bread for herself from last night's loaf.

Julius leaned back on the bench, against the wall, observing Miriam as she ate, noticing the new way she had arranged her hair and the gray shadows under her eyes. All the width of the table was positioned between them. He drew his hand slowly through Marcus' curls again and watched Miriam until she had finished her bread and had lifted an earthenware cup, filled with watered wine, to her lips. When she was done, he set Marcus on the ground and said, "Miriam, will you step out with me to get some morning air?"

Miriam gazed up at him. She looked, he thought, as if that were the last thing in the world she wanted to do.

Julius stood. "Come," he said softly, and held out his hand to her. "Marcus," he said, touching the boy's curls with his other hand as the boy opened up his mouth to complain, "your mother and I will return very soon. In the meantime, go out in the courtyard with Noemi and play." Taking Miriam's hand, holding her firmly by the elbow, Julius walked with her to the door.

Outside, the sky was blue and the sun shone brightly on the fantastically shaped white buildings surrounding them. Bright white and pink and yellow flowers were planted everywhere, hyacinth and narcissi on the ground, small wild tulips, and early single roses climbing the walls of the houses, on wooden trestles. Only a few people were out on the street with them, walking abroad. The neighborhood was quiet.

After a few steps Miriam stopped and looked behind her, back at the house. "I don't want to go too far, Julius," she said.

Julius tightened his grasp on her elbow and started walking again. "There is a square up ahead. I saw it last night on my way here. We can sit there and talk in private, outside of the house." Julius looked at Miriam, her face brightly lit by the morning sun. Her beauty was undeniable; even today, when she was not at her best, the evenness of her features, her beautiful skin, her wide-set green eyes. "All right?"

Miriam nodded and they walked together until they reached the sun-drenched white marble square, surrounded on each of its sides by low buildings. There was a round fountain in the middle encircled with low marble benches. Julius and Miriam sat side by side for some moments, deliciously warmed by the sun, breathing in the sweet floral air, watching the water chime and bubble as it trickled out of a tipping urn held lightly around its rim by a naked river nymph. The nymph had gorgeously carved breasts, Julius thought, the marble luminous and enticing to the eye as new fallen snow. Her nipples, fully illuminated by the angle of the sun, were delicate and erect. Julius removed his gaze and looked around at his modestly draped wife with her beautiful fair hair bound up in braids around the crown of her head. Frowning, he turned his face fully towards her. "Noemi informed me, when I asked her about it this morning, that you finished your cycle some days ago. That's accurate, yes?" Julius peered at her face and could feel the expression on his own face hardening.

Miriam colored, but said nothing.

"I thought so," he nodded. "I didn't think that Noemi would lie to my face. She's much too scared of me. I imagined, however, that it was possible that she had less than accurate information. But I suppose not." Julius looked away from his wife, back to the white river nymph. A light wind had distributed droplets of water over her body and the sun glinted and played over her nakedness. He listened as the water spilled out of her vessel and trickled down her lower limbs, gathering into the pool below that swirled amidst the white and pink and yellow flower petals. A rough laugh penetrated the air from one of the houses near the square and then, further away, down the avenue, he heard a merchant hawking ceramic wares. He could feel Miriam's eyes watching him.

"So, tell me Miriam," Julius said after a while, turning his face back to her. "What did you mean by the scene you enacted last night? Why lie to me?"

"It was late," Miriam said and turned her head and shoulders to look at Julius. "I didn't know how you would react to what I was going to say. I was tired and I didn't want to have to fight with you."

"If you didn't want to sleep with me last night you should have just said it flat out. Never lie to me. I hate lying."

"It's more complicated than that, Julius. Yesterday, during the delay on the road I had a lot of time to think. You must know that there are several things I am not happy about with our arrangement. You too, as I recall were not entirely happy." She swallowed. "Since we aren't actually going to be legally married under Roman law, I want to follow some of my own rituals. To my mind, that's fair." Miriam shrugged. "By the law of my people, after I bleed, I have to immerse myself in fresh water before I can sleep with you. Otherwise, the act is impure before God. It's a sin." Miriam angled her left hand over her eyes to block out the rays of the sun. "I know how you feel about my rituals, Julius." She shrugged again. "I didn't think it was likely that you were going to indulge my request if I asked you to abstain last night and told you the true reason. Particularly, since it was late when you arrived, and you gave the impression you were in a hurry to proceed." Her mouth was taut.

"Wait a moment, Miriam. Not so fast. I haven't agreed to anything yet."

Miriam crossed her arms over her chest. "You see, Julius. I didn't misjudge you. This reaction is precisely why I didn't tell you last night." Looking at his face, she paused and then relaxed her hands into her lap and began to speak slowly. "I don't see a just reason for you to dissent, Julius. It will be little extra trouble for you, and I have made up my mind."

Julius reached out with his right hand, gripped her left wrist tightly and held on to it. "I don't care if you have made up your mind. Think again, Miriam. It will be trouble for me because I want you available for screwing whenever I want you. Is that clear enough for you? That's one of the few advantages of this union, as far as I am concerned. And I don't want to be forced to subscribe to the laws of a religion I don't believe in. A fact, let me point out to you, which you know already."

"Don't get angry, Julius. Think calmly. You told me yourself you are going to be away a lot of the time in the first year once we reach Antioch, establishing contacts, riding patrol in the area outside the city. This is no different. A few more days, here or there. It will be very little trouble to you, I promise. And it's very important to me." Miriam relaxed her left arm, the arm that he continued to grasp tightly, and placed it in her lap so that he was touching her leg. After a moment, she lifted her free right hand and began softly to stroke his jaw, still unshaven this morning. "It is just a bath, Julius, a long ritual bath. That's all. And very occasionally, some restraint on your part. You won't ever have to do anything else." She reached up and lightly fingered his ear and then the hair on the back of his neck. "Seneca, I believe, admired restraint. Didn't he?"

Julius slowly permitted himself to relax. After a moment, he closed his eyes and leaned the back of his head into her hand. The water from the fountain behind him played delicately, gushing and burbling. Julius turned his head and gazed at the naked river nymph once more as Miriam continued to caress him. He took a deep breath and the air he breathed in was perfumed with the scent of spring flowers.

"Just a long bath," he said at last, voice half hypnotized.

"I'll be very clean afterward." She smiled and the sunlight sparkled in her eyes and glowed on her young skin.

Julius kept on staring at the river nymph. At last, he unbent enough to say, "Truth be told, I was planning on spending a few hours at the baths myself today." He let go of her wrist and placing his arms in the air languorously, he stretched his shoulders and back.

"I'll be ready for you early tonight, an hour after sunset. I promise." She leaned in close to him and whispered. "Can you arrange for Noemi and Marcus to spend the night elsewhere? Perhaps with Silius?"

Julius looked her in the eye, and slowly nodded, listening as the water behind him trickled down the water nymph's long legs into the undulating pool below. "Tonight," he said. And reaching across all the distance that lay between them, he placed his hand on her breast and squeezed.

PART IV

CHAPTER 6
Scenes from Childhood

For the most part, Marcus had only general impressions of the years he lived in Antioch as a child. He retained broad strokes, a floating panorama of background color and noise. He remembered the shape of the house he had lived in, formed of sunbaked white and brown stones, radiating daily warmth. The yard which surrounded the house was tiled in terracotta. He recalled those same earthen tiles drowning in blood one day when he fell off the outdoor gate and gashed his head open, reducing his world to the smell of sticky red, salt, earth and his mother's tears. Daily, sword clanged against javelin in the weapon yard, as soldier trained against soldier, in a blur of movement, too fast to decipher. The men, short, medium, tall, with their pungent scents and raucous speech, shouted at each other in Greek, Aramaic and Latin, their voices low or loud or deep. Skinny army children played with Marcus and fought against him regularly, with fists and wooden swords, younger than him and older; they were white-skinned and olive and brown.

A tall, featureless rabbi with a sonorous voice and a sparse ginger beard roamed through Marcus' memories. The beard waggled continuously when the man spoke, fascinating him. Mysteriously, Marcus thought, the man materialized only when his father, Julius, was not at home. And yet his father must have known about the man because, Marcus seemed to recollect, he was the only person during those years whom his father specifically gave him permission to address in Hebrew, that is, besides his mother. The rabbi brought to the house portable treasures: scrolls and papyri, wonderful tales, legends and bits of law.

And finally, Marcus remembered a covered marketplace, a wonderland for his eyes and nose. There were booths made of glittering gold, containing columns of jewels and stacks of silver shaped into cups, large platters, tiny gods and goddesses. Other booths contained grown-up weapons, swords and bows and arrows and nets and shields. Elsewhere there were booths built on top of each other that displayed piles of aromatic red powder and orange and yellow and furious black that made him sneeze; booths that showed off luscious melons and apricots and dates; sweet green figs and red grapes; spicy roasting meat, animal carcasses and tall earthenware vats of clotting blood. Dogs squabbled madly over the bones, rats and mice frolicked in their wake. And men and women, wearing short tunics and long gowns, wandered everywhere, indiscriminate, in a babble of constant movement and undifferentiated sound.

Yet, Marcus retained only one scene of his early childhood that he could paint, scene by scene, detail by detail, with startling clarity: the day when he was newly turned seven years old that his father had taken him to a Roman ceremonial procession to worship Emperor Trajan.

As the sun, already risen above the horizon, pierced his southeastern window, and shone full in his face, Marcus awoke and opened his eyes. It was early yet, he thought. He shut his eyes again, but it was no good, with the sun shining over the horizon. He sat up, and

70

when he started shivering in the cool winter air, he pulled his plain brown tunic over his head.

Downstairs, Marcus looked around. His father was not in sight, nor his sword, nor armor. Julius slept more often in camp than he did in the house, and when his sword and his armor were gone, that meant he was also. Marcus turned to his mother.

"Father's gone?"

"He left already," his mother answered, "to inspect his century before the parade begins." Marcus' father, Julius, was a centurion of middle rank, not a common soldier. Julius had been promoted to centurion years ago, and again, within the Legion, two years back. His father was hoping for still another promotion soon.

Marcus walked over to the table and sat. "He said he was going to take me with him this morning."

His mother did not answer him.

He should have realized, Marcus thought to himself, because he had heard shouting again late last night, after he was already lying in bed. And that generally meant that something one of his parents had promised him was not going to happen after all.

Marcus began to eat the food laid out before him, fresh baked flat bread, smelling of fresh ground flour and herbs, golden green olive oil, salty fish paste, soft sheep cheese and fruit from the cold storage. Marcus ate quickly. Then, bolting from his seat, he ran to the door, ignoring his mother shouting at him to stay inside. But when he looked outside, the square was deserted, eerily quiet. No one was playing, not even the girls. None of the other army children were in sight. Their fathers all must have taken them along with them, Marcus thought. Only he was left behind.

He stood at the open door for a while. It was chilly, he realized, even though the sun was bright. Wintertime. At least, it was not pouring buckets, with driving wind, cold and damp, the way it had all last week. But afterward, when the rain had stopped, there had

71

been such wonderful mud to play with. The children had made huge mud forts, and lobbed mud projectiles at each other for hours. Marcus had wanted to build a catapult to lob the mud more precisely. He was learning how to build simple catapults in the army engineering shop. But the very next day, before his catapult was finished, one of the children had been hit in the head with a mud ball that had a stone buried in it. The child, knocked unconscious, had bled all over the ground and the mothers had rushed outside and made all the children stop their play. Later that afternoon, the boy who had thrown the stone had been punished by his father. Days afterwards, the boy was still black and blue from the beating he received.

Marcus had kept on building his catapult, however. It might come in handy at some later date, he thought to himself. A lot of the things he suggested to the other children often came in handy. But that, he assumed, was because his father was a centurion and most of the other fathers were common soldiers. This meant that he had to do a lot more lessons than the other children. And there were lessons of an entirely different sort from his mother as well.

In the square before him, Marcus could still see the remains of one fort, its ramparts dried and half fallen. As he watched, the wind blew fiercely and toppled over the last bit of high wall. It fell to the ground, and burst apart in a shower of dirt, scattering everywhere. The wind rose again, lifting the dust with it. He watched, fascinated, as the wind carried the dust straight towards him. It came nearer and nearer. He ducked, but some of it struck him square in the face, stinging him. Marcus closed his eyes and rubbed them hard, then opened them and looked around, shivering. There were still no other children in sight. He stepped back inside. Closing the door behind him, he turned around to face his mother.

"Marcus," she said, calmly, taking him firmly by the hand. "Stay inside now. You're freezing and if you let any more wind inside, I will be too."

Marcus sat at the long marble table, carved with acanthus leaves, slowly reading a chapter of the *Iliad* in Greek. Achilles was his favorite hero, but his father preferred Aeneas since Aeneas was a Roman, not a Greek. Julius was a Roman and Marcus would also be a Roman when he was older and joined the army. But he still liked godlike Achilles best, not dutiful Aeneas. His mother, he thought, must like tricky Odysseus best of all.

His father had explained to him that, unlike him, his mother and Noemi could never be Romans. It must be because they were girls, Marcus told himself, and could not join the army. But he knew that was not the reason because his father had told him why.

As he read, thinking dreamily of Achilles' deeds, his mother sat beside him, writing letters. Correspondence with his grandfather. Marcus had known his grandfather years ago, but remembered him only hazily now, even though his grandfather had given him a precious scroll to keep.

His mother's maid, Noemi, sat silently by the fire, weaving a covering for the wall. She had been weaving the same covering for months now.

"Marcus," his mother said, finally. "Go upstairs, change your tunic and put on your head gear.

There was no point in arguing, so Marcus ran upstairs, put on his fine white tunic with the blue stripe and covered his head. When he got back downstairs, his mother had cleared off his scroll, her papyri and the inlaid bronze inkpot she had used. She had covered her head as well with an embroidered linen scarf, hiding all the braids she normally wore looped closely around the crown of her head. Marcus preferred his mother the other way because she had such pretty fair hair. She was still pretty like this, he thought, but less than usual. Noemi did not have to cover her hair when the rabbi came because she was a girl and unmarried still, even though she was all grown up.

The rabbi knocked a few minutes later. Noemi ran to the door and let him in, smiling. "Rabbi Samuel, please come in." Noemi always smiled at the rabbi. But Marcus had noticed, the rabbi rarely smiled back at her.

Today, before they began their lesson, his mother, Miriam, took the rabbi aside and whispered to him for a few minutes. That was unusual. The rabbi smiled at her the whole time, Marcus observed. It must be because his mother was so beautiful, thought Marcus. Men always smiled at her, although his father did not always do so.

Finally, they all sat down around the table, even Noemi. Although Noemi was his mother's maid, Miriam let her sit at the table when the rabbi came. His mother had explained to him that unlike herself and Marcus, Noemi had not been fortunate enough to have teachers when she was younger, so it was her obligation as a Jew to see that Noemi was taught about her people now. His father had scoffed when he had first heard about that, but his mother had argued with him and changed his mind. Marcus had noticed his mother was very smart. Even his father sometimes asked her for help when he had to negotiate a deal with merchant men around the city. She was the daughter of a merchant, Julius had explained to Marcus once, so she understood how commerce worked. That was all there was to it, Julius had said. Marcus, however, had his own opinion.

The rabbi had brought a small scroll with him today and some notes written on sheets of papyri. First, he unrolled the scroll carefully, and Marcus began to read from part of a copy of the Hebrew scripture. This week, they were continuing to read from the story of Joseph. The rabbi had explained to him previously that in three years time, at this pace, he would read through the entire Torah. At the end of it, they would hold a small celebration for him. To Marcus, three years seemed an awfully long time to have to wait.

When Marcus had finished reading his portion, the rabbi rolled the scroll up, lay it carefully to one side and opened the sheets of papyri.

And then it was Noemi's turn to read. She read much more slowly than Marcus did. Mother had told him that was because Noemi had not learned to read until she was already grown, which was harder than learning to read as a child. That must be true, Marcus thought, because he could already read in four languages, Hebrew, Aramaic, Greek and Latin. So could Miriam. His father only read Greek and Latin and Noemi read only one language slowly, Hebrew. A lot of the army children he played with could not read at all and probably never would.

His mother looked him in the face. "Marcus, pay attention. You are daydreaming again."

Marcus looked up at her and yawned. He tried to concentrate on what Noemi was reading, but he was tired and his eyes swam with tears. They would not focus properly.

At last, Noemi finished her portion and let herself breath again. She was always tense while reading. The rabbi put away the sheets of papyri. He sat back in his chair and closed his eyes and then, in his resonant voice, he began to tell a story, about Abraham, the patriarch of the Jews.

Long ago, chanted the rabbi, at the beginning of time, ten generations after Noah, in Ur of the Chaldeans, there lived a man named Terah who had a son called Abram. Now this man Terah was a maker of idols which he sold in the marketplace. One day, while Abram was still a lad, Terah left his shop in Abram's charge. After a while, an old man wandered into the shop. "I want to buy a mighty god," he said to Abram. Abram took down the idol that was placed on the highest shelf, standing taller any of the others, and gave it to the old man. When the old man asked whether, indeed, this god was the mightiest of them all, Abram said to him, "Did you not see that this one stood taller all the others? Have you not heard that that is the sign of a mighty god?" The man paid his money but as he was turning to leave, Abram asked him, "How old are you, good sir?" "Seventy years," replied the man. Abram said to him, "Seventy years, and yet you are ready to worship a god made only yesterday in my father's shop." Angrily, the man demanded his money back and left.

After the man had been gone for some time, Abram had an idea. For even though he was still a young child, God had already spoken to him. Seizing a stick from his father's shop, Abram smashed all of the gods except for the biggest of them all. He placed the stick in the hand of the idol that remained and waited for his father's return.

Sometime later, his father came back to his shop and, shocked, looked around at the destruction Abram had wrought. He asked Abram, "Who came into the shop and did this to all the other gods?" Abram replied to him, "Father, the mightiest god, the one you still see with the stick in his hand, rose up and destroyed all the others. Is he not the most powerful of them all?" Terah looked at his son. "These gods are but earth and wood and stone," he replied. "They do not have the power to do any such thing as you describe." Abram looked at his father. "You are right, father. These gods are but earth and wood and stone. They have no power to do anything. So, why do you worship them and continue to offer sacrifices of animals and wheat cakes before them?"

The rabbi's voice lingered then died as he finished reciting the story. Marcus sat very still on his chair, absorbing the tale, and looked at the rabbi, his eyes shining. This was a hero totally different than Achilles, but a hero nonetheless. A hero who fought for the truth. Marcus opened his mouth to ask for another tale, but at that very moment, a knock sounded on the door.

Startled, Miriam rose and opened the door. Silius, his father's chief aide, slipped into the room. Miriam nodded to him. "Hello, Silius."

"Ma'am," he said. "I'm sorry to disturb you, but I have orders to bring Marcus with me to attend the ceremonial procession. If we are to make it in time, before the procession begins, we must leave now."

Marcus jumped up from his chair, gleeful. He had forgotten all about the procession. Then he looked at his mother to gauge her reaction.

Miriam was still standing facing Silius. She turned back to look at Marcus. "Yes, of course, Silius," she said, while facing her son. "Marcus, you may go. But remember to think about the story the rabbi told you today."

Marcus grinned up at her. "Yes, mother, I will," he said glibly. He had gotten his wish to go to the ceremony. Right now, he'd say anything. After a moment, he remembered to add, "Thank you." Marcus looked next at the rabbi, who was scowling at him through his ginger beard. Marcus' manner became more formal. "Thank you for the lesson and the story, Rabbi Samuel." He nodded politely, as his mother had taught him. "Until next week." Then forgetting his dignity, he ran to the door and grabbed Silius by the hand. At the last moment, Marcus jerked off his head gear, and threw it onto a chest stationed near the door. With one rueful backward glance at the rabbi, Marcus exited.

Before he met up with his father, Marcus had to wade through a flood of folks in the center of Antioch. The city center was packed with townspeople, in a riot of color and noise, waiting eagerly, excitedly, ecstatically for the yearly procession to begin. Someone was blowing a war horn loudly. And there were vendors selling food everywhere. Fresh bread, bottles of wine, cooking pots of fava beans and roasted lamb that smelled so tasty, his mouth began to water. He looked around hungrily until he caught sight of his father in the distance.

Julius sat on horseback, at the head of his troop, stationed just aside the main gate to the city. His soldiers positioned behind him on the road into the city, he waited at the beginning of the procession route for the signal to march. Julius and his troops were formally garbed, wearing their ceremonial dress and sparkling half armor.

Julius frowned when he saw Marcus up close. Marcus looked down at his fresh white tunic. It was unlike his father's that was stitched with leather straps.

"I didn't have time to change into my army dress, father," he said, explaining. Julius had had a special tunic made for him to wear to official events that looked just like his father's army dress, but his mother did not allow Marcus to wear it when the rabbi visited them. "It's too Roman," she had told him. "Remember, you are a Jew. You are not a soldier, yet. Nor a Roman either. You might never be a Roman."

That last comment still rankled him.

Julius was still frowning. "It can't be helped now. We'll have to hide you in the middle of the troop, so you won't be seen. You can't ride in front with me as I had planned." Julius detached his surcoat. "Here, son, throw this over your clothing. You'll be less noticeable that way."

Vincius, another of his father's aides, lifted Marcus on to the small horse provided for him. Marcus liked Vincius a lot. He often came to the house and laughed with mama. Mama always fed him and sometimes when he was there Vincius gave him private lessons with his wooden sword in the yard.

Marcus looked about him as the procession began to march forward. Julius' century was stationed behind the wagon bearing the oversized statue of the Emperor God Trajan that was to be placed in the temple to Mars later today. Marcus was situated some ways back, in the middle of Julius' men and behind the tallest soldiers of his father's century who rode toward the front as an honor guard. He sat his horse alone with his thoughts in the riotous crowd. It was too noisy to speak.

Mounted on horseback as he was, the painted marble statue atop the wagon was so tall, as it glistened in the sun, that Marcus had it in sight the entire time during his ride from the *agora* to the new temple of Mars. He peered at it and frowned, thinking hard.

Finally, Marcus looked over at Vincius, riding beside him. Pointing to the statue with his chin, he shouted, "To me, it looks brand new."

Vincius leaned closer towards him. "Fresh from the marble worker's shop, last week," Vincius shouted back. "I had the story from the man who carved it while my soldiers were moving it onto the wagon. It's a beauty, no? Though the joke's on the sculptor, for Emperor Trajan surely wasn't."

It was beautiful, Marcus thought. A beautiful statue of the Emperor God made of stone. Could he smash it with a stick? Probably not, he thought, it was much too hard. But if the statue fell off the wagon, it would shatter into pieces. He wondered if his father and Vincius thought this was a real god. The people who had filled the wagon to the brim with offerings of fruit, wine and garlands of flowers certainly must, he thought. Yet, it did not seem real to him. Marcus contemplated what it must feel like to have God appear to you directly when you were a boy so you could be sure about things like this.

The procession swept into the rectangular forum and paced decorously all around its interior, finally halting before the temple of Mars. Built in Grecian style, its portico held up by Doric columns, the gleaming white marble temple radiated balance, grace, and the sturdiness of Roman Imperial dominance. An impressive building, the temple stood detached from all others in the vicinity, majestic in its solitude. The crowd milled all around the open porticoes of the forum, jostling each other, as they celebrated.

Marcus dismounted along with the others around him and waited until one of the soldiers came to lead his horse away. He ran over to his father and touched him on the arm.

Julius looked down at him and smoothed his dark hair, smiling. "Marcus," he said, "follow me." Julius headed with the other notables inside the temple, away from the constant din in the forum, the people shouting, the horns blowing, the drums beating. Outside the temple, the festival continued in full cry.

But inside, although there was a crowd of people waiting, the tone was hushed, expectant. He caught a glimpse of priests, far in front, dressed in white, and officiating at the ritual in low voices. Marcus heard someone in front of him piping sweet music on the flute. He did not possess a clear view ahead of him in the crowd. The grownups in front of him blocked his view. Marcus took Julius by the hand and held on to him tightly, tracing the colored circular pattern in the inlaid marble floor with his foot. He breathed in deeply. The air, he noticed, was laden with frankincense, piercing, woodsy and sweet, overriding the smell of the pyre on the central altar.

The line ahead of them moved slowly. When Marcus and Julius reached the front of it, Julius placed a copper coin in a bowl and took two small cakes from a platter heaped high. One Julius kept for himself, and the other he handed to Marcus. Marcus opened both of his hands to hold the cake and carefully watched what his father was doing. He knew Julius expected him to do everything he was doing.

There was a lighted pyre on an altar below the raised statue of Mars. Julius placed his cake on the fire and stood back to watch it burn, mumbling some words that Marcus could not hear. When the cake was entirely consumed, he signed to Marcus to do the same.

Marcus moved closer to him. "But father," he said in a low voice, meant only for Julius. "It's only a stone god. It has no power. Why are we giving it food? It can't eat the cake."

"Marcus," said Julius, giving him a look that froze him to his toes. "Do your duty as a Roman citizen."

In front of them, to their left, the pipe music rose higher and higher into the perfumed air, sweeter and sweeter, then fell and fell and fell, drowning the silence.

Marcus tried to explain again. "But..." he said.

"Marcus," Julius barked in the voice he used when commanding his men.

The people around him were all silent now. Marcus could feel the faces behind them all peering forward, examining him.

Flushing, he walked slowly up to the altar and put his cake in the fire. He stood back, exactly like his father had done before him, watching his cake burn. There was nothing he hated more than disappointing his father. Still, he refused to mumble any words.

When only ashes remained in the pyre, Marcus turned to his father, looking for his approval. His father nodded once and began to walk forward, away from the crowd, into an empty niche in the temple, between two interior columns. Following, Marcus walked over to him and stood beside him. He stared at the ground, closing his eyes on the tears that welled. He would not cry. His father did not permit him to cry. Marcus could feel Julius looking down at him. At last, when it was safe, he looked up.

"Okay, Marcus," said Julius, touching his hair lightly and then his shoulder. "It's over for now. But I never want to see a repeat of your behavior here again. Do you understand me?" Julius inserted his finger under Marcus' chin and raised his face so that his eyes stared solely into his father's.

"Yes, father," said Marcus dully.

Julius' finger was still placed, inexorably, under Marcus' chin. "Whatever nonsense your mother tells you about the gods, or, for that matter, whatever anyone that she pays to teach you says, in this matter you are to obey only me."

Behind their backs, in front of the crowd, the flute music was rising again.

Heroes, Marcus thought stubbornly, his chin jutting forward, do not always do just what their fathers tell them to do.

"I see that look in your eye, Marcus. So let me tell you now, son, the next time you flout me in public, I will beat you so hard that you will have to stay in bed for days. Is that absolutely clear?"

"Yes, father," Marcus repeated automatically, his eyes wide open, shocked. He was not sure whether he really believed what his father had said to him. Julius yelled at his mother a lot, but he never hit her. And sometimes mama yelled right back. His father had hit him, that was true, but he had certainly never beaten him that hard. But then, thought Marcus, his father had never threatened to do so before either.

Julius released Marcus' chin and, without looking down at him again, started walking forward, to the entrance of the temple, back into the light. "And now we go to your house, Marcus, and I'll discuss your behavior with your mother. I imagine she was the one who put you up to this."

And to that, Marcus took exception, for several reasons. He glanced over at his father and touched him on his arm, so that Julius would look down at him again. "Father," he said with absolute sincerity. "Mama never said a word about the ceremony. It was all my idea."

His father continued to study him. Marcus could see his father did not altogether believe him. He wondered again if his father realized just how clever his mother was. And what Julius thought of it if he did.

Yes, he was right, Marcus decided. She must like tricky Odysseus best of all.

PART V

CHAPTER 7
Family Reunion

The muscles in Marcus' shoulder were cramping again. He rotated his arm carefully, trying to uncramp it, hoping no one around him would notice. It was too soon for him to lower his arm. That would be seized upon. So he kept his arm where it was, extended, a slight bend at the elbow, with a short iron sword stretching out straight from his left hand and a small round shield on his right arm. His stance alert, on guard, his muscles tense, Marcus ran through his exercises in the private gymnasium set apart for military use.

The practice salle, crowded with men and an occasional boy going about their training, swirling around and around each other as they practiced fighting, reeked with male sweat, constant use and a lack of attention to cleanliness. Gritting his teeth as he held up the sword, Marcus looked about the room with focus as he moved about its perimeter practicing his drills, his back to the wall. He was waiting for Rufinus, the Syrian master at arms, or one of his assistants, to advance on him relentlessly whenever they spied an opening.

This sword he held in his hand was new. Closer to full military weight than his last one, he had received it only a week ago from his father, in acknowledgement that he had mastered the weight of his old sword, if not yet fully the technique. So, today, Marcus wanted to show he deserved the new sword. But standing on guard with his arm fully extended as he used it had become excruciating. Especially since practicing at the master's school always capped several hours of rigorous training in gymnastics and running. Usually, the additional training presented no difficulty to him. In fact, it was Marcus' favorite part of his week. But, today, he could not wait until he finished.

A loud noise in the observer's gallery behind him drew his attention. Curious, keeping his sword arm extended and his shield up, Marcus turned on his heel and looked up. His father's aide, Vincius, was standing there with some men he did not recognize, garbed in a variety of exotic dress. Visitors, he assumed.

The Greco-Syrian city of Caesarea where Marcus now lived was a jewel of a port city on the coastline of Judea, and foreign guests and other dignitaries visited frequently. Over a century ago, King Herod, master builder, had erected the magnificent city in twelve years on the site of Strabo's Tower, with a sparkling palace jutting towards the sea, a magnificent hippodrome next to it, also overlooking the sea, a nearby theatre, a grid system in the city proper, streets decorated with statuary and a city sewage system that worked so well, it was the marvel of the region. And now Caesarea served as the capitol city for its Roman masters. Over the years, a permanent army camp with barracks and offices had been erected right outside its boundaries.

Up in the loge, Vincius waved at him and Marcus began to raise his sword in acknowledgement of that wave. He lifted his sword higher. Until, of a sudden, the sword met a resistance that should not have existed. Marcus wrenched his body around just as Rufinus, the master arms-man, knocked the sword out of his hand in a blow which sent painful shivers all the way up his arm, reverberating to the top of his shoulder. Marcus reacted at speed. He jumped backwards, maintaining an on-guard stance, both legs slightly bent, and positioned his shield forward to defend himself against the onslaught he knew he had just earned from the master. With his left hand, Marcus jerked his dagger free from his belt and held it out warily before him. Then the master moved in closer to engage him and thought ceased as bodily instinct took over.

Three minutes later, Marcus was poised against the stone wall completely denuded of arms. His right hand clenched hard against his stomach, he had placed his left fingers in his mouth, sucking them madly in order to temper the brutal sting. The master had disarmed him, propelling his shield hard against the wall where it had dropped like a brick hurtling down a well. And moments afterwards, a precisely placed rap to the finger bones of his left hand with the flat of the master's sword had caused his grip to open automatically as his arm swung hard left, releasing his dagger to fly through the air of the gymnasium. Breathing hard, his head down, Marcus stood still and listened while Rufinus dissected in chilling detail every error in fighting he had made today.

"And finally, you continue to fight, Marcus, with the muscles in your shoulders clenched tight as the body of an unsatisfied whore. I have already pointed out that error to you time and time again. If you do not force yourself to cease this practice, I tell you now, despite your speed and striking accuracy, you will never amount to anything as a fighter. Not only does it tire you out unnecessarily, but it renders your arm inelastic, unable to absorb any blows that I direct against you. That's the reason your left shoulder feels numb right now. Next time, do as I instruct you."

Marcus glanced up momentarily, his cheeks burning red. Rufinus stood regarding him, an unpleasant expression on his face as he looked down his nose. A veteran, short, white-haired with one filmy blue eye, the man had retired with a pension after the regulation twenty-five years of army service, but even now he stayed on to instruct fighting in the military academy in Caesarea. He was a master fighter, renowned throughout the Roman province of Greater Syria, his speed and reflexes still exceptional. But the skill that made his teaching noteworthy was that he instinctually tailored his fighting to each of his students, fighting every one of them in the style most suitable to that individual and on a skill-level targeted to improve their work.

"And finally, Marcus, a mistake so basic it shames me as your teacher even to have to mention it. A mistake you have not repeated since your first visit to this school. You stand here, knowing you're awaiting a sneak attack on your position by an enemy of superior force. And what do you do? You lose focus and turn around to wave at your friends, giving me every opportunity to cut your head right off your shoulders. Is this a social event you are attending, Marcus, or a fighting academy?" Rufinus' voice kept on hardening as he spoke. "There will always be distractions on the battlefield. Don't give in to them lest you miss the enemy sneaking up right behind you. The true fighter must stay alert whenever danger exists. Remember," Rufinus barked at him, "Constant focus!"

Marcus jumped. Rufinus, in response, kept right on glaring at him. "Perhaps your father and I ought to reconsider our decision that you are ready to follow a more serious training schedule and return your old sword to you so that you can keep on fighting with the babies? No?"

"No, sir," said Marcus, his eyes focused back on the ground. And the worst of what the master had just said, Marcus supposed, was that he would have to repeat it all in excruciating detail to his father in a few days hence when Julius returned home from campaigning. There was nothing Marcus hated more than disappointing his father when it came to military matters. But there was no possible evasion for this situation. Julius would expect a full and accurate report on his training. And on everything that pertained to Marcus' military training, he scented the slightest deviation from the truth, like a bird dog tracking grouse. Marcus had no idea how his father did it. It was uncanny, an innate ability.

"Show me your fingers," Rufinus commanded.

Marcus sucked hard one last time before pulling his hand away from his mouth. Wiping his fingers gingerly on the leathers he wore over his tunic, he held his left hand out to the master.

Rufinus took Marcus' hand in his, and gently tested the soreness of his fingers, one by one. Two of them were red and swollen to the bone. Marcus winced, inadvertently tensing his arm. Rufinus looked up at him. "Tell the slave to clean and soak your hand well in hot water before applying liniment and a bandage to it. Your dagger work continues to improve, Marcus. I am pleased with that, at least. Your next session will be in a week. And take care of that hand. Lay off practicing with that hand until it heals. Work the dagger and the shield with your other hand only."

Rufinus let his hand go, dismissing him with a nod. Marcus bowed his head formally in acknowledgement. Rufinus began to walk away from him. Yet, just before he reached the closest stone archway in the wall, the master turned back. "But no liniment for your shoulder until tomorrow," he snapped. "I want you to feel the pain this time, so that next time we fight you will remember to keep your shoulder muscles loose. And before you think me unjust, remember, perhaps, one day on the battlefield this exercise may save your arm or your life."

Marcus stepped through the heavy leather door hanging into the small bathhouse located just off the military practice hall. He breathed in deeply; the air in here was humid and scented with mint and cedar. And since this bath house was small, it had far less traffic than the main bath house in Caesarea. Men preferred to visit that one, built near the forum, to benefit from the extensive social life that took place under its roof, political discussions, exercise, gambling, study, adult diversions of every kind. But this one, quiet and semi-private, suited Marcus fine.

A bath slave approached him and Marcus spoke his orders to the man softly. Then he moved to the marble benches built next to the wall, stripped off his half armor and tunic and crammed them into an empty niche. He walked over to the caldarium and hopped inside, wincing as the hot water closed over his sore hand and left shoulder. He got out quickly and went to lounge blissfully in the tepidarium. Master Rufinus recommended that his pupils not use the frigidarium on days when their muscles particularly ached them; the cold water, he advised them, allowed a chill to settle in the affected area, preventing the muscles from healing quickly. So, when Marcus was done lounging, he stepped out of the pool, forgoing the frigidarium, and stood quite still, as the slave toweled him dry. Then, Marcus walked over to one of the marble tables in the middle of the room and lay naked upon a heated sheet, face down, as a slave boy rubbed sweet smelling almond oil into his skin.

He lay still, breathing in the scented air, as the boy massaged the muscles in his back with his small, adept hands. Marcus shifted his head slightly to watch the slave boy as he began to work on his legs. The boy, he thought, looked younger than him, but he found it hard to tell for sure since he was so skinny.

The slave boy finished his work, lifting his warm hands from Marcus' body, and draped him with a heated linen sheet before he departed. The boy did his job well despite his small stature, but that made Marcus wonder whether his master treated the boy cruelly. And what, if anything, he made the boy do during the long winter nights. A scary thought, Marcus decided. He shuddered once, wrapping the sheet tightly in his right hand. Julius, his father, had once caught an older man ogling him. Afterwards, his father had explained a number of things to him and from then on Marcus only went to the baths where everyone knew exactly who his father was.

There were times when Marcus wondered what would happen to him if he were ever enslaved. What if he went off to sea, like his mother's brother, but the ship foundered far away? Would the local people make him their slave and beat him? Not likely, Marcus thought. He had only to fight his way to a Roman military outpost, and the army would send him home to his father wherever he landed. Most of the time, being the son of a Roman centurion was an advantage. Of course, if he landed among enemies of Rome, the Persians far to the East for example, Roman descent would be no asset. But he could deal with that contingency as well. He would simply tell them quite honestly that he was not Roman at all. And then he would ask them to send for the representative from one of the well-known Jewish communities in Persia. And that community would eventually ransom him back to his uncle or his mother. His mother had heard about such cases frequently from the merchants she befriended around the marketplace in Caesarea. The stories made the rounds through the well-traveled sea routes. Jews were happy to rescue their own people from pirates and slavery when they could.

Now, if he landed to the west among the British Celts or Germans, that presented more of a problem. No obvious advantages to plumb there in his background. He would have to be more resourceful, figure out a way to live off the land as long as he could in order to evade capture by the enemy. He could eat berries and roots and make a bow for himself out of wood and sinew and horn to bring down game. He'd barricade himself in caves or hide under boulders or in the treetops if he had to until he got the lay of the land and found a way to escape either by land or sea. He would have to travel primarily at night, Marcus thought, when he found himself on the move. Eventually, if he evaded capture long enough, he'd get back to civilization somehow.

The slave he was awaiting arrived at last, bearing a steaming urn. Marcus stopped daydreaming. He pushed himself up with his right hand, then swung his legs over the side of the table. He held out his left hand cautiously. The man cleaned it thoroughly for him, removing all vestiges of weapon grease, before placing it in the hot water to soak for several minutes. Marcus closed his eyes, relaxing, as the slave pulled out his hand and rubbed in the liniment. The salve, with its notes of lavender, myrrh and forest honey felt immediately soothing. He opened his eyes when the man began to wrap his hand in linen strips.

"Marcus." Vincius, grinning, leaned against the doorframe, calling to him.

Marcus grinned back and let himself slide off the table. The slave handed him his folded tunic and he slipped it over his head as Vincius approached him.

"Well, lad, it looks like I got you into a mite of trouble today with Master Rufinus."

Marcus stuck his head out of the top of his tunic and shrugged, grinning all the while. "You finally had your revenge. Paying me back for all those times I got you in trouble with my father."

Vincius returned a smile. "Show me the damage," he said, holding his hand out, his open palm facing upward.

Marcus put his hand on top of Vincius'. "Nothing to see, now. It's all wrapped up already. Rufinus said to wait a few days before practicing again, that's all."

"Your mother will be thrilled, no doubt. I can't wait to hear her lecture me. I'll have to tell her your injury is her fault, since she sent me to find you in the first place." Vincius let Marcus' hand drop. "If you're done here, then it's past time to be off."

Marcus stood stock still, his back very straight, and looked up into Vincius' eyes. "Why did she send you to find me, anyway? She already knew I had a practice session scheduled. I have it every week at the same time."

"She has a surprise for you. I suggest we get back home so she can tell you what it is."

"With my father away, it's bound to be something like, 'Son,'" Marcus said, speaking in a feminine tone. "'A new rabbi has come to town. And it's very important to me that you study with him. Unfortunately, the only time he has available is during your swordsmanship lessons.'" The alluring voice stopped and the boy's voice returned, open and direct. "She's pulled that stunt on me several times already. I've been expecting her to haul me out of my lessons all week."

"So cynical, young Marcus." Vincius chortled as he thwacked Marcus on the head with a folded linen sheet. "But you can always say no."

"You try saying no to my mother and see how that works out for you," he said and stared up at Vincius with wide-open eyes.

"Hmm. I see your point," said Vincius, crossing his arms over his chest. "But from what I know of it, you may even enjoy this surprise."

Marcus stood with his left foot forward, his right hand on his hip. He tipped his chin slightly forward. "Tell me," he said, and a look flashed across his face, twisting his lips into the ghost of a smile.

"She swore me to secrecy," said Vincius, his eyes glinting in response. "But I fancy you might like it this time."

"I can't wait," said Marcus and rolled his eyes.

———◆———

Miriam leaned her elbows on the windowsill and stuck her head out as far as she could. "He's finally coming," she announced to Yehonatan, her older brother, pulling in her head, half turning her body back to him where he lounged on a divan in her atrium. Her face vibrant, Miriam began to dance around the room. "I've been waiting for this moment all his life."

Yehonatan looked over at his younger sister and then glanced across to Tullian, his traveling companion, seated upright across the room on a second divan. Dark complected and of middle height, Tullian dominated his corner of the room, his frame and bearing radiating an impression of compact strength.

Yehonatan smiled slowly at his sister. His skin color had considerably darkened too, Miriam thought. The long stay in *Arabia Felix* had done its work, and on top of that, the return trip to Caesarea, by boat and horse and camel, while the sun burned down on him.

"All this enthusiasm, Miriam, just over the fact that I'll soon see your son," he said, smiling at her. Yehonatan raised his eyebrows, sun bleached, like the hair on top of his head. She remembered it a light brown from Sardis, but now his hair was almost as fair as hers. Uncovered inside the house, she thought it formed a striking combination against his dark skin and green eyes.

"Wait until you see him; he's dark haired but his facial structure is almost an exact match of yours. I so hoped you would meet him while he was still young." Miriam rubbed suddenly at the corners of her eyes.

"What happened to you Miriam? You never used to cry for such silly reasons."

Miriam stopped dancing around the room to whack her brother on the shoulder. "How would you know, Yehonatan? The last time you saw me I was practically a child myself."

Yehonatan caught her hand in his and pulled her gently to him, so that she ended up sitting on the divan next to him. He put his left arm around her waist. "And now my very talented younger sister is helping to expand father's business on the coast of Judea. And it was all her own idea, not his."

"Your idea, you mean," said Miriam, pretending to glower at him.

"Well, it was your idea right after I suggested it to you," said Yehonatan, and ducked his head as Miriam moved her arm around to whack him again. "Motivated purely by self-interest, as I was, I wanted you working for me at a young age."

Miriam heard the lock on the door lifting. "Hush for now, Yeho-natan. And remember, don't speak of business until this afternoon." She turned her head back to Yehonatan and her lips slowly formed her most conspiratorial smile.

———◆———

Marcus shoved the door open and stood in the stone doorway as he looked into the house, Vincius towering behind him. His mother had guests with her, two men. They looked, he thought, like the wealthy merchants from the East that he had seen with Vincius that morning on the balcony of the gymnasium. Marcus stepped into the house properly, realizing with a start that one of them, a blond man, had his arm around his mother. Hoping vainly that Vincius could not see her, Marcus wondered what on earth she could be doing and why she was doing it here, in public, before him, her son. And poor Vincius, standing on the doorstep just behind him, in love with his mother for years now, would be torn between his own wounded feelings and his instinct to protect her. What would happen to Miriam if he reported it to Julius? And why, thought Marcus again, was his mother doing this before her only son? Marcus could feel his face hardening into a scowl as he stood still, staring at the man. The man sat there with his arm around his mother and had the effrontery to smile back at him. Marcus glanced behind him as Vincius moved into the room, and saw that his face, for some reason, wore a smile as well.

"Apparently, my dear, the resemblance between us is not striking enough for your son to have noticed it yet, so if you would return me my arm," said the man to Miriam, "I'll introduce myself and Tullian, who seems rather to be enjoying the dubious elements of this little family drama." Pulling his arm from around his mother's waist, the man rose smoothly from the divan and moved to stand before Marcus. Taller than him, the man had a lithe grace as he leaned in and took his left hand gently in his. Marcus, sensing something about the man just beyond his conscious grasp, found his presence disquieting.

"This injury, I'm afraid, is attributable to me," the man said. "In my haste to meet you, I directed Vincius to take me to the gymnasium in the middle of your lesson, against his judgment, I'm afraid. Your mother has already scolded me for it." He turned his head to smile at Miriam once more. "But not too hard since it was her idea to begin with, so eager was she for her son to meet his uncle mere minutes after he arrived in port from Alexandria."

Marcus' eyes slid from the man to his mother, still unsure. Miriam smiled back at him.

"Well met, Marcus. I'm your uncle Yehonatan."

"Prosy as ever, Yehonatan." The second man had risen to speak, compact, powerful and vivid. He looked to be a soldier, Marcus thought approvingly. "If you had only started your speech with that bit, your nephew would have been the wiser, sooner."

The man turned to Marcus then. "And since your uncle seems to have forgotten to introduce me, Marcus, despite his promise to do just that, I'll fend for myself. I'm Tullian, your uncle's trading partner and sometimes friend." He took Marcus' uninjured right hand in his. "Skillful work with the dagger this morning, lad. When that hand is healed, I hope we'll have time to go a round or two ourselves."

After all those years of hearing about him, his uncle had proven himself a disappointment, Marcus thought. Dressed in bright blue embroidered robes offsetting his fair hair, he was too pretty and simpering by half. And now the man had seated himself back down on the divan and was touching his mother again. Turning his head decisively away from his uncle, Marcus considered his uncle's friend. At least, he seemed solid enough, a fighter, maybe a military man. The kind of man he knew from his father's military camp and instinctively liked. He looked up at Tullian and smiled.

———◦———

That afternoon, Vincius sat near Miriam as she gave her servant orders to prepare a sumptuous meal for her guests. Before he departed, Miriam took Vincius' hand in her small one and extended an invitation for him to dine with them that night as well.

Vincius could feel himself smiling broadly. He had never been able to exercise control over his features around Miriam. He reacted to her presence too immediately; and after a while, he had simply stopped trying.

She knew how he felt, of course; his reactions to her were too naked for her not to understand. The night when he had escorted her away from Julius' tent, days before her arrangement with Julius began, his feelings for her had begun. She had felt so off balance that night, almost broken, yet stalwart and brave, like a female wildcat he had once watched in the mountains near his home. Half surrounded by wolves, she had fought her way free, as he shot at the wolves, killed one and wounded another, before the rest fled. The cat had withdrawn from the battle hurt, but very much alive and he had left a rabbit for it once outside its den. Afterwards, he had seen the cat occasionally. Then later its progeny.

Miriam had hardened up since that time, of course. That didn't surprise him. So had he, more so every year. Time under Julius' command, whether as soldier or army wife, would do that to anyone.

But having seen her spark during those early days of her marriage, he knew down to his toes that this side of her existed within, if only he could figure out how to access it reliably. It flashed out occasionally but only enough to be tantalizing, moments when he felt he was seeing the real Miriam. Her worth was limitless to him; whereas Julius saw her merely as an unfortunate bargain he had been forced to strike. That frustrated him to no end.

She used to know her own value, too. But Vincius was not sure it ever occurred to her any more.

"Miriam," Vincius said, "it's very kind of you to invite me as well, but you will want time alone with your brother. You haven't seen him for years. Marcus has barely met him."

"I'll have time to spend with him after dinner, and all day tomorrow as well," said Miriam. "He'll be off for a week or so after that, before he returns to Caesarea to spend some more time here before leaving for Sardis."

"Still, Miriam, that's hardly much time. You've told me before you hadn't seen him for years and years. You'll want the privacy now, especially," he said, lowering his voice, "as Julius will return in less than a week, and he might be less accommodating to your desires."

"Frankly, Vincius, he'll want a report of went on here with guests in the house in any case. And if anyone is to give him a report, I'd prefer that he asked you and not one of the servants."

Vincius looked sheepish.

"I know you don't like it, that you would rather not report to him. But he'll ask and I trust you to provide him with what he'll consider an accurate report," she continued, squeezing his hand. "We both know Julius."

"You know, Miriam, he does exactly this same thing in camp, not just at your house. He asks for a full report whenever he returns. He likes to feel he has complete control in every domain where he has authority. To his mind, control comes through knowledge, it serves as its foundation, as it were. An illusion, of course, in a domestic context, but he cannot admit that to himself. His conditioning runs too deep."

"I know all too well," Miriam replied tiredly. "After all, I've been married to the man for nine years now, practically speaking."

Her bitterness over their quasi-legal domestic arrangement, Vincius reminded himself, had never entirely abated. After all these years, he still found that knowledge wrenching deep down in his gut. But as a soldier himself, he had nothing better to offer Miriam, only the same quasi-legal arrangement. And here, with Julius, at least she had Marcus with her.

His hand still rested in hers. As he lifted it away, Miriam looked up at him, and her face softened. She lowered the timbre of her voice. "You'll come, then, Vincius."

"Of course, I will," he said. Turning on his heel, he left the villa, shutting the door gently behind him.

That night, the men lingered, talking with Miriam and Marcus for a long time over the ruins of their dinner. There were platters spread before them of fried fish bursting open with delicate white meat, poultry stuffed with fruits and almonds and ginger and roasted lamb rubbed with cardamom and cinnamon and mint. The wine, served so profusely, came from a famous vineyard in Aza, only a short distance down the coastline. The servants had lit an abundance of sconces and oil lamps before the meal and after it was finished, they took the platters away with them and distributed bowls of rosewater to the guests, to clean their hands. The bowls rested on a fine linen cloth made at Bet Shean, laid out by the servants along with the sweet final course, warm honey cakes and fresh apricots and peaches; and the scent of the rosewater wafted into the air, providing a delicate counterpoint to the lingering smell of the food.

"Thank you, Miriam," said Yehonatan when everyone had finished eating at last. Miriam had seated Yehonatan in Julius' place, at the head of the table. "A most welcome break from the rations Tullian and I have been subjected to recently."

Vincius sat in his usual place, in the middle of the table, across from Marcus. He had talked less than the other two men, observing Yehonatan as he proceeded to charm everyone in the room. Not even

97

the servants had proven immune from his effect. Certainly, Marcus'
early diffidence had melted entirely away early in the dinner; his own,
of a different order than Marcus', had not even lasted that long; it
had vanished during the afternoon.

More surprisingly, Marcus, who normally never revealed much of
his feelings, had tonight spoken of them in some detail. To Vincius,
the fact that Marcus usually kept his own counsel made sense as a
self-protective gesture in a household in which, at times, an open war
for his soul was being waged by his parents. Yet, the effect of Yehonatan's presence had somehow erased the need for such a defense.
It was as though Yehonatan had sent a magnetic plumb line down
Marcus' throat and it had returned to him with pure nuggets of gold.

It was interesting too, how alike and unlike brother and sister
were. Miriam could often be charming, but she seemed to exercise
that ability only as needed, not for the pure joy of it, as Yehonatan did. Hers was a defensive charm, he decided, while Yehonatan
wielded his charm as an offensive stratagem. Yet, you could register
all this about him and still feel utterly seduced by his manner and
the stories of his doings in Arabia Felix and in Africa, sailing the
trade winds far down the coast and importing back fine cotton, rare
minerals and gemstones in exchange for frankincense and myrrh, the
priceless unguents of Arabia. Vincius knew from Miriam he traded
murex as well, the precious purple die found in its finest form in
shells dredged up in the thousands and thousands off the coastline
of Syria. That was the part of the business Miriam oversaw here in
Caesarea working in concert with her cousin, who roamed between
Syria and the north of Israel.

"Marcus," said Miriam, "your uncle has not yet mentioned to
you that he is planning on traveling south for about a week, down
the coast, to oversee the delivery of some goods he has brought back
with him. We thought that perhaps you might want to accompany

him and Tullian. It would be a wonderful opportunity to teach you about facets of your grandfather's business."

Twisting his lip, Marcus glanced around the room warily, first at his mother, then at Vincius and finally at Yehonatan. "Father will expect me to stay at my training. He won't like it if I leave off even for a couple of days, let alone for an entire week."

"You are forgetting your injury, Marcus," said Miriam. "You'll have to take off some time in any case, according to Master Rufinus."

Score one for Marcus earlier in the day, Vincius thought. He had been correct. Miriam had been conspiring to haul him out of his military training one way or another; and she had succeeded in coming up with a plan so attractive to Marcus that he had not even noticed that she had outmaneuvered him.

Yehonatan glanced over at him with a quick warning look, before smiling at Marcus over the table. "Think of it this way, Marcus. You mentioned earlier that your father would be extremely disappointed at the report you earned today at the gymnasium from Master Rufinus. And that you are dreading telling him about it. This way, if you go with us, from what your mother has told me, he'll be distracted by the fact that you have left without his consent. I'll doubt he'll remember to question you about the details of your training at all." Yehonatan grinned at Marcus, a grin glittering with mischief and collusion and intelligence. "Think of it, to borrow a military analogy, as a tactical exercise in confusing the adversary." He paused, smiling, as he gathered in all of their attention. When he resumed speaking, his voice was lower, more authoritative, the voice of a leader. "And when we return, I'll talk it over with Julius. I doubt there'll be any problems at all, Marcus, and certainly none that will fall on your shoulders. I'll see to that. After all, at this point, you are one of the heirs to a rather complicated trading business. It's only reasonable you start learning about it, as I did at your age." Yehonatan leaned back in his chair, smiling. "Of course, if you are not interested in coming with us," he said, sweeping his hands wide for emphasis, "why that's another matter altogether. Then you must stay here with your mother, by all means, and enjoy your time off from practice."

Ha, Vincius thought! He wished he could watch the tactical maneuvering that would take place during Yehonatan's first meeting with Julius. They would be rare adversaries, Julius all moodiness, command and duty with competing passions hidden just underneath the surface; and Yehonatan all subterfuge, intelligence and charm. The gods only knew what lurked beneath his façade. One way or another, Vincius thought, spellbound by the vision he had just conjured, he would have to figure out a way to get a full report of what happened at that meeting, even if he had to bribe the servants. And he knew just which ones would be amenable to his coin.

Vincius now knew exactly why Miriam had insisted that he come for dinner. Not altogether a selfless act inviting him, but that was Miriam. For, as his personal military representative here in Caesarea while he rode to a meeting in Jerusalem, Julius would be wroth with him, not Miriam, for letting Marcus leave without his consent. Vincius suspected, that were Silius here in his place, he would never countenance this impromptu trip. But Silius was not in love with Miriam. And Silius had yet to meet Yehonatan.

Tullian broke the silence. "Didn't I ask you earlier, Marcus, to practice dagger work with me during our stay? How about I add some wrestling technique to that as well when we travel south?"

"You know, Marcus," said Yehonatan, "I first hired Tullian to guard me on one of my voyages to the east. It's very rough country there, and Tullian used to be famous, up and down the Arabian Peninsula for his wrestling skill." Yehonatan looked at Tullian and winked. "But when I discovered the man had a brain in his head, I made him a partner in the business as well. He still guards me now, but I made sure it's in his interest to keep both me and the goods safe." Yehonatan swiveled his head to face Marcus again. "And do you know he has

100

taught me some Greek wrestling moves as well? So perhaps we can simply tell your father you have gone with us for a seminar in advanced wrestling technique unavailable in Caesarea. Afterwards, if he is still disappointed that you went off with me, we'll simply throw him in with Tullian to go a round or two. What do you say?"

Marcus looked at Yehonatan, his face, by the light of the oil lamp, brightened into a wide smile. "Yes," Marcus said, "throw him in the ring and see if he survives. That's the kind of logic that most appeals to father. But I'll let you handle him if he beats Tullian."

PART VI

CHAPTER 8

The Family Business

A day and a half after Miriam's dinner party, in the very early morning, with the sky just lightening into a profound blue, and the pink tendrils of dawn not yet visible, Marcus rose from his bed and stepped out onto the terrace. The moon lay curled like a cat in the sky, its light diffuse as it sank gently into the sea. Throwing on a short tunic, Marcus hurried out of his room and descended the staircase into the atrium. Catching sight of his uncle Yehonatan alone in the *peristyle*, the enclosed garden behind the house, Marcus stood silently for some moments, watching him. Surrounded by a wall of concentration so palpable Marcus could sense it in the next room, Yehonatan stood, facing away from the sea, his eyes closed, swaying slightly. Marcus observed him for some time, speculating; then turning silently, he edged away.

Sometime later, still in the early morning, Marcus stood waiting at the back gate for Yehonatan to join him to set out together. But as the wait grew longer and longer, so did his impatience. Everything for the trip was packed. And Tullian had seen to transporting their goods to the port of Caesarea to get a start on loading them into the boat that they would sail down the coast. He was waiting for them there and the boat was due to leave port before the tide turned.

At last Marcus turned back to the villa with the determination to seize his uncle from his mother by force if necessary. Planning an ambush in his mind, he moved silently up the pathway and stopped suddenly as he heard voices carried on the wind.

"...would certainly be best for Marcus and I if Julius never knows. We must be very careful."

The next words were low and indistinct, a whirring zephyr, full of syllables that he could not quite grasp. After another moment, he recognized his uncle's voice replying in Hebrew, not Aramaic nor Greek. Creeping closer to the building, Marcus stood in the shade and darted his head momentarily around the corner of the villa. His mother and Yehonatan were speaking to each other in the colonnaded front portico bathed in slanting morning light and the long black shadows of cypress trees, crisp and exact. Wearing a saffron dyed robe, his mother was sitting on a marble bench, leaning back against the wall, gazing northeast at the view before her. There were other villas nearby, and in the distance, the hillocks of Carmel thrust up awkwardly out of the earth, like a new-born colt rising on its spindly legs, sheltered by its mother.

Yehonatan, dressed in a white tunic with a blue mantle draped over his right shoulder, belted in leather and tooled gold, stood facing away from Miriam. Looking idly north, his hands rested on the side balustrade. As he shifted from foot to foot, the gold on his belt shimmered in the sun, refracting into myriad points of light, an entire heavenly host dancing into life for one glorious instant before evanescing into the ether.

Turning back suddenly to face his sister, Yehonatan's face wore a slight shadow. "Miriam, I still don't like leaving you here alone to face Julius. I wish you'd change your mind and come with us. I'd be much more comfortable if I were the one to deal with the man first."

His mother gave Marcus' uncle a slight smile and reached over to touch his arm. "I'll be fine, Yehonatan. I've been dealing with Julius for years now. Don't worry about me. His temper can run fierce, but he is not unjust. He'll be furious to find that Marcus is gone, but by the next morning he'll be calm enough to listen to reason."

"The next morning, Miriam? No need, then, I suppose, to speculate at the methods you'll employ to achieve that end." Yehonatan's mouth twisted as he finished speaking.

"I'm not averse to it if it comes down to that," said Miriam. In profile, it looked as though she were pursing her lips into a small smile. "Why should I be? But frankly, Yehonatan, that's not what I had in mind." She shrugged. "Although, it wouldn't be the first time I had to resort to such means to change his mood."

"Don't sound so happy about it. You are not shocking me, little sister, but you are making me regret ... many things." There was silence for several seconds, and then lowering his voice, Yehonatan said, *That which is crooked cannot be made straight; and that which is wanting cannot be numbered.*"

Marcus could hear his uncle's soft, inexorable footsteps as Yehonatan began to stroll, slowly, leisurely, completely at ease from the north end of the portico to the south end. Marcus coiled himself tightly as he could, hunched down, his eyes turned up, watching. He remained quite still, holding his breath.

Leaning down over the balustrade quite casually, Yehonatan shot his hand out around the corner of the villa, grabbed Marcus by the scruff of his neck and hauled him over the southern balustrade. Yehonatan turned to Miriam. "Well, well, how very inconvenient for us. It appears that your son has been listening in on what we've been saying for the last several minutes. I assume from the look on his face that his Hebrew is fluent." Tossing Marcus roughly against the wall of the villa, his voice cold as the depths of the sea, he said, "I suggest you apologize to your mother, immediately."

Marcus regained his balance and righted himself. He looked straight up at his uncle, sustaining his gaze. "What for, sir? For listening in? Or for getting caught?" Involuntarily, his right hand sneaked behind his back and began to rub the raw skin.

His uncle stood staring at him, his feet and shoulders both square with the ground, his mouth held tightly in a straight line. "If it comes to that, apologize for both. If you mean to succeed as a spy, you certainly need to go about it more cleverly than you did just now. You displayed complete incompetence. That deserves punishment in and of itself. Notice, for example, how easily you were caught. And the consequences of being caught in some circumstances can be quite dire, more so than you might expect, let me assure you." With the slightest of movements, the left side of Yehonatan's mouth quirked down in distaste.

This stern Yehonatan was entirely new to Marcus. So far, he had only encountered the charming and adventurous uncle who had been interested in attracting his affection. Marcus was aware in the welter of emotions he felt in reaction to the conversation he had overheard that there was a distinct note of loss underlying his anger. He banished the feeling from his mind immediately but could feel it snaking deep down into his gut. And that made him angry, angry enough to lash out.

"I always accept the consequences of my actions," Marcus said belligerently. "In this case, I imagine the consequence to be that I won't be accompanying you south after all. Very well. I'll stay here where I am supposed to be, where my father expects me to be, and I'll keep on studying. Roman law and Roman military arts and Roman spying techniques if it comes to that. All very useful for my future career as a centurion in the Roman army."

Yehonatan did not change his posture by as much as one iota. His mouth pulled taut, he responded. "Nothing so easy, Marcus. Oh, you'll still be coming with me. Only now I know better the nephew with whom I will be dealing. It's one thing, Marcus, to spy on an enemy but it's quite another to spy on your own family. *The path of the just is like the shining light... and the way of the wicked is like darkness.*" Yehonatan pointed his head at the dark corner, sun barren, in which Marcus had lurked. "One knows a man best by his deeds, and best of all, by his private deeds, the ones he does in the shade, beyond the sun's light, known only to God."

Silence fell over the portico. In the distance, Marcus could hear gulls crying to each other as they swooped, brawling in the air, and then diving into the sea, plumes of froth rising in their wake. A tendril of hair fluttered over his nose and he lifted a hand to move it away. There was a smear of blood on the back of his hand, he noticed. His back must have bled when his uncle dragged him over the balustrade; his uncle, whom Marcus had just learned the hard way was much stronger than he looked. And far more alert as well. Why had he ever suspected otherwise?

Yehonatan glanced away from him towards the sun, taking notice of its position, now perched far above the horizon. He said, "While this is a lovely family discussion we are having, nevertheless, you've reminded me, Marcus, that it is time we took our departure. But before we go, I want to hear you apologize to your mother."

Marcus, suddenly red-faced, forced himself to look Miriam in the eye. "I'm sorry, mother. I didn't set out to listen to you. But once I heard my name, I felt drawn to listen. I didn't stop to think." He stood before her, biting one side of his lip, fists lightly clenched.

"Marcus, enough said for now. It's time you left. But expect me, *O! son, to punish your sins after you return.*

Marcus looked up at her through his lashes and grinned. He said, *But not to the third and fourth generation*, I hope.

106

"I'll not decide until I see what fruits of the land you bring back for me. *Clusters of grapes born on the shoulders of men, pomegranates or figs?*" Miriam rose and leaned in to kiss Marcus on the cheek. Then, unexpectedly, she threw her arms around him, giving him a tight hug and rested her head against his for a moment. "You always make me proud, Marcus. And I know you will make your uncle proud as well when he knows you better. Learn everything you can from him." She released him then and turned her face up to her brother, eyes still twinkling as she raised her left eyebrow.

Yehonatan smiled back, and mirroring her, raised his right eyebrow. "Miriam, we'll be back in less than a week, unless the land eats us up or we turn into grasshoppers." He stepped in, leaning down to kiss his sister on the brow. Turning to Marcus, he said, "Come on *Caleb*, it's time we ventured forth to spy on the promised land." And then stepping beyond the sunlit portico, Yehonatan walked on the path towards the road, Marcus trailing behind him.

Together with Tullian, Yehonatan and Marcus sailed down the seacoast, from Caesarea to the port of Ashqelon, a short journey of some sixty miles south, in a wooden craft that they had hired for the trip, its cedar and oak frame stained dark from its yearly covering with tar. The back hull of the boat was crammed with his uncle's goods, packed tight in trunks and crates and urns. There were precious containers filled with frankincense and myrrh from Arabia and Ethiopia, cinnamon bark, ginger and ivory collected from the port of Rhapta on the East African coast. Still other ones stored black and white pepper from Barygaza on the Indian peninsula, and luminous pearls, twinkling white and gray, black and pink, brought from a country far away, farther east even than India. In the humid air, Marcus could from time to time smell the scent of some of the spices, leaking out of tiny fissures and cracks in their containers and blending in the air, fragrant, woodsy, sweet and sharp all mixed together.

Most of these goods, only a fraction of what his uncle had brought from Arabia, had already been secured for traders in Ashqelon itself. The details had been arranged in advance by one of his mother's agents, Marcus learned with disappointment. He would not, after all, get to enjoy the sight of Yehonatan hawking bargains on the street corner, dressed in blue samite and gold.

Marcus sat on his bench, perfectly at ease on the sea, and watched as the slaves rowed the boat north to the mouth of the port. Seamen steered her expertly around the tall ships docked in the spectacular haven of Caesarea, passing by each of the great watchtowers stationed along the southern mole encircling Sebastos Harbor. Last of all, the slaves rowed the boat past the temple of polished stones that Herod had dedicated in the sea, with its twin statues of Caesar and of Rome perched on columns far above their heads. As they sailed past, Marcus leaned far back on his bench and tilted his head as far as he could. Much later, when they were already far out at sea, he could still see the shimmering statues hanging in the air, the last tangible beacon of Caesarea.

All that morning, as the hours passed slowly amidst the sea brume intermittently dispersed by swift breezes, Marcus was made aware of his uncle's displeasure. His uncle sat comfortably on his bench, his legs spread before him, looking at no one, his eyes focused on the blue-gray sea, thinking. The entire world seemed shut from his focus except the one point on which Yehonatan was fixed. The short waves slapped and broke against the boat as it sailed steadily south, washing his blue mantle with foam and water and salt, but as far as Marcus observed, Yehonatan's expression hardly altered.

At first, Marcus stood up and walked carefully about the small deck, his movements circumscribed by the men and benches and packed goods, and the pitching of the vessel as it rolled east to west. The air smelled salty and damp and the wind blew fierce against his cheeks, roughening his skin. But, in the end, still somewhat restless, he settled down to listen to a discussion from Tullian on the techniques of Greek wrestling and its merits. He had Tullian's promise that once they had landed and their business was taken care of, he and Tullian would enjoy their first bout of wrestling together. But then Tullian looked over at Yehonatan for a long moment, still staring out to sea. When he turned back, his face had assumed a guarded look, instead of the easy expression it had worn while speaking to Marcus earlier. Tilting his head, Tullian said, "What in Hades happened while I was securing the boat?"

They landed in Ashqelon at noon. A much smaller port than Caesarea and far less magnificent in design despite its white marble flagstones, Ashqelon contained no natural harbor to shelter boats along the unbroken seacoast. Instead, the city perched above an underground river, its inhabitants gaining access to the precious sweet water through the digging of wells. Ashqelon itself, renowned for its wine and its green onions, both of which traded far to the West, had been endowed by Herod over a century before with marble baths and fountains and white colonnaded squares.

Marcus had stood silently watching everything that transpired as Tullian and his uncle sorted out their belongings and, then negotiating with the local men, had their goods moved into a small warehouse near the port. The next day had seen the disposal of almost all the goods they had brought along with them, except for one small trunk, earmarked for use where they were going next. But where they were going next, Marcus had not been told. Instead, he had been taken to a dizzying assortment of meetings that lasted from the early morning until early afternoon. There were meetings conducted in the back chambers of busy shops, squished in between stacked piles of bright carpets still smelling of desert dust, spices and the camels that had borne them west and bales of precious silk, brought through the Parthian kingdom all the way from China. Other meetings had transpired in warehouses and in the bustling covered marketplace. There he found a confusion of scents: spices, fruit and the pungent aroma of street food, vats of cooking beans and roasting meat. Once they walked down a street entirely hung with meat carcasses and clouding flies, as Marcus' stomach roiled from the rawness of the blood stench.

Yehonatan sat with Marcus and Tullian, one to either side, smiling, one knee draped over the other, holding a striped glass goblet of watered wine flavored with honey, or an earthenware jug, or a cast silver cup. He never drank the wine, although Tullian and Marcus always seemed to have some. Concluding past business transactions and negotiating future ones, Yehonatan balanced his every nuance, of speech or of implication, against his temporary opponent, his words wrought delicately like the finest work in filigree. After a time, and a substantial amount of drink, the meetings all blended together in Marcus' mind, a very long, complex negotiation, held in interchangeable rooms with people who metamorphosed one into the other, their garments flickering past his eyes, a stream of color. They were all a blur, none stood out in his mind, except for the last meeting of the day.

That meeting broke from the pattern in every respect. First, they were summoned to it by two armed Roman guards, short iron swords cased prominently in bright scabbards on their left hips, who left them no leeway to refuse or even to delay long enough to finish their current negotiation. Instead, the guards ordered them to walk through glaring white marble squares unrelieved by any shade, the sun at its zenith, to meet with the Roman military Administrator of Ashqelon in his palatial villa by the sea.

As they walked, Yehonatan surreptitiously leaned into Marcus, addressing him in Hebrew in an undertone. "I've no idea what this is about. As far as I know, we're all paid up in trade tariffs, so it ought not to be official. And I doubt it can be a message from your father so soon. It may be trouble. Or it may be nothing at all, just a show of force. Say as little as you can and speak neither Latin nor Hebrew

110

unless I cue you to do so explicitly in one of those tongues. And by the finger of God, stop drinking before you puke."

When they arrived at the villa, a guard directed them to an ante-chamber half full of people. There they were kept standing for over an hour, watched, in a room with guards, and little opportunity to speak without being overheard. Marcus heard Yehonatan and Tul-lian murmur an occasional word among themselves, but he did not understand the language that they used. At least it was cool inside, Marcus thought, as the wine-induced cloud fogging his mind slowly began to dissipate. He leaned back against the wall and kicked his heels until a guard commanded him to stop.

Finally, the wide cedar doors were thrown open once again, and a different guard emerged from the audience chamber. Pointing to Yehonatan and Tullian, the soldier barked, "You two, come along with me." The man's mouth curled upward slowly, his lips standing out red and full and wet against his dark curling hair. "And bring the boy."

Marcus stood on the threshold, behind Yehonatan. His first view inside the chamber showed him a long plain hall, sunlit and over-warm, looking out over the sea. Several couches were placed around the hall. At its far end, a man sat at a desk, brown haired, thickly built. The man looked up slowly from the pile of papers he was perusing at his desk and set down his stylus gently. Standing, he was no more an impressive figure than he had been sitting; stocky, unprepossessing in looks, he was, however, richly dressed in a white tunic with a purple stripe, belted at the waist and wearing magnificent scarlet boots. Moreover, he projected a supremely confident air. The man nodded once to the guard who had summoned them inside, curtly, in dismissal; the guard left, the door ringing closed behind him. Then suddenly, walking towards them from his end of the room, the man opened his mouth and began to declaim in pure Homeric Greek. "*Odysseus, man of tactics, reckless friend, what daring brings you down to the House of Death? – where the senseless, burnt-out wraiths of mortals make their home.* He finished his verse and stood before Yehonatan and Tullian, smiling at them wolfishly.

"Consulting Tiresias, for help on my journey home to rocky Sardis." Switching to modern Greek, Yehonatan said, "I must say, Achilles, that for a corpse who's lording it over the kingdom of the dead, you look well, all in all."

"Perhaps because it's a recent posting. I haven't been here long enough yet to assume a truly ghostly pallor, like some of my less fortunate compatriots."

"You're referring to the ones already interred underground? That's ancient history, Galenus. As you well know, all the recent bloody campaigns against Rome have been to the east of Judea or to the west."

"But if you're drinking daily blood," said Tullian, breaking in, "I hope to Hades it's from slaughtered sheep and not from slaughtered men. Galenus, you bastard, Iounathan may not admit it, but I will. You had us scared half to death out there in your antechamber. I could practically see him toting up in his head how long he thought we would last once we were thrown to the lions in Herod's arena for some crime against Rome we could not quite fathom that we had committed."

In a snap, Galenus' face turned utterly forbidding. "You are not, I hope, disparaging the Empire's rule of law?" He raised quizzing eyebrows, first at Tullian, then at Yehonatan. "The very threat of that arena works wonders, you know, on a myriad of seditious souls."

Yehonatan was looking full on at Galenus, his countenance smooth and inexpressive. "It's superb setting near the seacoast certainly provides a charming vista. Herod's engineers were surely worth whatever riches he paid them."

"Ah," said Galenus, "then you've been to Caesarea already? A beautiful city. Well worth a long visit." The Administrator's face, Marcus observed, had now returned to normal. Whatever threat had been fomenting in the air was banished. Temporary respite, at least.

"Yes," said Yehonatan, "we landed there from Alexandria. But, unfortunately, stayed only a day or so." He nodded at Tullian. "And I don't expect we'll be going back anytime soon to enjoy her further. We're due on a ship out of Tyre for the return trip to Sardis."

Marcus, who recognized that all this information was purposefully falsified, understood this as his uncle's signal to avoid talk of home, of Caesarea.

"Now, I wouldn't have minded being appointed Administrator of Caesarea," said Galenus, nodding his head wistfully back and forth. "The palaces, the hippodrome, the gladiatorial shows, the taxable wealth. Whereas in Ashqelon, one must console oneself with the splendid local wine. Of course, there are *other* native crops, if you know what I mean." Galenus mugged at the two men standing before him. "But that's a crop available worldwide. Although, in my experience, the regional differences always provide some local spice to savor." Galenus paused, looking closely first at Yehonatan, then at Tullian. "Regional differences can be instructive in other ways as well, a fact well known to the two of you. But speaking of excellent local vintages, I've been remiss. Sit, gentlemen, while my servant brings us some wine. And tell me, what brings you to Ashqelon just now?" Galenus walked to the door, opened it a crack, and spoke softly to someone waiting outside.

"It's a convenient transit point, Galenus. And we thought while we're here we might as well conduct some business as well," said Yehonatan. The smile was still on his face. He sat down on a couch and cocked his head slightly to the right as a young slave came into the room holding a silver tray, with the glasses of wine already poured. The boy, moving with a dancer's grace, set the tray lightly down on a small marble table, looked over once at his master and at Galenus' nod, scurried out of the room. Only then did Yehonatan resume speaking. "What else? Trade. The very same thing that once brought us to Parthia, Arabia, and points further east."

"That may well be true for you," said Galenus. "But I thought that Tullian here was a native of southern Arabia. One of the port cities, wasn't it? And what took him up to Parthia was you."

"I'm from Cana, on the Arabian coast," said Tullian. "But the only reason I was born there was because of commerce. One of the communities that sprang up around the spice trade."

Galenus handed around three tall goblets of wine, keeping the fourth goblet for himself. "And what kind of business brings you both here now?"

This time, Marcus was interested to see, Yehonatan drank deeply from his cup as soon as it was put into his hand.

"The murex trade, Galenus. As you know," said Yehonatan, pointing his index finger at Galenus' tunic, "royal dye. It's popular everywhere, inside the empire and out of it."

"Especially amongst those without proper standing to wear it," said Galenus and laughed as though he were truly amused. "Murex shells. Of course. I should have realized. Hence, Tyre, the queen city of the purple dye trade, stinking of fishy commerce."

"Hence, Tyre, as you say. From what we've seen so far, the quality of purple dye in Judea seems slightly inferior to that of Syria."

"It has that reputation, of course. Although, I cannot say I ever paid it any heed myself. Mithras be praised, I'm no tradesmen. That's what I would call dirty work. Give me some nice clean soldiering any day." Galenus finished his wine and filled it up again from the silver pitcher, looking about the room to see if anyone else's glass was empty. Then took the opportunity to refill Yehonatan's glass.

"So, Tullian," said Galenus, turning again to the fighter, "I see that Iounathan finally found a method of persuading you to give up your wrestling career in order to work solely with him in trade."

"Or you could say I finally grew a brain, though Iounathan takes credit for that too. Meanwhile, I'm older now," said Tullian. "The healing takes longer. And getting knocked about is more of a nuisance.

But I still fight. Exhibition bouts, and the occasional student. The pay is better, and the damage, well, hurts less. In fact, I've been planning on giving lessons to..." Tullian broke off suddenly and looked at Yehonatan.

"Yes?" said Galenus, looking back and forth between the two men, his expressions sharpening. "You were, perhaps, planning on instructing this young man who is accompanying you."

Yehonatan nodded slightly at Tullian.

Tullian said, "Just the basics, for now. He's uninstructed in the fighting arts as yet."

"And who exactly is this young man?" Galenus looked hard at Marcus, then back at Yehonatan. Of all things, a moue quirked its way onto his long lips. And vanished as suddenly. "I fear you've neglected to introduce him to me."

"Forgive the oversight, Galenus. My nephew, Marcus. He met us in Caesarea to start learning the trading business."

"So, young man, your home's in Sardis, with the rest of your family?"

Marcus glanced momentarily at Yehonatan, but could not read his expression. "That's right," he said at last, glancing to the left as he spoke. "Born there. And here to learn the family business."

Galenus looked back and forth between Yehonatan and Marcus once more, and then between Yehonatan and Tullian. He said, "He doesn't lie as well as you do, Iounathan. You'll have to train him up if you want him to succeed as well as you. But there's something more here, something you're not telling me." Galenus snapped his fingers. "No matter for now. If it's important, I'll ferret it out eventually. In any case, as you've doubtless guessed, what I really want from you is intelligence." He looked directly at Yehonatan. "You've been in Arabia more recently than I. What's the current situation?"

"It's been stable on the border of Parthia and Rome for years now, ever since Hadrian pulled back the border of the Empire to the west side of the Euphrates. *Abracadabra*. With a few words, the provinces of Mesopotamia and Armenia were dissolved," said Yehonatan. "And because magic's a known soporific, the whole region settled down to a long sleep. Brilliant planning in its way."

"You can keep the planning," said Galenus. "I preferred Trajan's aggressive expansionist policy and so did the army. If the man had not died, he would've conquered India next. Alas, the gods did not favor it. Perhaps they did not want a rival for god-like Alexander in their midst, so they took him before he achieved that rank." He breathed out once and shook his head. "Tragic in its way. The present regime is far more pragmatic. But how much less glorious!"

His goblet on the table before him, Galenus rubbed his hands together. "As for the current situation, do you care to share anything with me besides what the whole world already knows? Otherwise, it's going to be a long day for all of us and a very long night for you, Iounathan. Although it just might have some memorable compensations for me, and not, I suspect, only of the local variety." Tilting his head back, Galenus lifted the goblet to his mouth and finished his wine. "You understand me, I imagine."

Silence descended on the room. In its wake, Marcus could hear the slap of the waves on the shore. The sun glared into the room, glanced off of the silver wine pitcher and shattered into a hundred streaks of light. The reflection hurt his eyes, so Marcus closed them for a moment, and listened. A nerve twitched once, twice in his forehead. He became aware all at once that this morning's excess of wine had already degenerated into the makings of an exceptional headache. Outside the room, there was an occasional murmur of voices, and he could hear the guards patrolling, marching back and forth. Through the open terrace doors, the gulls squabbled for food, a familiar sound, and comforting in its way.

Marcus opened his eyes at last and saw that nothing had changed in the chamber, no one had moved by as much as an iota. Galenus still sat motionless, his face in shadow, expectant. And across from

116

him, his face ruthlessly lit up by the sun, Yehonatan sat mute, his breathing evenly paced.

Finally, Yehonatan glanced over at Tullian and turned back to Galenus. "We did hear before we left that there was some unrest within Parthia itself, a possible dynastic battle shaping up, led by a man called Tiridates, an ambitious nephew of the Parthian king; perhaps a useful opening to exploit if you Romans are planning an excursion to take Ctesiphon once again. But it was only a rumor. And that some months ago. We disbanded our team before we left and have received no further intelligence to that effect. In any case, the news is cold. Not the most successful fulcrum on which to pin a campaign, in my estimation."

Galenus smiled broadly, now like a hungry wolf whose large white teeth continue to show. "Well, at least you brought me one meaty nugget, even if I eventually find out the meat has already turned. Good, good."

Galenus turned his head suddenly to converse with Marcus again. "You might not think it, boy, if you've only just met him," Galenus said, "but underneath your uncle's delicate exterior, he's a mighty handy man to have around when you're planning a campaign. He and Tullian, here, ran the most efficient intelligence gathering team on the Arabian Peninsula as part of their trading business; better, in some respects I admit grudgingly, than the Roman army itself.

"And once, many years ago, your uncle's skills helped to rescue my cohort from a very tight spot we were in. We were facing a battle against superior native forces more familiar with the local territory than we were; it might have ended in a complete rout and our annihilation. But your uncle and Tullian stumbled upon us just then. And because they knew the land better than we did, your uncle came up with a brilliant plan for penetrating the enemy territory at night. He helped us destroy an entire Parthian detachment of troops, which outnumbered ours by at least half as much. Hence the private moniker

I bestowed on him, Odysseus." Galenus paused to smile in an oddly fond way at Yehonatan.

Odysseus! thought Marcus, eclipsing from his mind the strange tensions playing out between the three adult men here. Those had nothing to do with him. And with the headache, he had no desire to follow it down all its twisting, fetid channels, like a neighborhood of urban sprawl thrown together by poor squatters and the dispossessed. But this made sense to him personally. He'd always thought of his mother as Odyssean as well. Now it turned out to be a family trait. Marcus wondered when his own full measure of cunning would eventually arrive? But then, in certain areas of his life he had already learned to deal with his father with greater wiliness. Was wiliness a talent, like swordsmanship or allegorical interpretation, that one had to practice frequently before one attained excellence? Or was it a family trait and inborn? Either way, he promised himself, this coming year he would spend time learning to master it.

He focused outwardly again only to catch an expectant Galenus continuing to stare at him. Mercifully, the man seemed unaware of his lapse in attention. Marcus breathed in quickly, affixing his mind, like troweled cement, onto the Administrator.

"Not that Iounathan rescued my cohort for free, mind you," continued Galenus. "Once he came upon us, we didn't give him much of an option to depart unless he went to work for us. But as I recall, he ended up negotiating a rather large fee that included reduced tariff rates with the Roman emissary for quite a while after that, with some small help from myself. It ended up being a very profitable job for him."

Galenus paused and looked around the room, at each of them before returning his attention to Marcus. "To be frank, my dear boy, that expedition, however long in the past, is the reason I forgive your uncle and his friend the little secrets that they are holding out on me now." Galenus leaned in and lowered his voice. "Although, if they stay in Ashqelon, I may not always be so lenient."

118

"As I recall, you did quite well out of the deal yourself, Galenus." Yehonatan's voice sounded casual, almost bored. "Controlling the crossroads east of the Euphrates for a few years. Very profitable, is it not? Not to mention that you came out of it with your precious Legion intact."

"Did I imply there was no advantage to me?" Galenus smiled devastatingly at Yehonatan, then allowed a silence to develop. "A million apologies if I did. Naturally, I think no such thing." He rose, sweeping palm against palm three times, in dismissal. "Well, that's enough for now. I've other business to conduct and I'm quite sure you do as well."

Marcus stood up abruptly. Yehonatan and Tullian, however, lingered some moments more before they rose in concert from their couch. Yehonatan actually smiled at Galenus, raising his eyebrows, before accompanying the man to the door. Was that a challenge, Marcus wondered, or a complicit look?

"I'd set a spy on you, but I've no doubt he would be detected the moment he started work," said Galenus, smiling slowly back. "Complete waste of time. And to be truthful, at the moment, I'm short of reliable men to use for specialized business of that sort. I'll have to trust you for now, more's the pity." He put his hand on Yehonatan's arm and let it linger there. "Meanwhile, if anything else that I would find useful comes to your attention, here or in Sardis, send me a courier immediately. I'll see you're well rewarded." As Yehonatan moved backward, out of his reach, Galenus stepped forward to open the door. "It's been a pleasure seeing you two again and meeting your nephew. If, Iounathan, Marcus is your nephew. Although I've no idea why you would lie about it, except out of a corrupt natural proclivity. The coloring is different, yes. But, otherwise, the boy looks enough like you to be your own son. Though he feels rather Roman for a son of yours, which surprises me somehow. I never found you so fond of us. Lucky woman, whoever his mother is. Perhaps I'll meet her one day too. I'd enjoy that greatly, I believe."

That threat Marcus comprehended immediately.

Galenus stepped in, raising his index finger to touch Yehonatan's cheek, but then, meeting the expression in Yehonatan's eyes, he thought better of the gesture and let his finger drop. "Why so shy, Iounathan? Oh, of course. You don't want the boy to see." He pursed his lips, aping bafflement. "Or could it be that Tullian is...shall we say ...jealous of his prerogatives? And him, a world class fighter, so it's in your interest to keep him happy." Galenus' lips and cheeks fluted into a provocation. "Well, no matter, as I presume that you're on your way out of town today in any case. And if you're not, I advise you to be." Galenus nodded once to himself, then standing back from the door, he gestured for his guests to move past him, into the antechamber.

Outside the room, near the threshold, the next group of petitioners were waiting to meet with him, a threesome of Roman matrons dressed in red and white and black, clustering at the door. Galenus took one look and retired back into his long, empty hall, muttering to himself in Latin as he passed, "*On the threshold, the awful goddesses of vengeance squat.*

Diverted momentarily from the tension in the room and his own drumming headache, Marcus wondered whether Galenus could produce a fitting epigram on the spot for every set of guests he entertained.

As for Galenus' tales of the past, he wondered how much of it could be true and what stratagem Galenus was pursuing in apprising Marcus of it. A simple tactic like divide and conquer, perhaps? For in Marcus' experience, no one in power freely distributed military information that flattered other people's skills. And certainly no one gave out such intelligence to a youth such as himself without a very good reason for it.

Yehonatan made only one comment as they mounted up to ride out of town in the lingering light of the afternoon. "I assume that that was sufficient warning to keep us alert for Galenus' special friends all afternoon and during the rest of our trip," he said. "My God! Speaking of rank incompetence, how in *She'ol* did I fail to discover in time that that utter bastard was the Administrator of Ashqelon?"

They departed the town silently, riding along the seashore, breathing the humid air laced with salt brine and sun-baked fish. They rode past small fishing boats and men with nets bringing in their catch and passed entire battlefields of fish corpses swept out to sea, their skeletal heads bobbing white as they jostled each other amidst the foamy crests.

After the first mile on the beach, Yehonatan and Tullian stopped their horses, scrupulously observing the clearing behind them. It seemed empty of rocks, trees, and mysterious shadows. Only then did they ride hard, at a gallop, racing the sun that had just started its long afternoon descent, stopping periodically to check the way behind them. Once they rode past a thick stand of evergreen trees, the spicy-sweet resinous tang pungent in the humid air. Yehonatan drew his horse off the road to mount a rear guard, sending the other two ahead of him. Marcus looked over his shoulder as they rode past. He saw Yehonatan, erect and intent, a solitary figure, dwarfed by his setting.

Yet within the hour, after making certain that the road behind them was empty of suspicious traffic, Yehonatan caught up to them. But though they all three kept to a swift pace, they only approached Yavneh, the city that housed the great academy of Jewish learning in Israel, just as sunset was subsiding into twilight.

As they rode up to the gate, Yehonatan slowed his horse to a walk. The horse, a bay, undistinguished in looks and in gait, was breathing hard as was his own. "They won't think much of our piety," said Yehonatan, "descending upon them after the Sabbath has already begun."

"Don't let it worry you overmuch," said Tullian. "We're only minutes late. And today we've an unassailable excuse. Where's your head, Yehonatan? Not stuck in Ashqelon still?"

And that for some undetermined reason merited a reaction glance from Yehonatan that would have quelled anything else he himself had to say.

Luckily it did not succeed in quelling Tullian. "Think," he said. "We were taken away by Roman guards at sword point and held for hours. No one in this academy will find fault with us for that."

"Some will. Of course, they will. Moreover, we traded intelligence for the favor of a prompt release," said Yehonatan. "Let's not forget that."

"But they won't know that. Moreover, it was lukewarm intelligence about Parthians, Yehonatan, not about your own people," said Tullian. "Don't discount the difference."

"The Parthians were our allies."

"Even so," said Tullian. "There's a difference."

"It doesn't excuse it, though. Moreover, this time, that's all he asked for. But the next time he catches up with us, he'll be expecting more valuable intelligence. And that time it'll be about Jews and Judea. He still thinks you're an Arab and I'm a Greek, adopted into your tribe," said Yehonatan, "so he's going to find it very puzzling the next time we fail to play along with his dirty game. And if there's anything that Galenus won't let alone, it's a puzzle he's not yet solved."

PART VII

CHAPTER 9
A Sabbatical

The voice rose high and sweet. Marcus shut his eyes, concentrating on the words as they leapt into the air, expanding in breadth and power until they filled the entire room with their sound. Then the voice fell away and there was silence. Into the sudden hush, there came the whispers of men and the twittering of birds, delicate and mellifluous, calling one to another in harmony. *Holy, holy, holy is the Lord of Hosts.* Only then, the other voices resumed their chanting, earthly, deep and true.

Marcus opened his eyes and looked about as the men around him stirred from their prayers and meditations, eventually sitting down on the hard stone benches. Here and there, the sun, penetrating through the leafy cover outside, filtered into the room in warm golden spots, lighting up bits of the mosaic floor and the walls and the men.

The Sabbath prayer service ended. The lull that had fallen on the congregation began to dispel as men stood and conversed amicably. Then a man stood up from among the congregation and moved to the front of the room. Silence swept the room into renewed stillness, and in its hold, the man began to speak. White-haired and white-bearded, blue-eyed, with white skin translucent and smooth as a baby's, the man radiated perfect calm. His voice was low, monotone, at times indistinct. He used a dialect of Aramaic that Marcus did not understand perfectly. But as the man spoke, Marcus gradually began to feel unburdened, then completely relaxed. He followed every movement the man made, Marcus' eyes moving back and forth as the man turned slightly to address the audience, to the right and to the left, then back again. Eventually the man looked straight at him, directly into his eyes, holding his glance as he spoke. Locked in his gaze, Marcus sat rapt. And soon, he felt himself in a rising tide, borne aloft on the words and the bits of scripture recited. Disengaged from his body, he let go and followed. Until, a calm point amidst the whirlwind, he left all sense of self behind and soared.

There he floated at peace as though in a chamber of white light until the light flowed towards a spectrum of vivid color. Streaming through channels of yellow and orange, one distant part of his mind signaled to hold on. Ignoring that, he moved into a huge marble hall of red, a hall vaster and more magnificent than any he had seen in Caesarea. Unearthly. Gliding through the red palace, undefined, boundless, there were no walls or direction. Until beckoning him onward to the far end of the Hall, he had heard a still, small voice like the singing of doves.

There, at the end of the room, an open gate led to another hall. The light inside was softer, purple melting into a serene blue, infinitely desirable. The singing grew louder, bell-like in its perfect pitch. Marcus moved slowly towards the blue hall, yearning to enter, this time against an unseen counter-force. He reached the gateway and stopped only to listen to the disembodied voices. *Holy, holy, holy is the Lord of Hosts*, he heard, and felt himself pushed away hard by something intangible, out into free fall. Startled, unsteady, Marcus opened his eyes and gazed fully up into the sun for some moments, as its rays angled downward into the gray stone hall, now unblocked by leaf or bough.

Sun dazed, Marcus finally dragged his eyes away and then glanced slowly, carefully about the room, as he came back to himself from far, far away. Everywhere he looked, there were bright pools of light so intense, they hurt his head. He closed his eyes. When he reopened them, moments later, his vision had cleared. He could see things again, the way they truly were. Marcus slowly breathed in and out, in and out, the same technique he used to calm himself down after a bout of fighting when the blood swirling inside possessed him with anger.

The talk had finished. The hall had mostly emptied out. Yehonatan sitting by his side seemed aware of his state and waited for Marcus to speak. Marcus, though, felt unaccountably inarticulate. He managed a long, sideways glance at his uncle.

Yehonatan reached across and drew his hand over the back of his hair until he touched the nape of Marcus' neck. It felt warm and comforting and, despite himself, Marcus was glad that Yehonatan let the hand linger on his skin.

"I felt it too," Yehonatan said at last. "But, perhaps, not as strongly as you did, since it was not my first time, and I already knew what to expect. It didn't take me by surprise."

"You knew what to expect?" said Marcus. There was a certain difficulty in communicating.

"Yes," said Yehonatan. He nodded his head to where the man had stood. "Rabbi Chanon bar Hisda was my teacher when I studied at Sura in Babylonia years ago, before the massacres. He escaped them and resettled in Cana, where I studied with him again between expeditions." The planes of his uncle's face shifted, became impersonal. "He's a well-known rabbi, a learned man and a mystic with an unusual following. He also happens to be one of the reasons I brought you to Yavneh. I wanted him to meet you and vice versa. I had not, however, envisaged this." Yehonatan paused. "As to whether you consider your susceptibility to such an experience is a blessing or a curse, that's for you to decide."

Marcus sat mute.

That elicited a smile, a true one, warm and dazzling, full of understanding and camaraderie, like his mother's. And it affected him the way his mother's smile sometimes did. All at once, Marcus felt open, unbalanced, simultaneously happy and sad. Tears came into his eyes, so he bit down hard on his lip before they could fall. His father would have reamed him, he thought, for showing weakness in public, something he had not done since he was a young child. And on that thought, the tears dried up automatically.

Still observing him, Yehonatan removed his hand from Marcus' neck and stood up. "Sit and relax in peace for a little while longer, Marcus," he said. "I want to go speak to Rabbi Chanon for a few minutes, to set up a time to meet him a few days from now. When I get back, we'll go together to the mid-day meal."

"I couldn't possibly eat right now," said Marcus, feeling dizzy, elated, and somewhat scared.

"Don't be silly. It's the festive meal of the Sabbath day," said Yehonatan. "The point is to enjoy its blessing with other people. Of course, you'll eat."

"Where's Tullian?" said Marcus, looking around him.

"There's no escape that way," said Yehonatan. "He'll be at lunch too. You think he'd miss a chance at holiday fare?"

"Why didn't he come this morning, then?" asked Marcus.

"He's still recovering from his last encounter with Rabbi Chanon." Yehonatan leaned in to whisper, "To tell you the truth, he's terrified of him."

Later that day, electing not to return to the chilly stone hall for afternoon prayers, Marcus spent some time walking around the city of Yavneh with Tullian. A town of mixed population, Greco-Syrian, Roman, Idumaean and Jewish, Yavneh was not as large as either Caesarea or Ashqelon. Yet, like Ashqelon, it was a city of great antiquity. Located inland, it possessed a port city some miles from Yavneh proper.

Since the Great Revolt, Yavneh's importance had increased. At the end of that revolt, the Second Temple – rebuilt magnificently by Herod as his chief work and greatest architectural accomplishment – had been thrown down. To Yavneh the rabbis had come to establish their law court, called the *Sanhedrin*. And there, every day but the Sabbath, the rabbis came to teach the Torah. In its wake, many smaller schools of Jewish learning had formed, like clusters of tiny islands around a mainland.

Tullian and Marcus walked down curving alleyways, high walled on either side and crowned here and there by archways that opened into luxurious marble and limestone squares. An occasional fountain played in their midst, encircled by the foliage of early spring, bright flowers and spring-green leaves. People surrounded them at times, men and women and children promenading in Sabbath clothing, their finest tunics and gowns; others bustled through town in ordinary working garb. At times, an open gate would give a view unto a fine villa and garden.

After they had strolled through several squares in silence, an occasional word murmured here or there, Marcus turned to Tullian. "How come Yehonatan didn't take your hand and lead you to prayers this morning," said Marcus with asperity. "That's what he did to me."

"See, that's your problem. You're his nephew. In his eyes, he has an obligation. Because of your father..." Tullian met his glance. "Well, enough said. You understand me. But in the general way, I leave all this matter of prayers to Yehonatan. Speaking to God on our behalf, that's his concern. I think of him as my personal amulet, warding away evil and attracting good luck. My business in the company always had to do with mundane things. Training the guards to protect our merchandise and so on."

127

"Weapons work, you mean?"

"In the main. And being sure those guards had good intelligence, knew the territory we were traveling through, knew who potential enemies were, knew alternate routes in case of trouble, knew that it was best to stay honest themselves. I'm an earthy type. I think in terms of practical matters."

Marcus digested that for a moment. "He said you didn't come because you're scared of Rabbi Chanon."

"It doesn't surprise me. I let him think that," said Tullian, with a malicious grin. "It's his way of explaining to himself why, even after the subduing of Dura Europos and Sura, I don't take more of an interest in praying to our ethnic god. He can't really grasp my lack of interest, so he puts his brain to work to come up with a rational explanation. And one that doesn't flatter me, I might add. Then, with an explanation in hand, he can let the problem lie. It suits us both, see, to let him think whatever he wants."

When he finished laughing, Marcus considered the essence of what Tullian had said as they continued their walk through the small city. Reaching the wide limestone steps of a public building, he sat and peered up at Tullian, eyes squinting from the sunlight. "Yehonatan knows the Rabbi well then?"

"Ah, yes, I heard about your interesting encounter with Rabbi Chanon bar Hisda earlier." Tullian, leaning against a balustrade, his back towards the sun, examined his sunlit face closely. "I believe they were quite close once. Yehonatan was the Rabbi's prize disciple for a while in Sura, more than ten years ago. But sometime later, the Rabbi acquired a more brilliant disciple. From what I gleaned, Yehonatan didn't like playing a subordinate role." Tullian winked at Marcus. "Not that he explained it quite that way. Soon afterward, he left Sura and began to put his energy into developing his father's business. That's when I met him, down in Cana, trading."

Tullian paused. "Sometime after that, we were up in Parthia, doing tactical surveillance, when Galenus netted us into doing business with him. Galenus didn't know us. He'd heard of us from some of his contacts. Afterwards, a report about us got back to Sura, that Yehonatan had betrayed our allies to do business at a cut rate with the Romans." Tullian ceased speaking for a moment. "In fact, we had done just that. Yet, at the time, we hadn't any choice. Not if we wanted to live. And I was rather stubborn, I'm afraid, about my insistence on avoiding martyrdom." Tullian shook his head. "Yehonatan never forgave Galenus for using us that way, forcing us to do his bidding, even though it cemented our cover for a few years and it gave us a chance to spy inside a Roman camp." Looking at Marcus, Tullian shrugged. He moved to the left, examining the steps fastidiously before sitting down on them, his legs stretched out in front of him.

"Some people considered him a traitor for that. So, we couldn't go back to any of the communities up north, Jewish or Parthian for some time. But then Yehonatan learned the Proconsul, Lusius Quietus, was on a rampage, exceeding his orders from Rome. On the plane between the Euphrates and the Tigris, no community of Jews was safe." Tullian spat on the ground. "Lusius Quietus. Hadrian executed him for that, too. Eventually. And never a man deserved it more, the scum. If only it had been more painful and drawn out. Lasting days with vultures eating his guts and spitting them out. I wish we'd crucified him and his boys. What he did. Full out massacres, town after town, the women raped before and after their throats were slit, the young boys slashed end to end, and also raped, the tiny babies staked on plows and left to rot. Purple bloated bodies, unrecognizable for the most part. Heads without bodies kicked around for sport. Bodies without heads used for target practice. Never walk into a town, Marcus, where everyone's been dead for days. The smell alone is enough to drive you wild for a time. And if you've known all the people there, you go insane with grief. You don't recover from that very soon, I tell you."

Shielding his eyes from the sun with his right hand, Tullian looked at Marcus' face. "Lusius fought that rebellion with some men from your father's Legion too, you realize. He took some soldiers from here, and others he brought with him from Africa, where he had served before."

"I know." Marcus spoke in an undertone. "I heard about it. Thank God it happened years before my father arrived. Thank God. So how did the rabbi manage to survive?"

"Ah, the rabbi. He probably wouldn't have survived at all. Except Yehonatan organized a rescue for him and his students. Being completely immune to Rabbi Chanon's charms myself, I told Yehonatan he was a fool to put his life at risk. Again. And mine of course. And those of our men. But he paid no heed. Typically. In truth, considering the insane things he made us do on that expedition, I don't think he cared much just then whether he lived or died. Or us either." Tullian looked down at the ground. "He was out of his mind, a bit."

"I suppose too, the rescue was his way of doing public atonement for our idiocy, two years before, in letting ourselves get cornered by that rat, Galenus." The wrestler met Marcus' eyes. "So Yehonatan proved his deviousness as a tactician. And that he had the biggest ballocks on the peninsula. And returned, if only momentarily, to Rabbi Chanon's embrace as his well-beloved, first-born son. Now the rabbi thinks of him as a kind of prodigal, returned to his bosom to do God's will. That's a mistake. But then the man's too pigheaded to accept he was entirely wrong about Yehonatan for those few years. He knows it too; just can't admit it to himself straight out much of the time."

"And after that? What happened next?"

"Oh, we took off east for a while. Sailed to India, then came back and rode the trade winds south to Africa. We stayed there for a time. But after a while..." Tullian shrugged. "Well, we didn't belong there.

After some time, we both felt it. Eventually we went back to Felix Arabia. That's it really until we came west."

"That's quite a lot." Still, there was one tiny thing that Marcus wanted to know. "After all that, it doesn't seem possible the Rabbi could do anything that terrified you." he said. "So, what did he do?"

"I'd say, Marcus, the likelihood of your finding out about that from me doesn't exist. Your one hope, as far as I can see, is to broach the subject with the Rabbi himself. Because Yehonatan won't tell a thing."

Marcus cast a sideways glance at Tullian and found him smiling. "Well, that's blocked my advance."

"Securely. Like I wanted it to," said Tullian.

"On the other hand, I could change my ground. If *I* become a disciple of Rabbi Chanon, perhaps I may find out one day."

"Marcus, if you ever become a disciple of Rabbi Chanon bar Hisda, I'd gladly plan a mission to rescue *you* from his clutches. And not to belabor the point, but your father might have a thing or two to say about that."

With a little jolt, Marcus realized that Tullian had stopped joking, and now spoke from his heart.

"It's not that I think he's a charlatan, like a Greek magician, muttering incantations in Hebrew that he doesn't comprehend. No, I've seen his power. It's real enough. At moments." Tullian stopped himself, as though internally he was in some debate. "But the man has a certain whiff of zealotry to him. Best to avoid it."

"Zealotry." Marcus clucked his tongue. "And my uncle doesn't think that's a problem?"

"I never convinced him of it. But then he's got a streak of it himself, like granite seepage in a rock wall, spoiling a pure deposit of lapis lazuli."

"But you're a bit of a pagan, Tullian. That is, from what I've seen, you're even worse than me. You're lax on most of the commandments. Maybe the whole thing is less of a problem than you believe?"

131

"You think so, lad? It's a problem because fifty-five years ago Rome walloped us here. Because of the extremists among us forcing us to rebel. And nothing has been right since the Temple fell. Had we waited only another few years, crazy Nero would have died, and the problems abated. Somewhat. Not altogether. Enough, though. Certainly, in our own country, our position would be stronger than it is now. And all those rebellions since, they wouldn't have happened. Oh, Rome would still rule us, but not with the brazen fist she shows today. That's why, to my mind, zealotry is the most dangerous option before us."

"Worse than Rome smashing our country to potsherds? How? I don't see it?"

"How? Because if we follow its lead, it'll force another war against Rome. At the moment, that's a war I can't see us winning. See, Marcus. Jacob fled Esau and didn't return until he was strong enough to win. Even then, he deferred to his brother to avoid problems he did not need while his family was with him, the women and the young. That's our common patrimony. And like Jacob, I prefer to be wary, wise and alive. And my council to you, Marcus, is to do the same."

PART VIII

CHAPTER 10
Administrative Justice

From Caesarea, the military and administrative headquarters of Rome in *Provincia Judaea,* Julius frequently crossed Palestine and Judea with his troops. Usually, he rode east to Jerusalem and southeast into Arabia Petraea, a wealthy desert province, whose capitol city, Petra, was built into the cliffs of the desert wadis. The magnificent facades of these edifices, banks, temples and municipal buildings, were chiseled into rockface. Clever bastards, the architects they had hired from the Western Isles to do that work for them. But then, a hundred years ago King Aretas IV had had the money to squander, so why not. That was back when the Nabateans controlled the trade in frankincense and myrrh in southern Arabia. Their traders had traveled as far East as India, for pepper, ginger, sugar and cotton.

No longer, though. More than twenty years since, on the death of King Rabel II, Trajan had annexed their kingdom to Rome. Now Rome controlled the spice trade. And they ran it by sea, primarily through Egypt, no longer through the Moabite hills. Little merchandise came through here now, except what those Nabatean scum managed to smuggle in for themselves. Not like you could trust that lot with money so tight. Sometimes they fought you, sometimes they fought against each other for money. You could never be sure ahead of time.

But then that's the way it was everywhere in this corner of the East. The only ones here you could trust were the farflung bits of your own army, though not all of them were competent either. And even that only held true as long as the succession in Rome stayed clear.

The last few weeks, stationed at his Legion's villa a few miles outside Jerusalem at Ramat Rachel, Julius had discussed the state of affairs in the Eastern provinces of Rome with colleagues from all the Legions in the region: a small detachment of the III Cyrenaica had come north from Egypt, several senior centurions from the VI Ferrata had come down from Syria, along with the senior centurions of his own Legion, the Xth Fretensis, whose main force was split permanently between Jerusalem and Caesarea. In times of quiet, these informal sessions were an exceptional way to trade information on consecutive provinces, on upcoming problems, on training techniques. And then they could all relax at night in an expansive way with their peers. Considering how stretched they were out here for intellectual manpower, these rare sessions were fast becoming an addictive pleasure, for the mental stimulation as well as the late-night outings.

While Julius liked traveling, the truth these days was that he preferred home duty. He missed his family when he was away. Well, he missed Marcus. His son's precocity for handling weaponry continued to delight him; a joy like none other he had known in his life. And those moments late at night with Miriam when they weren't shouting or fighting or ignoring each other. Bedtime always solved their problems. At least until, regular as sunrise, they started up again the next day. Not that he deprived himself of much pleasure when he was away. Which was another thing he and Miriam fought about regularly. He had finally committed to not sleeping with other women while stationed in Caesarea. Still, it hadn't been that much to give up. Rarely did those times with tavern whores come anywhere near to matching what it was like with her. Especially *after* one of their memorable fights. And this way, the normal course of both their lives ran more smoothly, which was worth a lot. It made his homecomings sweet too; something to savor well in advance. Especially, and here he smiled to himself, if she were just a tiny bit angry about the women he had enjoyed while he was away.

Their detachment rode straight towards camp. Julius dismounted and handed the reins to one of the stable boys who ran up to him, snapping a salute, right hand to chest. "Silius, come," he called to his chief aide. Walking rapidly, he entered the long, unadorned military hall that contained his office. Julius had already decided, at least for today, to forego the mountain of official paperwork that must have built up in his absence. Instead, he would ask Vincius, whom he had left in charge, to accompany him on a review of the camp while reporting in detail on the state of affairs during the ten days past. The first moment he had free, he already planned to walk to the *gymnasium* and discuss his son's progress with Rufinus.

Tomorrow was soon enough to start on the reports.

When Julius and Silius entered Julius' office, Vincius was sitting at the large wooden desk, hard at work. He looked up from the papers he was reading and stood up smartly. "Sir," he said, and his glance shot past Julius and focused momentarily on Silius, standing slightly behind. "I hope your trip proved enjoyable."

"Enjoyable enough, Vincius," said Julius. "And here in camp? Any problems of note?"

"Everything in camp is in order, sir."

Again, Vincius glanced at Silius. Julius looked back and forth between the two men but could read nothing in Vincius' expressions. Clearly Vincius was hiding something. He would have to take extra care in sniffing it out.

135

Returning later that afternoon from his tour of the camp, Julius felt perplexed. His review had been thorough, brutal even. But he had been unable to detect the merest whiff of anything out of place. Nothing, as far as he could tell, had been hidden from his observation or covered up. In fact, Vincius' command skills continued to impress him. The men liked and respected him as a junior officer, responding well to his orders. Still, Julius sensed that there was something that Vincius was keeping from him. And in such matters, his instincts had proven infallible in the past. So, it was only a matter of time before Julius rooted out whatever violation had occurred. "Vincius," he snapped.

"Sir," Vincius barked out like an overeager puppy fearful he'd done something amiss. Silius too, finally appeared to have noticed something astray himself, the way he was eyeing Vincius.

"Accompany me back to my office. Time for a full review of the reports that have come in and gone out while I was away."

And here it was at last. Vincius looked resigned, as though he knew he could not escape the net that Julius was about to throw around him.

"Yes, sir," said Vincius, and fell in line behind him and Silius.

And now the hand of Zeus will descend in punishment, thought Vincius, marching behind Silius. He felt oddly detached from all this, as though it were happening to someone else. Vincius had tried to capture Silius' attention during the review of the camp. But Silius had chosen absolutely the worst moment to notice that something was amiss. And he had done so without schooling his expression, in full view of Julius.

Julius was a prick, that's what it came down to. They all knew it too. He was a supremely efficient officer, but efficiency could be

136

managed in more humane ways, in his opinion. Still, right now, with the sweat seeping out on his neck and torso like it was the height of summer and not a chilly day, Vincius promised himself never under any circumstances to do another favor for Miriam that undermined Julius' authority, directly or indirectly.

But, at least, she won't have to face this, he thought, resigned. At least Julius' temper will have died down – to some extent – by the time he goes home. She won't have the full-frontal assault directed her way. He had done his part to help her. He knew she had used him for exactly this, but he was not sorry for it. He thought she deserved protection from Julius. Hell, he protected his own men from Julius, when they deserved it. So, plunging in headlong, Vincius said, "There is one other thing, sir, that I should alert you to. Though properly speaking, it has nothing to do with me."

Julius stopped in his tracks and turned fully around to look at him. "Yes?" he said

"About Marcus..." said Vincius, taking a very deep breath. "There's been a change in plan."

<hr />

Julius sat watching Vincius through narrowed eyes as the man stood at attention across the width of Julius' desk. He had already kept Vincius alert and responding to his questions for most of an hour according to the small water clock he kept constantly running in his office to measure the daily and nightly watches. Julius could feel the heightened color in his own face and the heat in his blood as it whirled through his body. There was an echo in his ear. Calm, calm, Julius thought, calm. The boy has only been away from his routine for a few days. Nothing significant will have changed before he returns. Nothing will break the bond between us in such a short time.

"As I already said, sir, I felt that since events arose beyond the narrow set of contingencies we planned for, my limited authority over your son had been exceeded. And that, in such a situation, it seemed permissible to allow the boy to travel with his uncle, whose familial bond surely..." Vincius' voice trailed off.

"Well, then, let's go over it again." They had been stuck on the same point for some time now. Over and over, Vincius' answers were failing to satisfy him. "I transferred authority to you at my departure in order to deal with unplanned-for contingencies. Frankly, Vincius, I don't see how you failed to make the leap from the set of events I discussed with you in detail to the event that actually occurred. Rapid adjustments to new circumstances, that's the essence of the military art. I've seen you apply that very skill on the field time and again. It never seemed a difficult skill for you to master. In fact, you generally excel at it. That's the reason I left you in charge." Julius voice was rising again. He paused to breathe, forcing himself to slow down. "I'm left wondering," he said, articulating every word carefully, "did you purposely choose to disobey my orders? In that case, I may be looking at a case of military insubordination." Julius sat perfectly still, watching Vincius' reaction.

Vincius threw his head up and looked Julius in the eye. "No, sir," he snapped. His body, Julius observed dispassionately, was now completely rigid. Only a little more time now, Julius thought, before he'll break and confess how Miriam persuaded him to allow Marcus to go.

"If I may interrupt," said Silius where he stood against the wall This was the first time his aide had spoken during this interview.

"Yes, what is it?" said Julius, discommoded by the timing of the interruption.

"Perhaps, sir, this line of questioning is becoming unproductive."

"Really?" snapped Julius, both angered and distracted.

"This was a private matter, not a military one. It's not military insubordination. Your family is not the field," said Silius.

"You make your point. Score one for Silius," said Julius still looking away from him. He gestured curtly for Vincius to sit.

Vincius continued standing, but relaxed his posture slightly.

"And do you have any further opinions as to how I might conduct my private life?" Julius said to Silius, staring at Vincius.

"Only that you might take Vincius at his word." Silius' voice was neutral and calm. He said, "He did not feel he had a valid basis to override Miriam's wishes. His honest opinion was that his authority had been superseded."

Aggravated, Julius thought, Silius has just quietly, rationally, pointed out to me that I don't have the right to confuse the boundaries separating my military responsibilities with the domestic sphere. I can run my home life by military fiat if I so choose. But I can't make my officers responsible for failing to impose military rule at home in my absence. Even when I believe the conditions warrant it. And inside Julius another voice countered, *yet, once I relax the rules at home, what then? I'd never be able to control the outcome. Everything would be completely subject to the rules of chance. And that could be a disaster for both of us.*

What torture human relations are, he thought. We carry around with us the conditions for pain whenever we love and allow ourselves to have expectations of other people. The trick, as he knew so well, was never to love, never to yield oneself to the emotions. He believed in the truth of this philosophy deeply, implicitly. Yet, so far, he had failed to apply it to his own life, except in flashes here or there, soon vanquished. And he found that to be tragic, his failure to will himself the conditions for a tranquil flow of life. *Whoever wishes to be free, let him wish for nothing which depends on others*, he thought. But never yet had he succeeded in working himself free. "Tell me, Silius," said Julius at last. "How did we end up with Vincius in charge?"

"Vincius, sir? You appointed him."

"My error, you mean." Julius finally turned his head to look at Silius, still lurking in an unlit corner of the room. And that annoyed him too. Even Silius feared him sometimes, feared his anger. And Silius had known him since he was a youth, had known his father, had helped to train him. Was this fact sad or useful? Julius could not decide. It felt sad, yet it was something that could be exploited at times, and that was useful. "But I promoted Vincius on your recommendation," said Julius finally, his voice calm, his complexion no longer red. "I remember distinctly you told me he was ready for command. Well, you've lost your wager, Silius. You were wrong."

"Yes," said Silius, mildly. "I was wrong."

———◇———

"Fool," Silius said to Vincius after they walked together a good distance from Julius' office. "First of all, you owe me 30 *denarii*. Secondly, I hope you think it was worth it." Silius looked him over, shaking his head. "I'll say this for you, though. You're not prone to *small* errors of judgment."

Vincius grunted his assent. There could be no argument with that. Plus, from now on in, he was going to owe Silius plenty for rescuing him from Julius' wrath and salvaging his career, even if the old man had stepped in to save him extremely late in the day.

"You know he's obsessed with controlling the boy." Silius was still shaking his head. "Why flout his commands on that one thing?"

"I liked the uncle," said Vincius, "I thought Marcus deserved the chance to know him. He's going to inherit that business one day. It seemed a reasonable request." Vincius shrugged, and then a sheepish grin lit up his face. "To tell the truth, when Julius and Yehonatan finally come face to face, I want to see the explosion. Personally, I'm betting on Yehonatan to wipe the floor with Julius. But with such subtlety, he won't even notice until Yehonatan is long gone."

140

"I hope you enjoy your moment," Silius, looked bemused; half angry, half exasperated. "I only hope it proves worth more than a month of your wages, you fool, and weeks and weeks of Julius' displeasure whenever he looks your way."

CHAPTER 11

The Uncircumcised Heart

The tiny house where Marcus was staying contained a gaggle of small children. Well, only three, but two of them were years younger than he was. He was not used to sleeping with other children, especially not four to a room, with a small girl amongst the company. Although she did have a thin curtain around her bed for privacy. But the parents, Tzipporah and Itamar had only a tiny chamber to themselves. There was nowhere else to sleep. Yehonatan and Tullian were staying in a different house nearby. His separate accommodation had been arranged by their hosts because they thought he would enjoy himself more staying with children.

The oldest son, Naphtali, was about his own age, only a year older. He was intelligent and rambunctious and far more rigorously trained in Jewish law. Considering that Naphtali lived at Yavneh, this was hardly surprising. Marcus lived in Caesarea, home to many a Greek school, so he knew far more rhetoric and allegory and mathematics. Not to mention every one of the martial arts. Although none of these seemed particularly prized here, so he kept them to himself. More or less.

Binah, the young girl, almost ten, sylvan delicate, had big brown eyes, and long brown hair. The first day he was around, she lurked in corners and archways staring at him silently. But she was not shy or fragile, not normally at least. Marcus could see that. When attacked verbally by her older brother, her return wit was as deft and cutting as a gladiator's blade. For that, he quickly grew to admire her. And once, when she and her brother tussled physically, and it went on too long, Marcus pulled Naphtali off of her and pinned him down on the floor, effectively ending their fight. Later that day, when Naphtali was at work at the glass factory with his father, he and Binah, giggling together, conspired to sneak off to a rare empty lot where he showed her what to do if her older brother hit her again. He even let her hurt him, the way she would have to in order to stop Naphtali, and more than once. He did not mind though; with all the falling down and rolling around on the ground together, he was having too much fun to care. And after that, the two of them had an understanding. Secret allies. They even agreed on the military hand signals he showed her in case of need.

In just a few short days, the ambience of familial warmth was spilling over onto him. And, like a sea sponge, he absorbed it all. It was altogether different from what existed in his own home, sunny, spacious, lovely, ordered, and, with its double handful of servants, far, far cleaner. Yet while he appreciated all that, particularly the cleanliness, by contrast, he realized viscerally there was much less tension here and far more warmth and affection. There was so much love here, it radiated back at him from the walls. Marcus liked having children around him with whom to play, he was discovering, even Gad, just five years old, who jumped on him from time to time and laughed and liked being tickled into submission. There was very seldom laughter in his own house, he realized.

143

Because of the gaps in the ages of the children, Marcus was curious whether others had been born who had died as babies. Or, if like his mother, Tzipporah used herbs to stop herself from becoming pregnant. But these kinds of things were impossible to ask. The father, Itamar, had already fulfilled the *mitzvah* to be fruitful and multiply, with a child of either sex.

Two mornings later, the day he was to meet with Rabbi Chanon, Marcus was changing into a clean light blue tunic. He slid his arms into the sleeves, pulled it over his head and opened his eyes to find Naphtali staring at him.

"I thought you were Jewish. You're not Jewish?"

"What?" The tunic was halfway on now, over his head, but not pulled down. "Of course, I am."

"Then how come you're not circumcised?" Naphtali leaned over slightly and stared at his genitals. "You're definitely not circumcised. Until now, I've never seen someone—" Naphtali looked back up at him, suspicion and doubt creeping into his eyes.

To that, he did not have an answer he cared to share. He shrugged, turning his torso away from Naphtali and pulled down his tunic the rest of the way.

"Come on. Tell me. Is there a reason? You weren't kidnapped when you were a baby, were you? Then you would have the legal status of a pirated child. But that can't be. Because you're living with your family now. And you didn't grow up in ignorance, so that doesn't explain it."

Behind Naphtali, Marcus saw Binah sneak from the doorway into the room to stand against the wall, wide-eyed and silent, the way she had acted the first day he met her. Completely mortified now, Marcus could feel the blood mottling his cheeks. He had no memory of being made to feel so unpleasantly conscious of his nakedness. His experiences so far had tended the other way.

Naphtali stood before Marcus, his brown hair falling straight and wispy, his thin, young face serious and perplexed, relentlessly ticking

144

off items from a tally in his brain. "You told me yourself rabbis tutored you while you were growing up. So how come your parents didn't circumcise you?" When Marcus failed to respond to that question, Naphtali lowered his voice, practically whispering to him, "Was there a ban on it where you grew up, and no one to perform it for you?"

And that was true in its way, but not at all as Naphtali meant it. He nodded, standing there like an idiot, with no idea how to slip out from this barrage. Not by telling the truth. The truth was too humiliating. And then he saw Binah signaling him behind Naphtali's back.

"Naphtali," she said loudly, "you didn't hear *abba* calling you to go to work? You need to leave. Or you'll be late. And he'll scold you. Again."

"What? I'm late already? You're sure?" When Binah nodded at her brother, Naphtali gave him one last assessing look. He opened his mouth to say something else.

"Naphtali, run!" Binah said. And Naphtali scrambled out of the room, like an awkward hind chasing its mother.

Then it was only he and Binah in the room. She was staring at him solemnly, with those huge eyes that dominated her thin face, the straight fall of her body still pushed against the wall.

His face was still pulsing bright red. "Thank you," he managed at last.

She dipped her head in his direction, so she was not staring at him any longer. "Naphtali loves the law. But you know how boys are," she said, her voice precociously knowing. A tiny smile with her rosebud mouth helped defuse the tension in the room. "*Ema* says he doesn't always stop to think." And then she turned and exited the room, leaving him alone.

Marcus sat back down on the pallet, feeling shamed. After that, it took a while to force himself to leave the room. But when he did, outside in the common room, he saw Binah again. She was in the kitchen area helping her mother prepare the midday meal. "See you soon," she said and waved at him, smiling and natural.

Even his father would be charmed by Binah, he thought, returning her smile. Could circumcision be worth it after all? Then, startled, he stopped his forward motion wondering where that thought had come from.

After that, Marcus walked the short distance between Binah's cramped house to the one where Yehonatan and Tullian slept. This house, narrow and unadorned, with a façade of rough-hewn white limestone, was occupied by an older couple, Demetrius Ezekiel and Justina, his wife. Demetrius, once a wealthy Alexandrian trader, had sailed east and south from Felix Arabia with Yehonatan and Tullian. And from that common journey into the unknown, a strong friendship had blossomed. Then, after the turmoil between the Greeks and the Jews in Alexandria, displaced and impoverished, he moved his family from Egypt to retire to Israel, the land of milk and honey. Neither he nor his son Justus, who had returned to Arabia to continue his father's business, had yet recouped their former wealth.

The door stood ajar; inside he heard voices. Marcus knocked lightly, but when there was no answer, he entered the house. Further in, he realized the voices were arguing. Someone he did not recognize said, "We need to start stockpiling our own weaponry. This tribute of the Romans, let's make use of it for our own ends. If we send them damaged armaments, the Romans will reject them and send them back. And then we can easily repair what they don't want."

"I see. So it will cost us less. And we can do it under their noses."

"Exactly. And when Hadrian fails to keep his promise to rebuild the Temple, as we suspect he will, we'll have enough weapons to fight them and take Jerusalem back."

"Enough for an army?" said someone else. "Hardly."

"In time. For a large army, a successful one, with weapons spread around the country; in truth, it will take years." That voice was

146

Yehonatan's. "This is a start only. It'll need to be supplemented by our own private efforts."

The first voice spoke again. "True. Yet we have to begin somewhere. The advantage of this plan is that it makes use of what the Romans are already imposing."

Suddenly cognizant of what Yehonatan had rebuked him with the morning they left Caesarea, Marcus went back to the front door, stepped quietly outside, knocked again and scuffed the door open loudly. So much for his spying career, aborted before it matured.

"Shhh...," another voice muttered. And only after complete silence fell did the curtain separating the bedchamber from the main room draw back and Demetrius Ezekiel stood looking at Marcus. Face white and serious he ushered him into the chamber where the men were speaking. "My wife," he said to the men in the room, "must have gone next door. I didn't realize."

The sleeping pallets had been pulled back to the wall, Marcus noted, to make room for five men, perched on small folding stools studying him, some of them nervous. And then, light on his feet, Yehonatan was standing. "Ah, Marcus," he said. "I was expecting you at any moment." To the others, he said, "Masters, you'll excuse us. My nephew and I are to appear before Rabbi Chanon bar Hisda this morning." Then Yehonatan took him firmly by the shoulder and led him from the room. In the outside chamber, he picked up the last small casket that remained after Ashqelon, the only one unsold.

They walked several blocks to the house of study and entered. All around the room, men sat in pairs or triads at rickety tables discussing law. In another corner of the room, there were wooden benches, where a different rabbi was giving a talk to several others. So many streams of conversation were going on, that save where one voice sounded high above the others, individual voices cancelled each other, creating a general hubbub of noise. There was only one small brazier lit for the entire room, so the outside chill seeped everywhere.

The room smelt of parchment and ink and smoke and some earthy scent Marcus did not recognize.

At the front of the room, near a window with southern exposure and bright light, Rabbi Chanon was seated alone, reciting a passage to himself from sheets of papyrus laid on the table before him. Only when the rabbi took note of them and nodded, did they proceed in that direction.

Standing before the rabbi, he bowed his head slightly, Roman fashion, as Yehonatan presented him formally. The rabbi moved his hand, momentarily, towards the bare nape of Marcus' neck. As it connected to his skin, the touch jolted Marcus slightly. Neck still bent, he raised his eyes, enough to see.

"Ah, yes," said Rabbi Chanon, leaving one hand on the crux of Marcus' neck while its twin sat delicately in his lap. "A mystical soul." He raised his eyes to the man standing behind Marcus. "I see. It runs true in your family, Yehonatan." And now those eyes were directed right at Marcus. Eyes unlike any he had ever seen, with a depth of fire within that drew him in. "But, my son, you need to study more. You think you have the soul of a soldier. But that's not entirely so. Be careful, lest you find your true self neither in one place nor the other. A soldier kills. And what for? It's a striving after wind, after nothingness, against God's law, except in necessity." He stopped for a moment, removing his hand from Marcus' neck and placing it gently on his lap beside the other. Then he raised his eyes again to Yehonatan. "Your uncle strove after wind for a while. Look at the good it did him, exiled from his people for a few years. His eye was not satiated with seeing, nor his pockets with money. Better for him had he stayed with us in Sura and not left to amuse himself." The rabbi's eyes were closed and he spoke slowly, summoning the words from an inner light. "To read God's words, learn his law, this you must do, at least for some time. And then we'll see. You're hiding your true light, Marcus, behind your father's need of you. He's the true soldier, not you."

Turning to Yehonatan, Rabbi Chanon opened his eyes and said, "He's got a mystical side, Yehonatan, like you. Stronger than yours, perhaps. It needs nurturing. Well, I've seen enough, now." The rabbi rose slowly from his straight-backed wooden chair. "Come here, child, let me bless you." He waved his hands about mumbling a prayer in a dialect of Aramaic. And then he finished. "Come back to me, young man, some years from now, when you have changed your current path. Seek God's light. Remember my words."

Then with a flourish of a hand and another inward glance from those eyes he was dismissed and Yehonatan stepped forward.

The rabbi spoke again, "Ah, Yehonatan, you brought me the frankincense I asked for? This is it, here in the casket? Good, good. If Hadrian's promises to rebuild the Temple can be trusted, we'll have to start stockpiling it again for use – a large supply. We'll need you again, perhaps, back in Felix Arabia, supplying it for us. But with this, God willing, when the Temple is rebuilt, we'll have enough on hand for a little while, at least."

"Rabbi," Yehonatan said, "the boy..."

"Don't worry about what the boy hears. I've felt his heart already," the rabbi said. "And though it's still uncircumcised, underneath its hard shell, it's untouched and pure. Have no worry that he will betray his people." The rabbi looked at Yehonatan askance. "You're still not married, are you? No, no. You needn't answer. I already know." He shook his head. "I've told you before. A man should be married at your age, Yehonatan."

"Yes you have," Yehonatan said.

"I'm considering what's happening to your soul because you choose to ignore this. You still mourn–"

"–Yes," Yehonatan said, before the Rabbi finished.

"What sorrow that was for you. Her love for you ignited so many of your deepest gifts. But you must accept at long last she was not the future the Holy One, Blessed Be He, planned for you. It's many years already that you mourn her. The Holy One now wants your heart to be whole. Moreover, you still have a commandment to fulfill, to be fruitful and multiply. Know there is someone else who will be your future." When Yehonatan did not reply, the rabbi said, "Come, I'll write a letter to the rabbi in Sardis. I'll have him look out for you. You'll find a fitting wife there if God so wills."

"If God so wills."

"I'd prefer if you stayed here a little while, studying Torah with me. And I would look out for your wife, myself."

"I can't stay," said Yehonatan, tilting his head to one side. "My aging father needs me."

The rabbi threw up his hands. "You won't fool God with that," the rabbi said, "and you don't fool me. The two of you with your fathers. They're your excuse, not your purpose. Your fate is here, Yehonatan, in Israel, with your people. But you'll return. About that, at least, I'm certain. You won't be able to stay away. Come here, my son, step closer to me," he said, as his blue eyes warmed considerably. "Let me bless you."

When Yehonatan stepped nearer, the rabbi closed his eyes and made the blessing. He spoke softly and for a long time, drawing fire from heaven, his quiet words fluent to the tongue. When he finished, he lowered his hands and opened his eyes. "We'll see each other again, thank the Lord and all of His Heavenly angels. I asked for that. And received word it was granted. Go now in peace, with the Holy One's blessing upon you."

Uncle and nephew walked away from the study hall in silence, side by side, neither speaking. Only when they had reached a good distance away, Marcus stopped walking and grabbed Yehonatan's arm. "Did you tell him to say that about me?"

"Hardly. As though he would say what I told him to in any case. You did hear what he said about *me* in front of you, didn't you?"

Marcus looked up at Yehonatan, quizzically. "I expect you'll marry one of these days. Most people do. But what does he mean I'm not meant to be a soldier? Of course, I am. I've trained to be a soldier from birth. Everyone – Rufinus, my father, all my weapons teachers – they all say I excel at fighting, at strategy, at engineering. A natural soldier. With a worried sideways glance, he added, "You don't believe him, do you?"

Yehonatan's green eyes had become impossible to penetrate, smooth, like the surface of a jade ring. "What I think or believe is not important, Marcus. In the end, the matter is in God's hands and your own. Though I wish I were staying nearby to be more of a guide along the way."

"Can't you?"

"My father and Sardis call me home."

"The rabbi said that was just your excuse. But it won't affect me in any case. I'm going to be a soldier."

"If you say so." said Yehonatan and then he added wryly. "So now you know how Tullian feels. He didn't like what Rabbi Chanon prognosticated for him either." Then, responding to Marcus' sharpened look, he added, a small elusive smile playing on his lips, "Ah, but you won't get it out of me that way. I've been informed that telling's worth my life."

Late that afternoon, Yehonatan and Marcus were soaking their bruises in a private chamber in a bathhouse. "There's something I have to discuss with you. It's rather important, Marcus." Marcus glanced over at his uncle. This afternoon, Tullian had finally made good on his promise to train Marcus in wrestling technique. Yehonatan had joined in at times to help Tullian demonstrate complicated holds and throws. The role reversal had interested Marcus, for this time Tullian had commanded and Yehonatan had followed his lead. Tullian was

151

outside, exercising still. Or maybe his uncle had told him to stay away for a while yet. Tomorrow, early on, they would set out together for the return trip home to Caesarea.

"I owe you an apology," said Yehonatan.

That was surprising, Marcus thought. He raised his eyebrows and waited.

Yehonatan said, "Galenus."

"We've come out from that unhurt, as far as I saw. He kept his word and sent no spies."

"I'm glad you paid attention. Keep in mind, though," said Yehonatan, "that it might not always be so easy to tell. But I think you're right. Yavneh's safe enough. In the short term, we emerged unscathed. Nonetheless, there might be a problem in the future. You heard what he said before he let us go, didn't you?"

"You mean about my mother? And you're worried about her?" said Marcus.

"I'm worried about you as well."

"But you're more worried about her?"

"Not as you imply," said Yehonatan. "In truth, in this situation I'm more worried about her because if trouble comes to you by way of Galenus, your father will do more to protect you than to protect your mother."

"What kind of trouble?" Marcus said.

"If Galenus ever discovers that you and your mother are Jews, he might put a very different interpretation on my activities in his camps several years ago, one that was not at all beneficial to Rome and her interests. He won't like that; he'll feel I took advantage of him. I did, as a matter of fact. He won't be wrong about that. But, if I'm not available, he'll want to take revenge on someone close to me in return. And if you and Miriam are in his purview, believe me, the hammer blow will descend at lightning speed. Julius will shield you from it, if he can. But shielding your mother is another story. He

152

might and he might not. Who can say right now with any certainty? It will depend, I imagine, on the state of their ... *marriage.*"

Marcus did not want to think about that. "What activities were you involved with in Galenus' camp?" he said, homing in on the other essential art of Yehonatan's speech.

A surreptitious smile lit up his uncle's face. "Marcus, Marcus," he said, "I understood you heard all about that yesterday, from Tullian. What more could you want to know?"

"Everything. Surely, he barely touched the surface?" said Marcus. And then he registered Yehonatan's tone. "Oh, you're being disingenuous again."

"You mean, I'm lying? No, no," said Yehonatan, "just teasing you a bit." His grin dissipated slowly like the fading of bright starlight behind a moving front of clouds. "The fact is Galenus' future reprisals do worry me. Short of dragging you both home with me to Sardis, which I've seriously considered, all I can do is prepare you for the possibilities facing you. And so, I have a favor to ask of you."

"To ask *me*?" said Marcus.

"Yes, you. I'm asking you to keep certain information you've learned on this trip from your father. If he ever found out about some of my activities in Arabia, that also could bring trouble. I never meant for you to learn of them, at least at this stage of your life. And if not for Galenus, you wouldn't have. That's my fault and my responsibility. As it turned out, I've been ill prepared for several of the things that occurred on this trip. But it's you who must bear the burden of silence. At your age, that's a hard task. And perhaps an unwanted one. I apologize to you. What I'm asking of you is unfair, but there's no way around it, and it might shield your mother." Yehonatan studied his face.

"I agree," said Marcus.

"So easily?" said Yehonatan.

"You heard the rabbi." Marcus grinned. "I have a pure heart."

"Underneath the uncircumcised shell. I see in some things he made a rapid convert of you. But in that case," said Yehonatan, scrutinizing him, "there's one other thing."

"Yes?" said Marcus.

"If you've started putting together any information from the bits of conversation you overheard today, mention it to no one."

"Another of the things for which you were unprepared?" said Marcus.

"Completely unprepared," said Yehonatan, smiling ruefully. "I wasn't expecting any adventures at all on this trip, just some simple trading. And that information, Marcus, might prove even more incendiary than the extremely censored account you had about my spying activities. So, please, for everyone's good, say nothing."

Marcus lay in the bath, side by side with Yehonatan, enjoying the silence. He put his mind to piecing together bits of conversation he had been privy to earlier in the day. He suspected he knew what Yehonatan had just referred to, but he had no certainty. And Yehonatan was not going to confirm his guesswork, he had made that clear. After a while, Marcus' mind began to drift and to pursue other avenues, until finally he became riveted on one point. And there his mind stayed fixed for some time.

Finally, he got out of the bath, and sat on its edge, with his legs dangling in the water. "Uncle." His voice sounded very small in his ears.

"Yes," said Yehonatan, turning to look at him. "Is something wrong?"

"You know I'm not circumcised?"

Yehonatan gestured at Marcus' naked body. "The evidence does present itself to the eyes."

"Naphtali asked me about it. I didn't know what to say to him."

"You didn't feel you could tell him the truth?"

"No," said Marcus. "I didn't want to say who my father is. Or explain why, lest he think ill of me." He drew his legs up to his chest and curled his arms tightly around them. He took a deep breath. His

154

eyes remained fixed downward on his linked hands. "Uncle," he said again, his voice even smaller.

"Mmm," said Yehonatan.

"I've never seen what a circumcision really looks like. Up close, I mean." He had Yehonatan's full attention now. He could feel it focused on him, even though Marcus did not dare look straight back at him. Marcus' voice sounded so thin to his own ears that it was barely a thread. "Would it be possible ... that is, would you mind if I ..." Marcus cleared his throat and started again. "Do you think ... um ...could I look at it ... I mean ... yours?" His voice had sunk to a whisper, and he could feel the blood pulsing in his face, burning his ears.

Silence fell in the small chamber. The room felt warm, too warm suddenly, and moist, humid, scented with thick lavender and mint. Marcus could feel the sweat rolling in little drops down his torso. He wanted to sink back into the water again, to cover his body and his face underwater. After a while, he glanced to his left. Yehonatan had risen from the bath and was looking directly at him.

"The things I do for love," said Yehonatan, and gestured downward, encompassing his lower body. "Come, look, if you like."

Marcus edged over slowly and bent his head slightly toward Yehonatan's genitals.

"I pray to God," said Yehonatan leaning away, "that no one walks in on us inopportunely, while your *examination* is ongoing." Pursing his lips, he managed to look amused. "The appearances are rather against us, wouldn't you say? And all I need, with the rumors still circulating about me having been a traitor, is to have someone contend I have been committing what the scripture refers to as abominations with my own blood nephew. I recovered from being named a traitor, but I doubt they would let me live down incest and abominations as well."

"My father wouldn't like it either. But then, you could always arrange to rescue someone else," Marcus said. Yehonatan's banter, meant to relax his embarrassment, was starting to work.

155

"Even I don't think I could pull off another rescue like that. And Tullian absolutely would refuse to help this time. I nearly got him slaughtered last time. He's still got the scars. Afterward, I had to spend months working into his good graces again. I'm too lazy to do all that twice."

Marcus, fixated, was staring at Yehonatan's genitals. Then his eyes moved back across to compare it to his own, and back to Yehonatan's again."

"Did it hurt?" he whispered at last, before moving across the bath to sit on the ledge on the other side.

"As I was only eight days old when it occurred, I can't say I have any memory of it at all. But babies don't seem to cry for a very long period, afterward. Though, that's not conclusive evidence. Perhaps they are simply too much in shock at the cruelty fate had in store for them."

"Would it hurt me if I did it now, almost full grown?"

Yehonatan's voice responding was now completely serious. "Adult witnesses all attest the pain is excruciating for the first little while. But there's wine and opium and we could import some Syrian dancing girls to distract you while you lay convalescing."

"But I'd hardly be in a position to enjoy them fully, wouldn't you say?"

Yehonatan looked at him and laughed. "Yes, in that respect, they might be rather a waste. At your age, though, I'm sure your mother would count that as a blessing."

Marcus drew his knees to his chest, crossing his arms on top of them. He buried his head in his arms, closing his eyes, thinking. Warm water rushed in from the pipes, thrumming, creating eddies in the *tepidarium* at his feet. The water traveled to the far end of the pool before trickling down to a lower level where it cooled off.

"I'm not afraid of the pain," said Marcus at last, raising his head. He looked into Yehonatan's eyes knowing he was unable to mask the conflict he was undergoing, that his face openly mirrored it. Yehonatan looked back at him, and Marcus felt at that moment he could tell his uncle anything. He lowered his eyes. "I can't do it to my father," he said. "It would shame him too greatly. Everyone, his entire Legion would find out almost as soon as it happened. I couldn't fight with them or train or bathe without them being reminded daily, or my father either. They all sense what's at stake between my parents."

"Marcus, look at me," said Yehonatan. "You love your father, and it's God's will that you honor him. Then do so. But soon you'll be thirteen, a man grown according to Jewish law. You'll have to make your own decisions in freedom. The only thrall you owe is to God. As a man, you're responsible for yourself under God's law. Honor your father. I think your desire to do so speaks very well of you. Just remember to honor your mother equally."

As though he could ever forget that, thought Marcus. They were three sides of a triangle, his parents and he; and he was the fulcrum point that kept them all aloft.

That night Marcus dreamt of the vast purple-blue hall. A sphinx stood inside the gateway, wings furled, beckoning him onward. But when he approached, the sphinx rose up and carried him through the air, held fast in his front claws. He dropped him and Marcus floated on a current of ether into the amphitheater in Caesarea.

Suddenly, the sphinx transformed itself into a lion. Then the lion drew himself up, roaring, and began to attack. As the crowd around them cheered madly for his blood, for death, Marcus, barehanded and stark naked, fought back viciously. He jumped on the lion's back and rode the beast around the amphitheater. Grabbing it from behind, a chokehold around its neck, he anchored one arm and tightened the hold with his other. Then, as suddenly, the lion changed back into a sphinx and began to taunt him with an insoluble riddle, "What are you, Marcus? Lion or eagle?"

He froze. He could not move a muscle until he solved the riddle. Marcus looked into the sphinx's black on black eyes, as flat and unyielding as wrought iron, and knew the sphinx would eat him. Even so, he could not move. Instead, the sphinx began mumbling indecipherable incantations in Hebrew and flew away.

And then the amphitheater disappeared and he was all alone in a cold dark place.

Marcus jolted out from the dream chilled to the bone and scared stiff. It took a moment to realize he could move again. Then he began to shiver, like he had fever. He tried to lie still as he could on the pallet, breathing in and out, forcing a state of calm over his body, just as in the fighting exercises Rufinus had taught him long ago.

What was he? Who was he?

He had no idea.

PART IX

CHAPTER 12
Family Reunion

The knock sounded on Julius' office door at mid-afternoon.

Vincius raised his head and glanced at Julius, glad of the excuse for a break, however short-lived it would prove under the draconian conditions that his life had been subject to in the last three days.

"Come," said Julius, without looking up from the sheaf of parchment on his desk. Julius handed Vincius the report he had just finished checking without so much as a glance at him.

The door opened and a sentinel walked forward. Arianus, Vincius thought. What's he doing here? He's supposed to be standing guard at the southern road to Caesarea.

"Sir," said Arianus.

"What is it?" said Julius, his eyes on his papers still.

Arianus gazed briefly at Vincius, shooting him a brief commiserating look, before turning his eyes straight ahead, to Julius. He said, "You asked to be informed as soon as Marcus returned."

It was his own good fortune, Vincius thought rubbing his hands together under the desk, his face expressionless, that Julius had assigned him to work in his office today, under Julius' nose. It meant he could observe Julius' reaction to that news first-hand, to gauge what was coming.

Julius raised his head a few seconds after Arianus finished speaking. "Ah," he said. Sitting back in his chair, Julius placed his hands on the desk, before him. His right hand was smudged with ink. "He's back!" Julius nodded once. Leaning forward again, he set his elbows on the desk and squeezed his hands together, hard. "Where is he now?"

"We weren't sure where you wanted him. I was going to bring him along with me, but the man with him said surely I wasn't going to treat Marcus like he was under arrest," said Arianus. "He's not, sir, is he? Under arrest?"

"Of course, he's not under arrest," said Julius, his voice scathing, the blood high in his cheeks. He looked at the small water clock on his desk. "Tell Marcus to present himself here, alone, in one hour. As for the others, I'll deal with them later, at the villa." Julius nodded his head curtly at Arianus in dismissal.

"Sir, I'll go tell him." Arianus turned, and this time only his eyes met Vincius', no betraying grin discernible on his face. Arianus left the room, shutting the door soundlessly behind him.

Julius looked over at Vincius, sitting diagonally across from him over the table. Leaning in towards him, Julius' voice was low and hyper-articulate, always a danger sign. "Have you observed everything you wanted to, Vincius?" He stared straight into Vincius' eyes before speaking again. "Dare I suggest," he said, raising his eyebrows and lowering his voice even further, "that you return to work?

"Sir," said Vincius. And dropping his head, he hid the small smile that bloomed on his face in the crook of his right hand.

160

Walking from his home to his father's office in the permanent military camp outside Caesarea, Marcus felt a certain amount of trepidation. He thought his father would probably be very angry with him for leaving without his express permission, but he was not sure about it. True, Arianus had proven uncharacteristically close-mouthed in the few minutes of chat he had spared Marcus back at the villa. Arianus had been so uncommunicative and so brief that it had alarmed his mother into sending Yehonatan along with him. This, despite the fact that the one point Arianus had transmitted clearly was that Julius wanted to see only Marcus in his barracks' office.

If his father were not already furious, Marcus felt sure, his uncle's undesired appearance on the scene would do nothing to preserve his equanimity. And his father's temper was volatile enough without additional provocation. Looking straight ahead of him, Marcus rolled his eyes for the second time that day.

In the brief time he had been home, Marcus had read the signs. Julius must have laid down the law to his mother, or tried to at least, never an easy task. He could imagine the argument they had. By sending his uncle along with him, Miriam was trying to spare him the same kind of treatment she had received. The trouble was, he did not want to be spared, at least, not like that. Sighing, Marcus wished, once again, his mother did not constantly interfere between him and his father, making him feel like a small child. Nor, to Marcus' mind, would Julius view the intervention with kindness either. Above all things, Julius wanted Marcus to act like a soldier in training, not like a child hiding behind his mother's skirts. Since this was completely clear to Marcus, and most of the time he was happy enough to oblige his father, it baffled him why his mother, normally so astute, failed

161

repeatedly to understand the obvious. He shook his head in annoyance and quickened his pace.

"For what it's worth, I don't feel any happier tagging along behind you, than you are in having me tag along," said Yehonatan, a step behind him on the path. "But I promised your mother before we left for Ashqelon that I'd intercede in the case of trouble. Since she held me to my promise, I imagine she's expecting trouble."

"If there is going to be trouble, you'll just make it worse. Besides..." Marcus stopped arguing as Vincius came into sight a distance from his father's office. Vincius was leaning against the doorframe of another building, watching for him. He grinned when he caught sight of Marcus and Yehonatan.

Marcus walked up to him. "So how bad has it been?" said Marcus, grinning back at Vincius, his voice low, careful.

"Your father has relegated me to the lowest level of the underworld, but besides that..." Vincius shrugged. "I've got my health, if not the full pension I was looking forward to a month ago. And, by Dionysius, I'm still alive."

"A last-minute rescue by Silius?" said Marcus.

"Something very like," said Vincius nodding, half shame-faced, half-amused. "I notice, Marcus, you're in no hurry to step into the lion's den, yourself."

"Oh, Marcus is just reconnoitering the ground before he launches his attack from above. He has his troops already stationed, down to the placement of the catapults and the repeating ballistae," said Yehonatan. "I'd call it good strategy on his part." He nodded slightly at Marcus, an encouraging look on his face.

"And he brought you along to lead the assault for him?" said Vincius. He turned his head slightly from Yehonatan to Marcus.

Marcus glowered. "I don't need anyone to lead the damn assault for me," he said. Walking away at a furious pace, Marcus stepped alone inside the hall.

162

Just as the guard was changing, precisely an hour after Julius sent Arianus away, Marcus presented himself at Julius' door. "Father," he said, as he stuck his head in the doorway.

"Come in," said Julius softly. Marcus looked, Julius thought, as if he had hurriedly bathed. His hair was still tousled with damp and he wore a sparkling white tunic. "Punctual as ever," Julius observed to his son, his face melting into a smile at the very sight of him, despite himself, despite the words he had planned for this occasion. Julius was still smiling at his son when he saw the shadow materialize over Marcus' shoulder.

Vincius watched Marcus disappear inside the hall. Sucking in his breath hard, he turned around to face Yehonatan. "That one hit too near the mark, I fear." Shaking his head back and forth once, he said, "So who are you here sacrificing yourself for, Marcus or Miriam?"

Yehonatan looked straight into his eyes. "Marcus, of course," he said and paused. "I received the strong impression elsewhere that Miriam had already engaged your services for herself." Yehonatan crooked his head slightly to the left.

"You have to give her credit, that lady does plot."

"But sometimes, wouldn't you agree, her plotting lacks a little finesse?" Yehonatan murmured. He stepped in closer to Vincius and smiled across at him, a full smile, winning. "Tell me," he said, clasping his left hand on Vincius' right arm, his voice low and familiar, "how bad has it really been the last few days?"

Vincius shrugged. "I'm restricted to camp," he said, "so my information, you understand, is a little limited."

"Go on," Yehonatan murmured.

"Julius has only left camp twice himself, a few hours each time. He came back both times looking every bit as angry as he did when he departed."

"Miriam, I take it, did not get to apply her relaxation technique. I can quite understand why you're pleased about that."

"What?" said Vincius, his tanned features flooding a sudden red.

"No matter," said Yehonatan, slightly increasing the pressure of his clasp on Vincius' arm. "Go on."

Vincius looked away from Yehonatan, down at his arm. The clasp felt reassuring. It created a bond. So much from so little. Vincius shrugged again. "He's certainly showed no signs of relenting with me but give him time. The boy has just returned. Julius will be happier once he sees Marcus."

"In that case, we should let him see the boy in peace. But I suppose I better lurk in the neighborhood in case our speculation goes awry. I'll save my intercessory skills for tonight." Yehonatan smiled, an impenetrable look. "By the way, do you think we can wrangle you a pardon by dinnertime? It will be much more amusing with you there." Stepping back from Vincius, he released his clasp and dropped his hand.

"Let's see." Vincius laid his index finger across his mouth, his thumb below his chin, and tilted his face skyward. "I haven't sacrificed to the gods recently." Vincius shaded his eyes and moved his head from left to right. "Nor is Mercury manifesting himself anywhere on the horizon as far as I can see," he said and shrugged. "I'm afraid it's unlikely."

"Too bad," said Yehonatan, "we'll have to arrange some other way to keep you informed." Putting his left arm around Vincius, he led him toward the nearest pathway, away from the hall. "So, Vincius, how do disgraced soldiers spend their free time in Caesarea? Touring camp? Dicing? Drinking? Whoring? Making long lists of weaponry for their superiors?"

"We could tour camp, but there's not much to see here, just standard fortifications," said Vincius, slightly perplexed by the request. "The camp's square."

"That much the entire world knows already," said Yehonatan, lifting the corners of his mouth into a smile. "Oh well, just until we find a dice game in progress, then. There's not much opportunity to view a Roman military camp, let me tell you, on the southern tip of Arabia, where I've been stuck for the last several years. And it's always edifying, wouldn't you agree, to get a first-hand glimpse of the military force that rules the world."

———◇———

At twilight, Julius stood on the outside doorstep of the villa. The day, he thought, had had its manifold frustrations. The reunion with Marcus, aborted before it began; the long parlay with a military detachment from Alexandria arriving at his doorway on Marcus' footsteps. And now he was faced with this meeting. Groaning mentally, Julius held his hand out before him and pushed open the door.

Inside, the room was flooded with light. Set on the table, each branch of the huge glass candelabra brimmed with virgin oil, every taper lit. In the atrium, light from the two tall brass tripods bordering the silken chaise glinted off of the polished mosaic floor and sparkled upwards before being absorbed into the dark wall hangings. Torches flickered outside around the fountain, illuminating the splashing water in flashes, here, thither, yon, and the faces surrounding it. He heard the plinking notes of laughter and conversation in the courtyard garden, his presence at the villa yet unremarked.

Piqued, Julius thought, she never takes pains like this for me. For a moment, jealousy surged upwards in him. But then, he realized his error. Miriam had gone to this trouble precisely for him, not for her brother, but only to mollify him, as a salve for his nerves. Julius shook his head slightly, a small movement. He hated it when she interfered like this.

He breathed in sharply and realized that a subtle perfume hung in the air, a hint of myrrh, burning there in the corner of the room, light, fragrant, woodsy, soothing. Julius' mind momentarily caviled at the expense. But, of course, he thought bitterly, the brother brought that with him from Arabia. *It cost me nothing, or, at least, nothing monetary.*

Inhaling deeply, Julius trod on the marble lintel, and crossed over to the other side.

Yehonatan's looks took him aback.

All outside conversation had stopped as soon as Julius stepped firmly into the center of the atrium. One by one, the four people in the *peristyle* advanced into the house, the two faces he knew well and the two faces that he did not yet know: Miriam, Marcus, Tullian, Yehonatan.

"Julius," said Miriam coming towards him, her fair hair plaited into a knot on the crown of her hair. Dressed in a light blue robe, the material fluttered about her ankles as she traversed the floor. Miriam rarely failed to look beautiful, a consolation of sorts. "I've set out wine for you on the table, a new amphora from Aza. Shall I pour you a glass?"

Julius ignored her question and turned to look at the two men he did not know. The first, Julius thought approvingly, dark haired, dark complected, his body upright, powerful, compact, was clearly a fighter. And as clearly not a relative. He directed his glance to the far side of the room. The second, fair haired, taller than his friend, lissome, expensively dressed, the second, Julius thought dismissively, was as clearly not a fighter. Pleased, Julius stepped in for a closer look. And then stopped dead. He thought, *Marcus looks more like him than he does like me. I always thought my son looked like me. And* on the instant, the jealousy he had banished earlier, escaping, sang freely through his blood, *vibrato*.

"Where's that wine?" Julius growled.

"I'll pour you some, shall I, father?" Marcus stepped closer to him.

Julius could see the hated resemblance, stamped there in the bones of Marcus' face. For the first time ever, he felt a slight aversion to his son's countenance. Shutting his eyes for a moment, he said, his voice hard edged, "And bring some wine for our guest." Julius backed up one step, two, and sank gratefully into a hard wooden chair. His knife, he realized startled, was still on his right hip. He had not fully divested himself of his weapons when he entered the villa, the way he normally did.

"You," he said pointing at Yehonatan, "sit down on the chaise. The rest of you leave."

Marcus fetched the wine wordlessly, handing one goblet to him, a second to Yehonatan. His son headed toward the door then, following Tullian who had already departed. Yet, at the entranceway, Marcus stopped and turned around. Julius saw him look over at the two men and finally at his mother standing far off from the others. He watched as Miriam gave Marcus the slightest of nods, encouragement to leave. He felt his lip move upward in disgust. How she still babies him. There is something unnatural in it, Julius thought.

Marcus ignored the signal. He just stood there some more moments before nodding once firmly to himself, a decision of sorts. Exiting the room, Marcus climbed the stairs to the second floor two at a time and walked off towards his bedroom, all alone.

Julius turned his eyes back to Miriam who was still standing in the far corner of the atrium. He glared at her.

"I'm staying," she announced.

"No, Miriam, you're not staying. I don't want you here. And if your brother is any kind of a man, he doesn't want you here either."

Biting her lip, Miriam turned to look at Yehonatan.

167

Why hasn't the bastard sat down yet, thought Julius, the way I ordered him to? Annoyed he sat back in his chair, a frown molded onto his face, and watched as Yehonatan stepped towards Miriam.

"Miriam," said Yehonatan. Putting his arm around her shoulder, Yehonatan propelled her gently to the doorway. "Don't worry about a thing," he said calmly. "Go and entertain Tullian for a while. Julius and I are simply going to have a chat. I guarantee," he said, "we'll both be unharmed when it's over." Yehonatan waited by the door as Miriam left the room, took a few steps forward and then turned her head to glance at him over her shoulder. He nodded at her once, his arm raised, leaning against the doorframe. Only when Miriam moved beyond his sight, did Yehonatan turn around and look directly at Julius.

"I'd much prefer if we kept this civilized. No bloodshed, for example," Yehonatan said, staring pointedly at the knife on Julius' left hip.

"You're worried about this?" said Julius, his voice low. Grasping the stag's head hilt, he pulled the knife out its sheath and ran his left thumb lightly over the blade, again and again. The final time left a thin line of blood.

"I'd prefer not to have to change my own clothes again before dinner," said Yehonatan as he sat down on the chaise, arranging his blue silk tunic around him, "but if the damage is self-inflicted, who am I to stop you?" He smiled at Julius, but the look gave nothing away.

Julius felt his lip creeping upward in disgust again. He licked the trace of blood off of his thumb to cover his reaction. Switching the knife to his right hand, Julius set it on the table and pushed it away from himself.

"It's equidistant between the two of us now," said Julius. "If there is to be bloodshed, you'll only have to react faster than I do. Grab the knife first. Think you could?"

Infuriatingly, Yehonatan's small smile expanded across his face. "It's possible," he said slowly. "I'll do my best." Yehonatan leaned back on

168

the chaise and lifted his right arm along the back, completely relaxed. Picking up his wine from the side table, he took a sip of it, then held the goblet balanced on his left knee. "Miriam chose an excellent wine," Yehonatan said. "But enough with the games. Let us address the matter at hand, Julius."

"What makes you think you can take my son with you without my express authorization?"

"I had his mother's authorization."

"Not good enough. I'm Marcus' guardian."

"Not by law, you aren't. It's not as if your marriage were recognized under Roman law."

Julius chuckled mirthlessly. "You try enforcing a court ruling like that against an army man," said Julius, "and every soldier with a family will be against you. There's an entire army of men out there whose marriages are not legal according to Roman law."

"Who said anything about taking it to a court of law, Julius? I don't want to take the boy away from you. I simply wanted a chance to get to know him, to introduce him firsthand to my family's business. One day, he'll likely be my father's heir, my heir. It's a considerable fortune, as you know well," Yehonatan gestured around the room, "since it makes possible much of this."

"Why Marcus? Why not a son of your own?"

There was silence for a moment as Yehonatan removed his eyes from Julius' vicinity. He said, "My son is dead," and the timbre of his voice fell away mercilessly. "I've not had another."

Julius leaned back in his chair, spread his legs apart, and placed his right hand on his thigh. After a time, he said, "Miriam never mentioned you had children."

"Miriam doesn't know," said Yehonatan. "I never told her or my father. I was away for months trading before the boy was born and returned right after he died. Such news would not have gladdened them. I thought it best to let the matter lie."

"Then why tell me?"

Yehonatan's eyes targeted Julius' across the table. "Won't the obvious explanation do? You happened to ask. I was feeling expansive." His voice regaining tone, now sounded over-bright.

Julius stared at him for some moments more, his eyes narrowed. Coming to himself, he shook his head. "You're trying to distract me from the purpose of this discussion," he said.

Yehonatan picked up his wine glass from his knee, and held it cradled before him in both hands. Moving the glass slowly upward to his mouth, he took a long sip. As he moved it away from his face, the glass jerked slightly. Yehonatan looked down at the glass, still cradled in both hands, and lowered it with deliberation back onto his left knee. He sat still, his head bowed, staring at the glass. "You've a very uncharitable view of human nature if you think that," Yehonatan said at last and turned his head to the side, towards the garden, "though, God knows, on another occasion, I might have deserved it." He sat perfectly motionless. Next to him, the bronze tripod, aflame, tinged his colorless face with borrowed hues.

Julius broke the silence at last. "About Marcus," he said. "I mean him to follow my profession, to be an army man. To be a Roman. I won't brook your interference. I hope that's perfectly clear to you."

"He's going to choose his own way, one way or another, Julius, when he is grown. Maybe he'll be a soldier, maybe something else. But tighten the jesses too much now and he'll only fly further afield later on." Leaning forward, Yehonatan placed his wine goblet on the table and moved it away from himself. Shifting his weight forward until he just crouched, he stretched out his arm and picked up the knife on the table. Holding it by the blade, his index finger traced the intricate design on the golden hilt. He raised it closer to his face and examined it carefully.

"You violated my rule about the knife." Julius regarded him. "I placed it equidistant between us for a reason." A smile blossomed on his face, over-quick, a false spring, full of malice. "Should I be feeling alarmed?"

"Don't be a fool, Julius, we're hardly even at an impasse. No," said Yehonatan, "this is part of my profession, the examination and appreciation of luxury goods. I see you had the knife repaired once. Badly. You'd have needed a native craftsman from the northern wilds to duplicate this work. It's Scythian and quite old." He leaned back towards the table and laid down the knife. "The blade hasn't been sharpened carefully enough. You should hand it to your weapons master to work on, even if it is," said Yehonatan as he looked over at Julius, "merely ornamental." Cocking his head to one side, he said, "By the bye, it's a curious affectation for a Roman soldier."

"You know weaponry?" said Julius, surprised. From the man's demeanor, his dress, he had not expected that.

"Naturally," said Yehonatan. He lounged against the back of the chaise, the golden embroidery on the band of his tunic twinkling in the light.

Julius regarded the man as he sat there, perfectly at ease on the couch. For Julius' taste, Yehonatan's easy manners in his home at this moment were too insinuating. He was too relaxed, too confident. Julius could not decide what he thought of the man. He did not trust him. But he could feel his earlier hostility melting away. For a second, Julius regretted it. Hostility, he had found, was a perfect spur to quicken anger and, when necessary, even rage. A very useful tactic.

Standing up, Julius walked across the room to retrieve the jug of wine. He poured himself a second glass, considering. "You want some more?" he said, jerking his head in Yehonatan's direction. At Yehonatan's brief nod, Julius shoved the earthenware jug across the table over to him.

"You object to freedom of will on principle?" said Yehonatan, pouring himself wine.

"Hardly," said Julius. He snorted once.

"If not for yourself, then for your dependents?"

"It's a different case, isn't it," said Julius derisively, his eyes amused.

"Is it? Perhaps not for them," said Yehonatan. "In any case, I thought freedom of will was a point of honor amongst you Romans."

"Amongst some of us, yes. But so is professional continuity. My father was a centurion, his father was a centurion. I want my son to be a centurion or greater. He's got the talent for it. Besides," Julius said, "who, in this world, is ever free?"

"Free from what?"

"Constraint, responsibility, duty," said Julius. He lowered his voice to a whisper, "Unwanted feelings, moral failure, cowardice ... weakness." A half bitter smile landed on his lips and was trapped there. "Shall I go on?"

"It's a curious argument for pushing a young boy to a life he may not want," said Yehonatan. "You have learned your freedom is curtailed by human nature; therefore, you will not give your son the slightest chance for it. And why are you so sure, Julius, that if you loosen the restraints, he'll not choose soldiering in any case? As you say, with his talents, he's admirably suited for it."

"Yes," said Julius gratified. "Marcus is precociously gifted. A natural soldier, all his teachers say."

Yehonatan turned his head towards the garden, shifted his seat and settled again. "On the other hand," he said loudly, "Marcus has also developed a very unattractive habit of spying on his relatives. He's lurking in the *peristyle* right now, listening to us." Yehonatan turned to scrutinize Julius' expression and was satisfied by what he saw. He lowered his voice. "I wondered if he learned this from you, but I see now that I was wrong."

Julius faced Yehonatan, his eyes wide as he listened for a betraying sound. He did not hear a thing. "Marcus, spying? Here? On me?" he asked, astonished. "That's unlike him. You're sure?"

Yehonatan nodded, grimacing slightly.

Julius stood. "Marcus," he bellowed in the direction of the garden. "Get in here, immediately." Julius heard it now, the vines outside rustling as the boy disentangled himself from the shadows, in a blur of motion and sound.

Marcus sulked into the room. On his face was the most pronounced scowl Julius had ever seen him wear.

"It's my future you're discussing," Marcus said, standing squarely before his father, a bellicose, half-grown cub. "I have a right to know what you're saying."

"You should have asked me then. Not turned yourself into a sneak and a spy."

"You told me to get out of the room. You would have said no."

Julius leaped up from his chair, shot his hand out and gripped Marcus by the upper arm, hard, his muscles taut. "That is not license to listen in. Next time I tell you something, you obey fully. Every detail," he hissed. "Do you understand me, now? Am I clear enough for you?"

Marcus looked down at his arm where his father was holding him. The skin had already turned a mottled red from the pressure. He twisted his body around suddenly, applying a wrestling release. His arm instantly broke free from his father's grasp and he stepped back a pace. Marcus looked up at his father, his eyes fierce, challenging, exultant.

Julius returned the look, the anger molten in his eyes. "That was skillfully done," he said in a low voice, dangerous. "At least, I won't have to punish you for technical incompetence as well as disobedience."

"Ah yes," said Yehonatan, stepping suddenly between Julius and Marcus, causing the breach between them to widen. "Did I neglect to mention to you, Julius, that most days we were away, Tullian and I spent some time drilling Marcus in wrestling technique? Tullian mostly, of course, he's the expert. I'm afraid, he used me as a demonstration bag of sorts. I got thrown around a lot." For a second, Yehonatan sported a rueful grin. "But, Marcus, here," he said, draping his arm around Marcus and hauling him forcefully away from Julius toward the chaise, "Marcus managed to pick it up successfully." Yehonatan sat down across the small table from Julius and pulled Marcus down to the bench along with him. "Although, I admit, I had not foreseen he'd be stupid enough to apply the technique against his father. You'll have to excuse my lapse in foresight, I'm afraid."

Julius grunted. He was still standing, his face dark.

Yehonatan refilled Julius' glass with wine and pushed it across the small table toward him. When he looked up, there was a mischievous glow in his eye. "I've just had an idea," he said to Julius. "In addition to any punishment you mete out, send Marcus upstairs now. Make him compose a philosophical oration on the topic, The Virtue of Obedience in Sons. He can rewrite the bloody thing until both of us are satisfied with its Latin meter. It will take him days. The lingering memory, I feel sure, will help keep him in line on future occasions." The mischievous glow in Yehonatan's eye now shone over his entire face. "And when he's got it right, make him declaim it in front of company so that it becomes a lesson he never forgets! Think how much you would have hated that when you were his age."

Stooping, Julius picked up his wine and drank it down quickly. Yehonatan leaned over the table to hand the wine jug to him, and Julius slowly refilled his glass. By the time he sat down on his chair, the anger on his face had dissipated. He pointed his finger at Marcus and said, "You heard your uncle. Go! Now!"

"You cannot be serious," said Marcus to his father, balking. "I'm not going to do it. I'd rather a beating."

"That's a relief. Have no fears, I'm going to beat you also, but I'll do that tomorrow," said Julius silkily. "I'll spare your backside tonight, so you can sit and write for a few hours. I want the first draft of your oration downstairs tomorrow morning before I leave." Julius stared at his son, waiting for him to depart.

Marcus did not budge from the chaise.

"You're dismissed," said Julius. "Get out of here."

174

Marcus stood up from the chaise slowly. He looked back and forth between his father and Yehonatan, the two of them so strangely united against him. There was no solace here from either of them, no advantage he could exploit, no way he could see to play one off against the other. He was trapped between them, and disengagement suddenly seemed to Marcus the wisest course. Every good soldier, he thought, knows when to retreat.

They had been discussing philosophy before Yehonatan preternaturally figured out where he was and what he was doing. Philosophy, Marcus thought, in disgust. The way the conversation had begun with his father yelling for everyone to exit the room, Marcus had supposed they would end up in a brawl. He'd wanted to see that because he had absolutely no idea who would win. His father, to be sure, would underestimate Yehonatan, the way he, himself, originally had.

As he brushed past his uncle on the way to the door, Yehonatan touched him on the arm.

"Marcus, Marcus," said Yehonatan, shaking his head. "I warned you last time I caught you spying on me that the consequences of getting caught would be dire. Now you know firsthand what I meant." He looked Marcus in the eye, man to man. "I suggest you learn to control your rebellious streak. You understand what I'm telling you?"

Yehonatan was so smug at times, Marcus thought, disliking him again. For a few seconds he was tempted to defy the message Yehonatan had just conveyed to him, to loose his restraint like an arrow trained at Yehonatan's heart, to blurt out what he knew about the man to his father. What a pleasure that would be! At least, momentarily. Too bad the pleasure would not last. No, he thought, the consequences of speaking were too unpleasant to permit him to succumb to the urge. And Yehonatan knew that.

175

Marcus opened his mouth, not sure what he was going to say, but his father spoke first, breaking into his exchange with Yehonatan.

"Before you leave the room, Marcus," said Julius harshly, "one more thing. Who encouraged you to spy on me? It's an activity I will not tolerate."

"To be fair, Julius, perhaps no one person set Marcus on us at all," said Yehonatan, turning his head to smile slightly at his brother-in-law. "He could simply have picked up the habit at your camp. Every army pays professionals to spy on its enemies, Rome not least among them."

"What has that to do with this?" snapped Julius. "Marcus has received no training to be a professional spy." He lowered his voice. "And I am not his enemy."

"Precisely as I see it," said Yehonatan, looking directly at Marcus again. "What serves one's nation does not always serve one's family. You understand me, Marcus?"

Of course, he understood. Did the man think he was a moron? His uncle had just put him in his place. He, Yehonatan, was the professional spy and Marcus was not. Well, it was true enough. He had not managed to dupe his uncle either of the two times he had tried. Annoyed at the unaccustomed feeling of incompetence, Marcus set his mouth and jerked his shoulder around, cutting off Yehonatan from his view. He turned to face his father.

"Perhaps, Father," Marcus suggested half-maliciously, his voice lilting untrustworthily despite his effort to keep it steady, "spying is a talent I come by naturally."

"Oh, you mean your mother," Julius said disgustedly. "She put you up to it."

"What, Mother? Not at all. What makes you think so?" said Marcus staring upwards. For a moment, his hyacinthine eyes achieved a seraphic look, empty of guile. "But I'm sure it's a tendency I got from someone."

And having returned as much fire against Yehonatan as he dared under his father's nose, Marcus marched resolutely from the room, a small soldier, an army of one. He climbed slowly upstairs, there to unwillingly embrace the meager consolations of philosophy.

PART X

CHAPTER 13
Wounds

Relentless, thought Marcus. Today was relentless.

He lay on a deserted strip of beach with his head pillowed on a tussock in the sand, looking skyward, a few miles north of Caesarea. The late afternoon sun shone down on his half-naked torso, crisping his lightly browned skin. Marcus could feel the sweat as it pooled into drops before gathering speed to roll down his sides, tickling him. And then he felt the long, slow burn as the sweat penetrated the open cuts on his right side, by his ribs. He did not put his hands anywhere near the lacerations. He had at first, but it had only made the pain sharper when the salt and sand mixed in. Impossible to wash. The only water at hand was salty. Even the air smelt of salt when he breathed in. Sea salt and brackish seaweed. And blood. A metallic tang.

His right eye was a mess as well. He had not seen that shield hurling toward him, until it was right in front of his face. And then there was only time to wheel slightly and to duck. Even so, the shield caught the corner of his eye and his ribs, bursting open the skin in both places. There was a large bump on his head underneath his hair. He had no idea where that had come from.

The men were supposed to pull their weapons at the last moment in drills. Not to launch them with full force. In this case, Marcus was not sure what happened. But he suspected that Casio, the young man who carried that shield, did not like him very much. And he had succeeded in delivering that message to Marcus today.

He should have gone to the infirmary right after the drill. But all he had felt like doing immediately afterward was getting away. Off by himself. No attention focused on him. So here he was. Alone on a deserted strip of beach. A stupid thing to have done really, he thought. Like some pathetic, wounded animal who ran away to lick his wounds. Not soldierly behavior at all.

He already felt light-headed from the contusion and the loss of blood. Now with the sun shimmering down on the beach full force, he was beginning to feel immobilized. No shade anywhere in sight. He had to get out of here, he realized. Go home. Or get help. He needed water. His throat was constricting from thirst.

Marcus pushed himself up to his elbows. His horse, with his flask of water tied on to the saddle, was nowhere in sight. He whistled loudly for Argos and began to struggle slowly to his feet. But the dizziness grew acute and there was nothing to hold onto.

Marcus woke up a few minutes later, face flat in the sand. He still felt the pain. But, at least, he marveled, the dizziness was gone. Vanished. He turned his head to the right and spat out the sand. And then with his last conscious thought, he shut his eyes and willed himself to fall asleep.

When Marcus woke up before dusk, he saw two eyes before him. Two dark brown eyes. A thin face. Brown hair. A scraggy beard. A man hovering over him. Light colored clothing. He put his hand up to the bump on his head. When the pain surged, like small bolts of lightning exploding along a trajectory, he regretted it immediately.

179

He remembered only then where he was and why. He struggled to turn over, to sit up.

"Don't move," the man said. "You're hurt." He spoke accented Greek. Badly.

"I know," croaked Marcus, half leaning on his elbow. He answered in Aramaic. "Water?" he asked. His voice sounded plaintive. Dry.

The man called peremptorily over his shoulder to someone. Yared, a Hebrew name. Not Syrian or Greek.

Marcus could hear footsteps approaching rapidly, a boy about his age coming into view, carrying something. A flask of water. The boy lowered the flask toward him, to his mouth. Slowly, Marcus leaned forward to take a sip. Only a little one. He leaned away and felt the first man supporting his back. He pushed himself forward again and took a longer sip.

"Thank you," he murmured in Hebrew. It seemed like minutes had passed. Probably only seconds.

"What happened to you?" asked the man.

"Fight," he said. He used his hand and his arm to demonstrate tentatively. "Shield here. Face. Side."

"Romans?" the man said. He straightened up and spat to the left. "Why?"

Why indeed? thought Marcus. He had no idea really. Why had he been fighting? What was the point of it all? Sometimes, he hated everything about army life passionately. At other times, when he let himself, he remembered what Rabbi Chanon had told him a few years back, that soldiery was nothingness. On those occasion, when he collapsed the bulwark he had built up around himself, Marcus would make himself admit that the Rabbi had had more of a point than he originally thought. Once or twice, he had even permitted himself to agree with him.

Right now, he agreed with Rabbi Chanon with all his being.

He looked up and shrugged at the man. What could he say after all? He could feel his head beginning to thrum again. To cloud.

"They left you here like this?" the man said. The disgust in his voice was palpable.

"No." He shook his head slightly until the pain jabbed him again. And thought, do not set him off. Maintain the *status quo*. "No. My fault. Came here like this. On my horse." Marcus leaned in to take another sip. But this time the pain caused him to retch. The cloud in his head turned dense, heavy. His vision dimmed to a few points of light that began to twirl. For a moment, just a moment, he stood on the brink between realms and thought he saw a Seraph beckoning him into a midnight blue room. The doves were singing sweetly to him again. The blue room emanated wholeness and peace. He so much wanted to enter there. Marcus opened his eyes wider to grasp what he was seeing, to follow the voices. But the lights in front of him only twirled madly one last time before winking out. He was broken and there was nowhere to go. So, he surrendered to the dark.

The next time Marcus woke up he was in a bed of sorts in a house he did not know. Nothing about it smelled familiar. He could distinguish a fishy stink, newly scythed hay, goat skin. He opened his eyes once, looked about hazily, then shut them again. He heard murmurings, rustlings, a door closing. After a while, he woke again and felt hands on his body, at his right side. Someone was cleaning his wounds with water and an acerbic ointment that stung him. He smelled poppy in the room now, somewhere close by.

"You said he spoke to you in Hebrew. But he's not circumcised." Marcus did not recognize the voice speaking. "Strange, no?"

"Maybe a Christian, rabbi?" That voice belonged to the man who had helped him at the beach. "And look at the quality of his tunic. He seems wealthy enough."

Marcus ceased to listen, allowing his mind to drift. The same old story, he thought tiredly. He hated explaining his situation. Of late,

181

he avoided circumstances where he had to clarify anything personal. And so, he had slowly, inexorably shaped his life into an unvarying routine for the last three years.

Daily, from early morning to mid-afternoon, he spent hours in the *gymnasium* and the engineers' workshop, learning the rudiments and the more advanced requirements of an officer's position. Trained personally by Rufinus, he had gained considerable expertise with the short sword. He could fight with a shield and without one, on horse and on foot. His aim with bow and arrow was usually unerring. He could assemble and utilize catapults and ballistae. And he had started to master the rudiments of leading men in battle: to keep soldiers disciplined and in formation as they advanced to face an enemy and to inspire them to fight by setting an example of bravery at the fore of the troops.

Nightly, Marcus spent hours reading military treatises and reviewing military tactics with his father. And when his father was absent from Caesarea, as had happened frequently in the past months, he studied with men his father recruited to teach him, and on his own.

More and more, Marcus despised his own cowardice. Privately, he scorned the very safe life he had constructed for himself. The people around him, his parents, his father's men, assumed that soldiering was his calling, that he was exercising his natural gifts to the fullest. That he loved it. How that made him laugh at times. How easy it had been to fool them all. Too easy. Sometimes, he wished his uncle would return from Sardis for the sole purpose of seeing right through him. Yehonatan would set them all straight. One look, and all his deceptions would be over. He deserved it.

He wished it were over now.

When he had embarked on this project, he had not comprehended he had only to act a role slightly before people began to believe that this is who he was. A word stressed a certain way. The careful assumption of a manner from time to time. Most of all discipline.

And now he was caught. A trap of his own making. And slowly he had realized that he hated the lie he was living. But he had no idea how to extricate himself now. It had gone too far already. His father was overjoyed by his choices. Not his mother. But in this one thing, it was easier to disappoint his mother than his father. Most of the time, he stayed in his chosen role. There had been lapses.

And now here was the chance for another.

For the first time all day, Marcus felt a measure of hope. He opened his eyes. And looked up into the face of the man sitting by his side. Kind eyes. Light hazel brown with precise green flecks. Dark brown rims around the iris. Light hazel hair that matched the eyes, frosted with some gray. A chubby, lined face with a neatly trimmed beard.

"Ah. He's awake now." This last was addressed to the man on the beach. "Those were some nasty injuries, young man."

"Yes, Rabbi," he said. His voice sounded raspy. "I was in a fight." His head was still aching. Too much thinking, he decided.

The man from the beach approached the bed and handed him an earthenware cup. Marcus lifted it to his mouth and drank deeply and then some more. He tasted poppy mixed into the water. To dull the pain. Soon, he hoped.

"You were awake while we spoke before?" the rabbi said.

Marcus looked him in the eye. "Yes. For some of it."

"How did you come to be hurt like that?"

"I was in a fight," he repeated, adding nothing.

"With thugs?"

Marcus moved his head slightly, signifying dissent.

"With local soldiers, then?" asked the rabbi.

"With local soldiers," Marcus repeated. "Yes." He had to be careful here. There were political implications to what he was saying now.

"What happened? Did they attack you?" said the rabbi.

Marcus looked at the man's face. It expressed sympathy. Too much sympathy for his taste. "No," said Marcus. "It was an organized fight.

183

I knew what I was doing." When a shade of incredulity passed over the rabbi's face, he muttered. "Or, at least, I thought I did." Marcus raised his eyebrows. "I didn't realize how badly I was hurt until I was on the beach."

"Who taught you to speak Hebrew?"

He lowered his eyelids. Took the sheet that was covering him in his hands, twisted it slightly. First one way, then the other. "My mother," he said. "My grandfather originally. My mother's father. When I was a baby. He studied in Tiberias, in the Galilee. Years ago."

"Ah," said the rabbi. "Yes, I see."

Marcus forced his chin up. He forced himself to look right in the rabbi's eye. He forced himself to speak. "My father's Roman. A centurion," he said. "He wouldn't allow me to be circumcised."

The man from the beach spoke across the room. "A mamzer?" he whispered loudly. Shocked.

Marcus turned his head so quickly that the pain stabbed him again. "I'm not a mamzer," he half shouted, furious at the accusation. A mamzer. The worst kind of insult. The product of incest, or other illicit sex. Outcast. Unable to marry another Jew who was not of the same status. Marcus swallowed and put his hand to the lump on his head to help contain the twinges.

"Shush, Alexander," said the rabbi. "The boy is still hurt." The rabbi turned his head fully away from Marcus to face the other man. "In any case, the sage Rabbi Judah dissents. Holds the child of a Jewish woman and a non-Jewish man is a Jew, not a mamzer. His opinion is good enough for me. So here outside Caesarea, where my opinion holds sway locally, the boy is a Jew, whatever you have heard to the contrary. And that's enough said for now." He turned back to Marcus. "You are from Caesarea?"

Marcus nodded.

"Your father's own men attacked you?" The rabbi's voice was uninflected.

Marcus saw the trap, but still could not prevent himself from replying more honestly than he had meant to. "Practice session. But it got out of hand."

"Then to whom should we send word on your behalf?"

All of a sudden, Marcus was not sure he wanted to go home. To face the barrage of questions. To go back into his role so soon. To submit to the mundane, the everyday. He so much desired to escape from it for a while. He closed his eyes, felt a dogged look settling over his face.

"If they know you are hurt, your parents are probably very worried about you," the rabbi admonished him. "Think of your mother."

The call to responsibility. He was too familiar with that argument already. Marcus hardened his heart and kept his eyes closed for a few more moments.

"It's already quite late in the day," the rabbi said.

Marcus lay still, trying to smooth the scowl from his face.

"Your father may start a search for you. And if you are found here, there could be trouble for Alexander and Yared, his son."

Marcus opened his eyes regretfully. That was an argument he could not resist. "Why would there be?" he said. "They didn't hurt me. They helped me."

"In any case, you can't stay here," Alexander said. "Tell him so, Rabbi Ariel."

Marcus sat up. His head was feeling clearer now. "Of course," he said. "I'm sorry. I wasn't thinking." He told them his name. Explained where to find his house. "My father is away. Ask for my mother," he added. "She'll know what to do. She won't make a fuss. Speak to her in Hebrew."

"Alexander," said the rabbi. "Go."

The expression on Alexander's face grew stony.

"It's too late to send Yared on this errand," says the rabbi. "Have your lad come inside when he finishes his work. He can sit here with me and Marcus."

"Ride my horse," said Marcus. "He knows the way."

"What horse? There wasn't one on the beach when we located you," said Alexander acerbically.

"He most likely went home, then," said Marcus. "In which case, it's true. They will have started searching for me by now."

Alexander turned to go, lifted the latch of the door, spun on his heel. "It's a long walk, Rabbi, on a chill night," he said begrudgingly.

"Ask them for money, then, for helping me," Marcus said contemptuously. "That might make it worth your while."

"It's good to know, mamzer," said Alexander, "that you aren't as worthless as you look." He smiled tauntingly and walked out of the door of the small house.

"That was uncalled for, Marcus," admonished the rabbi as soon as Alexander left. "You only set him off." The rabbi waited some more time in silence. Finally, he said, "You were badly hurt. Are you afraid to go home?"

"Nothing like that. I'm not afraid," said Marcus. "I just wanted some time away, to get clear in my own mind." He started to shrug, stopped when he realized that even through a slight drug haze, his movements still felt constricted. Turned his head gingerly to face the rabbi. "It was an organized fight," he explained. "A drill. There weren't supposed to be any injuries." A few moments of silence. "I don't mind being hurt. If that's what you are thinking. I've been hurt before. It's just that I..." Marcus stopped himself from speaking. He looked down at the rumpled sheet in his hands.

"That you what?" said the rabbi, his voice sonorous, encouraging.

"Sometimes there doesn't seem to be much of a point to it, is all," said Marcus. "It's always the same thing. Lately there are times when I hate it. They all think that because I'm good at military things, that

186

I love it. But it's not true. You don't have to love a thing to be very skillful at it, to master it." Marcus looked up at the rabbi, checked his expression. Saw that his mien was still sympathetic. "They tell me it's a gift, but right now it feels more of a curse." Worried suddenly by the way he had let the conversation drift, Marcus added, hurriedly, "At least that's how I feel now. But it's probably because I'm not feeling well." He shut his mouth with deliberation, forcing himself to stop speaking.

"Have you considered that if your heart is not in it," suggested the rabbi, "maybe you're fighting on behalf of the wrong party?"

"It's not as if they need me. That's true. But what other army is there?" Marcus inflected his voice slightly. "Parthians? The Germanic Tribes? The Northern barbarians in Britain?"

Rabbi Ariel let a pause develop before speaking. "You are right, after all," he said. "There is no other army worth considering." A moment passed and all the while he looked solemnly at Marcus. "Yet," he added, in an undertone so low it could have been merely a puff of breath escaping from his lips. And then Rabbi Ariel subsided into silence. After a while, he said, "Sleep. It will be hours before anyone comes for you."

Marcus lay back on the bed, weary and hollow, thinking about what had just been said. And more importantly what had not been said. Possibilities rose in his mind like sandcastles. He pondered them as they dwindled slowly, eroded by reason. There was a message here, though, one he had still not uncovered. Something subterranean. He needed to figure out a way to avail himself of better sources of intelligence in Caesarea. Most of what he now knew about the political situation was filtered exclusively through a Roman perspective.

"Rabbi," he said at last, trying a smile on his face. "May I come to visit you?" He closed his eyes, encouraging himself, thinking, this is not unethical. "Sometime when I'm well again?"

"You may."

He remembered the torrent of information that had rained down upon him that one week traveling with Yehonatan. Realized he had allowed himself to be content with less, with a suppression of information from alternative sources, because of the discomfort he had felt. The way he believed it might threaten his family. Another trap, he thought, though this one is not entirely of my making. But he had submitted to it, he thought bitterly. If he wanted to be free, he had to know the truth, whatever that was, however it made him feel. What was the point of living life as a coward? Even if it put everything he held dear at stake.

Whole minutes later, Marcus wiped his face surreptitiously, cracked open his eyes. Cursed his weakness. Saw the rabbi turning to regard him from across the room. "I'm not really crying," Marcus said. After a moment he added. "It's only because I don't feel well."

"I assure you, Marcus. I saw nothing."

Marcus smiled tentatively. "We both know that's a lie." He heard the latch on the door being jiggled, then, and saw the door starting to open. Yared appeared, the boy he remembered dimly from the beach as a dark outline, carrying water. Marcus turned his head slightly toward him. He tried to smile. But thought, what could I possibly say to a stranger now? Instead he blocked out the world.

Sometime later, he woke and heard his mother's voice outside, high and cultured. Then Vincius' deeper voice, speaking to Alexander. He should have realized she'd bring Vincius. It seemed obvious now when he thought about it. It was full nighttime. She would need a guard. Marcus sat up in the bed, swung his legs over the side and stood. Too fast. He still felt a little dizzy. He closed his eyes and rode it out. Mastered the spell. Stood naked, looking about squarely on his feet for his tunic and trousers. The rabbi handed them to him and he slipped into the trousers. And sat back down onto the bed, the tunic in his lap, his head in his two hands, waiting.

188

"Perhaps you should have stayed lying down," Rabbi Ariel admonished him. He handed Marcus a glass of very watered wine.

"No," said Marcus. "I'd rather face this dressed." Marcus took the glass, drank it down in two gulps. There was poppy mixed in it again, slightly acrid on the tongue. At least, that will be useful for the ride home, he thought.

The door opened then, and his mother swept in, Alexander behind her, the malicious smile he had worn previously now banished. Marcus lifted his head slightly from his hands and watched Miriam advance into the room. She was dressed plainly, wearing a simple white under-tunic, partially covered by a loose, light blue robe. The linen fringe of her tunic peeked out at the bottom. Her fair hair was half veiled. She was dressed like a Jew, not in the more fashionable city garb she normally wore. Marcus was used to Miriam dressing traditionally when she interacted with Jews. Privately, he used to loathe the Janus-like approach. But right now, he was thankful, appreciated the gesture she had made on his behalf. It would facilitate this encounter immeasurably. His mother knew this, of course; that was the reason she did it.

"Marcus," she cried, stepping purposefully to his side.

"Hello, mother," he said, smiling painfully. "Don't worry about me. I'm fine. I'll be all right."

She slid over to the bed and stood next to him as she looked him over. The bruises on his face, his complexion, torso and side where the bandaging bulked under his tunic. She put her hand up to touch the side of his head, but he raised his hand more swiftly and blocked her.

He said, "Don't touch me there," and watched her face change, saw the hurt in her eyes become acute. Marcus lowered his voice. "I'm sorry. But it hurts," he said by way of expiation. And then to switch the topic, "You brought Vincius." His voice still sounded disapproving, gruff. He had intended to disguise that.

"I brought Vincius," she said shortly. "You'll need his help on the way home."

"I don't need any help," he said. "I'm okay. I can ride by myself."

Miriam looked him over again. Shook her head slightly at him, half exasperated, half worried still. "We'll soon see, won't we? I'll let Vincius decide, not you. He's a better judge of these things than either of us. More experience in the field."

Marcus disagreed, violently. He was about to voice his feelings, but caught the rabbi looking at him again, this time reproachfully. "Mother," he said, modifying his tone, speaking respectfully, "this is Rabbi Ariel. He cleaned me up and bandaged me, as you see. You met Alexander when he came to find you. He found me in the first place. On the beach. And brought me here."

Miriam stood up and walked over to the rabbi. She started to hold out her hand, then stopped herself as she recalled that in some religious circles men and women did not touch outside of marriage lest it lead to adultery. "Thank you both," she said. "We're profoundly grateful. I hope all this was not too much trouble."

Alexander grunted in assent at Miriam's words. The implication was clear to Marcus. It had been too much trouble. Even with the reward he had received that Marcus could now hear clinking in his purse.

The rabbi, Marcus was gratified to see, shot Alexander a reproach-ful glance as well.

And then Vincius arrived, his right arm raised, leaning into the doorframe. He was frowning. "Marcus," he said, and strode into the room. He was wearing a simple tunic, not his military dress, Marcus noted. But there was no disguising the sword at Vincius' right hip or his ramrod straight bearing, his short military haircut and his powerful presence. Vincius had risen in the ranks of Julius' men in the last three years. He now worked directly under him, as his optio.

190

Vincius halted in front of Marcus. He placed his left hand under Marcus' chin and began to tilt his head up and to the left.

Marcus crooked his head slightly, trying to evade Vincius' touch, and attempted to stand. But after he rose from the bed just a little, Vincius placed his right hand on Marcus' left shoulder and leaned into it firmly, pushing him back down to the bed. "I'm glad, for your sake, that you're not injured on your left side, Marcus. Otherwise, you'd be screaming by now," said Vincius, speaking in Aramaic. "And you'd deserve it too, I might add, pulling a stunt like that this afternoon. When your horse arrived without you, and bloodstains all over him, you had your mother half frantic." Vincius paused. "And me," he said finally. "And me."

"I know," said Marcus. "Dereliction of duty on your part. However, would you have it explained to my father when he returned?"

"Marcus!" reproved Miriam. She was still standing across the room, at the rabbi's side.

Vincius glanced at her, looked back at Marcus. "Shut up and lie down, you rude bastard, before I wallop you. Injury or no. I can see your head looks bad enough. Right now. I'm going to examine the rest of you."

Marcus raised his eyes. "Vincius," he said levelly. "I'm fine. I swear it. The cuts on my side bled a lot, and there is quite a bit of bruising, but they were superficial in the main. They might need some stitches. But the rabbi cleaned them well. There is no point in undoing the bandages until I get home. Xenon will see to it. After we're home, I promise to do whatever you like."

"Lie down now," Vincius growled at him.

Marcus opened his mouth to appeal.

Vincius raised his voice. "Marcus, lie down," he commanded.

There was never a reprieve from that tone of voice, so Marcus slowly lay back down on the pallet. Vincius leaned over and put his cool hands on him, started to unravel the bandages. But all Marcus could think was that he wanted to leave. He could feel Alexander's hostility like a battering ram from across the room focused on Vincius and himself. Vincius would not bother to pick up on something as intangible as that. As a Roman solider, he was professionally immune from reacting to the offended feelings of the people whose houses he was violating at any time. So, Marcus glanced at his mother instead, caught her eye. He moved his head toward Alexander and raised his eyebrow slightly. And was gratified to see Miriam look at the man and read him precisely. His mother excelled at gauging unspoken signals.

"Vincius," Miriam said, starting across the room. "Marcus says he's all right. He's pale, but his mind seems like it's still intact, worse luck for us." She was looking at Marcus and smiling as she said this. "Let's take him home before examining him."

"Just a minute," Vincius said, his back towards her, still bent over Marcus. "This will take no time. Better to be sure."

Miriam stepped up behind Vincius and laid her hand on his shoulder. She squeezed it lightly. The gesture was so rare and unexpected that Marcus actually saw Vincius' cheeks flood with color and his posture stiffen perceptibly. Marcus removed his eyes from Vincius to spare him any embarrassment and looked around the room instead. He saw, unfortunately, that Alexander and the rabbi had both noted Miriam's familiar gesture as well. Marcus could read in their eyes what they thought this implied about his mother. He did not like that at all.

"Vincius," Miriam repeated in a low tone of voice.

Vincius had already begun to refasten Marcus' bandage. "Yes, Miriam," he said. "We'll depart as soon as I finish tying this back together." And then giving his hand to Marcus, he said, "Can you walk, or should I carry you?"

Marcus swallowed. "I can walk," he snarled. He propelled himself up from the bed quickly and then the dizziness struck again. His head began to swim. "A second," he said and closed his eyes, standing squarely. But he felt Vincius move in next to him and put his arm around his shoulders. "In Jupiter's name, Marcus, lean on me. It's what I'm here for."

Marcus heard Alexander's drawing of breath across the room. The man would detest having a Roman soldier invoking the gods in his house, Marcus reflected. Slowly, with his eyes half closed and his head swimming still, Marcus leaned on Vincius, slowly drew his tunic over his head and then put one foot in front of the other mechanically until they reached the doorway. There he turned, looked individually at the rabbi and at Alexander, tried to smile. "Thank you both, sincerely, for finding me on the beach, bringing me here and tending my injuries." There was a brief pause. "And rabbi," he said laconically, "I meant what I asked earlier."

Marcus saw the rabbi glance at him, acknowledge his remark and then look past him, toward his mother. "Perhaps," suggested the rabbi, coming forward, looking worried, "we oughtn't to move him so far away tonight, after all. My house is quite small, but it's close by. I can offer it to you for the night."

"No, no, rabbi," Miriam replied, "I assure you this will be best. Xenon, the army physician who has known him from birth, will see him when he returns. And Marcus is very strong, thank God."

"Thank God," the rabbi echoed, stepping outside into the darkness after them.

"Alexander," Vincius called loudly, "if I could just have some help from you getting Marcus up on my horse, we'll be on our way directly."

From the doorway, Alexander turned his head just past Vincius and spat. The saliva, Marcus noted, glistening pale and globular in the moonlight, landed not far from Vincius' boot. There was a sudden moment of tension all around. This time, Marcus was quite sure, Vincius noticed it too.

Marcus looked around at the four faces standing with him. In the distance, he saw Yared in the moonlight peaking his head out of a nearby building. It was past time to be gone. "Where's Argos?" he said. "I'm not riding with you, Vincius."

"You think you're riding your own horse home tonight?" asked Vincius, studying his face. "How many times have you fainted already today, Marcus? Five or six, at least? You get up on my horse when I tell you to. And that, my boy, is an order."

Vincius turned from him then, curtly gave an order for Alexander to hold onto Marcus for a few moments as Vincius lifted Miriam onto her horse. When she was settled on top, her narrow undertunic pushed high up her thighs, but her loose-fitting overdress and her mantle still carefully covered her bare legs. Vincius turned and vaulted onto his own horse in one neat movement. "Ready?" he said to Alexander. "Lift him now."

Marcus insisted on helping the two men until it became apparent, even to himself, that he was impeding progress. At which point, he looked back and forth between the two men, both of them exasperated at him, relaxed his body completely and let himself be lifted into Vincius' arms.

"Can either of you please explain to me what just went on back there," said Vincius. They had passed far beyond the small village some time ago. Marcus was leaning back into Vincius' chest. Vincius' left arm draped protectively around him, was holding him steady. He was so close he could smell Vincius' scent, earthy, mixed with a residual smell of leather, and underlying that, barely discernible, a sharpish bite of sweat. It was an agreeable scent, familiar. Vincius must have bathed after the drill, thought Marcus lazily. He let his body slacken into Vincius', felt Vincius' arm tighten around him a little more.

"He doesn't like us," Marcus babbled to him. "He didn't like me because I'm of mixed descent. He thinks I'm a mamzer. That's about the lowest slur imaginable to a Jew, for your information. And he didn't like you because you're a Roman soldier, and you blasphemed in his house. He wanted us out of there." Marcus' head felt hazy again from the poppy drink the rabbi had administered and his body felt far, far away. He was only dimly aware of pain. But in other ways, his senses seemed more acute than usual, even in the dark. His mother's mute distress at what he had just said to Vincius leapt out at him, like a mountain lion in the dark. The awareness of it washed over him, so tangible he could almost touch her pain. He looked over at her, then, but found it hard to discern her features in the blackness.

"And you think that mattered?" said Vincius. "Who cares what he thought? You shouldn't have stopped my examination. I'd have beaten him if he gave us any trouble."

"I rather think that's the point, Vincius dear," said Miriam. "Marcus didn't want you using brute Roman force on his nice, new friends."

"Mmm," said Vincius. "But it would have felt so satisfying."

Vincius must be joking, Marcus finally decided. The sensation of warmth from Vincius' body was lulling him back to sleep. He could hear the clink of the horses' bridles and the regular thud of their hooves as they cantered along the earthen road. And below that, he was aware of Vincius' heartbeat, the merest vibration, in counterpoint to the other sounds. It was so restful. Marcus relaxed completely and shut his eyes.

⸻❖⸻

"Is he asleep?" Miriam asked sometime later.

"I think so," said Vincius. He switched the reins temporarily to his left hand and drew his right hand gently through Marcus' hair. Then bent his neck slightly and kissed Marcus on the top of his head. Vincius glanced shyly toward Miriam. He had not done such a thing since Marcus was a young child. She did not appear to take it amiss, however. So Vincius asked her, "Are you okay? I've rarely seen him so battered."

195

Miriam slowed her horse to a walk, and Vincius, to keep pace, followed suit. He turned to assess her properly. Her face, a pale splash in the moonlight, looked worried and tired.

"Marcus' practically in the army now," she said dully. "I suppose I better habituate myself to it."

Vincius nodded, sympathetic, but all the while his senses were distracted by something else. The moon, just past full, had reached the zenith of the sky and was shining straight down on the three of them, unimpeded by any shadow. To their right, as they rode, the sea rolled onto the beach, an illimitable darkness, punctuated here and there by moon-drenched foam. The waves rose and fell back, grinding into the sand in ceaseless rhythm. Vincius contemplated the scene for some moments as they rode together in parallel to the beach, and his body fell vulnerable to a tempo of its own. He expelled his breath once, a staccato sound, and forced his mind back to the subject at hand. "Still," he said to Miriam, "it was strange of Marcus to go off like that if he needed care. I'll address the situation tomorrow, find out who was responsible and why. And if he provoked an attack in any way."

"There's no point," said Miriam. "He won't tell you. He'll want to deal with it on his own."

"He'll want to, but that doesn't mean that he will. I may not let him." Vincius turned smiling to Miriam. He met her eyes. And succumbed for the countless time, a falling action. Very gradually, to give her time to hinder him if she wished, he moved his hand to her reins, took hold of them capably and halted both their horses. As she turned bodily to face him, questioning, he shifted both sets of reins to his other hand, and moved his horse next to hers, so that their thighs were touching. Slightly rubbing. In delicious friction. Vincius clasped her hand in his and, looking into her eyes, raised it slowly, to his lips. Surprisingly, she did not stop him. He tugged gently on her arm, reeling her body closer to his, her face next to his, her lips onto his. And kissed her for a very long time.

196

"Not now. Not with Marcus in your arms between us," Miriam whispered at last and began to withdraw her hand incrementally from his. "For God's sake, Vincius."

"He's asleep," Vincius protested. Marcus has always been a barrier between us, he thought half bitterly. But he let go of Miriam's hand just the same.

He was not asleep. Not yet. Nor was he surprised. By anything that had happened on the ride home. For one, it all felt so distant. There had been a moment when he had had the strangest feeling that he did not mind sharing Vincius' warmth with his mother. His mind, probing, found that thought disturbing, but his body felt so relaxed from the medicine that it failed to elicit a wilfull protest. He knew he might feel very differently about this later on. But for now, he let go of the problem and fell asleep.

CHAPTER 14

Fight Club

Escaping from behind a cloud, the sun sparkled unfettered, signaling its victory in the sky. Precisely at that moment, the angling sunlight, peering through the columns of the *gymnasium* and into the open hall where the men were training, registered on Marcus' mind as a problem. He pulled his shield up toward his face and, under that cover, let his eyes dart left for the merest second to note the position at which the sun was hanging in the sky. His eyes forward once more, he targeted his shield to deflect the sun's rays straight into the face of Critias, his opponent. Then he lunged and hit. A light touch only, but sufficient. Critias stood back from him as they saluted each other perfunctorily and then began to fight once again. But now, of course, since he had played his trick, he had to be aware that at any moment Critias was likely to use the stratagem against him.

As he fought on and on, Marcus' mind emptied of every tangent, every exigency but the scene before him. The anger that had been driving him for weeks after his physical recovery vanished from his conscious mind. He lived in the moment only, in the perfection of the details of his fighting abilities. Utterly focused, his weapons moved with precision, an extension of his body. Each separate movement that he made connected inexorably to the next. The gliding of his sandalled feet on the polished mosaic floor, the ringing of his heavy short sword against his opponent's, the twisting of his body as he ducked, retreated, turned, struck, paused, saluted and began to fight again. The movement too fast for thought, in that realm where instinct and tuition merge and mind and body flow as one. Unsustainable for long. But a joy to experience when it occurs.

This heightened state of concentration cannot last. Muscles begin to pall, individual senses reassert themselves. There is a first break in concentration. Eventually, mind and body disconnect from their flow and pull apart. And the body becomes vulnerable to error. Its brief, unfettered moment of unity finished, mind is returned to mortal status.

Today, as Marcus fought, this decline, this retreat from invulnerability, was signaled to him first by a few beads of sweat sliding down his short, dark, curly hair onto his forehead. The sweat trickled down his skin and then, as he twirled away from his opponent, Critias, it sprayed into his eyes. Momentarily blurring his vision, the drops stung him into awareness. The urge to use his hand to rub his eyes overwhelmed him. As neither of his arms were free, he forced himself to refrain. Instead, backing up rapidly, away from Critias, Marcus cocked his head and shook the sweat out of his eye. At best, a temporary palliative. And he had slowed down enough to become aware of the rate at which his heart was thudding in his chest. He continued to back away, to give himself some more moments to breathe easily. To ease the pain in his side he had not felt until now when his body's limitations began to intrude on him again. His brief escape from mortality was over for now, he realized. Until the next chance arrived to leave behind his mundane state for however short a duration. The need to do so recently had been driving him hard.

At that moment, Critias leapt once, twice and lunged low to the ground, his sword held straight out before him, his legs fully extended, his taller frame granting the illusion of boundless reach.

Marcus, sensing the shadow of movement before it occurred, bolted into action. Advancing, he parried the whisper of Critias' sword almost before the thrust arrived. He feinted right, ducked below Critias' counter, and then instantly jammed Critias' thumb knuckle with the flat of his sword so hard that Critias' palm jerked open, and he dropped his sword. Hooking Critias' overextended left leg with his own, Marcus knocked him off balance, then kicked him forcefully onto the hard polished floor. And kicked him again. He followed through by placing the point of his sword precisely at the vulnerable point where Critias' jaw was connected to his neck.

"Marcus, enough!" The peremptory voice intruded on the scene, descending from above his shoulder, high up in the balcony.

Pursing his mouth, holding his jaw tight, Marcus chose to look straight ahead, to ignore the voice. He had been ignoring that voice, or expressly countermanding what it said to do, for weeks. Since he woke up on the day after his accident, in fact.

"Do you yield?" he barked instead at the young man on the ground. In breach of the practice code, he pressed his dull practice sword point a little deeper into Critias' neck until a bud of skin, sundered by his blade, began to blossom pink, then red. For moments, he stared steadily down at his opponent, seeing someone entirely different on the ground, an entirely different scene. Moonlit. His senses drugged into compliance. The salty smell of the sea in the spring air. A heart beating comfortingly that was not his own. Until slowly, the tide of red blood on Critias' neck overran the ghostly white haze in his mind's eye.

He came to himself completely as Critias enclosed his left hand around the sword, exerting pressure to push it up and away. Marcus shook his head in bemusement. And in a rush, he released the pressure on his blade, allowing Critias to ease the sword away from his neck.

"Of course, I yield, you bastard," Critias snarled. He sat up slowly, ignoring the blood, nursing his right hand in his left, against his chest. "What the hell did you do to me just now? I think you broke my thumb." He glanced up, grimacing slightly. But looking as if he were working very hard to suppress a much fuller grimace. His short brown hair was coated with sweat. And his upper torso. Marcus saw him shiver slightly, once.

He stood still, his jaw stiff, looking down at Critias. In the background, Marcus heard the drone of conversation, the clatter of metal on metal, the fall of feet pacing back and forth. He thought, what was I thinking just now? Why have I done this? He knew, of course. His mind remembered fractured portraits from that moonlit night. But the answer was too disturbing to chase down.

He was still standing over Critias looking down at him when a hand gripped his shoulder hard from behind and pulled him back several paces. There was nothing gentle about that grip. Marcus identified the feel of Rufinus' presence without looking around. Rufinus, his sword master, his favorite teacher. A consummate professional. Not someone who would look kindly on this violation in the practice bout with Critias. Justly so.

Instinctively, Marcus twisted out of from Rufinus' grip. He ducked down rapidly, and rolled forward, head over heels, toward Critias. Coming up on his knees next to him, he offered him a hand back up. "I'm an idiot. I lost my head," Marcus said, his eyes wide, sincere. He attempted a smile, but it stalled on the threshold. "Forgive me." He glanced once back over his shoulder at Rufinus, noting that his complexion was beginning to suffuse. And jerked his head forward again. He had better, Marcus thought, behave very carefully for the rest of the day. For the rest of the month. By Charon, for the rest of his natural life. Otherwise, he would be crossing the River Styx much sooner than he had planned. He had seen the results on other students when Rufinus' complexion turned that particular shade of red before. They were not pretty.

"Ouch. Not that hand, cunt," yelped Critias. "If you are going to try to make amends, at least be careful." Very gingerly, Critias extended his left hand into Marcus' left, allowing himself to be pulled up.

Side by side, they turned and walked the few paces across the sun-drenched hall to face Rufinus, to listen to his exposition of each one of their fighting errors. Just before they reached him, Critias surreptitiously ran the fingers of his left hand over Marcus' forearm, a light touch. It signaled something. Forgiveness perhaps? Marcus hoped so.

Rufinus stood stock still as they walked up to him, his left fingers curled tightly around a wooden practice staff. He looked grim, his habitual expression. There was nothing to be read in that. He nodded at both of them, stepping up to Critias and examining cursorily first his neck and then his right hand. Rufinus handed Critias a rough linen cloth to staunch the sluggish discharge of blood at his neck. "It's doesn't look too bad," he said.

Critias put his hand to his neck and felt the wound, then placed the patch of linen on top of it. "It'll heal," he said. Critias shot Marcus a look, then turned back to Rufinus. "It's little more than a nick."

Rufinus' lips curled upwards slightly. "Oh, I think it's more serious than a nick. Don't underplay it on Marcus' behalf." He nodded and shut his eyes. Marcus knew from prior experience that Rufinus was revisualizing the fight, replaying the succession of moves in his head. Rufinus' capacity for evoking details, dissecting problematic bits of a much longer chain of action, was legendary, a trait both feared and admired by his students.

Only recently had Rufinus paired Marcus with Critias, a youth from a Greek merchanting family in Caesarea. Critias' family had lived in Caesarea for four generations, a part of the Greek-speaking majority that controlled civilian offices in the city. His family's villa, an immense two-story affair fronted with a formal portico containing twelve Corinthian columns, was nearby Marcus' own. They were on the same street, overlooking the sea, although Critias' was much closer to the town center and was by far the grander. The two families knew each other slightly from his mother's trading associates and his father's political connections. But they had not socialized together until now, when the first tentative contacts between Critias and Marcus had taken place after their training sessions at the *gymnasium*. There was too much of a gap in their social circumstances.

The inhabitants of Caesarea, Greek, Jewish and Roman, still retained bitter ancestral memories of the causes leading up to the Jewish Revolt close to sixty years ago. Before the war, the Jewish colony in that city had been an affluent minority of some 20,000 people primarily belonging to the merchant class, a wealthy community, richer than the Greco-Syrian majority. And uniquely among the Greco-Syrian cities of Judea, the Jewish inhabitants enjoyed equal status as citizens of Caesarea. This state of affairs had continued in a rough sort of stasis for decades. Finally, motivated by Greco-Syrian bribe money, Emperor Nero had promulgated an edict rescinding the rights of the Jews in that city, an action that only succeeded in heightening the tensions between the Greeks and the Jews. Street battles had erupted, in which at one time Greeks, another time Jews were slain. At last, the Greeks conspired with Florus, the Roman procurator of Judea, to incite the Jews to riot on a Sabbath. As a result of this action, almost the entire population of the Jews was slaughtered. And those who escaped were sent by Florus to the galleys to be sold into slavery.

Afterward, as the war against the Jews spread from the municipality throughout the entire province of Judea, the townspeople of Caesarea were well rewarded for their alliance and their loyalty to Rome; first by Vespasian and then by Titus, his successor as General in Judea and, later, on the Roman Imperial Throne. Rome elevated Caesarea to a *colonia*, veterans of the Roman army were encouraged to settle in its environs, and its Greco-Syrian inhabitants were granted a cessation from certain onerous taxes. These privileges were additional to the ones the Caesareans had already secured for themselves.

Unlike Marcus' previous sparring partners, Critias had no connection to the Roman army. Yet, he attended the gymnasium fanatically. Three years older than Marcus, eighteen instead of fifteen, he was several fingers' breadth taller than him, and weighed considerably more. His shoulders had already widened with corded muscle and hard training.

Insulted at first when Rufinus had paired him with Marcus, Critias realized his error soon into their first practice bout. The slender boy he had initially scorned disarmed him neatly once and then several more times in the course of their first long bout. Critias fought on, abandoning his cockiness, and then attempting, without any success that day, to salvage his shredded self-confidence. He had been practicing with Marcus ever since. But as Critias now had a distinctly healthy respect for Marcus' abilities, the results were generally more even than that first fight would seem to have augured.

Until today.

And that, Marcus reflected, was a shame. He would regret it for a long time to come if he had sacrificed Critias' companionship due to momentary recklessness. Marcus had worked very hard on making sure the tally of their fights remained close.

Rufinus said, "In a few minutes, Critias, I'll send you down to have the slave in the bathhouse look over your hand. It's already swelling."

He nodded his chin in Critias' direction. "But first, provide me with a critique of your own performance just now."

Marcus moved his eyes slightly and regarded Critias from under his eyelids. Critias' eyes were on the ground, and his color had risen. "Which part, sir?" said Critias, his voice low.

"The end, of course," said Rufinus, his lips twitching upward in amusement.

Critias nodded and raised his head slightly from its downward tilt. "I appear to have rushed the ending." He glanced at Marcus. "I thought Marcus was having trouble. But perhaps it was only a ruse. I didn't stop to consider that. So, I exploited my advantage, or tried to." Critias eyes were on the ground again. "I was impatient to finish him off and overextended, leaving myself slower to get out of position and open to counterattack." Critias raised his eyes and looked straight at Rufinus. "As happened, sir."

"As happened," Rufinus repeated. Rufinus' expression was scathing, his clear eye and his filmy blue eye were both directed straight at Critias. "Perhaps you will keep this slight embarrassment in mind next time you think you have the advantage, so you will be spared another such humiliation. It might save your life one day in a real fight. Hein?" His look roamed over the two youths standing before him. "Constant vigilance!" he barked. And even after years of training with Rufinus, both Marcus and Critias jumped at his words.

"Dismissed," Rufinus said to Critias. "As for you Marcus, you will accompany me to my office." The tone of voice in which he said this was not very reassuring.

Marcus had only time to register the furtive grin Critias directed toward him and his hand signal to meet him in the bath house before he turned on his heel. Following after Rufinus, he crossed the entire length of the sunlit hall, walking behind him toward the cramped, walled off section where Rufinus kept his desk and some of his possessions. Stored around the room were old and new swords. The blade of one of them, Marcus noticed, had broken off crookedly. There was a set of armor needing repair, as the bronze wire holding its iron scales together had twisted until the armor appeared misshapen. And sprawled across the chipped marble table there were a few scrolls, a stylus, a sheaf of parchment and a bronze ink jar enameled in bright green and blue. Rufinus was roughly literate, but he was not numerate. He had a Greek slave who kept accounts for him punctiliously.

The atmosphere inside the office had changed. No longer the fetid smell of drying sweat and salt in the gymnasium, instead, the air was infiltrated by dampness and must. There had been a collapse in the heating system recently which was not yet fully repaired. Marcus had heard that most of the damage to the hypocaust had occurred in this section of the hall.

He stood at attention and watched while Rufinus settled himself into a tripod folding chair behind his table, the wooden staff still upright in his hand. He waited a long time, his arms linked behind his back, as Rufinus stared at him, his eyes raking over every bit of him.

"Sit," Rufinus commanded at last.

Marcus backed toward another of the tripod chairs, standard military design for army camps, an unsurprising choice for the office of a veteran. He folded himself into the chair in one fluid motion, sitting upright, his legs spread apart, his eyes directed downward and waited for Rufinus to speak.

After several moments, Rufinus said, "There has been a change in you these last few weeks, Marcus. This fight today, for instance. It was both brilliant and deplorable. You made a brilliant recovery. That was no ruse, whatever Critias might suspect. But what led you to humiliate him once he was down on the ground? To draw blood from his neck in a practice bout, when he was already laid out on the floor? I thought he was your friend." There was a pause as Rufinus stopped speaking and looked disgusted. "Where is your head, boy?

I have never seen you do anything vicious like that." He shook his head. "It was gratuitous, nasty. There was no strategy to it at all."

Marcus remained silent. What, after all, could he say? He agreed with the assessment of his behavior. But he was hardly going to offer a reason for it when he did not want to think about it himself.

"Something has been goading you lately," said Rufinus. "I wish I knew what it was. Your fighting has been inspired, but I don't like the effect it's having on your character." Rufinus peered at him, but Marcus' eyes were still carefully directed toward the ground that lay between him and the master. He added, in the gentlest tone Marcus had ever heard him use. "Vincius believes you feel humiliated by what happened to you at the drill a month ago. And you are working it out on the men around you."

Marcus looked up. "Vincius," he scoffed. "What does he know about me?" Clamping his jaws shut, he stopped himself from scoffing. To have said even so little to the sharp-tongued master, Marcus realized, was enough to confirm to Rufinus that something had happened, to redirect Rufinus' suspicions where he did not want them to be. To alert him to something Marcus did not want him to know. He moved his face so that he was not making eye contact with Rufinus, shifting his eyes back down to the ground.

"So," said Rufinus at last. He nodded his head. "You should know, I asked Vincius for his opinion. That was the reason he was here today. Your behavior has been perplexing me. And with your father still away in Zeugma..."

Marcus picked up his head to find Rufinus still scrutinizing him. His teeth clenching, Marcus glared back at him. A shot at random? He felt sure not.

"I agree with you, however, that it was unfortunate he interceded when he did," said Rufinus dryly. "It had the opposite effect of what he intended. Although I don't suppose you are going to tell me why."

Marcus kept glaring at Rufinus, but he said nothing. The old man had an uncanny ability to read one's mind. He was not going to provide him any help.

"As long as you know the answer yourself then," Rufinus said. "I suppose you do."

Oh, he knew the reason he had reacted like that all right. If he were honest, Marcus admitted to himself, his anger had been growing for weeks. Maybe even longer. Now that was an unpleasant thought.

But a true one. To act on emotional grounds, he thought then, was the surest way to lose control in a fight. He had had a lesson in that today, one he would not forget soon. Emotions only fogged the issue. Cold, clear logic is what makes a man prevail.

Marcus looked up, realizing only then that Rufinus had sat quietly and watched the play of all these thoughts crossing his face. He cursed silently. To have imparted even this much made him feel unguarded. Unfortunately, he had excellent reasons for never revealing what he knew about this matter to anyone. Nor even hinting at it.

"I have something else to say to you before I dismiss you," said Rufinus. "I have always trained my young officers to fight cleanly. Not to invest their own hatreds into their fights with each other. Viciousness, in a commander, is something I cannot admire. And, indeed, in my experience, it works against the interests of everyone involved, the individual, his corps and of Rome. I'll not tolerate the merest glimmer of it in my school, Marcus. All it can do is breed bad blood, and to no purpose, among men who should be allies. For the next fifteen days, you will not be welcome here." Rufinus' eyes were scouring him now. "During this period, I expect you to reflect on what I have said. Think about what has been driving you these last weeks. And divest yourself of it. I don't want it here. Remember, a professional officer should never allow his personal feuds to encroach upon his command. Study your history, boy. Viciousness and revenge are extremely poor predictors of success in battle. And success in battle is what you must aim for, not any vendetta of your own." Rufinus stood up and so perforce did Marcus. "Now, go," he barked. "You are dismissed."

CHAPTER 15

Boys' Night Out

Marcus slipped into the small semi-private bath that serviced the *gymnasium*. He spotted Critias at once, at the far end of the pool, still lolling in the tepidarium. Marcus pulled off his sweaty tunic, knelt briefly to unlace his sandals and shoved them into a vacant cubby hole. He jumped into the steamy pool of the near empty caldarium. The water shot up in a jet, wetting his head, splashing over the rim of the pool and onto the stone walkway. The bath boy in the corner, dressed in a plain white linen robe, shot him a sour look before scurrying over with towels to mop up the floor.

The truth was now that Marcus was here, he felt a bit wary. But there was no point in alienating everyone in proximity. He fully planned on returning to the *gymnasium* as soon as Rufinus would permit him. And he preferred it when the help he received was not grudging. Marcus climbed out of the caldarium sedately enough and entered the tepidarium with hardly a ripple.

Critias was floating at the far end of the pool with his eyes closed and his thumb wrapped in linen and held aloft, half soaked despite his attempts to keep the bandage dry. "You're here at last," he said and smirked. "What did Rufinus do to you in the end? I've been savoring the thoughts of dire punishments meted out to you without even having to lift the finger you busted."

"Principally," said Marcus, "he warned me against the evils of pursuing revenge. Bad for Rome, bad for morale, bad for the soul. In that order." He watched the smile begin to fade from Critias' face. And added quickly, before Critias' visage had a chance to turn darker, "Don't worry, he suspended me for fifteen days as well. Time to read history and reflect on my misdeeds away from the *gymnasium*. Perhaps not dire enough, you're thinking? But myself, I'd have preferred something immediate and painful. For one thing, I could soak it away here in the baths and there'd be nothing to explain back home."

"But wasn't that your guard dog up in the balcony today? Watching over his prize pup? Surely, he'd report it back to his paymaster if you didn't."

When Marcus spoke again, the light tone that he had been working hard to maintain had entirely faded from his voice. "Ah, yes," he said quietly. "I was forgetting Vincius. How strange of me. It would have been painful and there would have been something to explain in any case. And this way, at least, I get time off to read history. Which pleases everyone. Critias, let's get the hell out of here."

"My dear boy. Still that impatience of yours. I'm not even completely bandaged yet."

"That's true," said Marcus. He grimaced. "You might as well let me see my own handiwork up close now that the blood is gone." He stepped closer tentatively, the water exaggerating his slowness as he moved forward, then leaned in. Critias was standing now, the water sliding down his chest. Some drops of water, not yet fallen, were still balancing on his shoulders and clinging to his hair. Raising his left hand, Marcus lightly touched the cleft skin below Critias' neck. Until Critias' fingers firmly enclosed his wrist.

"Marcus," Critias said in an undertone.

Critias' fingers were still folded around his arm. Marcus moved his arm away from Critias and looked up. Even with the warm water he was soaking in, it was plain to see that his friend's color had risen.

"What?" said Marcus, stepping back. He felt his color rising too. "What?" he repeated. "I do this in camp all the time." He jutted his chin out. "It's important for a commander to learn the seriousness of wounds, so he can judge his men's injuries."

"But I'm not one of your men," murmured Critias. "Not yet, at least."

"I'll live in hope." The light tone he had used previously had returned.

"Tell me something, Marcus. Sometimes I wonder how you tolerate Vincius. Today for instance," he said. "He's essentially your father's spy, isn't he, a threat to keep you in line?"

Marcus opened his mouth to answer. Took a long breath. And shut it without saying a word. He looked away. "Rufinus sent for him today, God knows why."

"So, it's a conspiracy against you. They're all your nursemaids, every last one." The mockery was back in Critias' voice.

He could beat Critias in a fight, Marcus thought. But he did not yet possess Critias' ability to cut any which way with his voice. It was something to aspire to in the future.

"In any case, you've misunderstood me. I'm staying a merchant," said Critias, "it's far more lucrative. But were I to enlist, it's not Vincius I'd need your protection from." As they were speaking, Critias had begun to lift himself out of the pool. Arms flexed, first his head and back rose fully out of the blue green water. Then, he levered his right leg onto the edge of the pool, and his muscles tensed, his rear and long legs appeared, the water sliding off of his skin. Pausing a moment at the edge of the pool, Critias bent to grab a linen sheet from a nearby marble bench. He stuck it under his arm and paced toward the massage tables on the other end of the hall. But before he disappeared from view, he turned his head back over his shoulder toward Marcus and smiled once. "It's your father."

Marcus stared at him. "My father?" he called after him. "Whatever for?"

But Critias had already gone. Marcus pulled himself out of the pool. And mused, I didn't think Critias even knew my father. Shrugging into the empty air, at no one in particular, Marcus stepped into the next room and dove hard into the frigidarium.

The night sky was airless and sandy, hot and dry. And for once, the breeze from the sea alleviated nothing, but only made things worse, as its fingers scattered sand and its voice hissed restlessly. The stars were swallowed up and the sky glinted red.

Despite the stifling conditions, and the incentive it created to stay indoors with shutters barred tight, Marcus found himself this night, a few days after his encounter with Critias at the baths, standing on the edge of the balcony outside his room, contemplating the climb down to the ground, his arm resting lightly on a pillar for balance. It was close to midnight. He crouched down, holding hard onto the edge and lowered himself until his legs connected to the fluted column on the story below. Gripping it, he shimmied down the rest of the way. Silently crossing the front garden, Marcus climbed over the gate and set off, a darting shadow in the deserted streets.

He identified music even before he entered the vine encrusted pergola, the sweet sound of strummed lyres rising above the discordant, trilling wind. And then, overriding the music, he heard voices arguing, the sound slurred, indistinct as it penetrated the wooden walls of the outbuilding. Marcus rested a moment, poised at the lintel. And then pushed the door to and entered.

Inside, the air felt dense with dust and smoke and wine fumes. Marcus shut the door and looked around. As his eyes adjusted to the half-light, produced by a mass of small oil lamps, Marcus recognized Critias reclining on a couch across the room. He spied three more couches arranged around an unlit brazier in the center of the floor, each of them already occupied. And that was somewhat disconcerting.

"Ah, you made it," said Critias, lifting a hand and beckoning him in. He signed next to the slaves standing against the wall to resume plucking their instruments. "I was just about to give up on you. And in this weather, no blame to you." Someone tossed a coin across the room toward Critias. Marcus caught a flicker of silver before Critias' left fist lifted up causally from the back of the couch to intercept it. He flipped it neatly onto the small table before him, into a small puddle of spilt wine, and looked up at Marcus, chuckling. "Marcus, stop standing at the door, brooding like Achilles before his ships, refusing to come out to war. *He would not enter the assembly of emulous men, nor ever go to war.'* Come in already. Join our assembly. Drink some wine."

"You were betting on me?" said Marcus and stepped closer, so that he stood just slightly outside the circumference of couches.

He watched Critias' eyes flash to the young man sitting to his side, the young man who had tossed the coin. They both burst out laughing. "Of course, we were," said Critias. "Well, perhaps, not uniquely on you. But so far, you're the only bet I've won. I speculated you were a sure thing, and I was right. This is Dion, by the way. He lost the bet so don't expect him to be too friendly." Critias gazed up at him, his eyes shining, and as Marcus approached, he handed him a goblet of wine. "Don't be shy. Sit here with me. These couches were built to hold two." Critias shifted his feet slightly, making room at the bottom end of the couch.

Marcus sat down on the very edge of the couch as far away from Critias as possible, hooking his arm casually around the fulcrum of the symposium couch. He was amused to note that the post at his end was crowned by a stallion and at Critias' end a mare. On a different couch across the room, he saw Silenus crowning one post, and at the other, a satyr with an ivory wreath. He took a large sip of wine, then another. It tasted strong, sweetened with honey and scarcely watered. Fortified, he looked to the side. Critias' right thumb, he noted, was still bandaged in linen strips. Looking up, he met Dion's eyes, watching him.

"So, this is your furious protégé," Dion remarked to Critias. "No wonder you admitted nothing to us." Classical featured, curly haired, with dark almond shaped eyes, like the living embodiment of a young god painted on a vase, Dion was still staring at him. "He appears a mere boy," he said finally.

"You wouldn't think so if you saw him fight," said Critias, "as I can attest to my dismay." He waved his thumb in the air. "He's dangerous enough once he has weapons."

"He's deadly with his own weapons on the field, and yet, by all appearances, uncertain how to parry your advances on the couch. What are you waiting for, Critias? *Carpe noctem.*"

Laughter pealed around the room.

Dion grinned at him then so outrageously that Marcus almost relented and grinned back. The man possessed an infectious smile.

"Critias, hoist your weapon and attack." The man lying to Marcus' left had broken into the conversation. "Otherwise, Dion may slip his sword in where you have left him an opening." The man was fair haired, with a finely chiseled, expressive face and a trim build. The kind of build that might conceal great athleticism. Or perhaps not. Best, though, to be on guard until one was certain, Marcus thought. He glanced at Critias and finished off his wine.

Critias did not meet his eyes. Marcus turned his head to gaze at the other two members of Critias' party. And realized, concentrating hard in the smoky air, that he was the youngest of the four guests in

215

the room by several years. Well, no matter, Marcus thought, he spent most of his time in older company.

The man lying on the couch across the room from him had dark hair and a beard, a thin, long face, his eyes too narrowly spaced to achieve beauty. A silent presence, he had not uttered a word since Marcus entered, though he had laughed once, his voice sparkling. He spoke now, however. "I'm Timnas," he said in a low voice, "originally from Alexandria. I'm here on business, mostly with Critias' father." Marcus noted the accent of his Greek, its uniquely Alexandrian rhythm discernible above the music.

The fair-haired man smiled at Marcus as he regarded him again. In that moment, Marcus suddenly knew him.

"You're Phoenix, aren't you?" he said. "You used to study at the *gymnasium* several years ago?"

"Yes, of course." The long smile still flickered on Phoenix's lips. "I was wondering if you would remember. Even all those years ago we speculated you would turn into Rufinus' prodigy. And now, from what Critias has said, you have. Well done!"

"What!" said Dion, broodingly, "Critias didn't tell me any such thing."

His index finger under his bottom lip, Phoenix tilted his light-colored eyebrows and looked at Dion. "Evidently not," he said.

Dion colored slightly and bit off what he had planned to say.

"Phoenix has just returned from a several year trip to Athens..." said Critias.

"Still the cradle of civilization, he was assuring us," Dion broke in, "and so much preferable to this backwater we all inhabit."

"...where he was studying philosophy at the Academy." Critias finished speaking as though Dion had not interrupted him.

Phoenix flashed a grin at Marcus. "Don't believe a word Critias says. The truth is, I only ever meddled with philosophy. It's much too dangerous to my family's holdings to embrace full time, a point

216

my father made to me repeatedly while he was still alive, in letters he sent me monthly. And at enormous expense, I might add. Speaking of wasting the family patrimony."

"Not that we were," said Dion. "Phoenix, beware, you are in danger of boring us again."

Phoenix turned suddenly and wagged his finger at Dion.

Dion flashed his marvelous smile in Marcus' direction. "Phoenix is slightly irritated with me, you see. Before you came in, he was regaling us with some miserable poetry he wrote himself on the voyage home and he did not like my commentary."

"Dion, typical critic." Phoenix turned to Marcus, *"His taste is keen, although his verse is harsh."*

The night wore on, with Marcus, in his self-appointed role of observer, keeping his eyes peeled wide. Dion and Phoenix remained endlessly locked in repartée, tallying hits back and forth. Critias, his voice slurring from the quantity of wine he had consumed, broke in from time to time, occasionally scoring a point of his own.

Marcus was used to a certain level of sexually laced badinage in the background from his time training among his father's men and from time spent talking to the men in the barracks. But listening now, he realized, how little of it had ever been directed at him. He had always known in one way or another that his father had made his protection over him very plain to his men. Marcus supposed Julius had done this indirectly, although he hadn't a clue as to how it had been achieved. He wondered, suddenly, if Phoenix had known his father during the time he attended Rufinus' weapons training at the *gymnasium*. His father had accompanied him occasionally then. Looking back and forth between Phoenix and Critias, he realized something important.

Marcus relaxed completely then. He sat back on the couch, listening to the voices squabbling in counterpoint to the music, and started drinking to catch up to the others. When Critias' sandal-less feet brushed across his thigh from time to time, he simply redirected them. At a certain point, he began to notice that Timnas, his face oddly lit in the smoky room, began looking at him pointedly. Odd how off-putting that felt. Critias had looked at him in a similar way now and then, and he had never thought twice about it until now. For the most part, he enjoyed Critias' companionship. That was the difference, perhaps. Tonight, however, his friend, drunk and abandoned, had not provided the best company.

Eventually, Timnas's continuing regard made Marcus extremely uncomfortable, and his relaxation ebbed. Chary and restless, he stood up to leave. Critias, who seemed ready to fall asleep on the couch next to him at any minute, barely lifted his head off the couch to say goodbye. He nodded slightly and sunk back into the couch. His arm flopped down off the couch, knocking over his glass goblet, shattering it and spilling the last of the wine. Marcus croaked a laugh, nodded farewell and turned to face the others. Phoenix looked, he thought, as though he wanted to stop meddling with philosophy forthwith and to start meddling with Dion instead. It was the intent light in his eye that gave him away. Whereas Dion seemed to flirt with equal generosity with everyone. Suspended in dialogue, chasing after Eros, neither Phoenix nor Dion lifted a head from their respective cushions to say goodbye. Though Dion did wave at him, airily, from his couch, smiling one last time. Marcus, half unsteady, his body in dissolution, slunk off to depart.

He opened the door and stood gazing out into the predawn light, breathing in the dusty, heavy air. More drunk than he had ever been in his life, Marcus walked through the garden, then treaded his way carefully up the deserted road. Finally, he stood before his house, staring silently up at the balcony. The thought of climbing all the way up the column of the portico was daunting in his current state, even with the help of the vines winding up to the balcony. He grabbed hold of the column before his nerve failed him and climbed up slowly without looking down once. When he reached the top, his breath was ragged and he felt nauseous.

Marcus fell into bed, but rose an hour later, in the full muted dawn light to vomit his guts up into a bronze ewer by his bed, over and over. He had not even tried to make it to the toilet.

PART XI

CHAPTER 16
A Villain Returns

Several days later, Marcus was sitting on a marble bench near the harbor of Caesarea, the breeze from the sea washing over him, bored and distracted.

His eyes wandered over the assortment of smaller wooden boats tied up close to the shore. And then he looked further out to sea, to the far end of the enormous harbor, where the ships were docked. He had sent a letter to his uncle last week by way of a courier, a man traveling on such a ship to Ephesus and then on to Sardis by post horse. It had cost him a small fortune. The courier was a business connection of Critias' father. Marcus had been worried about entrusting him with the document, but Critias, mocking his anxiety, had badgered him into believing that the man should be trusted.

His mother had her own network of couriers that she patronized. But Marcus had not wanted to use one of them. He had not wanted her to know that he was writing to Yehonatan. Or why.

Marcus finished his street food, bread and mashed fûl with olive oil and herbs, wiped his hands on his sky-blue tunic and stood, stretching lazily. Normally, he would be training this time of day. But he was still expelled. The lack of routine was beginning to drive him mad. His body craved some release, some hard physical activity. Walking about the harbor and hanging around with Critias' friends in the evenings no longer seemed a sufficient alternative.

He wandered off to the agora, a sweaty walk at mid-day now that the humidity had risen. There Marcus stood, his hand brushing back his damp hair from his brow, studying the contents of a fine shop, prominently placed along a portico, with an exhibit of weapons. It sold wooden swords for children to learn to fight, the way he had. They had leaf-shaped daggers with thin metal blades. The nicest of the daggers had sheathes beautifully decorated with inlaid silver and colored gemstones. There were short swords for fighting men, and longer swords for the cavalry. And then there were the bows. There was one, in particular, artfully wrought of horn, wood and sinew, and carved with antlers, that he had his eye on. What a dream to use that for hunting wild goat, roe deer and ibex from horseback instead of his father's cast-off bow, that he had to keep repairing lest it fall to pieces. When the merchant approached to inquire if he wanted to buy anything, he said, "Not today," and walked on. All his ready money had gone on sending that letter to Yehonatan.

Across the way, there was a shop containing jewels he had visited once with his uncle to buy a present for his mother before his departure. Today, on display, he noticed a chain, thick as gnarled grape vines. Attached to it was a small golden disk on which the head of Emperor Hadrian was coined in detail, his long straight nose, the curly locks on his head brushed smooth on top and his short, neatly clipped beard, unusual in a Roman Emperor. Some said the Emperor wore the beard to conceal a battle wound, others that he wore it to imitate the Greek philosophers he admired so much.

All around Marcus there was ceaseless bustle in the marketplace. He felt someone brush him, passing by in haste. But he had no reason to move down the avenue to see why the man was rushing. A procession of visiting dignitaries was about to sweep through town. There would be a bottleneck further up the street the man wanted to avoid. Marcus had already sensed, among the shopkeepers and pedestrians crowding near him, an undercurrent of excitement, a spontaneous ferment awaiting only the arrival of the procession down the wide avenue before it exploded into celebration.

And now Marcus could see the cavalcade arriving. He had an impression of a panoply of color. Men atop their horses, brown and black and gray. Dressed in red and brown and blue cloth. Their odd bits of armor glimmering in the white light. The horses swept along the crowds, their hooves clopping rhythmically on the stone road.

Yet, after the first seconds, alone in the standing crowd, it was not at the procession that Marcus looked, but the man at its head. A man who was little changed in the three years since Marcus had seen him last. Marcus gauged him perhaps stockier than once he had been. But the man's razored brown hair was cut in the same fashion and his round face with its pocky skin and the long, mobile mouth was otherwise unchanged. And the startling intelligence that molded his face and informed his eyes.

He stood watching, transfixed, as the man tramping past him on his Iberian gelding looked straight at him. After the first moment he smiled, full mouthed, exposing his teeth.

Someone put a hand on his shoulder and Marcus jumped. Then relaxed. It was only Critias.

"Look, the dolphin and the bull. That's the banner of the Xth Fretensis," Critias said. "Is that your father leading his men?"

Marcus was still facing forward, watching the front of the procession ride by him. "Where?" he said after a moment and turned his head. Until Critias spoke, he had not noticed his father's face in the mix, half a column behind Galenus, with Xenon, the company medic, by his side. Good God, he thought, if his father were planning on spending any time together with Galenus in Caesarea, it could turn into a disaster. He had to avert what might follow. He had recognized Galenus with no trouble at all. There was no reason to believe that sharp-eyed Galenus had not remembered him just as clearly.

Marcus turned his head to look at Critias. "I've got to go," he said, "quickly." Marcus started walking fast, dodging around people in the crowded streets. He looked over his shoulder. "Where did you come from, by the way?"

"From the harbor. Had a meeting with Phoenix, but he never came. Then I saw you across the market and decided to catch up." Critias paused to breathe. "Are you running off to join your father? Isn't it going to be a while before all this ceremony is over and he can actually see you?"

"If you must know," said Marcus, "I'm off to take a short ride on Argos. For a day or two."

"Good god, Marcus," said Critias. He stopped dead in the street and grinned. "Is this terror you are exhibiting? Of your father? You're that worried about what he'll do to you for getting expelled? You intrigue me."

"What?" said Marcus. "No, no, that's not it at all. What could my father do but beat me, and it's not as if he hasn't done that before. No, for imaginative and terrifying punishments, you'd need my uncle Yehonatan. And he emphatically is not here. I've not yet decided whether that's bad or good, given the circumstances."

"Which are?" said Critias.

"Disastrous," said Marcus. He nodded once and vanished in the crowd.

Marcus rode by a group of chattering horse boys mucking stalls, inhaling, as he passed, the familiar scents of hay and barley and manure. He exited the long, stone stable, directing his light gray Iberian horse toward the north gate of camp, towards the hillocks of the Carmel and the sea. He knew precisely where he was headed.

He thought of sea salt and seaweed and fish and a particular curve of coastline, as seductive to the eye as the newborn moon. Marcus had almost made it past the guarded entry when a voice he recognized too well shouted at him to halt. He spun his head about, then his entire body, nudging Argos to turn around in a tight semi-circle and making no effort to conceal the annoyance that he felt. The annoyance which, he was sure, was stamped on his face. Trapped by Vincius. For several cogent reasons, Vincius was the last person Marcus wanted to see just then.

"What now?" Marcus called; his tone as belligerent as he could make it.

Vincius, brown haired and vital, dressed in leather half-armor, his crested steel helmet tucked neatly under his left arm, crooked his index finger, and beckoned with it, repeatedly. "Come to me, Marcus. I want a word with you."

Marcus hesitated a few moments, then kicked his horse lightly, once, so that it moved toward Vincius.

"What?" he repeated. "I'm in a hurry just now."

"Too bad," said Vincius. He raised his eyebrows in question, but did not ask Marcus where he was headed. Until the silence between them grew taut and awkward. Then: "I simply wanted to see you, boy. You haven't been around for weeks. And I have been unable to get away to visit you." Vincius grinned at him then, warm, friendly, stalwart, and so very familiar. It was almost, but not quite, disarming. "Keeping this place up to par with both your father and Silius away for so long has been more work than I expected."

And modest. Marcus had forgotten to add modesty to his encomium. Everyone who knew Vincius was well aware he underplayed his strengths: his utter competence and his popularity with the men. The gesture on Vincius' part was so familiar and so grating just now that he had to restrain himself from rolling his eyes. For a moment, Marcus wished his father were here, just so that their eyes could meet, and they could share a knowing smile together. And then he remembered why he did not want his father anywhere near him and Vincius just then. "I've got to go, Vincius." He spoke quietly, and kept the anger out of his voice, letting logic override emotion, a charioteer forcefully reining in the black horse of rage.

Vincius stepped closer, laying his hand on Marcus' gray horse. He threaded his fingers through the Iberian's mane, gentling the horse, then looked up at Marcus and met his eye. "I'm sorry, lad, if my actions last week landed you in trouble with Master Rufinus.

Marcus held his hand up in check, palm outward. "Vincius, I'm not twelve years old anymore. You don't need to apologize to me for my own errors in judgment."

"Well, perhaps not." Vincius looked away, then eyed him again. "But my interceding in that fight only appeared to make things worse, not better. A feeling that was confirmed for me in the strongest possible terms when Rufinus personally escorted me out of the *gymnasium*, his arm draped around my shoulder, I'll have you know, without letting me talk to you." Vincius smiled ruefully. "Since he had asked me to come in the first place, it was rather peculiar. Wouldn't you agree?"

"Certainly, it was inconvenient."

"Yes. Inconvenient as well." Vincius' smile was still in place. "By the way, there was a courier this morning. Your father is due back here early this afternoon, although he will not be free right away. He's with a procession headed by the governor of Ashqelon who will be sticking around for a day or two, apparently. So, when you ride out, don't go too far. You'll be wanting to see him tonight, no doubt."

Marcus felt color surge into his cheeks. He could not help it. So he held his eyes very wide, looking at Vincius, and said, "No doubt. As do you." And was gratified to see the color spill into Vincius' face as well. Marcus smiled, half maliciously. "Goodbye for now, Vincius." Taking up his reins, he turned his gelding and rode hard for the gate.

But just before he exited, he looked back over his shoulder. "If you happen to see my mother," he shouted, "tell her I'm fine."

———◦———

Leaning back against the limestone wall of the stable, Vincius stood staring after Marcus as he rode out the gate, his right hand cupped over his eyes to shield them against the beating sun. He watched for a long time as the boy galloped northwest over the terrain leaving a train of illuminated dust motes dancing crazily in the air behind him before they sunk slowly back to earth. The young body was slightly lifted from the horse, the head and chest balanced forward for speed, the elbows tucked into his body, seamlessly displaying his years of training. The boy had always been a gratifying student. That much was true. Vincius was still watching as Marcus cut directly west toward the sea and vanished behind an outcropping of rock.

Finally, shaking his head, wiping the sweat that had accumulated on his brow with a hand grimy from weapon grease, Vincius pushed himself upright to head back in the direction of his office. He beckoned Scipio, his aide de camp, who had stood gossiping at the gate all this time with the soldiers standing watch. Frowning, Vincius handed the man his helmet, silently signaled him to follow in his wake, and began to walk to the barracks, the nails on the soles of his military boots striking crisply on the cut stone path, rap, tap, rap.

That something was troubling Marcus had been evident to Vincius. Yet, frustrating to him as a Euclidean proof he could not visualize, the solution had eluded his capture. Until just now. Why that thought had not occurred to him until now, he did not know. Marcus had apparently not been fully asleep that other night when he and Miriam carried him home from that rabbi's obscure village. Well, he had no time to mull over it now, the damage was already done. And he had business to do now, all the business of readying the camp to be handed back over to his commander's control.

At the thought of Julius' return, Vincius grimaced. He had been feeling anxious himself all day, his stomach muscles cramping at the oddest times, reminding him again and again of his vulnerabilities. To Miriam. And to Julius, if he ever found out what had happened in his absence, meager though it was. And more than that, Vincius was cognizant of how little he would like passing the reins of authority back over to Julius.

Fully trained and prepared for additional responsibility, Vincius had relished every minute of the power he had wielded these last two months. And to be reduced again to Julius' senior aide felt a humiliation, even apart from the emotional complications it created. Which rendered it a double blow. During a few moments in these last two months, Vincius had felt, actually felt, for the first time ever, that there was some hope for him as far as Miriam was concerned. But that had proven chimerical, a cruel illusion. And now, his hope turned back, shut from every shore, and barred from every inlet, there existed only his abiding passion for a woman with whom he believed he would never rest at port, and a return to a state of total restraint under Julius' constant eye and Marcus' ongoing hostility. Vincius sighed. The prospect ahead felt unbearable already.

CHAPTER 17

Runaway

In the weeks that had followed his initial meeting, Marcus had occasionally visited Rabbi Ariel. But, by now, the visits, which had been at best sporadic, had completely died out. So, he faced some embarrassment, both social and personal, as he made his way, slowing Argos to a dignified trot, to the small fishing village the rabbi inhabited. Just before he entered the hamlet, by a rough stone wall surrounding a grove of riotously fruiting olive trees, fuzzy and sun scented, Marcus stopped his horse to concoct a plausible excuse for his visit, unfurling his imagination like a gladiator casting a weighted net. He let fly, but the net came back empty. Nothing suggested itself to him; his inventiveness was in tatters. Thoughts slipped through his fingers, fragments of nothingness.

He proceeded some minutes later, propelled onward, not by desire, but by fear oozing up his entrails, which made him feel a coward and by sheer will power. Under the circumstances, Marcus decided, pragmatic at last, that social embarrassment was a necessary price to pay. At the edge of the village, he gave one last backward glance towards the vanishing marble grace of Caesarea, his home, and rode straight down a little incline toward the small stone house the rabbi and his family occupied.

The rabbi, he learned only then, was not at home.

———•———

Devorah stood framed in the doorway and watched as a Roman horseman approached the village, riding forward with aplomb. It was not until he stopped the horse right in front of her house that she realized, looking up at him, that the horseman was a boy and not a man at all, and, in fact, a bit younger than herself. She scrutinized him, noting clipped brown hair that still curled slightly despite its brevity, eyes a startling blue in his tanned face. He wore a sky-blue linen tunic edged in white, finely worked leather sandals and an over-confident manner. His tunic, Devorah noticed critically, dusty and sweat stained, and now undoubtedly smelling of horse, was long past appearing fresh.

She had brown hair herself, long and luxurious, although it did not curl. Right now, though, her hair was dirty and braided tightly around her head to minimize the effect. She wished she had covered it. And her eyes, to her chagrin, were a flat brown, not the color of the eastern sky at twilight.

In the end, it was his manner that decided Devorah and not his appearance. He was too self-possessed for a boy younger than herself. It impressed her which annoyed her. So, growling slightly, she held her rough linen gown closely to her body, stepped forward into the glinting sunlight, westering this time of the day, and confronted the Roman boy. "What do you want here?" she asked him in polished Greek.

He blinked and held up his hand, tented, over his eyes. "Dazzled by the reflection of the sun," he said and smiled at her. "I beg your pardon. I didn't see you standing there."

Devorah blushed. "And you are?" she said. Her voice was still gruff.

"Here to see the rabbi," he answered still smiling, polite. Not surprisingly, his Greek was native. "I understood that this was his house." His eyebrows went up. "It is his house, isn't it?"

She put her hands on her hips and pursed her lips, waiting.

His horse passaged, jerking the reins in his still hands. The boy steadied the gelding, turning him around and when he finished maneuvering, he looked down at her again, still smiling. Devorah decided that she did not like the smile. She felt something slightly mocking in it. There was silence as he looked her up and down, consideringly.

Finally, the boy said, speaking softly, "The rabbi invited me to come speak to him from time to time. Can you tell me if he is at home or out at work?"

He had switched to Aramaic, Devorah noted with surprise, because that sounded native, too. Finally, she brought to mind a bit of stray gossip she had heard in town. Something about a boy, Alexander, a neighbor of theirs, had found on the beach, bloodied. Her father had helped to clean the boy up. She had been away, visiting relatives, when it occurred. "Oh," she said at last. "You're the ma..." and clamped her mouth hard.

"I'm Marcus," he said, and swiped at his brow with the sweat stained sleeve of his tunic. "I gather you have heard of me already."

This time his smile was definitely mocking.

⸺⸺◆⸺⸺

Rabbi Ariel saw Devorah lingering at the door of the house of study soon after evening prayers finished. With the sun recently set, most of the men had hurriedly filed out of the solitary chamber,

230

tired from their day of work in the fields or in the sea. One or two lingered to talk to him for a few minutes. She waited quietly, peeking her brown head into the room from the doorway.

"Abba," Devorah said, when they had left. "We had a visitor. Or more properly, you had one. He went off riding, but said he would return after sunset. It's that Roman boy."

Rabbi Ariel thought for a moment. "Ah," he said, "Marcus," his mild hazel eyes lighting with warmth. "It's been some time since he came around. I wasn't sure we would see him again. And did you make him comfortable, daughter?

Devorah wrapped her arms tightly around her chest and squeezed. "He stayed on his horse, Abba. He didn't come in. But he said he would return." She looked up at him then and met his eyes.

The rabbi shook his head. "Devorah, Devorah," he said, half amused, half dismayed. "You must learn charity, child. *She opens her mouth with wisdom; and on her tongue is the Torah of steadfast love.*' You can't only be wise, Devorah, you must be good as well, kind. Make this verse your model." He looked his daughter up and down, noting the frown on her now downward tilted head, the downcast eyes. Was her regret sincere or was she merely hiding her expression from him? he wondered. With Devorah, it could be tricky to tell. "Come," he said, his tone exasperated and loving both. "And let us see what help we can provide the boy."

———◆———

As it turned out, Marcus elected not to return to the rabbi's home that evening, but came the next morning instead. On the short ride from hamlet to the beach some miles north of it, Marcus had passed a fisherman just returning home with his daily catch and willing to sell him a fish. The man's wife grilled it for him on an outside oven and served it to him on rough flat bread with some green Ashqelon

231

onion. There, too, at the man's house, he fed and watered Argos. And filled a flask for overnight.

Marcus spent the late afternoon hours leaning back against some rocks, his legs stretched out before him in the sand. Slowly, it settled into a balmy evening. Not chill. And clear. After a while, he stood to open the girth and breastplate of the thickish blanket that saddled the horse. He spread it on the ground and then resumed his position, sitting half on top of it, half covering his lap, sinking a little further down the rocks into the sand. Then he took out his dagger and lay it on his lap. After a while, Argos lay down near him. The horse was at ease, even if he, himself, was still on high alert.

He kept the dagger in his lap as he watched dusk settling in the sky, listening deeply to the lull of the surf, to the light wind and settling sands. These movements of the natural world shifted him, despite the worry he had felt earlier, into a deeply relaxed state where his thoughts came unimpeded.

It was late in Sivan. Already past the full, the moon was waning and had not yet risen tonight. But the stars, rising thick in the domed night sky, a swathe of white, glimmered fiercely. His eyes cocked, he watched their dance for a while, until he saw one star, then two, then three plummet towards the sea.

Marcus thought about his mother and father then and wondered if they realized he was absent yet and what they were doing about it.

He really should have stopped off and told his mother where he was going. Leaving a message with Vincius had been a mistake. The last thing Marcus wanted was Vincius anywhere near his mother.

But what could he have told her? Yehonatan had warned him never to discuss anything he had observed during their week together with his mother because it could endanger her.

And yet, if he hadn't left, if Julius had summoned him and his mother to attend the banquet, trouble would have descended forthwith on all of them. He had no doubt of Galenus' ruthlessness.

His mother would be devastated at his betrayal of his uncle and their people. And that he would never inflict on her. Better she suffer not knowing where he was for a few days than the ruination of the family and each of them individually.

The tricky thing was that he needed to keep protecting all three of them, without his mother or Julius finding out. At the same time, he had to keep the family glued together now that his mother was weakening. And that's why he had written to Yehonatan for help.

They were three sides of a triangle. And he was the one keeping them aloft.

When he did return home in a day or two, he needed a plausible explanation that his father would accept as to why he thought Galenus was a threat for all of them. Never for a moment did he forget that his father had a preternatural ability to sense lying, particularly when he cared to look deeply into a matter. Marcus had decided long ago never to lie to his father on important matters.

Yet he had sworn never to tell his father what he had discovered during the week he spent with Yehonatan. That there was a rebellion against Rome simmering among the Jews that his uncle supported tactically and financially. The fact that he had not only withheld this information but that he himself felt sympathetic to that cause would be like a dagger in his father's gut.

That information was too dangerous for him to hand over to his father now. For himself – because he had no excuse for not telling Julius three years ago when he had found it out. For Yehonatan, because Julius would judge him guilty and go after him and the others involved. And for his mother, who was innocent of all knowledge about it and caught in the middle of her family but would fully suffer the fallout.

Yehonatan had impressed on him that his mother needed to be protected at all costs. And that her best protection in the short term would be to keep her knowing nothing about this.

Sometime in the next day, he had to come up with an explanation that would satisfy both of his parents.

Yet his mind felt a complete blank, all invention squelched.

For the first time since he visited Yavneh, Marcus turned to prayer, for clarity, insight and help.

> *I cry out to you, O Lord.*
> *You are my rock; don't refuse to hear my voice.*

He woke early, lying motionlessly as the moon, a half sphere of translucence, passed from the gray sky into the blue-gray sea. Morning. The blessing of renewed light. He felt calm, calm as the summer sea. Sometime in the night, the dagger had dropped from his hand to lie forgotten at his side. Sheltered in his cleft of rock, chilled and hungry, Marcus kept still for a long time until pink streaks of cloud in the sky tinted the sea momentarily from gray to wine dark. A light wind rose blowing sand toward the rocks where he lay prone.

Marcus stood and shook himself off, brushing his dusty fingers through his short hair and wiping the residue of sand from his face and arms and legs. Argos was grazing a bit up the beach at a tuft of sea grass, so he whistled for the horse, then chafed his hands together and jumped up and down a few times to get his blood moving. Finally, Marcus buried his fingers in Argos' hair, and when the horse lifted his neck, he brushed the side of his face against the mane, chatting idly to the gelding as he warmed himself, breathing in his scent. Then he replaced the saddle cloth swiftly, mounted Argos and set off at a gallop over the pebble strewn beach. In the situation, strenuous riding was the best way he knew of to get warm.

Marcus met up with Rabbi Ariel later that morning where the man was laboring in a small wheat field. Marcus lifted his hand to greet the rabbi as he rode towards him from the edge of the field. There was an awkward pause during which the rabbi bent forward to lay his tools aside on the ground, then straightened up and scrutinized Marcus' condition, dusty, bedraggled and hungry. His hazel eyes shifted to Marcus' horse, also dusty and hungry, and in serious want of a brushing. And then he looked up and met Marcus' eyes. "You are not, by any chance, running away from home, are you?" Rabbi Ariel asked finally.

Marcus looked down at his filthy sky-blue tunic and laughed. "I suppose there's no point in denying it. It's obvious, isn't it?" he said sliding down from his horse. Lifting the reins over his horse's head, Marcus moved a few steps closer to the rabbi. "But don't worry. I have excellent reasons. And it's just for a day or two. I'll return as soon as I'm able to. I'm not running away permanently."

"For the moment there's nothing I can do about that. I can, however, take a break to get you something to eat. And something for your horse, as well. Follow me."

Ten minutes later, Marcus found himself back at the rabbi's small stone house with its dirt courtyard and rough stone fence. He watered Argos at the trough and set him to graze in an enclosed field behind the house with two donkeys for company. Then he walked over to the well and washed himself off as meticulously as he could with a bucket of cold water and a clean rag. His hair and face and hands, at least, were clean when he had finished, if nothing else particularly was. And the well water, cool and pure, had quaffed his thirst. He felt refreshed. Marcus sat down outside, as instructed, at a slatted wooden table curving completely around the trunk of a fruiting apricot tree. And waited.

In a few minutes, the rabbi returned with his daughter Devorah, bearing a platter of fresh bread and fish and fruit. Devorah walked across the yard to the well to fetch some water for the glazed pitcher.

"Eat," said the rabbi placing the tray down in front of Marcus. He sat down next to Marcus, took a green fig for himself, mumbled a prayer and began to eat the fruit lovingly, a small bite at a time.

235

Devorah, in the same rough linen gown she had worn the day before, placed the glazed earthenware pitcher on the table in front of him, then moved around to the other side of the table, with all the width of it between herself and the two men. She sat down, a scowl on her face, watching. At a certain point, Marcus noticed, the rabbi directed a telling look at her and the scowl began slowly to melt off her face until only a residue of it remained.

"So," said Rabbi Ariel at last, after Marcus had wiped his mouth clean, "I suppose you know the reason you came to me. How can I help you?"

Marcus glanced over at Devorah. Her presence still made him uncomfortable. He shrugged once, bit the inside of his left cheek until he tasted blood and said, hesitantly, "You said I might come to you from time to time, didn't you?" And then with more confidence as the rabbi nodded at him. "I want to learn from you. I've been to Yavneh already for a short visit some years ago. Just a couple of days. I thought... that is... I would like to learn more."

"But to what point? Why are you interested?" The rabbi's tone was pressing.

Looking down, his dark eyelashes flecking his cheeks, Marcus hesitated. He raised his eyes to the man slowly. "Did not Yosi ben Yoezer say, '*Let thy house be a meeting place for the sages; and sit amidst the dust of their feet and drink in their words with thirst.*' The house I can't provide, unfortunately," Marcus said with a downward swipe at his tunic, "but the dust I seem to have in abundance."

"A veritable feast of dust, if only it were edible." It was the first time the girl had spoken since she had arrived at the table.

"How lucky for me, then, that you provided me with living waters to drink." His voice snapped out the words before he turned his face back to the rabbi at his side. But he continued steadily enough. "You see, I traveled to Yavneh with my uncle. And while I was there, he took me to meet Rabbi Chanon bar Hisda."

"Ah, you've met Rabbi Chanon bar Hisda." Rabbi Ariel gave him a considering glance.

"You know him?"

"A little," said Rabbi Ariel. "By reputation mostly. A mystic with some following. An interesting, though complicated, man."

"Yes," said Marcus. He smiled soberly. "In retrospect, that's my impression as well. Although at the time, I was much too terrified of him to think anything at all. My uncle knows him quite well, however. He studied with him years back in Sura in Babylonia. He was his prize disciple for a while, I believe."

The rabbi nodded his head slightly before he spoke. "An interesting family, Marcus. Your grandfather studied in the Galilee, I think you told me last time we met. And your uncle in Sura. A prize disciple of Rabbi Chanon, you say." He massaged his lower lip with his index finger.

A brief laugh escaped Marcus' lips. But he swallowed the sound when the rabbi, clearly puzzled, shot a look in his direction before he continued speaking. "You have established your connections and you have shown me you have learned a little already. But you have not yet told me the reason why, Marcus, here and now, you yourself wish to study."

"I don't understand the question, Rabbi. Is it not my obligation to study Torah? Or at least, so I was taught as a child. '*He that learns not is worthy of death.*' It was forced down my throat until I had it by heart as a child. In the way of tradition, I believe, I am simply trying to remove myself from doubt."

"And you do doubt?" This time the rabbi's hazel eyes, examining him, were not at all mild.

Marcus met the look steadily. "Some things. Don't you?"

"Well, then," said Rabbi Ariel, and failed to answer him in return. "If we are going to begin lessons, we ought to start now. It's an excellent opportunity," the rabbi's look was still stern, "considering that you have nowhere else to go – for a day or two. I suggest we start with the prayer following a meal such as you have eaten with bread. And then we'll go to the fields for some work, and when we stop for our midday break, we will discuss Torah." The rabbi turned his head to his daughter. "Devorah, you may come with us today."

Devorah nodded her head at Marcus, but spoke only to her father. "He might not want to work, Abba. Surely, he has servants to do his work for him in town while he plays soldier and pursues not peace, but war."

Rabbi Ariel shook his head in exasperation at his daughter, but turned his head all the same to Marcus, a question in his eyes.

"Oh, I can work, Rabbi. Farming may not be my daily fare, yet I'm perfectly capable of it. Thank you all the same, Devorah, for your consideration." There was silence for some moments, time enough for his grating tone to reverberate, stillborn, in the air. When he next spoke, Marcus' voice was controlled and polite. "It's unusual, isn't it, rabbi, for girls to study law? I didn't see any in classes in Yavneh. Do not the Sages say, 'Talk not overmuch with women.'"

Marcus could not resist sneaking a look at Devorah after he said this. As he suspected, she was glowering at him in full force. He smiled back at her, a wide and seraphic smile, almost laughing out loud, but he caught himself in time.

"No, you wouldn't see girls at lectures in Yavneh, at least not publicly," said Rabbi Ariel shortly. "Privately is another matter. I've known other men who taught their daughters." The rabbi had caught the by-play, Marcus felt sure, between himself and Devorah, but was ignoring it meanwhile, curbing any trouble. "In any case, I have few people to teach during the day; the men here are hard at work and I have work of my own to do in my fields and sometimes in the sea. And I have no living son. So, Devorah has become my most talented, my most valued student." The rabbi smiled at his daughter and then turned his eyes to Marcus. "I hope it's not something you will find troubling." Rabbi Ariel said this politely; but it was perfectly clear to Marcus that if he did find it bothersome, it was his problem alone. The rabbi's pride in his daughter was palpable.

Marcus abandoned the fight, privately conceding defeat to Devorah on this issue, at least. "Hardly," said Marcus and shrugged. "My mother was my teacher for many years, after we moved away from my grandfather in Sardis. She studied with her father as well, at his knee; she remembers all his stories and knows quite a bit of law, herself. But my family, as you already said, is somewhat unusual. I was simply curious about the standard practice." This time, he met neither of their looks directly.

Yet, looking up a few moments later, he noticed that for the first time all morning, Devorah smiled at him. It transformed her utterly. Her face, Marcus realized, was quite charming when she smiled despite the dirty brown hair and the rough robe outlining her neck and thin shoulders. For some reason, he found that fact more than a little unnerving.

"First the prayer," said the rabbi and stood, "and then we're off to the field to work." He scowled at Marcus. "And if you don't want me sending a message to your parents, I'm expecting an explanation that will convince me you were wise to leave your home, however temporarily."

"You'll have it, Rabbi. Only not right now." He looked at Devorah significantly. "Although come to think of it," Marcus said tilting up his head, thinking, "a little message to my mother in Hebrew might be just the thing. She's not the one I'm avoiding today. My father is." He grinned flippantly. "With my family there is always something." And was abashed a moment later by the pitying look the rabbi turned on him.

After a few seconds, Rabbi Ariel ceased to regard him and began slowly to recite aloud the prayer for food. Marcus, committing the words to memory, repeated it after him somewhat impatiently. He had not come for rote prayers, which he found uninspiring, he had come for knowledge. For knowledge, not piety. Then, with the prayer finished, the three of them walked toward the field and began to work. Afterwards they sat together on a stone, below an olive tree for shade, and Rabbi Ariel began his first talk on the place of humility in wisdom. Which, if nothing else, Marcus thought, privately amused, provided an instructive gloss on Rabbi Ariel's thoughts about his two young students.

PART XII

CHAPTER 18

Julius and Miriam

Later that day, Julius stalked into his villa with all the purposefulness of a shark on a blood trail. He succeeded instantly in intimidating those servants unlucky enough to be in his purview when he arrived. The others, who had had the time or industry to scuttle out of his path before he entered, still scrambled to obey when he shouted orders at them across the courtyard. But the two people Julius had most wanted to impress with his anger were nowhere to be found. He sent out a young servant boy to look for them, but they were not in the large salon, nor the atrium; not upstairs in the sleeping chambers, nor in the bath complex. This did not have the effect of improving his temper. He sent one servant out on Miriam's trail and one out to trace Marcus at Rufinus' gymnasium. Then, bellowing for wine, Julius took himself into the garden to wait, seething.

Sitting down in the shade, he began to finger obsessively the long, sharp blade of his golden hilted Scythian knife. After the first inadvertent cut, three pearls of blood appeared on his brown skin. His index finger to his mouth, Julius sucked at them hard, thick salty-red on his tongue. He held out his other hand, and the servant, padding gently toward him on clean bare feet, placed in it a delicate blue tinged glass filled with wine. He tipped the drink down his throat, the entire glass at once and held it out again. As the man took it and poured him more wine, Julius began, instead, to toy restlessly with the elaborate antlered scrollwork of the hilt.

Julius had polished off his fourth cup of the sweet wine and already started on the fifth, when Miriam appeared before him at the entrance to the atrium. She was dressed in a celadon silk robe that heightened the greenness of her eyes. Her hair, sun bleached, was braided meticulously and twisted around her head, held up with a thin golden fillet. Chunks of emerald and gold hung about her neck. She looked cool and unflurried. As though she had not a worry in the world but him.

"Julius," she said advancing slowly towards him, the metallic fringe of her under-tunic humming over her white ankles, like bees bussing a rosebush. The sunlight illumined her breast. "The servants said you were asking for me. As it happens, I was in the middle of a negotiation and would have preferred it if you had not summoned me just now. The timing was extremely inconvenient. I'll have to return quite soon, in any case." She stopped a small distance away, looking down at him as he lolled back, half reclining on a leather chair, his knife abandoned in his lap. "But since I'm here, welcome back to Caesarea." She paused. "I had a message you arrived." Moments elapsed until she spoke again. "Yesterday afternoon."

A naked challenge if he had ever heard one. Julius weighed it as he rubbed his chin already slightly rough with stubble. Miriam's manner since she had entered, he noted, was polite but guarded. The bloody servant who located her must have blabbed about his temper. She was annoyed, however reluctantly, over his late return to the villa. Together, these two factors would account for the extreme chill in the air. Which, he mused, was not at all what he wanted from her right now with her standing there before him looking like a statue of Venus. Fully clothed. Unfortunately.

Julius, commander of Roman armies, smiled suddenly, a slight upward quirk of his lips and a certain intense glimmer in his eyes. Here was a challenge of another sort, and one that he would enjoy engaging in immediately. And winning. "Come here," he said in a low voice looking up at her out of half-masted eyes.

She eyed him back and then looked down at the near empty pitcher of wine. "Julius, it's only a few hours past mid-day and you're already drunk." Yet she moved in a step closer and proffered fingers in his direction. She did not move close enough to touch him.

"So I am," he said. Picking up the knife from his lap, he flung it from him so that it penetrated the fork of an espaliered apple tree spread-eagled against the limestone wall of the atrium. The knife hung in the wood, quivering for a few seconds, then stilled. Perfect accuracy. Julius barked a laugh, more than satisfied with his shot, and turned his eyes on Miriam, his next target. Half rising from his chair, quick as a striking asp, Julius grasped her arm. "Come here anyway," he said, and pulled her towards him hard, his powerful hand folded over the narrow bone of her wrist, the deep tan of his hand in stark relief against her white skin. She dropped into his lap half awkwardly.

"Julius," she said pushing herself away, trying to sit up and straighten her robe. "No. Not now. I have to..."

"Be quiet," he interrupted and put his lips on top of hers to still her voice, one hand on her breast, the other threaded through her hair. He kissed her furiously, like a priest fervently bombarding a cynic whom he senses he will soon convert. After some moments had passed, Miriam opened her mouth and kissed Julius back.

"I missed this," Julius said a long time afterward. They were in bed upstairs in their large chamber. The westering sun shone brightly into the room, a triangle of light, just missing the bed; but the cool sea air, wafting languidly, kept the room a pleasant temperature. Not

243

too hot. Just right. Perfect, in fact. Julius put his two hands on her shoulders and drew her under him again, rubbing his face in her hair, in the elusive scent he could never fully capture. "I missed this when I was away."

Miriam shifting her weight under him, twisted her shoulder and averted her face from him suddenly. "You didn't find the whores you used recently up to your standard?"

There was silence for a few seconds. Julius lifted his head, his upper body. Then: "Why buy a whore when I have you for free?" he said. He looked down at her still face and after a minute he added, "Why do you do this?" Minutes passed, broad and slow-moving, like a meandering river, like the Euphrates which he had watched unwavering, day after day, on the long march from Zeugma to Dura. And all the time she did not look at him. Dura. That brought a thought to his mind. But not yet. Not yet. Leave it for another time when his body felt less gripped. When what was at stake presently was not at stake.

Julius softened his voice, "Miriam. I was at an official banquet last night, not with a whore, if you must know. I didn't come to you because I passed out at camp, drunk." There was no response. She did not look at him. Shifting her body towards him again, he bent his head, and kissed her very delicately on the lobe of her ear, then nuzzled her face with his. "I'm sorry, Miriam. I should never have permitted myself to reply to you as I did." He smoothed her hair, long and unbound. "Can we agree, at least, to fight later?" Outside, the water broke on the shoreline, lapping mildly, wave after wave, a continuous rhythm, utterly impervious to human concerns. Julius spoke again, more directly. "Please speak to me."

Silence. He shifted his weight slightly, hesitating, before he got himself up from bed to exit the room, to leave the house, to go back to camp.

And at last she said, her voice completely neutral, "Did you enjoy the banquet?"

244

"No," Julius said and smiled, his eyes reflecting his relief, "not in the least. After three months away, riding and drinking with the men every singled god-damned day and every single god-damned night, I wanted to come here to relax, not to help preside over more government business in town. It was nonsense, governance at its worse; grasping provincial officials and ambitious soldiers and one uncannily sharp provincial administrator - very likely a murderer from early in my career - with whom I had spent too much time already, all sniping slowly at each other to prove their mastery. Why do you think I drank so much? I was seeking an elixir to immediate oblivion."

"You chose to be well-drunken, if not wise. My poor man. No lotus on the official menu, I gather."

"Oh, they served it, but I refrained. And I shut my ears when the Sirens sang. You see, Penelope, with Poseidon's help or without it, I aimed at returning as soon I could."

He waited patiently until she turned her head to him. Then he looked in her eyes and when he saw their expression, he exhaled roughly, in relief. He grappled her around the waist, his arms locked tight behind her, and one tensile hand sliding down the smooth skin of her back and below. Lowering his head to hers, he began to kiss her with passion.

Sometime later, Miriam lay straight on her back with Julius curled against her warmth in the great sun-splashed white bed, their bodies for the moment at peace. Her eyes open, fixed on the terraced window, Miriam registered small sounds the servants made as they went about their business downstairs; the brief slap of wet cloth on the inlaid marble floors, the high voice of a maid servant applying to the cook for orders, the intermittent patter of footsteps, light and heavy. Outside, the gardener's shears clacked as he cut flowers, while his young son raked smooth the white pebbled pathways, in long symmetric strokes, again and again. A homey smell of fresh bread and roasting meat drifted into the room. Outside, the small birds flew freely from tree to tree, warbling, singing, diving, at liberty to soar where so ever they desired. An irony, then, that for the most part, they stayed homeward bound.

A moment fit for meditative calm, Miriam reflected, if only she could reach it. But she could not, not today. She lay on her still bed, and all the while her mind assailed her for having succumbed to Julius yet again. She had thought, at times, to use the three-month separation from him to wean herself finally and forever from this difficult attraction. He and she were so unsuited in almost every way, so miserable with each other for the most part, except in bed, where they suited completely. A willow and an oak, whose roots had thoroughly married, but whose trunks battled each other daily for water and light, the elements of life.

Julius, however had the luxury of taking relief from the situation in a way that she could not. Or had not yet. In spite of the denial he had uttered earlier, Julius employed prostitutes. His disavowal, carefully worded, had only referred to last night, not any time prior to that on his trip. Julius never lied. She could say that much good of him. In effect, he had told her that he was coming clean to her bed, clean by the length of a night and a day, at least, and the meticulous bath he had, no doubt, taken this morning. Miriam hated knowing that fact, that he used his body with her the same way as he did with all his other women, that it had the same effect on all the others as it did on her. That the way they engaged was not unique for him as it was for her.

But there was nothing to do about it. Not now. She had already conceded the field to him and with all the jubilance of the returning conqueror he had taken possession of the ground again and again and again. She looked down the white sheeted length of her still body, listening as her breath and Julius' flowed in and out, in and out, strangely in rhythm.

The light in the room was more diffuse now, less piercing, as the sun had passed northerly and sunk lower on the horizon. Outside, beyond the terrace, Miriam could hear gulls crying as they swooped against each other, and then the sound of splashing as their bills impacted the water hard, penetrating its surface to capture the fish wriggling below. The birds rose into the sky, battling each other for the spoils.

Her brother also frequented whores. That had shocked Miriam when she found it out, a curious naiveté to which she wanted desperately to cling. It was an open secret that Yehonatan had taken Vincius to enjoy the most famous brothel in Caesarea, and the most expensive, just before he departed three years ago. Vincius had been suffering through the effects of her reconciliation with Julius, brought about by her brother's offices. Yehonatan may have thought that he was helping Vincius, but he had not, not even in the short term. A signal lapse of judgment on Yehonatan's part at which she still marveled.

Julius had laughed hysterically when he discovered it. It amused him that another man found his wife so attractive that he had to resort to a whore to cure himself and then failed to cure himself.

Unlike Julius, however, her brother neither possessed a spouse nor a permanent companion, as far as she knew. Miriam checked mentally, glancing at Julius under her lids. From time to time, she had had a suspicion that he knew something about that she did not. Once or twice, Julius had let slip something she did not understand only to turn the subject immediately when he saw the hungry response on her face, so that she felt like a hound baying in vain after stray drops of blood. It bothered Miriam that she had not yet found the means to ascertain what he knew, to pry it out from him or to discover it by other means.

She directed a semi-malevolent glance at him now only to find his eyes wide open and regarding her. He laughed briefly at her look, reached for her hand and kissed it. "Why so glum?" he said.

"Why so happy?" she responded acidly. Even replete from the effects of this afternoon, her fingers rejoiced anew in his touch. Miriam marveled dispassionately at her body's utter betrayal of her mind and soul. Of course, her mind equally and as ruthlessly tried to suppress her body. But that behavior was termed virtue and sanctioned by the world's sages, Jewish and Greek and Latin. Aeneas had given up his lust for Dido to go in search of his destiny and to found the line that would become the Roman people. But Dido, who could not escape, had killed herself. Dido had ruled Carthage. But a vengeful Venus had sent her own son to destroy Dido with killing lust and none of the gods had intervened to save her. An instructive, if disturbing, conclusion.

Still amused, Julius sat up next to her. "Surely Miriam, you know the reason I'm happy." He regarded her, running his eyes down the length of her body. "You were here for it, weren't you?" And he kicked the sheet down the bed with his left foot so that he could gaze at her body uncovered. He looked and looked, but did not touch, not now.

"Incidentally," Julius said, turning his eyes at last to her face, "What did your brother have to do with running intelligence for the XIIth Fulminata? The Legion stationed in Parthia some years back?"

Miriam sat up, reached for the sheet and covered herself again. She said truthfully, "I don't know." And then, because she could not resist, she asked, "What did he have to do with it?"

Julius' expression which had turned sober exuded a hint of distrust. "Actually, I'm not sure it is your brother." His eyes, looking into hers, had turned chilly. "Why, I ask myself, would your brother have supplied information for the Romans in Parthia?"

"He wouldn't," said Miriam carefully, watching the play of emotion across Julius' face.

248

"The same conclusion I reached," said Julius. "Still, the description..." He shook his head. "It matches too well." Julius had his knees up, with his elbows resting on them and his face in his hands, still thinking. In the end, he shrugged, shaking off the mood, and got out of bed. "Yehonatan, alas, remains an enigma." A grin appeared on his lips, shone for a second or two and twinkled out of existence. Walking naked to the door, Julius bellowed for a servant. A girl arrived some moments later, youngish, flustered and not particularly attractive, the new Syrian maid with cheeks turning apple red. Julius leaned against the doorframe, his weight on his right arm, bent above his head. Indifferent to the girl's embarrassment, he spouted off orders to lay out an informal supper for himself and Miriam as soon as possible; then to alert the stable boys to prepare his horse for departure within the hour.

Nude and noble, Miriam thought sarcastically. God knows she had tried; but she had never succeeded in instilling the slightest bit of modesty in Julius yet.

"I'm starving," Julius announced, his back still to her. "We'll eat soon and then I'm off back to the barracks. I hadn't planned on spending so long away this afternoon. I forgot what a temptress you are. My own sweet Siren, impelling me to bed and binding me to her for hours thereafter." The face he turned toward her moved in several seconds through an entire spectrum of feeling, from contentment to resentment. "Still, as always, Miriam, reality descends, eventually. Vincius handled most everything properly when I was away. But there are one or two little matters I brought back from the Governor in Syria that I must take care of immediately." His face frowned suddenly, expressing only disapproval, but not, this time, of her. "By the way, I heard about Marcus' escapades last night, at the banquet from Glaucon, the father of that boy, the one he hurt."

"Critias," supplied Miriam.

249

Julius nodded. "Critias, that's it. And then again from Vincius this morning, a more objective version likely. Still bad though. What was he thinking to act like that unprovoked?"

"I think Marcus must have missed you a great deal, Julius. He behaved terribly the whole time you were away."

The frown melted away, replaced instantly with smiling carmine lips, utterly transforming the arid landscape of his face; as when, after a rare, late winter snowfall, the stark hills of Judea burst forth into a carpet of poppy blooms. "Do you truly think so, Miriam?" Julius said softly. He walked back to the bed, leaned over, and kissed her gently and with affection on the forehead, a rare gesture. "Thank you for that. Although it still doesn't solve the problem of what to do about it."

Julius straightened and walked back across the room to look out at the ocean, a field of gray and scarlet, with the dying sun slipping beyond the bloody sky. He said, "In any case, where is Marcus? I wanted to bring him back to camp with me to accompany me to my meetings with the administrator tomorrow morning. I suppose he's out and about now, lurking somewhere in town, afraid of facing parental wrath. Whether he missed me or not when I was away, it's not very flattering that he has no desire to see me when I return. It's been over a day now since I'm back."

"You haven't seen Marcus yet?" Miriam sat straight up in the bed. She could feel the sudden pallor of her face and her blood beginning to run chill. "But Julius..." she said and covered her mouth with her two hands, laying one over the other. "No."

"Miriam?" He turned his face to her, his body still angled casually toward the terrace doors.

"I thought he was with you last night, in camp. He wasn't at home either."

"What are you talking about?" Julius was facing her properly now. "He always sleeps here."

"Not always. He's spent nights with you in camp before."

"But always by arrangement, Miriam. I always sent you a messenger beforehand."

"Not the last few times. Remember, just before you left. I sent you the messenger and you replied the next day."

"That's true." Julius' face changed. Miriam saw the precise moment he decided not to pursue the matter as an argument. "Don't worry, my dear," he said softly. "It's probably only a boy's prank to show me he has come of age. And he'll have his dagger with him. The gods know he can use it to defend himself well enough... if it comes to that. But it won't. Don't worry."

She studied his countenance and replied, "It sounds unlikely to me, Julius. If anything, Marcus seemed to be looking forward to your return." And thought bitterly to herself, the restoration of Roman rule, wherein all her subjects submit, rejoicing, to her flattening hand.

Miriam saw something else occur to Julius then. "Vincius mentioned riding." He snapped his fingers twice. "Yesterday, he saw Marcus take his horse and go riding. North, I think he said. Does Marcus know anyone who lives north? Do we? Anywhere he might stay overnight?" He scrutinized her face for a second, and then, looking down at himself, Julius barked at her, "Where in Hades are my clothes? Up, woman, and help me get dressed. I'm going downstairs to send a messenger to fetch Vincius here immediately. Get yourself dressed as well. If the poor man sees you like that, I doubt he'll be of any use to either of us."

Miriam leaned back against the diaphanous bed curtains allowing a smile to bloom on her small rose-pink mouth. Pleased, she thought, Julius, you hardly know of what you speak. If Vincius saw me like this, he'd... And then before she completed the thought, her heart jogged painfully in her chest. The smile faded instantaneously. She had forgotten for a moment that Marcus had gone missing.

Miriam scrabbled out of bed, then. Bending low, one by one, she located Julius' clothing where he had strewn them across the floor,

251

his white tunic, his fine brown linen riding breeches, his leather belt with the inlaid copper buckle sparkling red and gold and green, his golden dagger and his sandals. A small and useless act of expiation, utterly unrecognized by her God.

CHAPTER 19

The Prodigal Arrives Home

The door behind Vincius closed, its bolt rasping into place. The lock, it was plain, needed oiling, a treatment it would receive now that Julius had returned. There was a gentle swish of a robe as the servant behind him turned with the lantern in her hand. The maid servant held it aloft, and the flame cleaved the shadows and splashed light onto the frescoed walls, illuminating here a pale face against a deep red background, there a green grotto populated with fleeting maenads. The patter of their footsteps reverberated along the black and white marble floor. Otherwise, Vincius noted as he passed down the long hallway, the house was unusually quiet. Still, it was an odd choice of locale to manage a nighttime planning session.

He stopped at the portal to the atrium before entering to let his gaze sweep over the brightly lit room. "Julius!" Vincius nodded firmly at his superior officer seated squarely on the couch. The man wore a tunic and riding trousers; the same garments as earlier in the day, but less fresh. "Miriam." She was seated at Julius' side swathed

253

in a loose dress, the color nondescript in the candlelight, her arms crossed tightly over her chest. Her hair for once was knotted simply at the back of her head. Vincius' nod at her was accompanied by a brief smile, a mechanical upward tuck of his lips. Insincere, but it softened his face.

"You took long enough to arrive," said Julius. The criticism, uncharacteristically, was mildly stated.

Vincius shrugged half apologetically. "I was in a tavern with some friends, enjoying a night off. Your messenger took some time to locate me. Next time let me know ahead of time there's a minor crisis brewing, and I'll leave my address behind."

"Enough," said Julius swiping his hand upward, cutting off his chatter. "Tell me again the direction you last saw Marcus riding. Yesterday. I think you told me he went north. Along the waterfront, was it?" He lay his left hand down carefully along the back of the couch, behind Miriam's back. Julius' right hand, Vincius noted, was clenched to the wooden arm of the chaise.

Vincius drew the conclusion he should have reached earlier. There had been clues enough. "Marcus is missing," he said, and read his confirmation in Julius' and Miriam's eyes, both of them staring at him fixedly. "Yes. I saw him ride out of camp along the north trail. I told him that you were expected in the afternoon, so that..." Vincius stopped himself. "Have you checked with his friends? Critias, in particular. He's spent a lot of time with him lately. Nights, too, so it's been reported to me." His eyes carefully blank, Vincius looked at the space between Julius and Miriam.

"Nights?" said Julius.

The quality of the voice, interrogating him in an undertone, surprised Vincius.

"Marcus sneaked out of the house a few times, late at night." Miriam said calmly. And then in response to a look in Julius' eye, she added, "To get wildly drunk. And return. Nothing more. I told

254

you he behaved terribly when you were away. You didn't think I was exaggerating, did you?" She turned her face to Vincius, "We sent a messenger to their house already, but got a reply in the negative. Marcus hasn't been there."

Vincius moved his eyes to focus on Julius.

Julius said, "I spoke to Glaucon last night at the banquet. Critias' father. He addressed me at length, and not happily, about Marcus injuring his son. Well, what can you expect from a merchant, after all? If his son were with the army, he'd be used to injuries by now. In any case, if Marcus had been visiting them, I feel sure I'd have heard him complaining about that as well."

"He might not have known. I'm told there are several outbuildings around their property that the young men use."

Julius leaned his head back slightly to study Vincius, so that his square chin was underlit, his dark lashes casting magnificent shadows onto the skin below his brow bone. His nostrils flared slightly, suggestive of distaste and something stronger. "It only remains to think if Marcus knows anyone north of Caesarea with whom he might stay the night," Julius said at last, dismissing the comment entirely. "Remind me where Noemi and her husband live?"

"She lives too far south, between here and Joppa," said Miriam.

Vincius, standing straight, swallowed the implied rebuke. So, there were some possibilities that Julius was not going to consider. Certain kinds of friendship, for instance. In this matter, Julius was far more Roman than Greek. "North," Vincius repeated and glanced at Miriam measuringly. "Is it possible...?" he said and then bit off his words. For a moment, Vincius let himself taste the bitterness of Julius' reproval and kept his mouth shut. If Miriam had wanted it discussed, he thought, she would have done so. It hadn't slipped his mind; it certainly had not slipped hers. He changed course. "I'll go back to camp and arrange some soldiers to form a search party to ride out with me."

"I've already called up the men. We were waiting for you to get back to tell us the best direction to begin searching."

"You'll be riding with us, sir?"

"Miriam," said Julius, turning frontally to her. "It would be better if I went along. You'll be all right on your own." He withdrew his left hand from the back of the couch and stroked her cheek delicately.

Miriam closed her eyes, bending her neck toward Julius.

Vincius' right hand jerked involuntarily. He clenched it on the hilt of his sword and started to turn around. Damn the gods. He did not want to suffer Julius pawing Miriam before his face. "Sir," he said loudly. "If that's all, then, perhaps I will go ahead to arrange…"

"A minute, Vincius." Julius brushed Miriam's cheek one last time, leaned forward, his hands reaching to hold her hands in her lap and said, "Don't worry. Marcus is all right. We'll find him. I'll find him. And when he's back…" He broke off, shaking his head, and brushed a hand along her cheek again before kissing her softly on the lips. Miriam, Vincius noted, leaned her head into Julius' shoulder, her eyes closed. And then opened them and stared straight into his own, green into brown. She sat perfectly still, her eyes wide, as Julius disengaged from her.

"I'll either be back late tonight with Marcus in tow or I'll send you a message." Julius levered himself to his feet. "Tomorrow morning, I have to meet with the administrator of Ashqelon before he departs," he said grimacing. "The timing could not be worse."

Julius walked up to him swiftly, and for a moment lay his right hand convivially on Vincius' shoulder. It had never happened before. Then the light pressure was withdrawn, and Julius was preceding him down the long, frescoed hall. "Come," he said.

Vincius slowed his weary Arabian mare on the outskirts of the hamlet he had visited once before at night. The sky, thankfully, was

256

brightening from black to midnight blue. Soon it would be dawn. But it was not yet light enough to distinguish much without a lantern.

Privately, Vincius had been skeptical about the efficacy of searching the road at night when it was impossible to see whether any tracks led off the road. All that his men could have noted during the moonless hours of their long search with tall firs obscuring their path, casting long shadows that hedged them about on all sides, was something as substantial as a body lying by the side of the road. No other telling hints, such as footsteps leading off into the woods, discarded clothes, jewels or even the signs of a struggle. Finally, Vincius had sent his men, exhausted after searching fruitlessly all night, back to their sleeping quarters.

Julius had headed back already to prepare for his meeting in town, still half convinced this was a childish prank on his son's part, nothing more. A new team of men, headed by Silius, would resume searching in an hour or two. But Vincius wanted to check this one village on his own. He was not sure why Miriam had not mentioned the place, only that she had not. A signal to him or only a preference that Julius not find out about Marcus' tie to this place and how it had come about. He had no business indulging Miriam like this, but to be fair to her, she had not asked him to do it. It was only a request he had inferred, perhaps erroneously, through her silence. Then there had been that kiss that he had witnessed last night. He did not feel like catering to Julius right now even if Marcus' safety were at stake.

Vincius nudged his horse along slowly around the perimeter of the houses before him. At any moment, the tiny cluster of houses would stir into life, into its familiar morning activities. So, he had best get on with the task at hand. He sent his mind back to that moonlit night and tried to discern his whereabouts in this shadowland, whether there was anything he recognized here at all. And he did eventually. The slope of a hill came slowly into focus, and he edged the mare downward. At the bottom of it, Vincius found himself in a clearing with a stone wall bordering it on one side. He dismounted and placed his lantern carefully onto the wall. Then, because his muscles ached from carrying the torch extended out from his body for so long, he shook out his arm from the wrist while looking about. As his mare twitched her head, noisily jangling her bit, Vincius winced, cursing under his breath, and moved to muffle her.

A horse whinnied close by, startling him. Over the stone wall, Vincius heard the loud clop and swish of an animal moving towards him through some obstructed ground. Then, moments later, his own mare, snuffling the air, nickered in response. A greeting, not a challenge. He relaxed minimally. Only to jump the next moment when a shadow materialized out of the dark a hand's breadth away and touched him.

"I've been observing you for the last while, Vincius. You're very noisy when you scout. Contrary to your instructions I might add."

Marcus. But he had known that already from the horses' familiar greeting. Vincius exhaled loudly, just resisting the impulse to grab the brat across the stone wall separating them and shake him until his brain burst. His head lowered into his neck, Vincius leaned his arms onto the wall, closing his fists rigidly over its loose uppermost stones. "I might add that if you do not stopper your mouth..."

"You will do it for me. With one of those stones, perhaps. Let us take it as noted." Above Marcus' head, there was now no lingering black. The firmament had turned a deep midnight blue. Vincius could make out the boy's features, his dark curling hair, his highlighted cheekbones with shadows underneath and the bright blue eyes staring hard into his own.

Vincius' breathing was still tight. "What are you doing here, Marcus?"

"It's a small house. I slept outside to give them privacy."

Vincius found himself raising his arm, his fist still curled about a granite stone. He glared at Marcus.

Marcus, however, was not looking back at him. His eyes were riveted on the stone in Vincius' hand.

"Don't be silly, Vincius," he said. There was a brief pause in which Vincius unclenched his fist and slowly lowered the rock. "My father sent you here to find me."

"Not precisely."

"My mother, then." Marcus' color had risen.

Vincius laughed. The sound, to his ears, came out a little wild. "Is that what is exercising you? Then you will be gratified to find out your father never gave me the chance. He kept her all to himself since yesterday morning. Marcus, I repeat, what are you doing here? Why aren't you at home?"

He was met by a level stare. After a moment, Marcus responded, "I had something to attend to."

Vincius chortled, half choking on sudden mirth. "You are quite delusional if you think that excuse is going to pass muster at home. Socrates sitting among the clouds, no less, confabulating with idiots. Your father has a search party out looking for you. And another to start in an hour or so. You need to be practical, Marcus. Apply your brain and think." He let his words sink in before finishing. "Now that I have seen you, I'm starting back for Caesarea. I suggest you come with me."

"Not yet. I'll be heading home soon. Later today."

In the distance, beyond a stand of trees, a team of donkeys began braying. The sky had lightened; it was near sunrise. Vincius did not need the lantern any more so he leaned forward and blew it out. Straightening, he looked around, noting a field where Argos had grazed, the grass grown tall and dry, and a pallet with Marcus' saddle cloth lain on top lying in the shelter of the wall. To his left, at a distance, there was a small house, and an outdoor table built around the trunk of an ancient apricot tree. The enclosed yard was neatly kept;

it contained a raised well at its center, covered by a slab of stone, and welded onto the stone a bright metal ring to lift it.

"I'm starting back," Vincius repeated firmly. He could see that the door of the house had opened and a man – he thought he recognized the rabbi – was standing on its doorstep, observing the scene. Vincius pointed his head toward him and redirected his glance to Marcus. "I assume he knows you are here without leave. You are not lying to him, are you?"

Marcus looked over his shoulder. "He knows. He also knows I am returning today."

"Then, I'm letting you know that an hour after I return to camp, I'm telling your father where you are." Holding his reins steadily, he clambered onto the wall, the easier to mount the mare. After riding all night, Vincius was bone weary. "Well, Marcus?"

"I'll be back today. This afternoon. Without fail."

Vincius gathered the reins and signaled to his mare to move forward. He was halfway up the little slope before Marcus called to him and he stopped his horse, allowing the boy to come even with him.

"Is Galenus still in Caesarea?"

"Galenus?"

'The administrator of Ashqelon."

"I know who he is, boy. I'm just surprised you do. I believe he is leaving the city later this morning. Your father should be meeting with him before he departs. Why? What have you to do with him?"

Marcus nodded. The expression on his face was deadpan. It gave nothing away. "Thanks for finding me, Vincius. I promise you I'll head back in a few hours. Without question." And now for the first time in the encounter Marcus looked unsure. "Would it be too much to ask you not to say anything?" The pup actually smiled encouragement at him. "You must know it's best to say nothing at all to my father. If there's a price to pay, and there will be, you may as well not be caught up in the middle of it."

The specter of a grin slid across Vincius' face dissolved some seconds later by the bright light of the rising sun. "You're learning, my child," he said. Then, with a flick of his reins, he was gone.

———◦—◦—◦———

Miriam stood, her right hand leaning on a column for support, on the wide front portico and watched frowning as Marcus strode through the gate. He approached her fast, striding at speed down the marble path.

"Mother," he said, and, laughing, stepped up to kiss her, the most ungodly smile fixed on his lips. Her son, her son, had the gall to look pleased with himself! Two days gone without a word, and he returned looking sleek and self-satisfied, like a household cat who returns at last to his master's heartrending calls after catching a bird, swatting off its feathers one by one and then consuming every morsel of meat, a pleasant night's work. Over this she had worried and woken every hour to stand guard at the door, a lantern in her hand, more fool her. Miriam checked her desire to lash out, a physical effort. Then she half turned away from him, feeling as though the hand of God had removed a prop, provided by His mercy all through the night and now no longer necessary.

"I'm sending a message to your father and then I'm off to sleep," she said. "And you are to go off to the bath house. Have the servants deliver that disgusting tunic to the fuller's and then go to your room. And stay there. I warn you. '*Turn from my words neither to the right nor to the left.*'"

"As if my life depended on it," said Marcus, his face already changing. And at a further look from her, he lowered his eyes and grumbled, "which, you remind me, it does."

Miriam declared, "*Hear me, be afraid and do not act presumptuously again.*" And turning her back completely this time, her face stern, her

261

shoulders slumping, she withdrew to the inner court, leaving him still outside. All alone.

"Mother," she heard him call, but by then the door was already shutting. Unlike Lot's wife, she was not in the least tempted to look back.

———◇———

Marcus' final meeting of the day, with his father, took place in the late afternoon, some five hours after he returned home. The long bath followed by a period of enforced rest and reflection had restored him to himself. He walked downstairs with the jauntiness that had carried him through the last few days no longer evident in his gait.

———◇———

There was a firm knock at the door of his small office in the villa. Julius picked his head up from his desk and wiped out his eyes. Lack of sleep was making him sloppy. He pushed the reports he had meant to examine squarely in front of him, caged his head between his two hands, his elbows on the desk, and began to peruse the cramped Latinate writing on the top paper. "Come in, Marcus," he said.

Glancing up from under his eyelids, he was glad to note the boy did not skulk into the room but walked in with an upright carriage. "Sit," said Julius, "until I am ready for you." He forced himself to finish reading the full report, a brief describing infighting amongst the branches of the Parthian royal family, subtly encouraged by agents of Rome who were working to sow chaos along the Euphrates. And then he critiqued the implications of this policy on the north-eastern front of the Empire, the quadrant of territory that concerned him. Only then did Julius raise his head, slide his elbows off the desk and scrutinize his son.

"Hello, Father. Welcome home." Marcus spoke softly, his voice unconstrained as far as Julius could hear.

"In view of the circumstances, perhaps, I should be the one welcoming you home. Not the reverse." Julius' voice was equally low.

"Perhaps," the boy added with a gentle smile. "But you were gone longer. Surely that counts for something."

"It depends," said Julius, "on who is doing the counting." He picked up the small knife on his table, held it so that three fingers loosely encircled the smooth lapis hilt, and began to run his index finger lightly down the blade to test its sharpness. To his chagrin, he noted there was some dirt encrusted on it. He rubbed it with his nail, then wiped it off on his sleeve. Bending his head, he examined a small nick at the end of the blade. None of his knives ever remained pristine for long, a source of continual annoyance to him. "In any case," Julius resumed, "there was a legitimate explanation for my absence. I've yet to hear of one for yours." He looked up suddenly, the expression in his eyes turned hard. "Know that if you rely on an excuse, you had better make it unassailable. An unbreachable siege tower of reason. I know, already, that Vincius had alerted you to my return before you went off."

"Guilty, Father. But it's worse than that. I caught a glimpse of you during the procession march through Caesarea before I left." There was a smile on the boy's lips again.

"You don't say," said Julius, holding his jawbone tight. "And now you are boasting to me of your ingenuity in escaping my company for a few extra days. Do you mean me to applaud you?" Julius found himself looking straight into Marcus' hyacinthine eyes. "I assume, having no reason to think otherwise, that you were afraid to face me for your behavior while I was away. Perhaps it only occurred to you after you left that I would regard your desertion as cowardice and punish you harder for it. Eventually, you found the *courage* to return."

The boy had finally ceased his enraging smile. One aim accomplished. "You think no better of me?" he demanded.

Julius sensed an easy victory, an early night. "Have you given me reason to? I judge by what I see and by what I know."

"And you know me no better than that, Father?"

"Then tell me, Marcus. Why should I think better of you?" Julius leaned back against the cushion of his hard wooden chair, biding his time, watching the small movements in his son's face as he made the decision finally to confess.

Marcus' eyes were focused downwards, towards the floor. At last, he spoke. "On your march through town, there was a man proceeding you on horseback."

"There were many, as I recall. Of what possible relevance is that?"

"I knew one of them, that is all."

"You knew many."

"I'm not speaking of one of your men, Father. This man rules in Ashqelon. Before that, he was a tribune in Arabia. He used to lead the army there."

There was silence for a moment, time in which Julius' mind quickened and his features pulled sharply into focus: the blue-black glare beneath his angled brown brows balanced his straight nose, like a sparrowhawk gliding in the sky with its dark brown wings at full extension. A momentary dread crept into Julius' mind that some of his suspicions were about to be confirmed in ways he had never yet imagined. Nor would he like what he heard. He collected himself, then spoke. "You refer to former tribune Galenus? He's not a pleasant man. What could you know of him, son?"

"I met him once, a while back," said Marcus. And then, in response to the skeptical look on his father's face. "In Ashqelon."

Julius grunted a laugh. "You were never in Ashqelon to my knowledge."

"I was once. With Yehonatan and Tullian. You weren't pleased about it at the time, as I recall."

"Hmm," said Julius, "now I remember." And he thought, so Galenus does know Yehonatan. His expression was all inner directed now. "I forgot you ever visited the city." His elbow on the table, Julius placed his fingers on his temple and cheekbones and closed his eyes, thinking. Then he dropped his hands and lifted his head like a hound scenting a blood trail. "I admit, Marcus, that you have succeeded in distracting me very neatly from your situation. But even if you do know the man, it hardly gives you leave to run off for a few days without asking my permission first." He waved his hand. "What made you think this story would suffice?"

Marcus' eyes met his. "Just this. When I saw him in the procession, he looked straight at me. He recognized me, Father, just as I knew him."

"And if he did? Why is that important?"

"I felt a risk. To the family. To all of us. Not just myself." Marcus swallowed. Looking straight down, he spoke between his lashes. Softly. "Three years ago, he paid attention to me in a way that made me extremely uncomfortable. As if one day he would have more business with me." The boy glanced up for a second into his father's acute gaze. Then he looked quickly back to the floor.

"Go on." Julius' voice was soft, but its quality was insistent.

"He flattered me in a way I did not deserve. I didn't understand it at the time, just that his attentions made me anxious. But I thought about it later and came to see what it meant, Sir." Some moments later Marcus added, "I didn't like it."

There was profound silence in the room, time for Julius to hear every breath that his son drew. He stared at the boy, trying to see him as a stranger might. The dark curls on the downturned head whose color and texture he had bequeathed him; the periwinkle blue eyes, their whites pure as twin narcissi, which surpassed in beauty the

265

remarkable eyes of his mother and his own, as he well knew; the precisely turned cheekbones, which, over time, had more and more come to resemble his uncle's facial structure. That his son was tied by looks to another man still bothered him beyond reason. He felt it like a morass in the pit of his belly, curdling his mind whenever he pondered it. With a kind of biting distaste, Julius said, "And where was Yehonatan when all of this happening?"

"Sitting near me on a couch. Galenus was paying attention to him too." And then, in response to a flash in his father's eyes, he said. "Yehonatan didn't like it either. But towards him, it was plain for all three of us to see. Not sneaky like with me."

"If you noticed it as a lad, why assume Yehonatan did not? He's not a simple man." Julius snorted, cutting off a mordant laugh. "Did their past dealings give Galenus leave, then, to treat him so?"

Something flicked across the boy's face too fast for him to read properly. But he thought he saw shock and horror blunting a second later into dismay. "They met before. In Arabia. They had business dealings. Sir. That's what I know." Marcus shrugged his face into natural animation again.

"You told me nothing of this then. Why not?"

"Nothing happened. To any of us. I thought no more of it then. Only, there was a reason I was reminded of the thing recently. I thought it through. Then, when I saw General Galenus riding in front of you, Sir, it all came home again. I worried about what would happen if you forced me to meet him. Say, if you brought him here before I could speak to you."

"Perhaps," Julius demurred. He shrugged his shoulders. "What I don't understand is why you thought I wouldn't protect you from him? Why say nothing to me and disappear? Why not trust me?"

"I wasn't worried about the present. You would protect me now. But I won't always serve near you." Marcus finally looked up. "And Galenus isn't the kind of man who will accept no unless he wants to. If it's in his interest. I saw that clearly enough the first time I met him. I thought it better for him to know nothing more of me than what he knows already."

"That's all?"

"To tell the truth, Father..." Marcus looked at him consideringly.

"Go on."

"I didn't think it would do you any good either for him to find out Uncle Yehonatan was your relation by marriage. Things being in the state they are here. Politically, I mean."

"That was prescient." He looked straight back at his son now, his expression Jovian, a stern god of justice. "I see you were well intentioned, Marcus. But next time let me take care of it. It's presumptuous of you to think I need your intervention in such a matter." Then, searching the boy's expression, he relented a bit, "But you were correct enough, after all. It's not in my interest to let him know that." Julius paused. "There's another thing I would like to know. Where were you staying all this time?"

"The first night I camped on the beach."

"And then?"

"I was visiting one of the men who rescued me on the beach. You'll have heard of that already, I imagine, from Mother or Vincius."

"Judeans, I think your mother mentioned?"

"Yes, Father. I wanted to thank him properly. He cleaned up my wounds and bandaged me. I stayed over at his cottage." He could see Julius watching him carefully, judging every word. "The man's a rabbi. He's educated. He knows law and history. We spent some time discussing them."

"I don't see the need for you to study Jewish law. If you want to study law, Roman law should suffice you."

"We've been through this before, Father. It interests me." Marcus shrugged his shoulders. "What harm could there be in studying it?"

"*A great book is a great evil*," Julius snapped out.

Marcus smiled reprovingly. "Callimuchus, Father? He wrote at least 800 short works and was speaking about epic poetry, not learning in general. Judging by your taste for Epictetus, you don't believe that yourself."

"I suppose I don't." Julius sat still, his face forward, frowning at his son. "In any case, I doubt he showed you any books. Still, if he taught you well, I hope you offered recompense. I believe Vincius mentioned that the village where they found you is quite poor."

"I didn't pay him, Father. I worked in his fields with him while I was there."

"Don't do that again. You are not a peasant to work the field. Pay the man next time. You hear?"

"He's not a peasant either. He's a well-spoken man.

Furious at the continued insubordination, Julius breathed out loudly. Just then something else occurred to him. "Wait a second." His eyes narrowed slightly. "Vincius and your mother must know exactly where this man lives. Why did neither of them mention it to me so we could bring you home last night?"

Marcus ran his tongue over his upper lip. "I don't know," he said.

"Perhaps, you don't," Julius enunciated neutrally. He kept his focus on his son. "I'll have to ask them." Julius stood up, placing his two fists on the table and leaning forward. Following suit, Marcus rose, positioning himself behind his three-legged stool, waiting for his father's judgement.

"I don't forbid you from seeing this man again, Marcus. He helped you without thought of reward. There may be good in him. But I don't want you to see him without my express permission. You must ask me before you visit him again. I'll brook no disobedience in this. Is that understood?"

"Yes, Sir. I understand."

Julius waved him away. "Good night, son."

When the door had shut tight, Julius sat back down on his wooden chair, stacked fist over fist on the polished cedar surface of the desk and laid his forehead on top. "Galenus," he said aloud, like the name was a curse. "Mithras be praised that Marcus had the foresight..." To what? he thought. To run and hide? To deceive him? Certainly, to get the measure of Galenus in one brief meeting, a meeting that neither Marcus nor Yehonatan had told him about previously, a meeting that sounded alarming.

That he had not been told was intolerable.

But why? he asked himself. Why should that enrage him?

Why didn't Yehonatan and Marcus want him to know about a meeting with a man they did not know he had a connection to, however dubious and long ago? Why would they refrain from telling him unless they were hiding something? What else had happened on that trip? Yehonatan, he admitted to himself then, had distracted him so much he had not even asked. Given what Julius had guessed about Yehonatan over the past few weeks, there was a past history between him and Galenus. And what had transpired at the meeting had been alarming. Dangerous too. Galenus would tell him straight up, he felt sure. But would want to know why he wanted the information. And that, as Marcus had realized, would reveal the relationship between them.

Did Miriam know about what happened during that meeting, he wondered. Because that would be insufferable. He, alone, was responsible for the safety of his family. Not Miriam. Not her brother. Not Marcus.

He'd often thought that Miriam and Marcus were too close, that it was wrong for a mother and her grown son to remain so intimate as the boy grew into his late teens. There was an impropriety about it. A young man should live with other men who could train him up for combat and other work.

But then Julius had never known his own mother. Either she had died after his birth, or his father had simply taken him away from his mother when his Legion left Germania, then hired a local nursemaid to care for him. One or the other, he didn't know the truth. His aunt, with whom he had lived during part of his childhood, had told him both stories. The aunt who did not like him much and with whom he had had a fraught relationship.

In the end, it had made him strong and resilient.

Marcus needed more strength and resilience to deal with the adversity that would come to him as he fought his way up the military command structure. He would have to send Marcus away soon to redirect that relationship and to create toughness in him as well. It was way too soft, his relationship with his mother.

His own journey with Galenus from Zeugma had been ... fascinating. The man was a repository of political and military know-how and dynastic maneuverings.

But he rang danger signals as well, from sundown to sun-up, every damn day.

Then there was that little voice that whispered in his head that Galenus had most likely killed Marcellus near seventeen years ago. That murder had made him centurion before his time, which he had ridden to a more powerful position in the army and a higher status marriage than he would have otherwise enjoyed. The murder that his cohort had never been able to pursue. There never had been direct evidence for it, only suspicion on their part. And they had been told, time and again, that suspicion and a dead mouse in hand were not enough to proceed. What could he possibly do about the murder now with Marcellus forgotten except by a few of his staff and himself? And with Galenus ensconced in power?

He had done nothing in the time since Galenus had been installed.

What could he do if he wanted to do something?

Stop drinking for one, so his mind was clearer.

But if he stopped honoring Dionysius by drinking freely, would the god continue to look on him with favor? Would all the years of favor he had experienced by propitiating Dionysius finally turn into a curse?

To that he had no answer.

This was all more complicated than he would have wished.

———◦———

Marcus walked out of his father's office. A few sconces in the hallway glimmered still but most of the villa was already washed in deep shadow. He was tired, grateful that this meeting he had dreaded was over at last and that he had escaped so lightly. It could have been much worse. In fact, he had expected it to be worse. From long experience, he knew the pattern the examination was likely to take. Fortunately, most of the questions his father had asked he had prepared himself for. But there were one or two at the end he had not anticipated. Foolish of him. Now, it was late, and he was tired out. It had been tricky going but the day had had its blessings. Given the outcome of events, he felt all too conscious of their source.

Earlier that day, wending his way home, Phoenix had hailed him near the forum, diversion incarnate beckoning to him irresistibly. Dreading the moment he must arrive back home, a smiling Marcus hailed Phoenix back, rode over to him and dismounted his Iberian. The fellow, leaning back against a sparkling white marble wall, surveyed him up and down and visibly refrained from quipping on the state of his dilapidated sky-blue tunic. Instead, his eyes alight, Phoenix told him of a lecture he had just attended at one of the schools given by Lucan, a philosopher he knew from Athens. Drunk this day on words alone, Phoenix had done his best to reconstruct the argument. "Oh, but I'm sloppy," Phoenix said, "I haven't the verbal facility, the literary balance, the poetry to convey his talk in all its intricacy. You

271

know, Marcus, tomorrow he plans on presenting a counterargument. There will be a chance at the end to argue with him or to talk to him, as you like. You ought to come with me to see what you think."

"Both positions?" Marcus repeated. He raised his eyebrows. "Not just the one he believes is true? Your man's not a charlatan by any chance?"

"You haven't guessed the reason? For the sheer pleasure of doing it brilliantly. The man's a latter-day sophist," said Phoenix. And then with another appraising look he said, "I think you will enjoy it if you come. It's verbal play of another kind. If you like, meet me here at noon."

A sophist. Marcus had read some of their writings. Gorgias naturally. There were several copies of his *Epitaphius* in the great library of Caesarea, musty scrolls with small cracks webbing their ancient seams. But this would be his first chance to encounter a sophist arguing in person. "Tomorrow, unfortunately, might be impossible." Marcus shot Phoenix a waggish grin. "But I'll make the effort." He held out his hand to his friend, sprung up onto his saddlecloth, gathered his horse, waved farewell and set forth feeling curiously lightened.

The air had been pleasant then with a fresh breeze blowing in from the sea, the sky a whitish blue. As he rode on, the hawking voices from the marketplace receded, the insistent odors faded behind him, the foot traffic on the ground waned. Presently, the houses grew larger, the expanse of land surrounding each one more spacious. Here and there, through gaps in the clematis covered gates, he watched the sea, the rhythmic surge of its waves, its light spume floating skyward. The Iberian's hooves fell to earth with precise clops. Marcus considered the argument Phoenix had laid out for him, noticing one or two points of attack. Odd, he thought, that Dion was nowhere in sight today. He was not used to seeing those two far apart from each other of late. In fact, a few days before Critias had told him an amusing story. He considered Critias for a moment. Once, not long ago, his friend had also made a stray remark to him about his father.

Marcus reined his horse to an amble for a few moments, reconstructing the few words that Critias had spoken. And what he had expressed by looks rather than speech. He ran his tongue over his upper teeth considering it. Eureka, the boy thought, his eyes suddenly alight, a small smile forming on his mouth. He clucked to Argos to step up from the cross street to the wide lane that led to his house. The solution he had been seeking about what to say to forestall his father had finally emerged.

He had failed to play around with his hypotheses. And now that he had, a fullborn solution to his dilemma had arisen in his mind, like Athena birthed from the head of Zeus. It was that simple. An unexpected line of defense had opened before his eyes with the advantage of preserving intact all the territory he wanted to guard. This was a classic flanking maneuver.

After all, he decided, it had been extraordinarily auspicious for him to have run across Phoenix just then. Although the idea of that fellow as a godsend of any sort made Marcus want to roar with laughter.

PART XIII

CHAPTER 20
Devorah

Marcus held the reins in one hand as he angled his other hand over his eyes to shield them as he squinted into the sun now descending towards the horizon. That uneven brownish lump under a stubby tree far ahead of them really had just moved. It wasn't a rock, but a person or an animal. And then, as his small party rapidly approached the crossroad, it suddenly came to him who it was: Devorah, sitting in the dust of the road. He still could not see her face distinctly. Yet, she became instantly recognizable. Perhaps because she always wore the same drab clothing.

Twenty paces away, Marcus maneuvered Argos out in front of his two friends angling his horse across the road so that he was blocking their advance. He looked at Dion and Critias' startled faces and said, "I know that..." and pointed his thumb over his shoulder. "You'll both wait for me a moment while I make sure everything is all right." Sliding down from his gelding, he stepped a pace towards Dion, the better horseman of the two, and handed him Argos' reins to hold.

274

Astride his horse, Dion leaned down slightly and took the reins in his elegant left hand, then straightened, looking over Marcus' head at the undistinguished brown girl near the crossroads. He shook his head slightly, his curls diffusing a hint of lavender. An incredulous grin played on his face, but he refrained from saying anything. Instead, wrapping the reins around his hand, he flicked it gently against the rich linen tunic covering his thigh. "Go ahead," he said. "We'll wait."

Marcus walked down the empty road and crossed over to her. She was sitting ramrod straight now, her legs tucked underneath the shapeless garment and staring right at him, her eyebrows uplifted. A market basket filled with goods lay behind her, he noticed, a few of its items tossed out at her side.

She turned her eyes from him and looked past him. "So those are your friends," she said in Aramaic, examining the two men on the road. "Well, I'm not surprised." Her gaze moved dismissively back to Marcus. "I saw you in the distance. I was sure you were planning to ride right by me without saying hello."

The expression on his face was his only response, a slight lilt of his lips that was not a smile.

"So why did you stop?"

He stepped closer. "To confound your expectations of me." His expression barely altered as he spoke. "Could I have had any other purpose, do you think?"

She nodded sagely. "Seeing it's you, it sounds very likely."

He looked at her impatiently. "What are you doing out here alone, Devorah? It's late in the day and you're still miles from home."

"Having my expectations confounded, seemingly. Why are you here?"

"I don't like to mention the obvious, but it is late, you are all alone on the road and far from home."

"Yes. That is obvious."

"Devorah." He was growing annoyed.

"Marcus." She echoed his tone back perfectly.

"Get up and hand me the basket. I'll take you home. Your father would not like this."

"What? And leave behind your Roman friends and countrymen?" She sneered at him. "Or are you planning on having your friends escort me as well?"

"What a treat that would be for you and me both. Unfortunately, it might just be less pleasurable for them." He leaned across her familiarly and put his hand on the basket's handle to hoist it up."

She lay her hand over his urgently. "Don't," she said.

"Why ever not?" he said and began to lift it.

"Don't," she said once more, pressing the basket down with her weight. She was looking past him to the grouping of men and horses. "The bottom is about to fall off."

He let go of the basket and stood upright. "I see," he said. "Well, if nothing else that certainly explains why you are sitting here idling." There were tears in her eyes, he noticed surprised. He modulated his tone to sound less astringent. "Don't worry. One of us will have something to repair your basket well enough. And then I'll escort you home on Argos."

She looked up at him, her brown eyes big, and for once did not utter a word.

Marcus turned silently and trod back to face Dion and Critias. "You two go ahead. She needs a bit of help. I have to take her home."

"You are going to leave us on her account? Marcus, you're not serious! And what about tonight?" said Critias. "Look, if it is that important to you, we'll ride back to town and I can send a slave." He looked at Marcus impatiently. "Or one of your servants. Why trouble to do it yourself?"

The expression in Critias' eyes was transparent. Marcus directed his eyes away from it. "She's a young girl. I am not leaving her here unescorted for hours, with night coming on."

"Marcus, look at her," said Dion, amused. "I hardly think that will be a problem."

He stared up at Dion, his expression inimical.

Dion snorted. "I only meant someone would have to notice her first. With that hair, with that dress, she's barely distinguishable from the landscape." His eyebrows rose. "I must admit I didn't see her until you pointed her out."

Marcus' face was stony. "And you're always so observant."

"Nor did I," said Critias. "Who is she to you anyway? A servant, a family retainer?"

"Does it matter?" said Marcus. "Look, I owe her family a debt. The kind you don't repay by leaving one of them in potential danger." He looked up into their faces. "I'll see you tomorrow. Or maybe," he added under his breath, "not." Stepping to the side of Dion's horse, Marcus pulled up the edge of the man's saddlebag and pulled a cloth out of it. "Dion," he said, "I'm taking this cloth." And then in reply to his friend's look. "I need it. I'll replace it, I promise."

Dion barked a laugh. "Marcus! As though I care about the filthy cloth." Dion handed Argos' reins back to Marcus and gathered his own horse beneath them. "Take it, it's no matter. Goodbye," he said, kicking the mare lightly to start her moving.

Critias lingered a moment more, glancing from the girl back to Marcus who stood before him, holding Argos by the reins, Dion's cloth draped over his shoulder. The look in his eyes had turned hostile. "I see it now," Critias said. "I had not quite realized..."

"Critias, whatever you are thinking, that's not it." He paused a moment. "Her father... He's my teacher."

Critias nodded curtly, as though that information confirmed his thinking. And with the reins tucked into the palms of his hands, he breathed out loudly once, touched his horse lightly then rode fast to catch up with Dion.

Leading Argos, Marcus walked back toward Devorah.

"So those are your friends," she said again.

Her tone stung him hard, like angry wasps defending their nest during a summer dry spell. "They were," he said. "They may be again. One day." He shrugged. "Or perhaps not." Then he sat down on the ground. Devorah took the basket and emptied it out. And he started ripping the cloth into long shreds with his knife. When it was done, he said, "Hand me the basket."

"I'll do it," said Devorah and stuck her hand out. "Give me the cloth."

"I like fixing objects," said Marcus and shrugged. "Years of spending times with engineers." When she handed him the basket, he turned it over, examined the broken part at the bottom and then placed it between his legs and began to interweave the cloth tightly through the space between the spokes of the basket so that it would hold the weight of the goods that she had brought with her from town.

Devorah inched away from him, settling herself against a boulder. Hawk-like, her brown eyes flitted up and down his body and over to his horse, observing in the stillness that descended every detail in view. His tunic had grayed with hard use. There were darkened smears of dirt on his legs and arms. Scratches, a scraped knee. His fingers twirling the basket round and round possessed a cleverness of their own, the magic of knowledge mated with speed.

The air felt fresh and light today, fragrant even, not oppressive with heat and drought, as it sometimes did. The autumn rains had just begun this year. Above their heads, a bronzed turtledove landed on a nearby tree, and began to coo. A second one landed and, together into the prismatic sunshine, they purred forth an entire dialogue. Shaking his head to ward off a buzzing horsefly, Argos blew out noisily into the tall grass he was grazing, jiggling his bit.

"Why are you so heavily armed today?" The girl's voice broke into the quiet.

"What?" said Marcus, his attention focused entirely on his handi-work with the basket. He looked up to her then back down at himself.

"Bow, knife," she nodded at the horse, "sword."

"We went out hunting."

"And that's why you're the filthy one? Because you played prey for the two boys?"

His glance shot up, disbelief vying with amusement. "And the reason you ask is?"

"From the evidence of my eyes, you don't seem to have caught anything at all."

"If you must know, *my strings sang, my arrows flew gladly*," said Marcus continuing to work, a grin now touching his face. "Critias has two slaves transporting the carcasses back to Caesarea."

She thought about that for a second. "Oh." Her voice changed as she spoke the word, her jibing tone sinking now into total disapproval.

"What? What did I do now?" said Marcus. He glanced up from his basket once again before resuming his work. "I see. Although it's odd that that bothers you more than the other." He smiled again, this time coldly. "Of course, you would think that about me." His voice had chilled. "I don't eat the animals I shoot, Devorah. Critias and Dion are splitting the carcasses among themselves."

"Why bother then? It seems awfully bloodthirsty to kill animals if you aren't going to eat them."

"But so much less bloodthirsty than practicing on men." Marcus looked at her again noting that at the angle she was now sitting, the sunlight showed her face brushed with sweat and dust. "I like distance shooting from horseback. It's more challenging than practicing in the yard." He smoothed back a stray curl that had fallen forward onto his forehead. "Besides, it's not a total waste. I'll send some of our servants over for a share of the meat later on. They are not permitted to cook the meat at our house, you see, because my mother will not

279

let them bring it into the house, not even in the servant's quarter. It's not kosher."

Devorah snorted.

"Yes, I thought you realized that. And now you see I know it too." He stood up. "Come on. This should hold for now."

"Let me see that," she said and grabbed the basket from him. "Not bad," she concluded grudgingly, testing its weight. "You do have your occasional uses, Marcus." One by one, she replaced the new earthenware platters and cups she had bought in the city into the basket then laid the vegetables and spices on top of them.

Marcus chuckled. "Thanks," he said. "The first genuine words of praise you've ever uttered about me." When she finished arranging the goods in the basket, he spoke again. "Stand here by my side. Time to lift you up onto Argos."

"You ride. I'll walk."

He glared at her a second. "You'd like that, wouldn't you? It would bolster every prejudice you already hold about me."

"Well, yes," she said, shrugging. "But if you prefer it the other way, I'll ride and you can walk."

"As though you could possibly control him! Have you ever ridden a horse before? Or only donkeys?"

"You can hold the lead."

"The reins. Not the bloody lead. And I'm not going to walk miles to your house when I can ride. It will take hours. I want to be home later tonight."

"That's right," she sneered. "Your evening with your friends. What a waste to miss it."

"Yes," he sneered back, "my evening with my damned friends." He ran his fingers under Argos' mane, back and forth, stroking the horse's neck. "Devorah, what is this about? Is there some way I have offended you today?"

"No," said Devorah.

280

"Then come over here and get up on the horse."

She set her mouth. "No."

"Why not? What's the problem?"

"You know it as well as I do, Marcus. You're just not thinking." After a moment when he said nothing, she put her hands on her hips, closed her eyes and recited, "'*Be deliberate in judgment, raise up many disciples and make a fence around the Law*.' One of those fences is that we oughtn't to sit so close by each other, male and female. Touching. On top of your horse. It isn't modest."

"Is that all? Well, stick the cursed basket between us."

"It won't fit," said Devorah. "And I'm serious."

"I know you're serious," said Marcus. "I concede your point. But I don't see the choice. Look at the sun." He jerked his chin to the west. "Your father's no doubt extremely worried by now."

She exhaled loudly. "There is a choice. You just don't want to take it because it's inconvenient."

"Or because in this case, it's irrelevant." Marcus leaned his forehead into Argos' mane as he lightly stroked the horse's ear. He twisted his head and looked at the girl. "Devorah, you don't seriously fancy yourself in any danger of falling for my advances on the way home, do you? I mean, it is not as though you can stomach me most of the time."

"That's not the point and you know it. I'm talking about a way of behaving that you must practice all the time. Acting modestly. It's got nothing to do with you and your advances. You idiot. And, no," she said, glaring at him with her face furious, "I'm not afraid of falling for you on the way home."

He stared back at her, his face expressionless, unbudging. "That's my point exactly. So then, there's no point in worrying about it, is there?"

"You mean there's no point in arguing about it anymore, don't you? Since we aren't getting anywhere. And won't." Her voice still

281

scathing, the girl stepped closer to Marcus. "All right then." Overhead the doves twittered still.

"Oh, yes we are," Marcus said nastily. "You may not realize it yet, Devorah, but this is the first time you have ever let me win an argument so cleanly. Victory at last. However trivial. I'm planning on savoring the feeling the whole ride back to your house."

He bent slightly at the waist, and with a nod, waited until she lifted her left foot into the grip made by his interlaced hands. Then touching her arm and shoulder with delicacy, enough only to keep her balanced, he hoisted her up carefully onto Argos' back. Handing her the basket, he levered himself in front of her onto the gelding. Sitting, he dug in his heels. "Hold on," he said and urged his horse into a run.

A half a mile later Marcus slowed Argos into a walk.

"Can you move that basket? It's damn uncomfortable sticking into my back."

"Where should I put it? There's nowhere else I can hold it comfortably."

Marcus looked over his shoulder. "Here, hand it to me. And move in closer behind me. Hold me, not just the back of my tunic. Otherwise, you'll slip off. As it is, Argos doesn't like you sitting that far back."

"He's a horse. How can you tell?"

"Because he's my horse. I can feel what he's telling me, just like he knows what I tell him." He glanced back at her face over his shoulder. "Look, we were exercising hard all morning. And now he's running more heavily than he should be. So, it would help if you sit as close to me as you can."

The road entered a large stand of cedar trees and Marcus stretched his shoulders, breathing in with relief at the respite from the glaring light that marked the sun's descent toward the western horizon. The air here was filled with a sticky sweet resinous scent, earthy and deep, enjoyable. Before them, long shadows fell intermittently across the road. Marcus angled his gaze back toward the sea. Perched just above the skyline he saw long, thin golden clouds. He shifted his seat slightly.

"You know, this basket is damn uncomfortable. Why I bothered to repair it, I don't know. We should have left it, and I could have sent you whatever you needed tomorrow."

"I only want the things I bought, Marcus. Not anything else."

"It's plain earthenware, right? You can get pieces like these, a thousand thousand, any day in the market. What does it matter?"

"The difference is that I bought these."

"Now that went straight to the point. So, tell me, Devorah, how were you planning on getting these things home if I hadn't stumbled across you?"

"I was waiting for twilight, and then I was going to carry them home in my overdress."

"Ever the pragmatist, you. But why not carry them in your dress during the daylight?"

"My under-tunic is... Look, Marcus, I had my reasons. Nor is it your concern."

"Your under-tunic. Hmm."

She punched him in the lower back.

"Ugh," he grunted. "Right in the kidneys. What was that for?"

"Don't imagine anything," Devorah said. "Just kick this beast so it goes faster than a crawl."

"Okay, for a bit." Marcus anchored the basket firmly between his thighs. "But since you've now decided that we are permitted to touch..." Reaching behind him, he grasped her under the knees and jerked her towards him. "Now you're finally sitting close enough." Grabbing hold of Devorah's left arm, the boy tucked it firmly around his chest and pinned it under his own arm. "Lean forward into me and this time hold onto me tightly."

A mile later, Marcus slowed the horse again. The road around them was shadowy and deserted, empty enough for him to hear the resonating clop of Argos' hooves, the noisy huffing of the horse's breath. Together with the girl, he floated through a cloud of milling gnats. Marcus ducked his head, swatting them away, still grasping the basket with the muscles in his thighs. Behind him, Devorah was hiding her face in his tunic. He inhaled sharply and then surprised, he seized hold of a hank of her hair, sliding it through his fingers so that it just brushed over his nose and mouth. "Is that perfume you're wearing?" he jeered.

"I went to the baths today," she said snatching her hair away. "And if I am?"

"Nothing. I'm surprised." He laughed out loud. "It's usually my male friends who are scented, not the female... I mean, that's the same bath oil that Dion wears. Ordinarily, you smell..."

She sniffed out hard. "Of the farmyard, you mean." The hurt in her voice was palpable.

"You're not customarily sopped in lavender oil, Devorah. That's all I meant." And then before she had a chance to stew, he said, "Tell me, what did your father teach you this week?"

"If you want to know, why don't you come anymore?"

"I don't always have the chance, that's all."

Holding his ribs firmly, she leaned in and snorted in his ear. "As past-times go, Nimrod, I'm sure hunting is much more enjoyable."

"Hunting has its moments," he said. "The stimulation of the chase for one thing. Loosing the arrow cleanly into the heart of the animal you're trying to kill. Though that's a sentiment," he half glanced over his shoulder at her, "that likely you don't admire. It also happens to be an arena in which I excel. And what, in this instance, may be most to the point, it's sanctioned parentally, if not divinely."

"Your father's giving you trouble again?"

284

Her hands were holding his ribs. She could feel him breathing and the moment that his breathing caught and when he restarted it.

"Loosed the arrow smack into the heart," she said and laughed. "And to think, you believed I would not enjoy the feeling."

"How much that is praiseworthy we have in common," he quipped. After a moment he lowered his voice. "I've been obvious, then?"

"Not at all," she said. "What pleasure would I find in that? You underrate me."

They rode together in silence until Marcus moved Argos into a trot.

"Why so upset that I know, Marcus?" she hissed in his ear, jouncing painfully behind him. She grabbed him harder around the waist. "You've let fall clues now and again, you know. It's trickier coming to us with your father around full-time, isn't it? Why make it such a mystery?"

"Weren't you going to tell me something," he said sharply elbowing her left hand away from his body, "about the Torah portion last week?"

"On one condition," she said, slipping behind. "That you stop this damned horse. Or let me get off."

"Then start talking." He reached his left hand in back of him and steadied her again.

"Okay then," she said. "Do you know the story of how Jacob stole the first-born blessing from Esau, his brother?"

Marcus snorted. "Of course."

"Because I wondered if you knew," she said, "that Esau lost his father's blessing when he went hunting, armed with quiver and bow, on behalf of his father?"

Marcus snorted. "I see your implication. And while it's true that my father encourages hunting, I have no brother. Also, Isaac sent Esau. My father is no Isaac. Though perhaps," he added in an undertone, "I now better understand your dislike of hunting."

"My father told me once that some learned rabbis in Yavneh whisper that Rome is descended from the heirs of Esau," Devorah replied, "therefore the antagonism between us will be eternal."

"How does that work?" asked Marcus. "Rome is on the opposite side of the world from Edom."

"Because Herod the Tyrant was an Idumean by birth and Idumeans descend directly from Esau. He worked for Rome and handed us over to them at his death."

Marcus considered that point in silence as they continued their ride northeast.

Devorah said. "And here's a different point altogether. Have you never thought it strange, that Rebecca knows to whom the blessing belongs, but Isaac does not?"

"It's toward the end of his life," Marcus said. "Isaac's sight has dimmed. Perhaps his inward vision too."

"The story states only the sight of his eyes. If it meant something else it would be less specific," she countered. "Even so, why do you think that Jacob knew that his mother's voice was the correct one to listen to, not his father's?"

"Surely, he knew his brother's nature as well as his own. He could tell which of the two of them was better suited."

"But how could he know it wasn't his own pride urging him to accept?" she said.

Marcus flexed his thigh muscles to steady the basket, then twisted his upper torso around. He said, "I don't know. Do you?"

"My father said that there's a tradition that Abraham told Jacob beforehand. But I think that detracts from Rebecca. When pregnant, she consulted God. And God answered her prayer. She knew which child would inherit. Perhaps Jacob realized that."

"Jacob seems extremely close to his mother, the tent dweller, the scholarly lad who stays home to study." Silence fell for a moment as they both considered that point. Their thoughts led each of them into their own private territory. Then Marcus continued. "As a couple, Isaac and Rebecca don't seem to have discussed the inheritance with each other, crucial as it was. I wonder if they got along at that point."

"Of course, they got along," Devorah snapped. "He's a patriarch, she's a matriarch."

"You're joking, right?" he snorted. "Or perhaps you don't know the other stories? Hagar and Sarah, Jacob and Esau, Joseph and his brothers. Never a dispute amongst them!"

"I don't agree," she said, "But we'll argue that point later. Meanwhile, why do you think that once Isaac finds out he's been tricked, he can't take the blessing back and give it to Esau?"

"Words change things," said Marcus. He spoke softly. "They shape reality. *God said let there be light and there was light.*' An extreme example, but you see the point. Words have power. Once spoken, you can't ignore them or take them back."

"But, spoken before God? And when they are based on a lie?" said the girl. "On its face, it doesn't make sense."

"Sometimes a person speaks a word, and you know it's true, even if you don't want it to be. You can't deny the truth of it, afterward," he said. "It has its own power."

"Odd. My father said something like that. He told me of a holy man his father knew, who could tell whether his prayers were accepted by the way the words flew from his mouth," said Devorah. "If they flowed smoothly, his prayer would be effective, but if not, the prayer always failed."

"I met a holy man like that once who told me a thing. I've been worried ever since that he was right."

"What thing?"

"That I have a mystical bent."

She laughed raucously. "You," she said. "Is there any doubt? You're going to be a soldier. It's what you were born to do."

287

"I..." The sound died in Marcus' throat. He shrugged. "That's what my father thinks too." Marcus patted her thigh to grab her attention then pointed forward. "Look up ahead. Lights from your village. Do you know, Devorah? One day when you are in Caesarea for market day you should come with me to hear this philosopher whose talks I attend, Antinous. He's quite a brilliant man, trained in Athens but from the West. You would enjoy it, I believe. I could sneak you in. It would not be impossible to arrange if you wanted to come. There are a few women who attend. Or we could hide your hair and put boys' clothes on you."

"A lecture on pagan philosophy," she snorted. "Me? You cannot be serious."

"Of course, I am," he said, his voice derisive. "You're such a shark you would devour it whole."

She punched him in the kidney again. "You're not thinking again, army boy. I could not possibly wear boy's clothes. It's forbidden."

He jerked slightly but said nothing. Starring ahead, letting the merest hint of a smile inform his lips, Marcus mused about the thing that Devorah had not said was forbidden. In no other way did he allow his body to reveal any clue as to what he was thinking.

They rode uphill through the dregs of twilight, odd bits of illumination still fracturing the sky. The shadows above them shifted and stirred, encroaching, elongating. Until at last Marcus grazed her thigh with his fingertips, then lifted his hand to point the way forward. "Look over my shoulder. That's your father leaning in the doorway. Waiting for you. I wager he's furious."

"Hardly," she snorted. "It's my father. Not yours."

⸺⸺◆⸺⸺

Shadows hovered all around the walls, pressing into the center of the small room. They crept downward from the smoky ceiling and up from the floor, converging near the oil lamp on the table, which, spitting its flame upward and out, vanquished them in a continuing battle. He sat in his house across the crude wooden table from the two young people, watching them gobble their food, gulp after gulp. The room was utterly still, except the repeated clanks as they ladled the thick bean stew into their dishes, the slight crackles as they broke their rough barley bread and plopped it into the stew, over and over. The aroma of the long simmering stew, piquant rosemary, lima beans and olive oil lingered comfortingly in the air.

Rabbi Ariel sat until the room was silent, until the food was entirely consumed, until the boy looked at the girl and smiled. And then his daughter relaxed her grimace and managed a slight smile in return. And that too, was unexpected.

"Thank you for dinner," Marcus said. He scraped back his wooden chair. "I should be returning home now."

Devorah rolled her eyes. "You're not thinking again, Marcus," she said.

"What?" he said. And then, "Oh." He shifted his eyes downward and quickly mouthed a prayer of thanks to God for the food to finish his meal properly.

Rabbi Ariel had already observed some little signs that there had been a change, however slight, between the two of them, when Marcus had politely helped Devorah to dismount his horse, holding her body a few seconds too long. Or perhaps not too long, but as though he were comfortable touching her. Neither interpretation of the event, he groused silently, pleased him overmuch.

"And thank you as well for helping my girl," Rabbi Ariel said. He pushed back the bench he was seated on and stood up. "Let me see you to your horse."

"I didn't need the help, Father." Devorah's face was serious, insistent. "I keep telling you that."

289

He looked at his daughter, frowning, slightly shaking his head, until she turned to Marcus and said, "I didn't need it, but I do appreciate that you helped me." Then dropping her voice to a mumble, she added, "I felt much safer with you escorting me home."

"Thank you," he said as he rose from the table. "An admission at last."

"You have your uses, soldier boy. I'll grant you that."

"For one," Marcus drawled, raising his eyebrows, one hip jutting forward, "I got you home to your papa with all of your goods still intact." And then pursing his lips into a victory smirk, his eyes brilliant, the young man strode to the door and took his departure.

His daughter, he was chagrined to notice, actually bit off a laugh as he turned to face her.

Later, Rabbi Ariel sat alone pondering the recent past. Before him on the table was an oil lamp whose wick he was trimming. As he worked, the shadows above him were lengthening, winning their battle against the light.

The mistake, he realized, had been to pair those two together for learning. He saw it now. A more traditional teacher, a more righteous man, never would have. Pride had motivated him, his pride in his daughter's accomplishments, not the desire to serve God. He was a simple man, a man who had not considered where this might lead. There was a solution at hand, of course; to unpair the two before, God forbid, he or his daughter had unpleasant consequences to face.

Personally, Rabbi Ariel admitted to himself, he was quite fond of Marcus. He had a good heart and a strong will to learn. But there were daily influences on the lad which he knew nothing of except the incontrovertible fact that they were unholy. He closed his eyes and pictured the boy's face as he had seen it tonight, then his daughter's.

A new face of the moon had come to light, one of the seventy-seventy, in semi-eclipse. Nothing good, the rabbi sensed, would come from more intermingling of the two.

PART XIV

CHAPTER 21
A Family Scene

A light knock sounded at her door, one that Miriam recognized. "Come in," she said, her voice bright, as she began winding closed the scroll she had been reading. Euripides's *Hippolytus*. The play was touring the city just now with Marcello of Tarsus as lead actor and she wanted to compare his company's interpretation with her own impressions. Keeping the carnelian-colored woolen throw tucked around her torso for warmth, she changed her position on the couch from reclining to vertical. The tall tripod lamps behind her head began flickering as the door slowly opened.

"He's gone for the night, is he?" Marcus asked as he slipped his head, then his body into her room.

"He's gone for now. Hence the peace. He may return later. Your father so often is unpredictable." Miriam looked her son over carefully, noting the old cloth tunic, the new dirt stains, the dusty boots, the earthy aroma of horse and sweat and leather. "You're only now getting home? It's late. Have you eaten yet?"

"I ate at Rabbi Ariel's," said Marcus, sitting down near her on the couch. "Bean stew. Humble, but very filling."

Pleased, she smiled at her son. "So, the hunting was only an excuse, then?"

"No. Can't you tell?" He held his two palms out showing the ingrained dirt, flipped them over and then looked down at the rest of himself. "I'm filthy." Tossing his head back, he raised his eyes to look at her. "But afterward I got diverted."

Miriam leaned over and lightly touched his short, dark curls, sliding the slightly textured hair through her fingers. Such a pleasure it still was, the warmth from his hair.

"Mother," he said, protesting. But he barely moved his head away from her caress.

Miriam lowered her hand, nevertheless, to rest on the couch, and leaned back against the cushions. "Did you want to see your father, then," she asked, "or me?"

"You," said Marcus. "I was hoping not to see my father tonight. At all." He exhaled pointedly through his nostrils. "I don't think he would fancy my extra-curricular excursion. I didn't ask his permission first."

Miriam recognized the bitter tone in her son's voice. "He's keeping you on a very short rein?"

"As though I'm a bloody stallion he's trying to break." Marcus leaned his head to the side and rubbed his neck.

"But he hasn't yet?"

Marcus slowly cocked his head sideways, his face etched in light and shadow, a smile playing on his lips.

It was answer enough for now. Miriam reached over to pat his upper arm, to reassure him, but stopped herself in time. He would not like it. Fortunately, he had not seen the gesture. He was looking straight ahead, his eyes enchanted by the intricate pattern on the carpet. Yehonatan had shipped the carpet to her from Persia several years ago. It displayed fine craftsmanship, silk threads intertwined among the wool, delicate flowers and leaves brought to life in peach and green, brick and turmeric.

"Mother," Marcus said at last. The lit bronze tripod to his side cast elegant patterns below her son's cheekbones, heightening the chiseled relief work of his face.

"Yes," she said brightly, encouraging him.

"I have a somewhat..." Marcus stopped and made hedging motions with his hands in the air. He glanced at her.

"Yes," she prompted again, making her voice soft.

"A somewhat delicate request to make of you." He glanced at her quickly and then away, toward the light. "You know Devorah? She's, well, they're very poor. Not hungry or anything. They live on a farm. But there's money for little else." He turned his face to her again.

Miriam made an encouraging noise in her throat, unsure where this was heading.

"She has no clothes." The color surged into his cheeks and he amended. "I mean, obviously she has clothes, a horrible brown robe or two. But I'm not even sure her under dress is, well...adequate. I ran into her today with Dion and Critias. They mocked her so cruelly I was disgusted!" He was drumming his right foot against the floor, his face staring down, his lip slightly curled, rueful. "I had a thought, since Rabbi Ariel is my teacher and he's uncomfortable accepting payment for studying Torah with him. I mean, I couldn't. But could you? Find a way to get her some decent dresses?"

His face was burning scarlet. "Marcus," she said gently.

Reluctantly he turned his face up to hers.

"That's a very kind thought on your part." With an effort she refrained from asking him if he had an interest in the girl. It would only deter future confidences.

"Thank you, Mother, for teaching me charity." After some time, Marcus spoke again. "I hardly like her. That's the odd thing," he said.

"Most of the time she's difficult and unpleasant. Like a vicious camel that only wants to bite."

Miriam leaned across and touched his knee. The insistent drumming ceased at last.

"Marcus. You needn't excuse yourself to me. It's a very kind impulse of which I approve. I'm proud of you. And I promise to think of a way which touches the pride neither of the girl nor her father."

"Thank you, Mother." He leaned back against the cushions, his head against the wall, his arms raised and tucked, triangle fashion, behind his head. She saw the more vulnerable skin of his underarm, soft and pale, the contoured bulge of his bicep muscles.

They sat together in comfort, the diffuse yellow light of the tripod flicking lazily on their faces, the orange blaze in the hearth warming them, the deep woody scent of burning cedar in the air. He leaned across, drawing an edge of her throw over his knees. "I'm tired," he announced, closing his eyes.

She was tired herself. The last thing she remembered was the sound of him yawning.

———◇———

Sometime later, Julius stood outside of Miriam's room poised to enter. It was completely silent. She's probably asleep, he thought, and opened the wooden door hard enough so that it clattered against the wall. Inside, it was dark. The fire had burned low, leaving only pale ash and black embers sporadically glowing red.

"Where's Marcus?" Julius said, his voice pitched to boom across the room.

Two shadows jerked awake on the couch, disentangling themselves. For a moment, Julius' heart constricted with rage and pain. She dares, he thought, his feet frozen, his hand stuck fast to his dagger, she's threatened before but finally she dares. A second later he recognized the second shadow as Marcus. "What in hell is going on here?" he roared, snapping his fingers at a servant down the hall. "You. Bring light. Immediately."

Marcus sat up ramrod straight, then relaxed a little, shaking himself awake. "Father. I was hoping you would come. I must have fallen asleep while I was waiting. Sir, I apologize." He rose, the woolen blanket cascading off of him in waves like water tumbling from the heights.

Julius stood in the doorway, dominating the front end of the room, radiating anger like death fumes from a three-day-old corpse. Waiting impatiently for the servant to bring light, he was in no mood to be analytical. The plain truth was he had not liked what he saw.

"Marcus," he snapped.

"Yes, Father. Here I am."

"The hunting today," Julius asked. "How was it?"

The boy stood still, but his eyes darting once towards his mother and then back again, betrayed him palpably, like a fox that knows he is trapped looking for an outlet.

"The hills were flush. I brought down two harts and some rabbits. I'll come with you and tell you about it, shall I?" said the boy, and leaned down to kiss his mother's cheek goodnight, brief, impersonal. Marcus said something Julius could not hear, and Miriam whispered a word or two in return. He shook his head, in the negative. "No," the boy said and stepped around the pink veined marble table toward his father.

"And the ride home?" Julius asked.

Marcus stopped mid-step, then, placed his leg down carefully.

"Julius," Miriam interjected. "Marcus is weary. He hunted all day and dropped off here from pure exhaustion. Perhaps you could let his account wait until tomorrow?"

The boy's head shot around to her, his eyes narrowed, his cheekbones sharpened.

Julius looked back and forth in painful triumph. The both of them had made a hash of it. They were clearly hiding something from him, but with very little coordination. "You've interfered enough already, Miriam," he shouted. "Look how soft you've made the boy. Sleeping cuddled with you on the couch at night, like he's an infant." And at last, the demon of fury within Julius, struggling hard against its bonds, burst free. His voice deepened. "Or a degenerate. Treating him like he's your lover."

Miriam's derisive laughter peeled across the room.

Midway towards Julius, Marcus had stopped. For a moment, he snapped his head back towards his mother. Then he turned to face Julius, his head cocked forward, a furrow ploughed between his dark brows. "Father, what? You're not serious. You can't believe that."

"Have you given me reason not to?" He watched his son's narrowed eyes change from shock to disbelief then harden into anger.

"You're blind, Father. You use your eyes to see only false pictures that will feed your rage."

"Marcus," Miriam said from the couch. "Your father is drunk again. You go to bed. I'll deal with him."

"Or I was blind and now I see." Julius sputtered, staring at his son with naked hostility. "I ran into Glaucon today, Critias' father. He invited me to dinner where I had a long talk with him." The servant behind him now held out a torch that illumined the room. And Julius stepped into the room with palpable menace, his titanic shadow advancing on his wife and son like a fleet of scavenger birds. "Suppose you tell me, Marcus, my son, my only son, where you went after the hunting."

"It was nothing. I ran into Devorah, Rabbi Ariel's daughter. That is, all three of us did. On our way home. She needed some help getting to her house. So naturally, I..."

"Naturally you went with her, despite the fact that I forbade you to do any such thing without my permission."

"She needed help." He shrugged. "Would you have preferred me to pass her by without saying a word? The action of a virtuous man."

"The virtue of a soldier is to obey his officer," said Julius, dominating his son with his eyes, the tone of his voice, his commanding posture. "Without question."

Marcus opened his mouth. "But I am not–"

"And the virtue of a son is to obey his father," Julius said in carrying tones.

"And the virtue of a friend? To pass by and do nothing to aid his friend in need?"

"These people are not your friends. You pay the father. He works for you. He's your bloody servant."

"And that means I have no obligations?" Silence. "As you well know, he helped me, saved my life perhaps, before he knew anything about me."

"And that accounts for why you dawdled at the task, countermanding–"

"I dawdled because I enjoyed it. Unlike here, it's pleasant there." Marcus' eyes hardened. "Or, wait. It was pleasant here before you arrived. Very pleasant." He darted his tongue out between his lips for a second, then turned back to smile lingeringly at Miriam. "Right, Mother?"

Still seated, Miriam stared at her son as though he were a stranger, then turned to face Julius. Her small hand, resting on the back of the couch, flew up to her mouth like a startled bird taking flight. As Julius took another step forward, she rose to her feet. "This abomination," she said, "has gone far enough. Stop it now. Both of you."

"But Mother," said Marcus, "you know Father doesn't like it when we lie to him."

Julius advanced further into the room and, when he was close enough, he threw his right fist out, hard and fast, straight towards his son's face. Marcus used a side block on that, a smile glimmering on his lips, and slid easily away from the next punch, laughing.

Julius stepped in closer, crouching slightly to throw an uppercut. But before his fist reached Marcus, unseen by him, Miriam stepped between the two of them. Julius had just enough time to pull back slightly, so the blow that landed on the underside of her jaw was not at full force.

Her hand on her jaw, her left hand raised to Julius' shoulder, Miriam said, "Stop it now. Stop Julius."

"Miriam," Julius said, stepping backward. "I'm so sorry. Here. Take my arm. Come sit. Sit."

Miriam did not budge. She did not take his arm. "What is this about, Julius? Why did you come here tonight in this foul condition?"

Julius looked at Marcus, disgusted. "Marcus knows what it's about."

Marcus looked back at his father, face and eyes hostile. "I know you're so drunk you're raving. How like a bull stung by bees you are, seeing red before your eyes and destroying everything in sight. Heedless." He put his arm on Miriam's back and said, "Mother, come sit down."

She allowed herself to be led to the couch, her hand still on her jaw. Marcus stayed by her side with a hand on her shoulder.

"I have no idea what Glaucon told you tonight," Marcus continued. "But I can guess. I'll tell you this, Father. Critias had your number before ever we became friends. His father does too. You do know that in some ... matters, your opinions are well publicized throughout certain circles of Caesarea. You're far too easy to manipulate."

"And what does that mean?" Julius shouted at him.

"Glaucon manipulated you. Critias figured out at last that I'm not all Roman in my tastes and habits. And that instead of having Greek habits, like him, I might add, I have Jewish ones."

"What does that mean?" Julius shouted at him.

"It means he's so angry that he took his revenge by lying to his father who promptly reported it all to you. It also means that I am going to continue to learn Torah with Rabbi Ariel when I want to."

"We'll see about that," said Julius in a threatening tone.

"Yes," said Marcus, facing up to his father squarely for the first time in his life. They were almost of a height now. "We shall." Then he turned and walked straight towards the door.

"Come back here!" shouted Julius. "We're not done."

"I'm done," said Marcus, turning to look back at him. "I'm going to get Xenon to come examine Mother. Which you would be doing yourself if you had any decency left."

CHAPTER 22

Vengeance is Mine

"I'm just telling you, there is no point having me fighting Critias again today." Leaning over the balustrade, Marcus peered down below into the training salle. It was still mostly empty with a few men standing together in tight clutches buckling on their practice hauberks or running through drills with their swords. He had arrived early today to make sure he had time to have this discussion.

When Rufinus said nothing in reply, Marcus straightened up, stood shoulder to shoulder with the master at arms, both their heads facing downward, watching the men trickle in through the doors like a broken line of ants, each moving to his assigned task. "I've been holding myself back for weeks now."

"Longer."

"You knew? And said nothing."

Rufinus coughed dramatically.

"Okay, it was obvious. But it's not like you to let me get away with taking the easy way out. I thought you would call me on it."

"It's not like you to want to take the easy way out." Rufinus flicked a glance at him over his left shoulder and then went right back to looking down at the room below, evaluating the men, keeping watch on everything going on down below him. "I was curious as to your motives."

Marcus snorted.

"And, perhaps, I made certain assumptions." Rufinus drew away from the railing, stepping back into the covered gallery. "For example, I thought you enjoyed him partnering you. Hein? A friend to spar with, here and elsewhere?" He leaned his back against a limestone wall. His face half illumined by the light of a wall scone, Rufinus turned his head to Marcus. "Was this incorrect?"

Marcus looked him squarely in the eye. "It had its moments. But lately it's become a bore. I'm better than him and there was no progress. So, it's time to cut the losses and make a switch." He resumed his pose nonchalantly, his upper body hanging out over the balustrade. "You've had it under consideration a long time, sir. Did you choose someone new for me to fight?"

The small man barked a laugh.

"What?" said Marcus.

"My boy, your defense work is quite admirable. You engage your opponent on his own ground, while giving nothing away."

Marcus turned to face Rufinus, allowing himself a small smile in return. "The credit belongs entirely to you, Master Rufinus. I've studied your methods."

"Yes, son. I know very well what to credit to my own account." He cleared his throat. "However," he said, "while compelling, your offense work still lacks the finesse of your defense. In light of which, why don't I let you choose your opponent today." He swept his hand from side to side. "There are the men. Pick someone down below for offense work."

"Me choose? Choose anyone?" said Marcus. "Anyone at all?" He looked down below to the arriving men circling around the room, moving into position to fight. This time when he turned back to Rufinus the surface of his face had fractured into planes, the dark surfaces overshadowing the light. "Offense work," he said, pressing his lips into a cold smile. "I see just my man."

Marcus stood on the bottom rung of the stairs, some steps off from his chosen sparring partner, eyeing the man, snaring his focus. Pacing up to him like a mountain cat stalking a bear, he let a smile break slowly over his face. "We fight together today. You and I. Face to face."

The man was half a head taller than he, stouter through the chest and with longer reach. His nostrils flared slightly and his lustrous brown eyes narrowed for a few seconds before he snapped, "Another time, Marcus. Today, I already have a friend lined up to fight..."

"Disengage. You're fighting with me. No shields, swords only."

Casio looked over Marcus' shoulder to Rufinus still standing on the staircase. "Master, I have a partner pre-arranged. I'd prefer to... "

"For today, Casio, you are to fight with Marcus."

"But, sir..."

Marcus stuck his hand up into the space between the Master's face and Casio's. He snapped his fingers once loudly, then drew his two fingers back sharply, pointing toward his eyes. "Focus on me. You're fighting me today, soldier. Is that clear? Draw your sword and salute." Casio's gaze wandered for a second longer behind Marcus' shoulder to Rufinus and then, with a bewildered expression still hovering on his face, they came to rest on him. The man lifted his right hand and rubbed it through his short, straight brown hair.

Behind him, Marcus heard the Master's steps receding. He raised his own practice sword then, holding it straight up before his face to salute Casio before they engaged. Marcus waited a few seconds until Casio slowly brought his sword up to his face to salute, until they had rapped swords together sharply. Then he rapidly advanced on Casio, once, twice, as Casio backed up. Stepping up again, his left shoulder relaxed, his grip tight, Marcus began his onslaught of blows. Attack, parry left, feint a counterattack, then slip the blade underneath Casio's garde and lunge. As he blocks, recover. Then, hedge left while moving forward, thrust, parry right, riposte. And there it was repeated, the first error in the man's swordplay, the telltale dipping of the man's shoulder before he thrust. Rufinus was testing him, Marcus thought. Well, just for Rufinus, he'd take Casio apart perfectly. Make Rufinus proud of him. Marcus lunged again, watching Casio's reaction time, testing his reflexes. People were always testing him, he thought, grimacing. He didn't like it any more than Casio was about to. Marcus spotted a new opening, a different line of attack. He ran through the moves again. Yes, definite weakness there. He noted this, Casio's second shortcoming for later. It was a fault he would enjoy exploiting.

Breathing harder now, Marcus pressed his lips together as he swept his sword down to the lower left. He moved back a small step before feinting twice and lunging. And here he found hard resistance, at least, initially. Try a new tack, he thought, reaching his sword high and stepping up to fight at close quarters.

Casio stepped away from him three times in succession hoping to catch his breath, but Marcus followed up immediately, not permitting Casio the respite. The glint in the man's eye turned intent and feral. With the force of a rock hurled into a calm sea, his anger radiated towards Marcus, breaking against him wave upon wave. The anger he recognized, blind, ferocious, a living force, though his mind had not yet penetrated the reason for it. He scrutinized Casio as a bead of sweat slid down the man's high forehead, down his curving cheekbone, down to his chin, where it hung suspended for a moment before falling into thin air.

It occurred to Marcus then that his father was a real bastard. What could he have meant last week by barging in and making that twisted claim about incest? And with his mother? God, it made him ill. Marcus gripped the handle of his sword, his shoulder muscles contracting tightly as he moved forward to reengage once more.

"Perhaps this won't be as easy as you thought," Casio taunted, moving in close, surprising him. As Casio thrust, Marcus rallied his sword to block the blow. Casio parried and, as Marcus was dodging right, he slipped his sword past Marcus' garde to strike. He hit not Marcus' heart, as intended, but his left elbow hard. Wincing slightly, Marcus felt intense pain ricocheting up along his humerus bone to his shoulder, and, beyond that, a sudden numbness. His fingers sprung open, losing hold of his sword.

Casio's sword was sweeping down in a perfect arc that would bang into the crown of his skull. Marcus slipped right, the whoosh of Casio's sword missing him by less than a finger's breadth. Dropping into a right-handed roll, he sprung up near Casio, took one more step forward. Just as Casio's arm swung at him hard, Marcus spun kicked, smashing the fingers of Casio's sword hand against the hilt of the sword from the opposite direction. Through his foot, Marcus felt the compression of Casio's finger bones against the hilt of his own sword and knew that Casio's fingers would drop his sword.

Even before Casio's weapon landed on the ground near his own, Marcus was rolling forward. As he came up, he used his bent left foreleg as a lever to knock Casio flat on the ground. There was a thump, oddly euphonious, as Casio's head pounded the wooden floor. Swift as a ballista bolt, Marcus straddled his opponent, his right knee bent to the ground, his right forearm and elbow whipping around to strike Casio in the ribcage. There was a resounding crack. The man grunted loudly, pulling sharply right out of instinct to cradle his broken ribs. As his head shot up, Marcus marked him with another elbow strike to his forehead. Casio's head thudded back to the ground, and he lay prostrate, unmoving as the becalmed sea. The anger now was all in Marcus.

304

God, he felt invulnerable, like he could fight at this peak forever. Blood coursed through him like sunlight piercing the morning sky. Marcus rose from the ground, his forehead splotched pink and red like dawn clouds. He exerted himself to steady his racing breaths. Inhaling deeply, he tasted acrid battle sweat in his mouth, on his tongue. Sweat tickled his scalp, permeated his hair. Marcus became aware suddenly that his entire body felt damp. All around him the crowd stood quiet, staring at him. He faced them, staring back. God, he was not yet ready for this fight to end!

Rufinus scowled at him with his one clear eye, and the foggy blue one. They were standing now in Rufinus' office, just the two of them. The room was over warm and humid. "Nice work, Marcus. Authoritative, even. Especially the part where you knocked the man unconscious. It took premeditation and craftsmanship to execute that plan."

Marcus held his tongue between his teeth, his lip swelling out slightly to the left. He lifted his eyes towards Rufinus, forcing himself to stand still.

The master raised his right hand and, before Marcus had time to react, jabbed him in the forehead. "What? You really didn't think I'd notice that the bruise you gave him on his forehead matches this scar above your eye. And same with the blows to the ribcage. Hah!" He breathed out of his nose derisively, his arms locked behind his back, angling his left foot in front of his right foot.

Rufinus was not expecting an answer, so Marcus did not give him one. He stood in silence as the little man glared at him, fury and wounded pride fighting for dominance in his aged face.

Rufinus tapped his foot. "You finally got your revenge. It took you long enough, didn't it?"

Marcus made his face blank.

"You used me, Marcus. The entire school saw me set you up with Casio for that fight." Rufinus kicked a tripod from his path and strode across his office, wall to wall. "I will not condone that."

Marcus stood by the wall, his head up high, watching Rufinus move back and forth, shaking his head from side to side. His blood still felt enriched, zinging within him like an elixir of the gods. It was taking considerable restraint to make himself stand still.

After a couple of moments, Rufinus stopped and looked at him. "Tell me, boy. What was your principal error in this fight?"

Marcus breathed out hard. At last, they were on familiar ground. "Shoulder tensed. I didn't absorb the blow well. And then I dropped my sword–"

"Idiot." Rufinus' voice sawed him off. "That was your third mistake, your fifth mistake. It doesn't matter which. It's unimportant either way." He swung his hands wildly above his head. "Tell me the first thing you did wrong today."

Marcus looked up at him, biting the corner of his lip, his color smoldering. "Rising from my bed to come here."

Rufinus raised his voice. "Arrogance, you fool. You underestimated your opponent, that's what. You became bored, lost focus, whatever it was." Rufinus stepped in closer to him, putting his face right in front of Marcus. "Where did you go halfway through that fight?" His finger up, Rufinus resumed jabbing him in the forehead. "Because you weren't in here. Were you dreaming of nymphs in the Elysian fields? Next time, that's where you'll end up, if you're not careful. The middle of a fight where your opponent wants to kill you is neither the time nor place for it."

Little flecks of saliva were landing all over Marcus' face. Smelling the wine and garlic on Rufinus' breath, he stood still, unresisting.

Rufinus grabbed him by the neck of his tunic and shook him hard. "Do you even know why Casio attacked you at the exhibition bout months ago?"

Dumb, Marcus realized. God, he was a fool not to have found out first. "It's not important now. I took care of it."

Rufinus stepped back, letting him go at last. "You don't think it's important to know his reasons before you attacked him back? You naïve brat." He shook his head, moving back a pace. "Don't expect you have solved the problem today. You've only made him madder."

"I didn't plan this, you know. I spotted him on the floor after you told me to choose a sparring partner. I took the opportunity. But I didn't plan it. How could I have known what you would say to me in advance?"

"Never lie to me, child. You obviously planned the moves in your head for whenever the opportunity presented itself." Rufinus made a sound of disgust in his throat. "But you should have realized what I would say to you afterward. You should have thought it through." He picked a dagger up from his table and began to twirl it about in his hands. "Just like your father, I might add."

"I'm nothing like him."

Rufinus' gaze forced Marcus' down. "So that's it." He nodded at the boy. "At last."

Marcus swallowed. "I meant—" He breathed out, his eyes moving left. "I'm a better fighter than he is, for one."

There was a blur of motion to his right.

Marcus jumped left. His eyes shot around to see Rufinus' dagger quivering in the wall right near where his head had been. Marcus turned back to Rufinus, his mouth an open gash in his face.

"Don't lie to me, boy, when I have a weapon in my hand."

Marcus caught his breath on an upswing and held on to it tight.

"Your father directs his rage at the people around him. You carry your anger into fighting. You're a better fighter than he is. But you're also a more reckless one. The risks you take without forethought!" Rufinus threw up his hands. "Only a fool loses concentration when he faces death. I tell you now, Marcus. You feel all powerful when

307

you take those risks because so far you have never lost. God help you the day the odds turn on you. And they will. I assure you of it. As for your anger, I told you before. Don't bring it here. Be very wary of the kind of man, the kind of commander it will turn you into. You fight, you take your revenge and that's all you'll see. But everyone around you will bear the cost."

"Mercy not vengeance, is that what you're preaching? What is this, Rufinus? You're turning into a Christian in your old age?"

"And if I have? Is mocking me for it going to stop you from turning into your father?"

Marcus opened his mouth to speak.

"Don't even begin to deny it. You gave yourself away earlier."

Marcus narrowed his eyes and looked straight at Rufinus. "I don't know what you're talking about. I respect my father."

"You may respect him. But you don't want to be like him by any measure. When your father's angry, he's not a moral man. You're shaping up to be the same, at least when you fight." Rufinus lowered his voice. "Which would be tragic for you, Marcus. As it's not the sort of man you admire."

Marcus lowered his eyes to the ground. Outside, he could hear the occasional clang of weapons, a voice bellowing, feet thudding on the floor. The air felt dry. The sweat on his body had largely evaporated leaving a salty residue in his clothes, on his skin, in his hair that prickled his flesh. He yearned for the bathhouse. "I don't understand you." Marcus started over. "You're telling me to give up fighting in order to be a better man? You?"

"Child," Rufinus said derisively. "Not in the least. I'm saying take control of yourself and make yourself a better man. Your men will fight better for you if they follow you out of love rather than fear."

"When did you become a Christian, Rufinus? I thought you worshipped Mithras along with everyone else in the barracks."

"I don't live in the barracks anymore, Marcus. I haven't for many years."

"Right." Marcus' brow remained furrowed.

With arms crossed before him, Rufinus said, "Well, if you must know, it was the wife who started. She dragged me along to one of her meetings. I thought it would be ridiculous. But then I liked what I heard. Fighting is what I do best. But at the end of a life spent viciously killing other men, it's a relief to find there may be something more." The words hung in the air for a moment. Then Rufinus swiped his hands together, swishing skin against skin, signaling a close to the conversation. "One more thing. There *is* one way I know of to clear up your concentration problem."

"Oh?"

Rufinus reached onto his desk and pulled out a long, thick piece of black cloth. "As of next week, you're going to learn how to fight blind." Rufinus threw his hand up in the air. "Now get out of here."

PART XV

CHAPTER 23
A Delight for the Eyes

It was a fine early morning, cool now, but with the promise of warmth in the afternoon. The sky shone cerulean blue. In the clear morning light, the *peristylium* looked perfectly tended. Foliage still lush this late in autumn; ripe apples hanging on the tree espaliered along the southern wall; the fine mosaic floor with the sphinx at the gate carrying a burnished sword that Miriam insisted was an angel, not a sphinx, though Julius could never understand why. The brushed pebble pathway lay smooth in its bed. Water from the fountain plinked into a pool free of algae and debris. In all the garden, not a weed nor a decaying leaf nor a splotch of mud was amiss. Julius felt a proprietary sense of satisfaction as he stepped through the arched doorway. At the far end of the garden, hidden behind a portal sat Marcus.

"There you are, son. I need to talk to you."

Marcus looked up at him, looked back down at his plate. "I'm eating," he mumbled.

Julius strode over to the table and stared down, like a sudden dark cloud lowering above a plain. He reached down, picked up Marcus' plate and flung it into the wall. The plate burst asunder, a shower of brightly painted earthenware, orange slices and purple grapes raining down atop the beds of blue asters. That easily, Julius thought with satisfaction, was the order of the garden shattered. "Well, now you're done." Julius pulled out a wooden chair and sat himself down opposite Marcus.

The boy shoved his chair back and pushed himself up to stand.

Julius reached across the marble table and laid his hand over his son's arm to restrain him. "Sit. I have business to discuss with you." His hand tightened as he felt the muscles in Marcus' forearm bunch to resist.

Two eyes met his, narrowed but expressionless. His son had this trick of showing little on his face. Julius envied the stoic demeanor, though he knew well his son's temperament did not match. He could sense the anger harnessed behind those eyes.

"I received an official complaint about you yesterday." Julius waited a beat. "Marcus. You really cannot beat up men under my command during your training sessions, even if you are furious with me at the time."

His son's silence deepened.

Julius pounded his fist down on the table, jolting the remaining dishes and silver spoons into the air. "You hear me."

Another beat.

"Yes, Sir." The eyes were summarily withdrawn from his.

Julius raised his hand and reached for an apple hanging from the wall, then drew his new dagger, silver hilted. He began to peel the apple smoothly, starting at the top. "I'm going away for some months. A trip to Jerusalem to reconnoiter with the rest of the Legion. I'm thinking I should take you with me. Keep my eye on you. Keep you

311

out of trouble. You need discipline." He pared round and round the apple, in one long strip.

Marcus was slumping back in his chair, informal and resentful. But his knit brow betrayed interest despite himself. "Why so long a trip?"

"Implementation of new decrees from Rome. There's a feeling above that they might prove unpopular in some regions of the province. This way we can coordinate a policy to stave off potential rebellion. Stop the trouble before it has much time to fester and it grows into something worse." The red apple skin lay on the table, one continuous piece, discarded. Julius began to slice the peeled fruit into thin, perfectly matched pieces. "This would be as good an opportunity as exists for you to familiarize yourself with more of the territory around here, get an overview of the land." He finished cutting the apple and bit into a piece. The flesh was firm and white, the juice sweet but tart, a superior apple.

Marcus shrugged uncommittedly. "Master Rufinus wants me for some advanced training in the next few weeks. One on one. He's planned it especially for me. I can hardly call it off now."

"There are plenty of experienced swordsmen you can work with in Jerusalem. Men with different approaches. Consider that you might learn something new." A pause. "Son, I'm very proud of your abilities as a fighter." He looked up and held his Marcus' eyes. "That is, when you are not beating up my men. But I want you with me for this."

"Yes, I'm aware of how proud you are of my hunting and fighting abilities."

Julius screwed his eyes shut as the scene from the other night flashed through his mind. He cringed slightly. Oh, the fault was his. He'd let his temper get out of hand again. He knew that. But if he got his son alone for a time, he'd make up for it. He would keep him away from bad influences. Critias, for example. A piece of work, that boy. And on this trip — "It would be an opportunity for you to see a great city."

312

"Formerly great. Now in ruins. Due to the fine fighting abilities of your Legion."

"Marcus. I know you want to see Jerusalem. You've mentioned it often enough. If you come, I'll let you spend some time in the city without me to do whatever it is you do when you —" Julius waved his hand in a circle. "Well, whatever it is. You have my word." Damn it. He hadn't really meant to go that far. And bribing his son, not ordering him about, made him look weak. But he could see his words had made an impression. Marcus' face was softening, he had unlocked his jaw and was moving it from side to side, thinking. Julius bit into another slice of apple. He closed his eyes, savoring the taste of triumph to come, so near now. "And it will be invaluable for your future career in the army." Julius opened his eyes to discover his son watching him chew, a telltale look on his face. With a sinking feeling, he pushed the plate of apple slices over to him. "Take a bite if you want one, Marcus. They're delicious."

"Good for eating and a delight for the eyes?"

The boy's eyes were steely now as he levered himself off his chair. He walked over the path, his sandals leaving troughs in the marble pebbles. At the far side of the mosaic, Marcus turned.

"No, Father. Not this time. I refuse to bite."

PART XVI

CHAPTER 24

A Pagan and A Fancy Woman

A few weeks later, Devorah stood outside the bathhouse in the center of Caesarea, waiting. Her full market basket, a brand new one this time, loaded with a new earthenware oil lamp, fava beans and a tiny packet of black peppercorns, lay upright on the ground by her foot. She leaned her thin shoulders further back onto the marble wall, exhaling through her nose, and scuffed her sandal repeatedly.

It was past mid-day; the sun high in the meridian radiated light, drenching the street in white heat. The rainy season had started a month since in a gigantic cloudburst the day after the prayer for rain was recited. A great blessing, her father had called it. But today was as hot as any day in summer. Here, by the wall, where there were shadows present, was the only shelter. They fell, black and cool, sharp and precise, elongated reflections of the upper world, distorting mirrors. Devorah kept her head down so that no one from her town chancing by would recognize her and stop to talk. Gritting her teeth, she thought again about leaving. She did not know why she stayed.

When she looked up again the boy was sidling towards her. She waited until he was close enough to hear her hiss. "I can't believe I let you talk me into this." He had a skinny, olive-skinned girl with round cheeks walking several paces behind him.

Marcus approached closer to her, his shoulder casually brushing against hers for a second. "It's good to see you too Devorah." Then he leaned over and breathed in her ear. "So, you got all dressed up to listen to a heretic. How shocking!" he said, and his voice sparkled.

"Not a heretic, a pagan," she shot back. "There's a difference." And then she mumbled: "Anyway, it's my disguise. No one would recognize me in this."

"I did."

She punched him in the arm and the boy laughed.

"Ow! You hit my sore spot." He pushed back his tunic sleeve to display a large bruise on his upper arm, black and green. He examined it a moment, exhibiting a strange pride, before letting his sleeve drop over it again. "And I hit yours, obviously. So, fought to a draw." Marcus said, "And now, time to go before we're late. Hamida, take her basket."

Devorah stared at Marcus and let her frown dominate her face.

"Not the look again. Devorah, I swear, you are like Plato's guard dog who barks at whatever is new." Marcus rolled his eyes. "I brought Hamida along because at the lecture, you will be more comfortable if you have a servant-girl sitting by your side."

She continued to frown at him and did not budge.

"For purposes of modesty only. Nearly everyone else is likely to be male." He took hold of her arm and yanked it lightly. "Come on."

It was a little too cool inside the stone lecture hall. Pulling her shawl tight around her shoulders, Devorah bowed her head slightly, tucking the bottom triangle of her face between her palms. Sitting here felt all wrong. She was too much on view, a female oddity in a swarm of male bodies turning to stare. There were no other women in sight, save Hamida. She doubted there was another Jew in the place except Marcus. If you could count Marcus, she groused silently. Oh God, Oh God. Why had she come? Why had she let Marcus persuade her? Why had he brought her here? Her leg jounced up and down under her robe, fluttering the fine fabric.

There was a flash of red cloth to her left, then a tincture of myrrh and rose drifted her way. Devorah pulled her face out of her hands and glanced up as a lady swanned by. Tall, straight-backed, slender, blond, the woman's posture bespoke a grace Devorah knew she could never possess and instinctively envied. Her eyes were far from the only ones to follow the matron's glide up the center aisle of the hall. But at least she was no longer the only female here except Marcus' maid. She relaxed a bit and sneaked a look at him. He caught the motion of her head and gazed back at her, a query softening his blue eyes, drawing her in. She felt herself melting too for an instant. Yet how uncomfortable a thought to rely on Marcus for shelter. Devorah jarred her head away from him, edged away on the limestone bench and did the only obvious thing in the circumstances. She began to listen.

"...what then is the nature of virtue, my friends? Can virtue only be expressed practically as the achievement of excellence in any field of endeavor? We say that the virtue of a soldier is to fight for his country as a hero, yes? And the virtue of an archer is to loose his arrow with so perfect an aim as to always hit the target."

Antinous, the philosopher shuffled his feet, his face raised to the ceiling, his eyes momentarily closed. He was mulling over how to say the next bit, Devorah decided. His voice was gruff, low and heavily accented such that she found herself wondering about the limits of his fluency in Aramaic. That seemed unnatural in a philosopher. And that baffled and embarrassed her for him. Nor could she place his accent.

"But does virtue itself have a higher calling, a recognizable essence that separates it from its many applications, its horde of particularities? Does being virtuous itself have a purpose? Why should a man pursue virtue, or live a virtuous life?" The man lifted his hand to his face. "For what end?"

She had guessed completely wrong about the lecturer's ability to speak Aramaic. He was short, with craggy skin and rough-textured gray hair. His tunic was worn and discolored. Even his laundress, Devorah surmised, was no longer able to bleach it white in the vats of urine befouling the air of the working quarters on humid days. It made him look unworldly, she realized. And that made an amusing contrast with the careful upper-class dress of much of his audience. The girl looked down at her lap very conscious of her own unaccustomed dress, the fine texture of the fabric, the blue dye, still bright after several washings, given to her last month by Marcus' mother. Too true, she had come in disguise.

"Once again, does virtue exist only in practical activities that can be mastered? Or does virtue have a higher purpose?"

A hush seized hold of the room, like a climber on the heights breathlessly gripping a smooth-faced cliff.

"Its purpose is to help us achieve our end of becoming like God."

This time Antinous scanned the faces of his audience. His eyes drifted from the right wing of the hall straight across to its far-left side. The man had cow eyes, brown and soulful, with no tinge of arrogance. It struck Devorah how rare this expression was among the educated Greeks she had encountered in Caesarea or Jaffa. But, of course, this man was not Greek. Perhaps, it was normal among philosophers? She did not know, never having seen one up close before today. None of the Syrian country folk who lived near her had cause to look arrogant, although some wore cagey expressions and others looked downright mean. Yet they were ignorant people with little to sustain them and not even a belief in a true God for comfort, as her people had. *Comfort, oh comfort, My people.* Devorah mouthed the words silently as her father had taught them to her.

"But how, you ask, is a human being to accomplish this? For it is true that it is no easy task. Plato mentions only one way. Contemplation of the primal good — and that is God. The soul that remembers truth and justice is eager to find itself once more on the Plain of Truth which will nourish all that is most noble in it, in particular its desire to dwell with Being itself. The purest of these souls, those who seek out what is real, belong surely to philosophers. Whereas, those others who are devoid of wisdom, remain in a dark cave, as if chained in place, seeing nothing real but only shadows dancing on a wall. So removed are they from truth and God."

The talk had ended. Devorah remained still, her chin resting in her palms, her elbows leaning on her knees. *Let every valley be raised, every hill and mount made low. Let the rugged ground become level and the ridges become a plain. The Presence of the Lord shall appear, And all flesh, as one, shall behold–For the Lord Himself has spoken.* So, the prophet had spoken hundreds of years earlier, Devorah thought. And what was level ground, land without mounts or ridges, but a shadowless land where God could be seen from every point? The Plain of Truth, she thought, considering the idea from every angle she could imagine, and shuddered once as goose bumps broke out suddenly on her arms. It fit so well.

Devorah felt cold. "You were right," the girl said and hugged her body tightly without looking up at Marcus. "In some ways, it didn't seem so different than the teaching of Torah."

He leaned down and spoke close to her ear. "In what ways did you think?"

Devorah scrunched her brow and thought. She remembered watching the villagers from time to time as her father led them in prayer, their faces uplifted, or wise rabbis she had seen speaking in Yavneh and Bene Brak. "But it differs too. Your man thinks only philosophers can know God. That appeals to you?"

"Broaden it from philosophers to scholars like your father, rabbis, mystics. That doesn't appeal to you?" He fixed his eyes on her, and she stared back. "If you won't admit it to me, then in some dark recess of your soul, admit it to yourself."

She looked at him blankly.

He threw back his chin. "I've told you before, Devorah," he said, perfectly mimicking her father's concerned tone, "you must learn that knowledge and wisdom are nothing without humility and the fear of God."

"You make my argument for me," Devorah said. Her belly roiled lightly, and she leaned away from Marcus, wounded that he had ridiculed her father to her face. And that made her angry. "Your philosopher friend doesn't realize he can't get very far if he doesn't know Torah. And you're not planning to tell him, are you?" she smirked. "Where, oh where, Marcus, have your charitable impulses gone?"

When she looked up at him, Marcus was actually rolling his eyes at her. She wanted to smack him. Aim hard for that bruise he had shown off to her, hit him where it would really hurt. Punish him for flaunting his weak spot like that to his adversary as though she were harmless. Devorah found herself standing, clutching her shawl about her. "I mean, it's not as though they are God's chosen. And what kind of God is their God anyway? A God of the mind, of thought. What does that have to do with the charitable impulse from the heart, or with the world we live in, where people starve and suffer and need help? Though I don't expect you know much about that."

Marcus straddled the bench. Looking up at her, he stretched his legs out straight to either side and leaned back. "And what kind is ours? A jealous God. And you think that's superior?"

"You should have discussed that with my father," she hissed. "That's a complex topic. And you're missing the point."

"So are you. Worse, you're doing it on purpose." His voice broke off suddenly, and he began to rise and smile, becoming an altogether new man standing at her side with his eyes now focused away from her.

Devorah turned about to see the matron in red she had earlier remarked prancing up to pose before Marcus.

"I trust," said the woman looking back and forth between the two of them, "that I am not interrupting anything important." Looking directly at Marcus, she lifted her shapely arm and touched him on the shoulder. "I told my brother that he had to introduce me to you today."

Marcus smiled witlessly at the Greek matron. Devorah's own face, she did not doubt, still looked furious. She tried to smooth it out. But she could feel her efforts had not worked.

"Not at all," murmured Marcus with charming insincerity. Or perhaps he was sincere. Perhaps he was glad their argument was over.

"He's been regaling the family with stories about you for some time."

Devorah grunted ironically, a sound in her throat too low for the others to hear. It was obvious to her that Marcus hadn't a clue who this was. Nevertheless, he was enjoying the flattery. Well, who wouldn't? For some reason, the beauty was practically fawning on him. God, but she hated the fact that the boy could shrug off his mood so easily when she still felt locked in the throes of their dispute. She looked down at the ground, and considered stomping on his foot to remind him their quarrel was not over. She raised her toes, her brain and her leg muscles twitching to strike before her courage deserted her. Belatedly, self-restraint rose to the surface to spare her dignity in front of such a paragon of grace and stupidity. More's the pity.

"And your brother is?" Marcus asked. The woman arched her neck around and smiled conspiratorially at a blond-haired man pacing up to her. "Ah, Phoenix, of course. I see the resemblance now."

Devorah did not. No resemblance whatsoever.

Marcus stepped up to Phoenix and lightly punched his shoulder. "Bastard. You never mentioned a beautiful sister."

"Perhaps not," Phoenix demurred. "But the parents banished Helen to Athens years back. I thought we were rid of her permanently."

Devorah swallowed a laugh. Of course, the paragon was named Helen. No other name would have fit half so well except Aphrodite.

"In other words," Helen interjected, "I married an Athenian."

"So, you see," continued Phoenix with little regard for his sister's words, "mentioning the sister was hardly a consideration. And only recently has fate, that harsh mistress, revoked the decree and let Helen return to the family nest."

So now Helen was a widow. And a wealthy one, no doubt. Surely, Devorah thought, she didn't seem very broken up by it. Nor was there much stirring by way of family affection between the siblings. She sensed hostility from the man and dismissiveness on the woman's part. And then she felt that same critical viewing prism turned on her. The woman stood next to her openly contrasting her refined robe with her cheap woven sandals and her ill-groomed face and hair as if it were a sordid puzzle she could not bother to solve.

Devorah turned from that visual flaying to discover that Phoenix was regarding her as well, and a little too warmly to suit her. She intercepted his eyes descending from her breast to her lower limbs and instinctively stepped back out of the circle. Mortified, Devorah bit her lip, waiting for Marcus to break the silence. But when she turned to look at him, he, too, was staring red-faced at her hempen sandals just now realizing what a visible lapse in her dress they were. Marcus forced to evaluate lapses in feminine fashion on her account – now that was a joke. At her expense.

Say something, idiot, Devorah thought viciously. Distract them. Even so, she waded through heavy seconds before Marcus caught on to the role she had mentally assigned him.

"This is my cousin, Devorah. She's visiting from the east." He looked at the two faces, the woman's disinterested, the man's skeptical. "From Tiberius," he added insistently.

Cousin! God, he was babbling. She could tell that neither of them had bought his story. Marcus tongue-tied to this extent was a sight she'd never seen before. Another occasion and she would have relished it, but not now when embarrassment over her was its cause.

"Are you hoping to speak to Antinous today?" Marcus asked Phoenix, changing tracks.

Helen interposed herself between the two men. "We've seen Antinous every night at our house for dinner for two weeks straight. I imagine he'll move in soon if Phoenix has his way."

"You needn't come hear him speak, sister, if his presence at the house irks you so much."

"Why, Phoenix, you have it all wrong. I don't mind hearing him speak about his theories at a school like this. I do, however, mind his droning on while I'm trying to eat my dinner; talking about the remedy of self-restraint while gorging on a fifteen-course meal. Even you must admit that has the virtue of being humorous. But it would be a trifle rude to laugh at table." She moued charmingly. "Still, Caesarea is a provincial backwater of a capitol. So, there's little choice in celebrity philosophers who are available for home entertainment."

"It's not Athens, that's true." Phoenix's eyes turned dreamy and reminiscent.

Thank God for that, Devorah thought and glanced at Marcus. He caught her look and snuck a grin in the corner of his mouth.

"It's not at all like Athens and still less like Rome," said Helen. "Here, you can't be too choosy about guests. For instance, just last week, my mother presented the man with a new tunic, but he insists on wearing that old rag he's got on. I fancy he thinks it makes him look more authentic. Still. At least he's not a stoic. Now that would be intolerable. Platonists at least believe in enlightenment, if mostly for themselves. But all stoics are grim."

"You know, you're right. My father admires the stoics and he's intolerable," said Marcus.

322

"And, grim. Logically, he must be grim," said Helen and they both started to cackle. Although a moment later, Marcus bit off his laugh suddenly, like a sailor grabbing for the deck as he missteps into thin air.

Devorah saw Helen's nostrils flare once in response to his uncertain look. Lifting her head, she homed in on the boy, like a hooded snake about to strike. "The truth is I prefer fighting men to philosophers. There's nothing more amusing than watching a good fighting exhibition or a gladiatorial show, don't you agree? Coincidentally," she purred, "my brother mentions you're a bit of a prodigy in that arena."

"Phoenix, what pap have you been feeding your sister?"

"Only the purest kind, like mother's milk. I told no lies," Phoenix said, "as you well know. I mentioned your exhibition fight the other day. Where Rufinus blindfolded you and made you fight against two opponents, and you still got in three hits out of five."

The color had surged into Marcus' cheeks. "True. I was *very* impressive." His voice and face were all deprecation now. "Until Rufinus thwacked my arm so hard I couldn't even lift my sword."

"Good old Rufinus. But then he only strikes the ones he loves."

"Pain as love. An interesting philosophy." Helen raised her eyebrows. "It certainly sounds more fun than an exhortation to seek the primal good."

"You'd be surprised. It happens to be a very effective conditioning technique," Marcus said, and then blushed scarlet anew. "In the ring, I mean."

Whacked by the master. So that was how he got that gigantic bruise, Devorah thought. So it was, as she had suspected, a badge of honor. Disgust tugged her lips downward. Yet no one, she realized, least of all Marcus, had ever mentioned to her that the boy was that good, a prodigy, not just a boastful brat with a manner about him that opened all doors. All her assumptions about him lay overturned. She felt hollowed out in the pit of her belly.

Helen stepped closer to Marcus, blinking up at him lazily. "And outside the ring?" she said in a voice so low Devorah had to strain to hear it. "Have you tested it yet?"

As Phoenix laughed, Marcus tilted his lips crookedly into a raw, suggestive smirk. The blood was still suffusing his cheeks, dyeing them red, the heat emanating from his entire figure in waves.

Devorah's face fell away. Not Helena, she thought. Me. Look at me. Her belly clutched painfully and she felt a terrible anxiety arise. Deep down in her chest she could feel each one of her heartbeats tolling loudly, like a flesh wound pulsing blood. Why hadn't she realized before the nature of her feelings for Marcus? And to realize it only now while he stood by her side, ignoring her completely, to ogle a widow several years senior to him as she dangled her attractions before his eyes.

Devorah felt shame more profound than any she had yet tasted in her life, that she should be reduced to wanting what? attention? love? physical pleasure? And from him! It was wrong. He was not the kind of boy she'd ever thought to want to give herself to. And yet at this moment her body was tugging her into his sphere incessantly, the moon to her tide. He stood by her side, absorbed so facilely in the pleasure that slut was arousing in him, oblivious to her. This was a humiliation too profound. The irony that it should be Marcus she wanted – or was it just her body that wanted him and not her soul? — mortified Devorah. She stood rigid, until the heat of her anger let her unfreeze.

"Cousin," Devorah said, and grasped his arm tightly, right on the bruise, with both of her hands. "Marcus. Have you forgotten? Your mother is expecting us to meet her. She said directly after the lecture," she added in response to Marcus' blank expression.

"My mother? What? Oh yes, now I remember. Of course," he said as her nails scraped deep into his flesh. "Well, then, we must fly, like bats returning to their cave. The mother hates to be kept waiting.

She'll feed me on rotten fish for a week straight. As it is I barely got permission from her to bring Devorah here in the first place."

Devorah held onto his arm on the long walk down the aisle maintaining the sharp pressure of her nails latched into his skin. Thus, they descended the staircase. When they reached the front hall of the building, he shook her arm off hard, angrily. "My mother? What is this?" he said. "I was enjoying myself."

"You were. But I wasn't." She thought of Helen in that tight red dress. That morning, she had passed a dove lying out on the marble forum, its neck broken, it's neat feathers gray and black, a dark eye. One perfect circle of blood lay on the marble spilled opposite that eye, the exact color of Helen's dress. As she looked on, a skinny cat had rustled the baskets as it wove in and out, yearning to retrieve the bird. But in the end, it only poked its head out with the one sick eye and looked at her plaintively, too intimidated to seize the dove from the crowded street filled with strangers. "Even now you have no idea. Do you?" her voice rose on the question. "Do you?"

"I see that I've offended you. I'm sorry for that."

Empty manners, that's all it was. "But not why?" She glared at him; her eyes two fiery rockets launched by a catapult. "Do you think I wanted to watch that fancy woman prance you off to bed? It's not as though she made it a challenge, even. Did you invite me here to show me that?"

His color, she noted had risen into his cheeks again. His eyes slid left. "That was just flirtation," he insisted. "Haven't you ever flirted? My God, it's not as though I meant anything by it. Her brother was standing next to her the whole time. A bit of fun, that's all."

"Fun for you, you mean. And if you didn't mean anything, which I doubt, she certainly did." She looked off, away from him, her eyes boring out holes in the walls. "My father was right about you after all. What he thinks of you."

"What do you mean?"

His voice was too neutral, too gray. And that enraged her. She said nothing. And then spitefully, "You must have wondered why I had to sneak to see you, why he won't let us learn together anymore."

"What does he think of me, Devorah?"

"I argued with him to change his mind, but it turns out he's right."

He grabbed her arm and for the first time she felt his full strength as her wrist was crushed in his grip. "What does he think of me, Devorah?"

"That you're not a good enough man for me to spend time with," she spat at him.

"Oh," he said and let go of her arm. "Is that all?"

But she had seen the desolate fall of his features a second before he blanked out his face.

She stood there stunned. *Learn charity, child,* her father had told her the day she met Marcus. *Be good as well and kind.* She had to try. Because with her foolish heart, no one now would ever think her wise.

CHAPTER 25
Too Late

Miriam sat at the marble table in the *peristylium* and perched her foot on its carved sphinx base. It had been a sunny day, but by early evening it was already cool. She wore a blue and silver woolen wrap over her light wool robe since even in the enclosed garden she had felt a chill breeze stirring. It was the heat from the small stove, lit at her back, that kept her warm. A parchment missive lay on the table, and she gripped it tightly between her two small hands lest it fly away before she read through the letter once again. When she finished, Miriam looked across the court at the fountain, splashing unconcerned, and watched the westering sun crystallize drops of water from its stream before they dissolved into the pool.

"I'm curious, Vincius, why my brother sends you a separate note?"

"We parted friends. It's not so strange." Her friend stood slouched, leaning his back against a marble pillar, his hand loosely gripping the pommel of his short sword. It was a striking acquisition, the metal still glistening, beautifully balanced, with two pieces of black onyx inlaid along the hilt and a piece of ivory in its center. In contrast, his white belted tunic looked like it needed mending. So, too, the red cloak he wore on top of it. Although the brooch that pinned it on the right shoulder, a golden coiled snaked, looked like fair work.

"Acquaintances," she amended. "And that was four years ago."

"Drinking partners."

She read his declination to engage further on the topic in his shrug, his failure to make full eye contact. Miriam continued regardless. "My brother is not the sort of man to write friendly letters to his inferiors for no reason." She felt rather than saw his wince. "Or those he thinks of that way to suit his purposes."

"You were right the first time. In every way that's important to him, I'm his social inferior."

She raised her eyebrows. "Which begs the question, Vincius. Why did he write to you?"

"What can I tell you, Miriam. Despite my lowly status, I'm a likeable man."

Never the truth about Yehonatan from Julius. And now Vincius, too, was suppressing information about her brother. She could sense it in his face, hear it in his voice. Damn Yehonatan for the secrets he kept with the men in her life, extending his control everywhere. Miriam sighed, breathing in the moist salt air blowing from the sea. She felt the salt on her skin, coarsening her hair, thickening her clothes. The direct approach usually worked with Vincius, but not in this case. Perhaps she'd try another kind of overture to see what it brought her?

"Stay and have a drink with me?"

"Of course." This time Vincius looked her fully in the face as he spoke, smiling.

Miriam signaled to Hamida, standing in the covered corridor, to pour another glass of the warm wine and honey aperitif, then to throw another log from the pile onto the stove before she removed herself.

Moments after Hamida left, Miriam crooked her finger, beckoning. "It's all ready. Come here and sit down."

Still smiling, Vincius pushed himself off the wall and slowly walked over towards her. He pulled out a chair across from her, sat down, then propped his elbows on the table. She smiled back at him with the merest hint of an upward tilt on her lips.

Vincius gulped down his wine. A shame, thought Miriam, since it was too well blended to waste like that, the sweetness of the honey perfectly balanced the flavor of the wine. Watching her, Vincius reached his hand slowly across the table and carried her own into his two palms. His hands felt harder than hers and warmer, larger, callused, rough, altogether new territory. Startled, overwhelmed by sensation, Miriam did not withdraw her hand. Only she turned her face back to the fountain and studied the water gurgling lazily from its spigot.

"God, Miriam, look at me."

"What?" she said, her eyes darting towards him and away as the color flecked her cheeks. "No. I can't."

"Do you want me to stop?" he said, releasing her hand.

She left hers in place and lightly, so lightly, pressed his thumb. Really, she thought, it could just have been her nerves jumping. But he closed his palm on her hand once again and this time drew it up to his mouth to kiss.

⸺◈⸺

The first hint Vincius had that something had changed was that Miriam began jerking her fingers away from his mouth. As he opened his eyes, he held on tight to her hand. Damn the gods, Marcus had just slipped noiselessly into the garden. Still, Vincius kept hold of her hand as she carried it across the table and for some moments more

329

until she tugged it free. He could feel the boy's eyes on them before he looked away.

At least, Vincius thought, Marcus had not yet staked him through the heart with the knife he wore at his hip. God knows, he had the skill and speed to do it. Nor was he stomping away in disgust this time at the mere sight of him. Rather, Marcus seated himself in a chair across the *peristylium* and almost at once began to talk. And that was unexpected, even tentatively hopeful.

"Nice sword, Vincius."

"It is, isn't it?" Vincius drew the shining blade from its sheath and ran his finger lightly over it, not deep enough to draw blood.

"Is it just for show, or does it strike true?"

"Want a feel," said Vincius and offered him the weapon.

Marcus cocked one eyebrow and laughed. "I'll resist that offer." A beat later, he asked. "Tell me, how went the military exercises in Joppa?"

"Actually enjoyable, this time. A leisurely two days march south, three days joint military exercises with the centuries stationed in Joppa, including exercises with the navy to defend the port. That, by the way, has been a vulnerable point for invasion in every major war in your people's history. A point well worth noting. We were a bit uncoordinated all around, but next time we'll do better. And the final afternoon, there was a series of exhibition fights for the troops to enjoy. You would have appreciated that. Two of them were at the expert level that you're aspiring to. Then, two and a half days march back up north. And all of it by the side of the sea with refreshing breezes. The weather was beautiful. We do it all again next week in a march north to Ptolemais, worse luck."

"Did Galenus show up to see it or advise?

"Still with your interest in that man? What is it between you and him?"

"Nothing," said Marcus and shrugged. "I had a thought to keep track of him for the *pater*."

An obvious lie. Marcus did not look to be obliging his father in much lately. Otherwise, how to explain him tolerating what he had just seen. "Did you mean keep track of him for Yehonatan? But speaking of your father—"

"Must we?"

Vincius raised his eyebrows. "I received a note from him today," he said. "He'll be away longer than he expected. A month or longer until he returns. I thought you should know."

Marcus' sharp glance encompassed both him and Miriam at the table. "Because I never would have surmised that without your say so." And he laughed on a dark and bitter note.

Every nuance of that laugh was reflected back in pain on Miriam's face. Her doubts, her shame, her hatred of Julius, of him and of herself. Another minute she was sure to kick him out. He loved her, he should go, make this easier for her. But damn it, not tonight. Not now, when he finally stood on the brink of what he had wanted for so long. Self-sacrifice had never been his favorite suit. And he had no will to leave unasked.

Laughing still, Marcus stepped over to the table and poured himself a cup of wine from the pitcher. Standing straight in front of them, he tilted his head back until he drained the cup. A bleak look surging across his face, like an ocean-scape in winter, Marcus replaced the cup then trod over to the wall to pluck the last apple from the tree.

"*A delight for the eyes*," Marcus said, as he watched the two of them.

Vincius heard Miriam's indrawn breath as though she registered something he did not in Marcus' words. Was it a quotation? The two of them were always throwing around scriptural quotes he did not know.

The silence that developed tried everyone's nerves. Until, at last, Marcus' voice again breached the void, like over bright steel. "Still,

331

children, we ought to be merry. Does not King Solomon say, 'There is a time for wailing and a time for dancing.' The wailing we had last month. Surely the time is now ripe for the dancing! Particularly under the sheets."

In one powerful motion, Vincius rose to his feet to seize hold of the boy and shake him until it hurt.

"Oh, Vincius, forbear," Marcus said with another laugh, flitting lightly out of reach. "I'm dancing too. Did you not notice? And if you use your sword on me, you can hardly sheathe it again with my mother's complicity." With his knife he snipped a lily from its bed and tossed it at his mother. "Though who knows? It's a time for dancing, so perhaps she wouldn't mind. But speaking of tossing flowers, I'm off to coax the charms of my own fair Hellenic bud to open into full summer bloom."

The pure white lily had landed on the table in front of Miriam. "There's a letter here for you, too," she said, her voice slashing roughly across his, to stop his torrent of cutting words. "Take it," she said, holding it up to him. "And read it before you leave." She handed him the flower back as well, gingerly and by its stem. "Give the bud to Devorah, dear." She raised her eyebrows. "That is, if you do intend to dance with her. And she with you."

"Not Devorah," Marcus said. "Helen." He moved in closer again, took the letter in one hand, but refused the flower before moving back to his position near the wall. Without referring to the letter, he merely commented, "How full we all will be of news!"

"Bastard," Vincius muttered under his breath. And then he said scathingly, "Are you drunk?"

"A little," said Marcus and laughed. "Does it matter?"

Miriam's voice persisted, now bright and cheery and utterly out of place. "The missive is from your uncle. He wants to see you."

"Right. To Sardis I shall go. Because it will be no trouble getting permission to travel there."

"Not Sardis," said Miriam. "Caesarea. He'll be here as soon as he can."

Marcus surveyed the two of them, his eyes waving at them a final time before they drowned. With a bitter laugh, he bit down on the apple and swallowed. "Too late," he said, and bit down again.

The core he jettisoned as waste.

PART XVII

CHAPTER 26
Fighting Blind

At the side of the aqueduct that brought Caesarea's fresh water supply from the foothills of Carmel, there was a lengthy dirt track. Marcus was running on it. Each time he returned to this spot, he was amazed by the sweep of Roman engineering, the precision, the structure, the balance and how pleasing it was to the eye. Like the buildings in Caesarea, it was built in the spirit of domination, to last through the ages.

Marcus liked running by the sea in the early morning, even as the weather grew colder; the beauty of sun and sea brought an even, expansive state. Truth is, he had been shocked to his core by the recent dressing down that Rufinus gave him. But the weeks since had brought a kind of revelation to him, both bad and good.

In the end, Marcus had let himself sidle up to the truths in what Rufinus had accused him of. Hard lessons but worthwhile.

To become a master fighter, he needed full control of himself before and during fighting; therefore, he must train not just his body to be superlative, but his mind and the seat of his emotions to be under

334

his control. Too often, he let rage slip through and gain the upper hand, like a black shadow at noon seeping through a gate and bathing the ground in darkness; or, like when a barbarian wrestles a Greek athlete and, against all civilized rules, uses every low method to win.

Rufinus had been right about that too.

He loathed his father's rage and how it had spilled onto their family, poisoning it.

He needed to change paths before that became his essential nature too. And he still could. Did not the prophet teach that *A bruised reed He shall not break.* These days when he prayed, Marcus asked for guidance on how to live his life well. He knew he was blessed with enormous gifts. How should he direct them so that they were not squandered? How should he direct them so that they aided his mother's people, his own people?

Every day, Marcus worked the drills Rufinus set for him to master the art of fighting blind. Nothing in his life hence far had challenged him physically to this extent. The skill level required was so refined, that to succeed, he had to perfectly balance body, mind, soul. This too Rufinus advised him on. No more could he fight while allowing his thoughts to attune to the siren song of wrongs done him, for this just aggravated his black horse of irrationality.

For all his faculties to flow as one, to reach and maintain his peak abilities, he needed to be surrounded by a wall of calm. That meant no more evening Dionysiac indulgences.

With Rufinus' aid, Marcus began building his surrounding wall of calm to be impenetrable, like Roman architecture. He let in nothing that would ruffle him. Early mornings, he rode Argos, swam in the Great Sea, or ran these trails near the aqueduct. Until midday, he trained. Afternoons, he studied philosophy and mathematics. He followed Rufinus' advice about eating light and healthy food with no indulgences. He withdrew from all social activities. Instead, in the early evenings, he sought out a local rabbi and began to attend evening prayer nightly, followed by meetings where he learned Torah and law.

Body, mind, soul. He worked on disciplining and improving each one of them, every single day. Like an Apollonian Temple, the apotheosis of Greek architectural beauty, he set himself to be disciplined and perfectly proportioned.

During those weeks, he existed in a cold, beautiful harmony that kept him separate from the seat of his emotions. He purposefully set his charioteer in charge of both his white horse and his black horse with a controlling rein.

His discipline became exemplary. And this brought him close to a feeling of inner contentment, carefully architected, the work of his hands, his mind, his soul.

With both his father and Vincius away, he always knew there would come a challenge to this Edenic period in time.

The first cracks appeared sooner than Marcus hoped, as it happened.

———◇———

"I received a message from Vincius," Miriam said late one afternoon as she and Marcus sat amicably in the atrium. Marcus was reading Plato's Parmenides, and she was staring at her accounts with her attention wandering off. "He'll be back in a few days."

"Hmm," Marcus said, ignoring her.

"He wanted to know if I need any commissions fulfilled in Dor, since he will be passing in a few days." Dor, some fifteen miles north of Caesarea on the seacoast, was the nearest center of the murex trade that produced the royal blue and purple dye that their family business traded.

Marcus finally looked back at her, his eyebrows raised. "And do you?"

336

"It's not the first time he has fulfilled commissions for me in Dor. I sent him north with some letters to our agents when he left to go to Sidon a month ago. He'll be bringing replies and gold."

Marcus looked at her another moment, his expression flat, and then looked back down at his book. A moment later he asked, his eyes still focused on the book, "What are we really discussing here, Mother?"

Miriam paused for a moment. "Yehonatan writes that my father now needs to be living with family full time, since he is aging."

"It's a good thing, then, that Yehonatan is living with him full time."

"It's been over four years and Yehonatan wants to resume traveling in the east."

Marcus finally looked up at her and met her eyes. "And?"

"He thinks I should plan a trip back home."

"By yourself?"

"No, dear. He thinks you should accompany me home to see your grandfather." Silence. "None of us want you to join the Roman army, Marcus. Especially not in this country, against our own people at this time of rising tension. If you accompanied me, it would take you away legitimately."

"Does Julius know you're planning a lengthy separation? Years apart?"

Since that awful fight Marcus and Julius had had in her chambers, her son had taken to referring to his father as Julius. Miriam took a very deep breath. And then another. "I'm planning more than that, precious one. I'm planning a formal separation." She waited a moment, then added. "A divorce. I would like you to come with me to live back in Sardis. Time for you to start learning to run the business."

For a long time, Marcus said nothing. Miriam waited. She could hear her own breath and his and the waves on the shore and the gulls squabbling for food.

Finally, he looked up at her and his blue eyes flashed fire, "And Vincius?"

"He wants to marry me."

Marcus' eyes flashed cold fire again. He opened his mouth to argue, but then took a deliberate deep breath instead and looked down at his book.

She reached out to him then and took his hand in hers. "Marcus, my darling son," she said and brought their hands up to her cheek. "The marriage with Julius was always a mistake. First, I erred." As she said this, her beautiful green eyes met his and held them unflinchingly. "My father was so furious at me, he compounded the mistake. He forced an ongoing connection between us." She took a deep breath to calm herself and then another. "Years ago, right before we left Sardis, my father, Daniel, apologized, but only because I was leaving. By then, Julius had compelled me to come with him to Syria because he threatened to take you away from me if I didn't." She shuddered once, as if in the grip of bad memories and her eyes revealed old pain. "To this day, I don't know whether he meant it or not." Miriam inhaled roughly once, then again. "It was very scary for me on the road with only you and Noemie. I was not safe. At that point, there was no choice but to marry."

Miriam had never spoken about any of this to her son before.

The silence between them built higher and higher, as when, after a sudden desert storm, the waters of a flash flood whirl down so ferociously between two sides of a stone chasm that anyone who enters therein is like to die, impaled on the rocks.

At long last, Marcus withdrew his hand. "Time for evening prayer," he said, stood up without looking at her further and left.

Miriam waited until the door closed softly behind Marcus. Then the tears that had been threatening began to roll down her cheeks, slowly at first, one by one. Soon they quickened and turned into a torrent. So many, she knew not how to stop them. These were the tears she had withheld for years as she built up her reserves and fought her battles with Julius. Tears had been gone from her life for so long, she had thought that she no longer had access to them.

But she had passed a milestone today in summoning the courage to speak squarely to Marcus. It had been painful and difficult to speak these words out loud to her son. But saying them had given her a resolve that had been lacking in her until now. As though the words had retrospectively willed her future deeds into existence. *Abracadabra, I create as I speak.* Miriam knew at long last the path behind her was closing. And her best way forward now lay open ahead.

Yehonatan's arrival would be a special blessing from God. He would help her with everything. Deep in her bones, in her womb, throughout her body, she sensed the truth of that. How fortunate that he was coming just now! A small miracle that fate had arranged perfectly to support her. For the first time in years, Miriam felt a prayer arising within her spontaneously for all that she desired to be accomplished with ease. *Lord, I know not how to accomplish my desire, except to rely on you entirely.* She shaped her bequest to the Holy One, then sent it aloft to fly towards heaven.

And the tears rolled down her cheeks once more.

"Marcus!" Phoenix hailed him near the forum on his way home that evening, "haven't seen you in months!"

"I've been training," Marcus said, crossing over to him. "Full time."

"What a shame you're not Greek-born," said Phoenix. "Because there's an Olympics next year. You'd be a sure candidate. Why not come over for some drinks and you can tell me all about it?"

Marcus turned down the drinking, but agreed to walk together towards their home quarter. The truth was he had no desire to return home so soon after that conversation with his mother. A short distraction would not hurt. Phoenix embodied the kind of diversion Marcus had denied himself for months.

And the black horse within Marcus, feeling Phoenix's presence, sensed that the rein holding him back all this time was finally loosening. Restive and fired up, the stallion reared, urgent to have its head and the rein slipped some more.

In the end, it took very little persuasion for Marcus to end up at Phoenix's home that evening.

For several hours, they relaxed in a lavishly decorated office just off the atrium, where frescoed walls in reds and blues and greens illustrated famous scenes from Greek history. A large one portrayed Achilles killing Hector, while a smaller one showed Socrates touching Phaedo's golden locks before he drank the hemlock. A fitting place to pass time drinking wine and discussing philosophy, though they soon passed on to arguing about technique and strategy in expedition fights they had both witnessed.

"And here's Helen to join us," said Phoenix, as his sister wafted downstairs in another striking robe. This time it was green with golden highlights that reflected the gold of her hair and deftly drew all eyes to her beauty.

"How is the wine tonight?" she asked.

"Rich," said Marcus. "From Aza, I believe."

"Join us," said Phoenix and handed her up a glass.

"I will," Helen said, and took the glass. She closed her eyes as she took the first swallow and made a sound of appreciation. Then, smiling at Marcus she crossed the room to sit down near him on his couch. "How delightful to see you again! Did I hear correctly you've been training even harder?" she said. "Your muscles certainly look honed." And as Helen ran her hand lightly down his arm, she made another sound of appreciation.

Across the room, Phoenix snorted.

Marcus, very aware that his muscles were chiseled to near perfection, was still unused to direct flattery from a beautiful older matron. He looked down at his cup, smiled quietly and took a long sip. For the first time he noticed the Greek inscription on his cup, *Be glad that you have come.* True enough, he was glad he had come. He let himself polish off his fourth glass of wine, then raised his countenance and smiled right back at Helen.

Inside of him, his black horse felt nearly free.

"We're going to the chariot races at the hippodrome later this week, said Helen, leaning in. Her breasts were more exposed in this position. "You really should join us."

"I take it you support the green team?" Marcus said, pointing at her dress. "I'll gladly come."

A short while later, Dion turned up at the door, and Marcus used the occasion to fill his cup once more and to stay far longer than he had intended.

The next morning, as Rufinus put him through his paces with the usual level of difficulty, sparing him nothing, Marcus' skin turned clammy white and he vomited. His focus had been off all session.

Rufinus looked down at the vomit in disgust, then back at him. "This is a discipline that brooks no trifling. The next time you come here ill from drink will be your last," Rufinus barked at him. "Drunkard is a fine profession. But don't waste my time."

"Rufinus, I apologize," said Marcus, shamefaced and still queasy. "It's that–."

"On the battlefield, no one cares about your woes or your nerves, except that it makes you easier to kill. Get that in your head," Rufinus bellowed. "Vigilant focus!"

Marcus jumped.

That day he went home early with bruises.

PART XVIII

CHAPTER 27
Cracks in the Defenses

Two months later, in late winter, Quintillus Rufus, the Senior Tribune of the Xth Fretensis, dispatched Julius back to the port at Caesarea to greet the general of the Sixth Legion. Turbo was arriving from Alexandria with some of his officers to confer on the security situation in Judea and throughout the Eastern Mediterranean. This time, Julius' posting back to Caesarea had come with no advance notice. He left without writing a message and sending it ahead. No matter, he thought. He would be there soon enough.

The general's warship was due to make landfall in a week or there-abouts. Calm seas prevailed, the report informed him. Pirate activity was at an all-time low in the area. Julius wished as much could be said for the roads. These days, they were less than fully tranquil with roving bands of men stealing money, goods and sometimes life itself from travelers. In winter, cold weather and chill rain kept the roads desolate for days at a time making wayfarers even more vulnerable. Bandits never struck at troops of armed soldiers riding on the main road. But all of Jerusalem had heard the tale of two sentries robbed and slain by brigands who left their bodies far off a dirt track, their skulls dented by stones, their organs mauled by swords. It was an ugly crime, the markings of political zealotry strong upon it, for who else but a madman or a zealot would strike thus at Rome?

Even now with Judea subjugated, on her knees and left begging, one still came across fools who did not accept that Rome's dominion was inevitable and invincible. Rome acted in haste to mete out punishment. Those particular thugs, apprehended after days of searching through barren hills and stony caves, were dragged back to Jerusalem in chains for questioning that lasted hours upon hours. Days later, the torturer confirmed that the leader of the band was still uncaptured, one Amidav Avtinas, the scion of aristocrats who still dwelled in the city, a priestly family now fallen on very hard times. With the Temple's destruction, the Avtinas' enormous income as the sole supplier of incense for daily Temple rites was reduced to a trickle.

Lucky for the family, Amidav was known to be outcast and degenerate, else Quintillus Rufus would have sent the whole lot of them to the arena to be mauled by lions, not just their son. But the times were too tense to risk making an entire priestly family into a symbol of Roman justice. Their martyrdom would have created more trouble than it was worth just now in small and large recriminations throughout the Jerusalem area and the Judean hills. Forces on the ground were still scant with little hope of persuading Rome to send in reinforcements. Julius had had to make this point over and over to the Governor before the man relented.

Instead, the priestly family was thrown out of their half-burnt villa – a prime bit of real estate in the center of the city now appropriated by Rome — while Amidav's men were dragged into the arena to stave off wild beasts with their bare hands. That was an entertainment Julius' men had enjoyed watching. The smell of terror and imminent death clogging the air, the tang of sweat and piss and flying red blood gashing the white limestone walls and gushing across the virgin sand. At the last, the prisoners ceased their screaming, their voices stoppered with pain. Julius, himself, had not taken pleasure in the spectacle; but by Mithras, those brigands had earned every moment.

Although he would have preferred to ride to Caesarea Maritima alone with Silius and Arianus, instead, Julius found himself journeying in the midst of a small detachment of men: Silius, Arianus, Flavius Antoninus, Gaius, Xeno and Orodes; the last three were a triumvirate of likely soldiers, rotated to his century several months prior from the VIth Legion in Syria. Xeno and Orodes were both Macedonian by birth, born fighters and practiced athletes. Flavius Antoninus was joining him from the command in Jerusalem. Arianus, meanwhile, had been rising in the ranks in Caesarea for some time and had even befriended Marcus. The young man possessed a hefty supply of nervous energy that occasionally exhausted itself. In appearance, he had smooth blond-red hair, a slightly florid complexion, wide-set almond eyes, a beautifully proportioned body and occasionally a haughty air that military service had not yet cured. He resembled nothing so much as an idealized statue of Alexander or the kind of expensive catamite one sometimes spotted at the gymnasium, toning his beautiful body. Orodes, in contrast, was mole-like; muddy brown in looks, barrel-chested and subterranean in habit. Julius kept wondering what he was hiding.

The bit of road they were traveling on still had its tricky spots, cutting from Jerusalem across the Judean hills to Neapolis. Beyond that, it was market day, and the people milling about the dusty villages were filled with hostility against Rome–not least due to last winter's drought – as though Rome's dominion extended to controlling the four winds. So far this winter, great storm clouds had rolled in with a whipping wind, but less rain had fallen than what was needed. The local people saw it as yet another curse on the Jewish people, symbolized by the military presence of Rome. As though he and his men were no more than a divine curse, visited on the people for their sins.

As it turned out, Julius thought, his mind skittering into abandoned chambers, it had turned out a very good thing Marcus had not come with him on this trip to Jerusalem. It would have been a disaster – for both of them: from the display of Roman force against Jewish rebels in the arena, to having Marcus observing the atmosphere that prevailed in the Judean villages. For he would have observed it. And on that thought Julius sealed off that dark portal, sucked in his breath and leaned forward on his horse, urging him into a run.

Julius and his men spent their first night at the small army garrison in Neapolis, 45 Roman miles north of Jerusalem and a smidge east. Julius was allocated an inner room with a soft bed and a gray woolen blanket, while his men arranged their pallets in a cramped antechamber outside his room. The floor was hard stone, but the hypocaust gave off ample heat into the room, exuding warmth from the floor and walls.

He awoke the next morning to a door creaking open. Silius stood on the threshold, bringing him a red earthenware cup of warm wine with honey. "Your drink, sir."

Julius shook himself awake, then lifted himself to his elbows and reached out with his hand to take the cup. Silius moved to uncover the window just a bit, enough so he could see outside. The morning was still lightless, foretelling another dark day. Their little troop would ride hemmed in by low clouds and a keening wind. His naked skin shivering slightly, Julius tipped back his head and swallowed his wine. "Swill." He licked his lips. "That's one good reason to be going home. Miriam stocks much finer vintages than this. Next time remind me to bring several cases of it."

"You did that, sir."

Julius glowered then finished off the drink. "Yes, well then remind me to send for replacements when I've drunk off the lot."

This time Silius said nothing and moved not so much as a muscle on his face. The man was humoring him, damn it. Julius remembered perfectly well that Silius had reminded him to send for more wine and Julius had nixed it because he had not wanted to send a missive back to Caesarea, had not wanted to waste a moment on it, nor concentrate an idle thought. He tossed the red cup hard at the man and watched Silius grab it handily from the air. The man was old, but his reaction time was still impeccable.

A beat later, Silius spoke. "The local centurion requested an interview with you, sir, after you have bathed. Drusus Priscus, his name is."

"I'm aware of that. And?"

"...and as far as I can tell, his men think well of him, conditionally, that he does nothing to make their lives more insecure. So far, he's seen as just, and a hard worker. Nothing out of the way. But then he's recently appointed. They don't have much to judge from yet."

"Of course. And that's all you have managed to discover?"

"Silius shrugged. "I've had a bare hour to work on it this morning."

Julius grunted and rolled out of bed. "Okay, get out. I'll take my bath now. If you should..."

"...happen to rout out anything else important, I'll come report it to you. Immediately. Got that already, sir. Know it off by heart."

Julius directed a stern eye at him, which he knew would impress Silius not in the least, then nodded a dismissal. After the door snapped closed, Julius flipped a clean tunic over his head, shoved his feet into sandals and left to search out the relative luxury of the bath house.

Later that morning, Julius inspected the military fortifications around Neapolis with Drusus. As they climbed the four-story gate made from great blocks of basalt, he looked the man over with a critical eye. Brown hair, still young, medium height, a sharp-featured, intelligent face. Of course, Julius reminded himself, that did not necessarily mean the man would be intelligent in a crisis or even that he was intelligent at all. Western accented Latin, a wealthy background, or at least an upper class one. And since his manner appeared seamless, it was instilled from birth. Quite obviously Drusus cared about his clothes. They were expensive and cut to flatter his upright military bearing. And as far as Julius could tell, the man possessed good reaction speed. A mixed review, but positive overall.

Since Julius' own manners were far from seamless, he cut directly to the point. "Permit a fellow centurion a blunt question. Did you earn this post or was it handed out as a sinecure or a favor to your family?"

"Well, all three, really." He grinned, displaying small, crooked teeth, and surprisingly little offense at the question. "But then I arrived. The garrison is small but it's an important trade city, with a large population, difficult relations among the different ethnic groups and all sorts of restive natives. Since I've been here, I've had more time to wonder whether I wasn't set up for an elaborate failure. I'm not," he said, "a fool."

Julius raised his eyebrows. "You consider your humiliation is worth more to Rome than Neapolis?"

"Put like that..." said Drusus and laughed. "I'm likely to be struck down by the gods for hubris, aren't I? But it's a much trickier post than it appeared on parchment."

"Not just tricky. It's a crucial point to hold if there's a rebellion."

"I realize that, of course." Drusus bristled. Then he checked himself. "If, you said?" Drusus swallowed. "And do you believe a rebellion is ... imminent?"

"Yes. Imminent. But who is to say how imminent?" Julius shrugged. "Days, months, years? Surely not days. It will be months or even years. Perhaps not at all if we're very lucky. But that would take superb restraint on both sides and a tolerance likely not to be meted out by everyone concerned." Julius looked at Drusus bluntly. "Tell me. Do you feel more or less tolerant since you've been posted here?"

Drusus' arms tightened across his chest.

Julius scowled. "Now multiply that feeling by the entire command." He waited a moment, but no more questions were forthcoming. "If we're done here, I'd like to finish my inspection. It's been several years since I've examined the city gates." He grimaced slightly, business-like. "A review seems in order."

Neapolis, at the mouth of the only mountain pass in Judea with direct access both east and west, formed the central point in a hub of ancient roads. In ancient times, it had been a capital city. Recently resettled as a city for Titus' veterans after the last Jewish war, it was now occupied alike by Romans, Samaritans, Christians and a small group of Jews. Its military value reflected its commanding geographical situation. Neapolis was still an important station in continuing east-west trade.

Julius made a point of walking around the battlements at all the city gates to gauge their strengths and their weaknesses, to observe where the stone and brickwork was shoddily constructed and where it needed repair. He made sure that Drusus knew this as well. For it was clear that if the city were ever laid under siege, her attackers would have had ample time to study her weaknesses from the inside as well. On the way down, Drusus pointed out to him a few things he had not, himself, remarked.

Later, outside the stable and astride his horse, Julius leaned down to say one final word to Drusus. "Figure out a way to have the council vote funds to get the southern wall repaired as soon as possible. In the next months. That's crucial."

Drusus nodded and waved them through the gate, biting his bottom lip.

The man looked less cocksure now than he had started out. One goal accomplished. To speak truth, it was a relief to articulate to someone else some of this formless anxiety that had seized his gut now for weeks and months. It was the coming rebellion, he reflected, tingling along his nerves, filling his stomach with dread. Perhaps his warning would even do some good.

That day, Julius set a leisurely pace on the road. His one goal was to reach Caesarea by sunset. He had six hours to travel a bit over thirty miles. There was no point in tiring either the horses or the men unduly. There was no emergency awaiting him once he returned to Caesarea. Besides, he thought, he'd come to rely on Vincius. Despite the man's personal eccentricities, he had a genius for organization and the men respected him. However, Julius had made sure they still obeyed him with greater alacrity. Fear, in a soldier, was a notable way to measure respect.

All that long afternoon, as the horses' hooves struck hard on the frigid road, and his lungs protested the cold, Julius allowed himself, at last, to ponder the problem of Marcus. Political trouble was brewing, that he knew. The Roman command was now anticipating a revolt by the Jews at some future point. In truth, Julius himself felt glad at this presage of war. The current state of continued restraint was proving frustrating to himself and his fellow officers. War was the one decisive method to establish lasting Roman dominion.

Aye, but his son might decide to join the rebels. That was the trouble! The best offensive solution was to send the boy abroad very soon to serve in the Western Empire. In Gaul or Britain or Germania, the boy would not be infected by the local madness. Get him away from his mother, away from here, and his son might still turn out all right. He'd made up his mind to do it as soon as he arrived.

A small animal rustled furiously away from them in the dense underbrush. Julius surveyed the site, but the animal never broke cover. Finally, he lifted his eyes from the road. Caesarea gleamed on the horizon, the palace jutting out to sea, the long marble forum, the amphitheater and Herod's Temples, towering above the earth. They were just a bit out of the city now. Julius exhaled, his breath puffing and raw, and reached for his third flask of strong wine. He took a long draught, then another and another. Silius was too far behind, so he tossed the scanty remains to Arianus who caught it, then held it up to his ear, jiggling it until he heard a faint liquid slosh. "Not much left, sir," Arianus said, laughing at him. True enough. There was little left. He had had a thirst. His face set forward again, Julius rode straight down toward the sea.

Too quickly. He'd drunk too much. The wine had gone straight to his head. Julius shook his head, looked up at the horizon and, for a moment, caught his breath. Above the gray-black sea, a small cloud of gulls hovered in the sky, downy gray-white against the gray blue sky, floating at rest, in slightly crooked lines, one after the other, their nether wings tipped in black shadow. The winter wind carried their small shrieks and caws, the flutter of their lingering wings, the scent of fish. Far off, the sky radiated pink. Sunset even now approached. One thing was sure, he had timed the length of the trip true.

A quarter of an hour later, Julius was riding through the poor out-skirts of town. Dusk had already washed over the limestone buildings, staining them a dark grape. Before him, rivulets of caked mud ran between the stones strewing the street. The stench of city life was all around them now. He smelled death and decay, food cooking and rotting garbage, the bitter whiff of waste from man and animal. In a dark alleyway, a cat interrupted its meal to turn its eyes on them, a long green feral gleam, before it yowled and skittered off.

And then, out of the corner of his eye, Julius glimpsed a shadow sliding around a bend in the road. No more than that. What alerted him, he never afterwards knew. A trick of light in the twilight gloom, a flash of motion that he recognized. His body would have sworn that was Marcus disappearing down a lane. Julius moved his horse into the crossroads in time to see the shadow slip through a far-off door. Why, he wondered, was his son slinking into one of the broken-down stone houses that littered this neighborhood? It puzzled him, too, that for such a destitute area, this house was lit by an extravagance of lamps. An oil lamp illuminated its outside and light shone brightly through the small window that faced the street.

Julius reined in, pivoting his horse to the right. "Silius," he called in a carrying whisper. "Was that–?" he pointed. "Did you see anything that way?

The little man came abreast of him on his brown horse and turned eyes glazed with dust and exhaustion up to him. Still, he managed to project his voice sharply. "Anything of what sort?"

Julius looked at the other four faces halted slightly behind him, with their tired eyes and their thoughts only of reaching their bunker to sleep or spend time drinking with their friends and fellow soldiers and camp women after months away.

"Arianus? No. Any of you?" Of course not. None of them had been alert. But then he, too, was tired. Julius pondered a moment. "I'll say goodnight to you now. Silius, check that a sentry has already been posted to the port to alert us when the general's ship makes entrance. If not, send one." He nodded to his men. "Any questions? No. Then I'll see you at the barracks tomorrow morning."

Wheeling his tired horse, exhausted himself, Julius set off after the shadow he thought had been his son.

After a bit, Julius dismounted so that he could lead his horse cannily over the stony rubble. The roads were not maintained in this impoverished district. He tied his horse to a post while still some way off. For a second Julius stood undecided as the gelding's head drooped and it snuffled at the rocky ground for fodder. Then, stalwart, stubborn, he approached the building carefully. A sound of uplifted voices emerged punctuated by a silence in which he heard the sweet even-song of birds.

Julius reached the dwelling. The door was left partially open, so he peered across the stone lintel. The room contained arched ceilings and a rough stone floor. The plastered walls were now a faded blue and the few windows had blue and green glass. Seats were built around

351

the perimeter of the room that was occupied by men both standing and sitting. Jews all, he could tell by their garb, who appeared to be praying, with downturned faces. Praying, always praying, for all the good it did them.

He ran his eyes over the lot of them slowly. And then his breath hissed out of his chest cavity. At the very back, off by himself, Marcus stood starring straight at him. His quicksilver son, in whom was stored all his pride of manhood.

"Marcus," Julius cried angrily, stepping inside. His short sword grated against the stone doorframe, and all at once every eye was turned on him, a Roman soldier, in half armor and helmeted, shouting fiercely in a Jewish house of prayer.

Shocked, Marcus took a step towards him, and tripped, his balance faltering against the foundation stone. He caught himself then, straightened his body and took no closer steps.

"Come here, I say," Julius shouted, his voice sounding thick even in his own ears.

Marcus looked straight at his father, his face ashen, and shook his head in abnegation.

Julius looked back at his son, his well-beloved quicksilver son, and tried to fathom what Marcus was telling him. After a moment he caught his breath and leaned against the stone lintel, to steady himself in turn, to regain his balance.

At that moment, a middle-aged man with short dark hair and a graying beard approached Julius. "Excuse me, Centurio, but this young man is a member of my congregation. And it's our time for prayers and study. Is there a problem? Can you tell me what you want with him, please?"

"The problem is," Julius bellowed, "he's my son. And he's coming home with me now."

Around the room, came sounds of shock and dismay from the congregants.

352

The middle-aged man slowly turned to look at Marcus. "Micha'el, this is correct?"

"Marcus. His name is Marcus," interjected Julius, "and he's my son."

The murmurings of the congregation became louder and louder.

"You're drunk again, Julius," Marcus said with asperity. And he quietly added. "Rabbi Yo'el, I apologize deeply for this display."

The rabbi looked between the two men.

Julius reached out his hand to grab Marcus and pull him towards the door, but his hand was immediately intercepted and held in an iron grip.

"I said no, Julius." Marcus met his eyes levelly, with such strength, will and fury apparent in them Julius automatically dropped his hand and took a step backwards. A second later, he realized what he had done and stepped forward again.

"Micha'el," said the Rabbi, "or is it Marcus? This man is your father?"

"It's both," said Marcus. "I'm both. And yes, he's my father."

"I see," said the rabbi, sounding uncertain. "Please go with him now then, settle this dispute elsewhere. When you next have time, if you wish to discuss it further or you need aid, come and see me, so I can understand the whole situation."

"No one understands the whole situation," said Marcus, on a bitter laugh. "Certainly not us." And though he followed Julius out the door, Julius, walking ahead, could feel his anger smoldering, like a blacksmith's hearth radiating heat.

Once out the door, Julius spun on his heel to confront him, with words and a closed fist to Marcus' face. "Don't you ever..."

Marcus stopped the punch again. "I'm not seven years old anymore, Julius. You can't intimidate me with threatened beatings. If I want to go pray, I will go pray. To my God, not your stone godlings." He stepped in closer to loom over his father. "Do you understand? I don't need your permission."

Julius did not understand. He was tired from riding all day and the wine he had recently consumed, starving from the long fast on the road and this insubordination now woke his rage. Scales were falling from his eyes and a black pit of desolation opened up in his chest that reached down to his guts and felt like fear. He used that to launch the biggest attack he knew on his son, the one he had always used successfully in battle, the one that had never failed him.

Marcus stopped him cold, then counterattacked with a blow to Julius' solar plexus, which knocked him backwards and off balance. The blow was so deep that he simply ran out of air and found himself kneeling on the ground, chasing his breath.

"Had enough?" taunted Marcus.

The truth was Julius had had enough. He was still having trouble breathing. But that did not stop him from roaring, "No," as he pushed himself up and launched himself full tilt through the air to land on Marcus' body. They both tipped over and then they were on the ground fighting each other.

There had been a time when his son was a boy that they had wrestled together in play. For Julius, it had been a game to teach Marcus. But it had been years since the two had grappled. Past the learning stage, they never had fought with any seriousness, and never with the level of rage incandescing both of them at this moment. The fight turned punitive immediately. Marcus was the better fighter, younger, stronger, more practiced. But Julius had fought in battle with many more warriors and against many different styles. He had hard won knowledge of practical survival techniques that Marcus had not yet acquired, and he used them to deflect attacks and to counterattack viciously.

At last Marcus, straddling him, punched Julius in the jaw so hard that his head rocked back and hit the stone road. "Enough," Julius said weakly. "Enough Marcus." And he placed his head back down on the ground.

Then someone pulled Marcus off from behind. Julius looked up to see the rabbi and another man from the synagogue who began to yell at his son in a flurry of shocked Aramaic in a dialect that Julius did not comprehend.

Marcus looked at them askance, looked down at Julius with a dark glance, and extended his hand.

"Too dizzy," Julius said and placed his hand back on his forehead. "I'm seeing double for the moment. Get my horse."

Marcus retrieved the horse and after a while, the three men got Julius seated upon it.

Then they walked, Marcus leading the bay horse through the darkening streets.

"Congratulations are due to Rufinus," Julius said at last. "That was very impressive. Though I doubt he was expecting you to turn those abilities against me first thing I got back."

"I doubt he expected you to attack me first thing you got back, either."

"Speaking of attacks," said Julius, "I've been thinking of your future. Son, this will be a sacrifice for me, but I am planning to send you abroad to join the army in a different country. With your skills, anyone will take you, and you will rise very rapidly. I am thinking of Egypt.

"Egypt's too close for your purposes. If there's a war, Egyptian Legions will likely be summoned here. Besides, you'll know soon enough so I may as well tell you now. My grandfather is ill. Mother wants to go see him before he dies and wants me along for the journey."

Julius took some time to process this. It should not have surprised him that his quicksilver son had already figured out what his purpose was in wanting to send him away from this land with its volatile populations. And that he had figured out a real objection to the legion in Egypt. "You can join the army in Sardis, then. That's not a terrible idea at all," Julius said.

"No, Father," Marcus said. "I am never, ever going to join the Roman army, because wherever I am sent, there's always a chance that I get transferred back here if there's a rebellion, just like you were transferred here."

Julius assimilated this. "Go to Britannia then. We had news in Jerusalem that Julius Severus, the best general in the entire army has just been appointed to govern the province. And it's so far away. There's not a chance in the world he will ever get transferred here."

"Julius," said Marcus patiently. "If you have never heard me before, hear me now. Considering what the Romans have done to my people, I am never going to fight for the Roman side." Marcus stopped moving and turned around to look squarely at Julius. "Ever."

Julius registered the words "my people," which he had never heard his son use before. And though it was almost dark, Julius could see his face and the determination therein. "But you've trained for it your whole life. I don't understand what you will do."

"Rufinus suggested that I could have a career for a few years appearing in expedition fights abroad. And that's appealing." Marcus shrugged. "I considered traveling east with Yehonatan. But mother wants me to stay and help her work the business in Sardis."

"Your mother!" Julius' last nerve snapped, and he bellowed, "Did she put you up to this? She's a twisted snake!

Marcus looked back at his father, his features twisting into a grimace. "The way you talk about her! No wonder she's di..." He snapped his mouth shut.

It did not stop Julius' ire. "Don't get ahead of yourself there, Marcus. She's hardly a paragon! Did I ever tell you how I first fucked your mother and got you on her? Both of us falling down drunk under an altar to Dionysius! Tell that to your rabbi. He won't think you're so pure."

"None of them think I'm pure. And if Rabbi Yo'el had any doubts about it at all, he doesn't after tonight. The shame of my conception shines right through me." Marcus pivoted away from his father then and spoke with eyes straight ahead. "Thanks for telling me that, though. Now I know the worst and it's not as bad as I had imagined. I'd assumed for years that you raped her, that she had no choice. Because I couldn't figure how she would have ever accepted you. You're from such entirely different worlds. But, instead, you met somehow and got her raving drunk, like Dionysius' mad Maenads." Marcus drew in a breath. "Quite an image for a son to treasure."

Julius took his time to answer. His voice went very low and very precise. "Had I not been drunk like a satyr and worshipping Dionysius, you wouldn't even exist."

"And you've been a drunkard ever since in tribute to the god," Marcus spit back. "How aspirational for me!"

"Stuck for life with the consequence of a wine-sodden mistake," Julius said.

A metal gate scraped open nearby, a male voice shouted a half-heard command, then the gate clanged shut and the caterwauling of guard dogs began in reply, a chorus of cacophony.

Julius reached his hand towards his aching head, closed his eyes, and trusted to his son, his only son, the one he loved, to lead him correctly.

The two men continued in silence for some time, each one alone with his thoughts, on this part of their journey home. Marcus guided in the dark and Julius allowed himself to be guided, half sleeping in the saddle.

When next he came back to full consciousness, his horse had stopped. Julius opened his eyes, squinting down at Marcus in the moonlight. It was so bright, he shut his eyes again.

"We've reached the crossroad," Marcus said, stepping from the east-west road onto the Roman coastal road.

Julius opened his eyes back up. Across the road, a big house had lit a torch in front of its gate that threw rays of light onto the road.

357

The light shone off white polished pebbles placed along the corner of the large stones lining the roads, to help night-time travelers traverse the roads safely. Right now, however, the light was refracting into his eyes. Julius shut them again and took a deep breath. He had made his decision. Now to follow it all the way through. He took a long exhale and opened his eyes. "Head south from here. Go straight to the house. I'll ride alone to the barracks."

"Father," said Marcus, stepping closer, "I'll lead you. Of course."

"Go," Julius commanded. "You already made your choice." There was a pause and the lights refracted into his eyes again and he felt dizzy. He raised his voice, "Go to your house." Even as Marcus baulked, he purposefully barked in the voice of command loathed by his son, "Go now. Leave."

Marcus slapped Julius' horse on its rump so that the horse leaped forward towards the northern road. "Goodbye," he said, and with no backwards glance, he turned and walked away.

Julius directing the reins lightly, wheeled his bay back around so he could watch Marcus recede. His eyes turned greedy, then, hoarding the last images of his son like treasured seeds that must be carefully preserved to outlast a lengthy drought; like the seven-year famine the Pharoah had endured, as he had heard Miriam and Marcus recount from their holy book. Julius wondered if that was a true story. He watched as his son became smaller and vaguer, until he evanesced into the blackness.

Something irrevocable had happened tonight. Would his own drought, like Pharoah's, find an end one day?

The wait that stretched ahead of him felt interminable already.

Perhaps if he drank deep of the spiced Dionysian cultic wine, he would dream the future and know how long he had to wait. But no. All this mess had begun, eighteen years back, with ecstatic cultic wine. Maybe he should regard this part of his life as finally over and done? Like an eighteen-year ellipse that had moved into completion. It was finished. Done.

One part of his brain looked at that thought for a little while and decided to test it. He said aloud, "And now I'm free." Then gasped as his heart contracted painfully three times.

He knew, then, surer than any prophetic dream, he would never be free. Nor did he want to be free. Mercury, the Wingèd One, had delivered that message to him in record time.

Only then did Julius take stock of himself. His head ached worse than it ever had, and his nausea was so intense he would surely vomit soon if nothing worse. Cold and alone, he turned his horse and rode laboriously towards the barracks.

He only hoped he would last the trip.

CHAPTER 28

A Paradise of Their Making

Near home, Marcus stopped off at The Dancing Dolphin Inn, tossed off two glasses of their famed ale and requested an amphora of the most expensive wine they sold. Then he repaired towards Phoenix's villa, amphora in hand, and asked the door servant for his friend.

"Phoenix is away, sir," said the servant, who recognized him. As the man turned away, Helen appeared behind him, a vision in blue and gold. For the first time, he dared to smile at her full on. It was, perhaps, the influence of the ale he had just imbibed. And the fight that proceeded that.

Helen smiled back dazzlingly, walked forward, and reached out both her hands to take his in hers. "Come in, Marcus," she purred. "Have you been fighting? You look a bit bedraggled tonight. Let's see what I can do about that."

Marcus continued to smile at her as a thousand reasons multiplied in his head as to why he should beg off. A vision of Rufinus stepped forward grunting disapproval of the behavior that was about to occur;

Rabbi Ariel took his place, shaking his head at Marcus' fallen moral state; Rabbi Yo'el tightened his mouth before turning away; while his own mother yelled silently at him; then Rufinus was back, hectoring him about his promise to commit to training. And last and finally, Devorah looked at him in disdain that slowly, oh so slowly, morphed into pain. Then she dissolved into tears.

Marcus shut his eyes and felt inwards and could not reach his center. The last thing he wanted to deal with right now were womanly tears. Or the constant push to better himself. All he wanted in this moment was equilibrium. Since that was impossible, then he wanted distraction so the recent scenes with Julius ceased to run through his mind.

If Helen possessed the key to oblivion, however brief, he would take her up on it. Eyes still shut, his hands leapt out to meet hers. Only then did he open his eyes to follow after.

Helen's inner chamber was a marvel of a room. The walls were painted burnt ochre with a large frieze of nymphs, lit by moonlight shining in from a terrace door that opened onto the Mediterranean. There were blush pink marble floors striated with gray. Sconces with soft orange light were stationed about the walls. On the table, a bowl of water, painted with heroic scenes, rested on a clay pot with a burning wick, diffusing the scent of lavender into the room. It was a warm and inviting chamber, displaying a side of Helen absent from public view.

Marcus stood transfixed at the lintel, uncertain now of his ground. He said, "My father often jests that relations between men and women is a different kind of battlefield; lady, it's one I am untrained in."

"It doesn't have to be a battlefield." Helen took his hand, held it palm to palm for a few moments and said, "Shall I guide you?" At his nod, she drew him into the room and sat him down.

Marcus spent that night in Helen's arms, letting her lead him to a paradise of their making. There was some awkwardness at first, then kindness, laughter, and much pleasure.

Draw me, after thee we will run:
The king hath brought me into his chambers:
We will remember thy love more than wine.

The next morning Marcus did not attend training.
Rufinus, resolutely, crossed his name off the list.

———◦———

Midmorning the next day, Miriam sat in the quiet of Julius'
quarters at the barracks. Early that morning, a messenger had arrived
at the villa to tell her that Julius had been found near the gates of the
barracks, fallen off his horse and unconscious. She had rushed here
with her maid, Hamida, hurrying through the falling rain, dashing
from portico to portico to stay dry.

But now she sat in her damp clothing, as Julius slept in his bed,
trying to warm up with the stingy heat provided by the hypocaust.

Miriam wondered why she had hurried so much.

Outside she could hear soldiers giving orders, an occasional clack
of weapons at the drill, and the ceaseless drum of rain on the roof.

Inside Julius slept on. When she looked more carefully at him,
she saw that he looked ill. His complexion, tending towards florid,
had instead a pasty tone and his hair, usually lustrous, was dusty and
matted flat around his forehead.

She was alone in this cold room filled with neatly rolled Latin
papyri. It was a thoroughly masculine environment, where Julius was
at ease, reminding her viscerally of those horrid months in her life
when she had traveled with the army. Neither place was one where
a woman might flourish.

Miriam walked over to his desk and picked up a scroll at random.
Seneca. She unrolled it and stopped at a well-worn spot. Miriam read,

"It is not because things are difficult that we do not dare; it is because we do not dare that things are difficult."

The truth of that hit her hard, like a brilliant marksman bringing down a gazelle from afar with one clean shot between the eyes. For years now, that had been true of her. Decades, really, if she were completely truthful. She had not dared to do the one thing to change her life she knew she needed to do; instead, she had developed an enormous resistance to daring anything at all. All during her walk to the military camp this morning, Miriam had felt like she was dragging that resistance with her like an unclean thing, felt it holding her back, to the extent that she wondered whether she would have the courage to talk to Julius honestly today. Dread filled her still.

Miriam rolled the scroll to another place and read, *"He who is brave is free."*

She let those words vibrate through her clear down to her toes which began to tingle. This, right here, felt like an unmistakable message from above. A deep part of her now felt she had been guided today by the Lord and His Angels so that she would follow through on what she had resolved.

Miriame suddenly felt deeply grateful, as though the prayer she had sent aloft to heaven weeks ago had been answered right now in this moment. Hope rose within her, a soft feeling of contentment that expanded from her womb to her heart to her throat, so unlike the warlike and sharp sensations she often felt around Julius. Inside herself, her tension began to unfold.

Miriam shaped another prayer to the Holy One, spoke it aloud and sent it off; then she sat in a reverie for a time, staring into space, the scroll on her lap, reciting psalms she had known by heart all her life.

I sought God and he heard me
And delivered me from all my fears.

Julius awoke shortly afterwards; he squinted into the light of the darkened room. When he noticed her, he grimaced and closed his eyes again. "If you're here, I must be in worse state than I realized," he said in a low voice.

In truth, Miriam had rarely come to this room. The villa was their shared ground. That had been their arrangement. "Come now, Julius," she said. "With me here or without me, you know you're in bad state."

He grunted a reply.

"I hear you fell off your horse on the way home, by yourself, and that's how the guard found you overnight." For the moment Miriam left the rest unspoken. That one slip from a horse was unlikely to have done all the damage she could see. She said, "You have to stop drinking while you ride."

Julius grunted his agreement and looked out his window at the gray world beyond. His eyesight had accustomed itself to the low light of the room now.

"What happened to you?"

"Not now, Miriam," he said, and groaned, "Did Xenon leave any potions? My head is killing me."

Miriam got up from her chair, went to his desk and found the potion Xenon had left, a tincture of opium mixed with other herbs she did not recognize. She handed it to him, watched him drink it and then waited for it to take effect.

Fortunately, the potion was strong and that happened rapidly.

"Stop hovering over me," Julius grumbled. "Go sit back over there."

With a pained smile, Miriam walked back to the chair she had sat in for the last few hours. "I repeat, Julius, what happened to you?"

"Have you spoken to your son this morning?"

She had not. Nor seen him either. "He goes to exercise before dawn each day. I rarely see him in the early mornings." And then she saw Julius' eyes veering away from contact with hers. "Hold, Julius, what are you implying? What about Marcus?"

Julius held her eyes and in return, Miriam's beautiful green eyes became very wide. "No, he cannot have done this. At least, not without reason." Her voice grew sharp. "What reason did you give him, Julius?"

He held her eyes again and at last looked away.

"What reason did you give him?"

"I told you I didn't want him studying with rabbis without my permission. He didn't have my permission."

"What did you do?"

"Pulled him out of some impoverished house of prayer. Why was he going there?"

"To pray and study. He's been going there for months. He enjoys it."

"I doubt he'll enjoy it again after last night. Or that he'll be welcome back."

Miriam stood up and her dark green woolen gown fell straight from bodice to ankles, one strong line. "Julius, this is no longer your decision to make. According to Jewish law, he's a man now, with a man's responsibility."

"Really? He told me you're dragging him to Sardis, a mama with her baby boy in tow. Not very manly. And that he refuses to fight in the Roman army. You're doing too, I imagine."

At that news, which Marcus had refrained from telling her, tears welled up in Miriam's eyes. "No. I didn't know he made that decision until just now," she replied, and she allowed the tears to stream down her cheeks.

Julius looked up at the tears disgruntled. "Why are you crying? It's happy news for you, surely. Your victory."

"Our son has grown up into a fine man, Julius. I'm sorry you cannot see it."

"Why must you go to Sardis right now?"

"My father is ill."

"Your brother is there."

"Father's ill now. I want to visit lest he die before I see him again." Miriam paused for a moment then plunged on, like a horse galloping heedlessly towards a ravine. "My brother is needed back in the east to tend the business with Tullian. He wants me to stay in Sardis for some time."

"Absolutely not!" Julius said. And then, "He put you up to all this!"

"No, Julius. No one put me up to anything. I want to go home to Sardis," Miriam said. Her green eyes became very big, she planted her feet and took a deep breath. "And I want our marriage arrangement dissolved." She added in an undertone voice, "It never was fully legal in either of our traditions, as you well know; so, dissolving it shan't be difficult."

Silence reigned in the room.

Miriam bit her lip hard, breathed in and out hard, shut her eyes and continued. "Lord knows, Julius, we've not had an easy time of it. Or been happy. And now Marcus is grown. Raising him was what we shared. It's a blessing how well he turned out, despite our foibles. And he's the true product of the best of us. But now that job is finished, it's time for us to part."

She snuck a glance at Julius. He looked shocked, like someone had punched him in the face. She supposed in a way she had.

Miriam opened her mouth to respond to him, to argue with him, but Julius closed his eyes and held up a hand. He took a breath and then another.

Miriam sat herself down and waited.

———◦———✦———◦———

Julius let Miriam wait. He was finding it hard to catch his equilibrium. The alcoholic rage that had fueled him last night had long since departed; he felt spent, empty, grubby. On top of that, his head and body ached from the fall off his horse and the effects of too much

366

drink. Everything felt flat and fuzzy as though he were far, far away; as though he were viewing the events in his life from atop a mountain looking down at teeny villagers below, small and indistinct.

When he was younger, he had wanted – oh, he had wanted so many things. Most of those desires he realized as a youth he would never attain. Thus began his love of stoic philosophy, which trained him young to discipline those wants. It was also a way to manage the chaos of army life.

He had been well down the pathway of acceptance, when out of the blue, on a day whose mystery far surpassed all other days in his mundane life, he had sired a son like an arrow from the god. And because of that wild consummation under the aegis of Dionysius, he had later married a beautiful woman who, over the course of years, became wealthy; and who allowed him to attain a higher status in the army and in society in Caesarea than he would have achieved on his own. Each, in their own way, had been divine gifts.

Now, in less than one day, both gifts had been withdrawn.

Had he lost favor with the god? Due to his own shortcomings? Or a lack of devotion?

Or was this simply the end of this stage of his life; and the god no longer chose to work through him?

"Julius?" said Miriam.

Julius opened his eyes and looked straight at her. "You'll have your divorce," he said. "Just as I promised you in Cappadocia, all those years ago. Though it will be a mite more complex than I imagined back then." He sighed. Time for plain speaking now. "Having you as my wife and Marcus as my son improved my life immeasurably. And I thank you for that." He met her startled eyes and held them for a long time. "Now I ask you for a favor in return. I want you to take Marcus to Sardis and keep him there for as long as you can. Forever if possible.

Shocked, Miriam said. "Why do you ask that?"

"Isn't it obvious?"

"Not to me."

"There's a very good chance our people will go at war."

Her eyes widened. "How soon?"

"In a year or a handful of years? If things continue this way, with Emperor Hadrian in charge, it's inevitable." He shrugged.

"What does this have to do with–?" Her eyes lit as clarity began to pour into her.

"With Marcus' martial skills, to what height will he not rise in your people's forces, if he so choses? Best he depart with you, for all our sakes. If he wants to waste his life on expedition fights around the Mediterranean and the Western Empire, believe me, I'm not happy; but better that than him fighting against Rome. That will end in disaster for all of us. Tell that to your brother."

She took her time to assimilate that.

Julius resumed, "You primed Marcus to leave. Last night, I prodded him harder."

"How did you do that?"

"Like Triton's trumpet raising tumult in the seas, I triggered his fury and his contempt.

"You pushed him away to make it easier for him to leave?"

"Never tell him that, Miriam. If the gods bless me and I see him again one day, I will explain myself."

"You know he'll take this hard."

"Not at the moment. His fury against me will carry him a long time. Years even." Julius sighed. "The gods know I deserve it."

Miriam did not say a word, but her eyes flashed agreement. She stood up and moved closer to the bed. "Thank you for making this so much easier than I ever imagined, Julius. I appreciate it more than you know. May God grant you perfect healing." She leaned in and touched his palm with her finger, a teeny gesture.

Julius felt her touch reverberate throughout his body.

"Why did we never speak this way when we were wed? The marriage would have been much happier."

Julius noticed her use of the past tense. And mourned it briefly. "Your boldness today inspired my truth-telling."

"If only," she said, lofting the words like a prayer. And her finger traced a small line on his palm, back and forth.

"If only," Julius agreed, wistfully. He closed his palm on her finger for a moment.

And then she was gone. And Julius was alone again.

Naturally.

———————◇———————

Miriam walked home briskly, Hamida trailing behind her. The rain had stopped, and the sun was peeking through the clouds. Chill gusts of wind began to blow, and she wrapped herself in her woolen wrap. Her feelings were whirling so fast, it was hard to know exactly what she felt. But gratitude at the ease of the experience was topmost among them. Her heart felt open and receptive to the blessing of the Lord. For the Lord had granted her prayer that Julius agree to a divorce with so much ease, it stunned her. Her own small miracle she would hold in her heart forever.

Then the rain started again, and she stopped in the forum for shelter. And there in a corner shop she knew well she spotted a necklace she had long admired, with amethysts and emeralds hanging in clusters from a golden chain. She was free, she reminded herself, to buy jewels she didn't need that pleased her. Or anything else she wanted to do.

When the merchant placed the necklace around her neck, Miriam laughed in delight.

She was free.

Later, today or tomorrow, she promised herself to send seven times the cost of the necklace to Rabbi Yo'el to distribute among his needy congregants; seven, the holy number of the Lord.

When Miriam arrived home an hour later, still more good fortune awaited. Yehonatan had arrived at last. All about the portico, there was a bustle as his goods were carried inside the house by servants.

She hurried to hug her brother. Then said, with an enormous smile, "You're looking at a free woman. Or at least I soon will be. Julius just agreed to the divorce." And she crossed her two hands over her chest, looked skyward and smiled radiantly.

"Praise God," said Yehonatan. "The maker of all miracles. Father, too, will be thrilled when he hears."

"He has only himself to thank for it in the first place," Miriam said with asperity. Then she remembered the blessing she had received this day and her joy. "How is he?"

"Stable for now, but withering into old age. You'll see when you arrive." Side by side, they proceeded inside. "And where is Marcus?" said Yehonatan. "The servants say he wasn't home all night."

Where indeed?

———◇———

When Marcus finally returned home later that morning, it was Yehonatan who greeted him at the door. They embraced like dear relatives who have not seen each other for years and who have faced trials and tribulations between times.

"It's too late," said Marcus to his uncle. "Thank you so much for coming. But it's too late now. Everything has fallen apart."

"I'll always come to your aid, Marcus, only send word. You know that, son. But for the help you sought here, it was always too late. From the day it began, it was so written in the stars."

370

Marcus took some time to accept that. Eventually he nodded. Then he said, "Mother doesn't know I invited you. Say nothing to her."

"She's distracted ... by the move."

Marcus snorted. "Not just the move. Did she tell you ...?" And he clamped down on what he was going to say.

"If she hasn't, she will. Now, son, I had a thought that instead of going northwest to Sardis, you could come east with me and learn everything about the business I did not have time to teach you last time. Tullian wants to go south to Sanaa to see his family. You could take his place and coordinate the guard, which will be an excellent chance for you to learn to lead men."

"You'll teach me the spy networks?"

Yehonatan smiled at him, wrinkles crinkling at the corners of his green eyes, a smile as blithesome as it was collusive. "Particularly the spy networks," he said. "We can go north to Ctesiphon and study the strategies the Parthians deployed successfully against Rome. Think of it as the start to an adventure."

Marcus took a moment to assimilate this. "I'm coming back to Judea, afterwards," he said.

"You will. We both will. Our fate," Yehonatan said, "lies here."

Epilogue

As usual, it was just the two of them seated at the rickety wooden table for the midweek evening meal, Devorah and her dear father, Rabbi Ariel. For the meals today, she had made thick lentil stew dripped with olive oil – which after their harvest was now in abundance. She served it in bowls with two-day-old bread, just softer than rock hard. The bread sponged up the stew perfectly, which in turn softened the bread and made everything taste delicious.

Earlier today, her father had lit more oil lamps than usual to provide the room plentiful light in the winter gloom. "It's the season for oil lamps," he had said cheerily. And it was, mere days before the celebration of Chanukah, when they would eat all their foods cooked in olive oil, savory and sweet. But Devorah was not at all sure that the extra light had improved the look of the room. Instead, when she looked around, she saw the flaws more clearly.

But then lately everywhere she looked she saw flaws. Not least her own.

"Devori," her father said. Like a startled bird rising from a half barren bush, Devorah looked up. Devori had been her mother's name for her when she was young, but she couldn't recall the last time her father had used it. In fact, she couldn't remember hearing it since her mother and younger brother died from fevers, some ten years past.

"Abba," she replied.

"I've noticed you don't seem happy lately," he said, and his soulful hazel eyes looked deep into hers. "I blame myself."

"It's not your fault," she said, noticing the circles under his eyes, that seemed darker than usual, and the accumulating wrinkles in their corners. And then the deep loving kindness of his soul penetrated her heart. And part of her wanted to flee and part of her wanted to soak up his love forever and still another part wanted to lower her eyes, shrink in on herself and cry. And that is what she proceeded to do, cry heavy salt tears right into her soup.

"I blame myself," Rabbi Ariel repeated and shook his head sorrowfully. "Selfishly, I enjoyed having you with me after your mother died, so much that I put off arranging your marriage far longer than I should have. But now, my dear, the time has come for you to have a husband and a household of your own to fill with children that will bring you joy; and will bring me the blessings of a grandfather." The rabbi paused for a moment, then continued more softly, "I've been in touch with a colleague from my time learning in Yavneh who has a son to marry. I suggested we should arrange a meeting between the two of you and our families. What do you say, my dear?"

"I don't know," Devorah said, still looking down at the soup while she leaked more tears. "I don't know."

"It will give you something to look forward to, a husband of your own, children to come..."

"But what if I don't like him?" said Devorah. Yet all she could think was how strongly she had disliked Marcus on sight. But now, by some strange alchemy, she could not lose the ties that bound him to her, even though she desperately wanted them gone.

So maybe her judgment was flawed.

She had heard Marcus had taken a ship with his mother and his uncle and his horse and sailed off somewhere exotic to the north. And that their beautiful villa on the seashore had been sold. His father, though, remained at the head of the Caesarian centurions.

"Of course, my dear, if you dislike this young man – or he you – we'll look elsewhere. I made it very clear there's no obligation. We will look as long as we need to for you to find a young man worthy of you, who will honor you as his valorous bride." And her father peered at her again with his deep kindness exuding from him.

Devorah had a sudden memory of her father singing Solomon's poem, *A Woman of Valor*, to her mother every Shabbat eve. On her death bed, before she expired, he had recited the poem of love and recognition one final time. "If only I could find someone like you, Abba. A rabbi and scholar who is kind. Then I would be happy."

"My dear, I know this young man to be a rabbi and a scholar. Together we will discover if he is kind." And Rabbi Ariel looked at her with a question in his eyes.

A week after Marcus had left on that great ship, two full wagons had arrived at her father's home, followed by several sheep and goats. The wagons were loaded with all sorts of fine household furnishings from the villa, lovely dresses that fit her perfectly, garments for her father, medicinal herbs, grains, wines, and a request by Marcus' mother for the rabbi to take what he wished for his household and to distribute the remaining goods among the local congregants as he saw fit, along with a substantial bequest for helping her in this last charitable act in the area.

Devorah knew the distribution of this largesse had changed the perception of her father in the village for the better.

A cynical part of her wondered whether the potential marriage he had just mentioned was only available now because of it, too.

Quite probably.

Devorah drew in a breath and thought of her unhappiness these last few months. Everything in her life felt unmoored and mundane. Nothing stirred up excitement. She dragged her discontent everywhere.

There must be a way to change all this.

She drew in another breath, absorbed some of her father's loving kindness for ballast, closed her eyes and leapt.

"Okay, then, Abba" Devorah said, as her finger traced a gash on the surface of the table. "I agree to meet him. And his family."

Stay tuned for <u>Matters of Love and War</u>, Book II
of the *Chronicles of Marcus* which continues the story
three years later, in the year 130 CE.

Acknowledgments

There are several people who deserve my thanks for helping me with this long-term project.

First of all, my thanks and gratitude are due to my mother, Rita Lehman Schiffren, now deceased, who gave me tremendous support when I was first working on this novel. I would also like to thank my father, Alan Schiffren, who helped provide me with enough freedom early on to be able to focus on writing *The Mistake*. My sister, Lisa Schiffren, helped me by reading parts of the manuscript at a vital time and giving excellent editing suggestions.

I also want to extend my gratitude to the members of the Writing Circle at Ruth Keeler Library, North Salem, NY, who have often heard me read excerpts of the book and given plenty of encouragement over the years to finish *The Mistake* and send it out for publishing.

Steve Eisner from When Words Count deserves my deep gratitude for accepting me into his program and encouraging me with his mentorship and coaching. That provided the necessary trigger for me to get this project up and moving again after it had been stuck in cold storage for many years. Similarly, I would like to thank his colleague, Alison McBain, for her warm support, her editing help, her patient advice, and her endless resourcefulness.

And, finally, my thanks are due to David LaGere and Christopher Madden and the rest of the crew at Woodhall Press, who agreed to publish *The Mistake*, encouraged me along the way, matched me up with great critiques and let me take more time than they wanted with the revisions!

With love and gratitude to all of them!

About the Author

Mara Schiffren, PhD, was born in New York City and moved around between the two coasts of the USA as a child. She grew up in love with myths and history and read widely. In college she competed in fencing and soccer, then moved to Israel for a few years to pursue her interest in studying Jewish history and religion. There, she became passionate about her studies and decided to pursue advanced academic work. This culminated in a Doctorate in The Study of Religion at Harvard University with a focus on Jewish history and theology during the Hellenistic and Roman periods. This was a time when three powerful cultures met and clashed and out of the cataclysm, modern Western culture began its formation.

She currently resides in North Salem, NY, with her dog and a cat, where she writes for local papers and coaches Peak Performance and Creativity.